THE TIDE OF RAINE

WHISPERS

=== *of* ===

WAR

BOOK ONE

First Edition - Version 1.0

Published by Whisper Stories
Cover design by Natalia Junqueira
Interior design and formatting by Natalia Junqueira
Map created by Natalia Junqueira based on original concepts by Tylr Kreiser
Edited by Salima Alikhan and Robin Fuller

ISBN: 979-8-9994651-1-5 (paperback)
ISBN: 979-8-9994651-2-2 (hardback)

PROLOGUE

IRA reached up to touch the hideous scabs on her right cheek. Two deep parallel lines were carved into her face from her ear to her cheekbone, just below her eye—the mark of a Rogue. Her body was covered in cuts, her bones were still bruised, and her muscles screamed with every movement. The remnants of war-torn trauma riddled every step she took.

Tall trees loomed over the forest trail, casting dark midday shadows that stole her gaze. She fell into each one of them, stepping into their shade only to relive the horrific moments that haunted her mind. She could still feel the thunderous booms from the clouds above, see arrows hissing through the air, and hear the deadly song of steel clashing while the flames of destruction danced across Abnor. The smell of scorched earth and seared flesh continued to linger in her nose. But soon, her body would heal, and the tragic scenes of devastation she could still see as if they were right in front of her would all fade into a distant memory… All except for one: the execution of her husband, Victor Raine.

She had been forced to stand helplessly by as a piece of her soul was ripped away right before her eyes. The swing of a sword that seemingly fell for a lifetime gave birth to a pain that she would carry forever. Never again would she feel the touch of her beloved, hear the strength of his voice, or be warmed by his laughter. Yet despite the abundance of atrocities that ravaged her, Fira remained strong. She had no choice.

"Mommy!" a little boy suddenly shouted.

Fira snapped out of her trance to see her son, Vincent, with his hands on his hips. Clearly, he had made more than one attempt to get her attention. "What is it, love?" she asked wearily.

"Can we go play in the creek?" Vincent requested, the sun gleaming off his golden-brown hair. He looked at her with emerald eyes full of youthful innocence. She hoped it was a look he would maintain forever. "Please, Mommy! I wanna show them how to catch the crayfish just like Father taught me!"

Fira smiled softly. "Of course. Go ahead. I'll be right behind you."

Vincent quickly turned around and waved for the other three children traveling with them, signaling them to follow his lead. Only one of the three followed Vincent as he hurried to the water's edge—a girl, the shortest of the bunch, raced after him with a broad smile painted across her face. Her long sunset curls, teeming with knots and debris, flowed behind her as she ran through the trees.

"It's okay. Go ahead," Fira said to the other two children, who had yet to follow.

The second girl, whom Fira believed to be the oldest of the three, nodded to the tall, dark-haired, shy boy beside her, signaling for him to go first. As the two walked past Fira to join the others, the girl glanced at her cautiously. Fira could sense the nervousness and fear in all three nameless newcomers, but this girl seemed especially wary. And who could blame her, Fira thought, considering that they had been brought into her care straight from a battlefield? Still dressed in filthy, tattered rags, they appeared to be around Vincent's age—much too young to have heard the screams of war.

Fira knelt beside the creek and was acutely terrified of her wavy reflection. Her sandy-blonde hair was disheveled and unkempt, with strands still matted together with dried blood that might not have been her own. Dark circles framed her heavy eyelids, refusing to fade no matter how many times she splashed her face. She winced as the cold water touched the two deep cuts on her cheek.

Her thoughts drifted to her comrades as she stared at her horrid appearance. She wondered where they were now and how they were adapting to their new lives. She did not regret their decision to defy the king; she knew she would make the same choice again if given the chance. Yet she understood that the other Guardians who had followed Victor into battle would likely never share her feelings. Why should they? The king had ordered everyone who accompanied their once-beloved commander to be marked as Rogues and banished from Meditas. Most had nowhere else to go, and Fira knew that people were not quick to accept a Rogue into their community. Rogues were ostracized, ridiculed, and treated as if they carried some infectious disease. Society viewed them as traitors to the Guardians' sacred oath, no better than the horrors that roamed the night.

"Does it hurt?" the wary girl asked, pulling Fira out of her thoughts.

Fira turned to see her sitting several feet away with her knees pulled up to her chest. Her blue eyes were fixated on Fira's cheek. Her brown hair fell over her left shoulder, resting on a disfigured arm.

"Only a little," Fira answered. "May I join you?"

The girl tensed up as Fira sat beside her, and she never took her eyes off the strange woman for more than a few seconds. They sat silently as Vincent demonstrated to the other two how to catch the small crustaceans by tiptoeing through the shallow water and carefully lifting rocks.

"You don't want to play with them?" Fira asked.

The girl shook her head. "I have to be ready."

Fira looked at her, confused. "Ready for what?"

"In case someone attacks us again."

Fira's already wounded heart broke even more deeply at the girl's words. She could not have been older than twelve, yet she concerned herself with fears no child should ever have to. Fira gently placed an open palm on the girl's hand, startling her.

"You're safe with me," Fira said with tears welling in her eyes.

The girl shrugged away Fira's hand. "Because you're one of those... Guardians?"

"Because I can see that you've been through enough pain already, and I would like to protect you. All of you, if you'll let me."

The girl did not respond, letting her eyes fall to the gravel beneath her feet. Fira had so many questions. She tried not to think about what could have happened to them had they not been brought to her, or where they would be if Victor's army had never defied the king's orders to stand down. Dahnkar would have almost certainly wiped out all of Abnor and its people. Even if the children had miraculously survived, they would have likely succumbed to starvation or worse.

While Fira was lost in her thoughts again, she was carefully studied by the girl beside her. The young girl followed the river of sunlight that flowed over Fira's features, from her dark eyebrows to the brown wells of sadness beneath them. She wore a leather breastplate that bore a large tree in the center with leaves resembling clouds. All over the woman's body, she could see a dark, dried liquid that she could only assume was blood, and even darker areas on her skin that were equally likely to be bruises or dirt. A tear in her trousers just behind the leather shin guard revealed to the girl yet another bloodied injury. From what she knew, Guardians all had incredible powers. There was no way this woman could be one of the breathtaking warriors she had heard about and be so wounded. Her curiosity rose just enough for her to break the silence.

"If you're really one of those Guardian warriors," the girl started, "don't you have powers? How can you be so hurt?"

Fira smiled gratefully at her. It was nice to see that she still possessed some child-like innocence after all. "Our powers are called Favors," she said.

"So, you *do* have powers?" the girl questioned.

"I do."

"Prove it," the girl demanded with narrowed eyes.

Fira leaned to her side, picked up a small rock from the ground, and showed it to her. Once the girl looked back, Fira closed her fist and raised her hand, pointing it at a tree about a hundred paces away.

"Do you see that tree? The one with the drooping branch?" Fira asked.

The girl nodded. "Yeah, I can see it."

With the girl's focus on the tree, Fira opened her hand. Faster than a bolt fired from a crossbow, the rock flew from her palm, stirring up dust and leaves as it blasted clean through the center of the trunk. The girl was amazed, but once she turned her attention back to Fira, she could see blood trickling out of her nose.

Fira wiped her face with the back of her hand. "It's true that our Favors are powerful abilities, but as you can see, we're far from invincible."

"Oh," the girl said, hanging her head, disappointed. She started fidgeting with the small rocks on the ground by her feet. A moment later, she looked back up at Fira as if to speak, but quickly returned her attention to the ground. Fira sat quietly, patiently waiting, hoping the girl would gain the courage to say what she wanted.

"Catch him! Catch him!" Vincent shouted from the other side of the creek.

Fira looked up to see the other three children thrusting their hands into the water, trying to snatch a fleeing crayfish.

"Will you... tell me about them?" the brown-haired girl finally asked.

"About Guardians?" Fira clarified.

The girl nodded.

"Well, what do you already know?"

"That you have pow—erm... Favors, and that you're the most powerful warriors in all of Sanora."

Fira smiled. She realized the girl's youthful spirit was still largely intact, despite what she had been through; she was only afraid to let it shine through.

"We're more than just warriors," Fira started. "Many, many years ago, four stars fell from their home in the sky and crashed into our continent." She began rearranging a small group of rocks on the ground. "One here, in what we now call Dahnkar. One here, in Limfas. One in Meditas, the nation I was sworn to, and one here in Abnor, where we found you."

The girl looked at the strange rock formation on the ground, slightly puzzled. "They all seem really close together."

Fira chuckled. "They are. But I assure you, it doesn't feel that way when you travel between them. After the stars crashed, at each of the now four great nations, a spring of raw energy was created that provides our world with the balance it needs for us to survive. We, as Guardians, swear our allegiance to one of those fountains and its nation in order to protect that balance."

"That's why you came to Abnor, then? To protect the fountain?"

"And its people."

"Does every Guardian do the swear?"

"Yes, they do."

"But if you swear something, that's the same as promises, right? Wouldn't that mean that the Dha-an-ker Guardians broke their promise?"

"Indeed, they did. King Netir wanted to take control of another fountain and try to obtain its power. Some people want all the power in the world and will do whatever they can to get it, promises or no promises."

The girl's eyes widened as she scanned over the rocks, piecing everything together. "Do you get the Favors from the fountains?"

Fira nodded. "When we take the Guardian's oath, we drink the water from the fountain we are sworn to protect, and if it welcomes us, it then grants us our Favors. But if it doesn't welcome us..." She trailed off, ultimately deciding to leave the darker aspects of becoming a Guardian unspoken.

The girl clutched her disfigured left arm nervously. "You stopped. Why'd you stop? What happens if it doesn't welcome you? Is it something bad?" Her voice was suddenly hurried, as if she were frightened.

Fira looked at her curiously. The girl was trembling, tears welling in her eyes. Fira quickly connected the dots. "You drank from the Abnor fountain," she said, almost to herself.

The tears in the girl's eyes started streaming down her face. "Am I going to die now?"

"No, honey, no," Fira said quickly. She was unsure how to comfort the girl while respecting her boundaries. She moved to put a consoling hand on the girl's shoulder, but the moment she lifted her arm, the girl threw herself into her and held her tightly. Fira gritted her teeth, trying to muffle her grimace of pain as she embraced the girl. She held her close while she sobbed, running her fingers through her hair.

In truth, she did not know what would happen to the girl, but what was she supposed to say? She had seen what occurred when the fountain denied someone, but the effects were always immediate. To her knowledge, nobody who was accepted had ever been left deformed. Still, the fountains affected everyone differently, and uncertainty gnawed at her.

"I only wanted to be strong," the girl said, pulling away with a sniffle. "So I could protect them."

"You look pretty strong to me," Vincent said, suddenly standing beside them.

"You're just a little kid. What would you know?" the young girl responded harshly.

"Well, that boy said you fought off a bandit, and you have to be pretty strong to do that. And that means you have to stay with us, because my daddy had strong friends, and I'm going to be a Guardian just like him someday. So, I need strong friends too!" Vincent waved for her to join them in the creek. "Come, come! It will be easier to catch them if we do it together."

Vincent grabbed the girl by the hand and pulled her into the creek with the others before she could refuse him. He then proceeded to demonstrate his tiptoe method of catching crayfish again—only this time, he slipped and fell with a splash. Fira watched as the brown-haired girl not only smiled for the first time since she had met her, but started to laugh. An uncontrollable expression of joy spread painfully across Fira's face as she watched the four children fumble about in the creek. However, the longer she sat alone on the bank, the louder her thoughts began to scream.

She knew without a doubt that Vincent would become a Guardian once he was of age. That would happen whether he or she wanted it or not. King Sentis had demanded one more thing from Victor before he died: his only son. An execution, a scar, and a banishment were not enough to fulfill the king's insatiable lust for punishment. In Vincent's eighteenth year, he was to speak the exact words his mother and father had spoken before him, taking the Guardian's oath.

As much as Fira loved to entertain the idea of escaping the king's demands by going into hiding or violently removing him from the picture, there was no point. Victor had made a soul oath with the king to ensure Vincent's service. It was a legend as old as time that was said to have been used throughout history, and although Fira did not much believe in the legend, if she was wrong, Vincent's life would be forfeited—a risk she was most certainly not willing to take. Besides, if Vincent wanted to become a Guardian just like his father, the world would be a better place for it, and what kind of mother would she be if she deterred him from chasing his dreams?

"Look, Mommy! She caught one!" Vincent shouted.

The brown-haired girl lifted one of the tiny crustaceans with a bright smile shining across her face.

"Can I hold it?" the sunset-haired girl asked. As soon as the small critter was in her possession, she thrust it at the tall boy's face. "Rawr!"

The boy quickly put up his hands and backed away with splashing steps. She then proceeded to chase after Vincent and the brown-haired girl with the crayfish held out in front of her, laughing hysterically. After she had finally had her fill of terrorizing everyone with the poor creature, she lifted it to her mouth.

"No, don't eat it!" Vincent said in a panic. He quickly swatted the crayfish out of her hand before she could bite down.

"Quick! Catch him again!" Vincent said to the brown-haired girl, who immediately started shooting her hands into the water.

With the sight of the children playing in front of her, all of Fira's physical ailments seemed to fade away underneath a blanket of bliss. Tears filled with a cacophony of emotions fell from her eyes. There was only one thing missing.

"Can you see them from the stars, my love? Are you watching?" she whispered.

Fira longed for the moment to last forever, and for the future to remain buried deep behind the setting sun. But in the end, she knew that one day was someday, and that day would surely come to be today's tomorrow much too soon. She believed that between Victor's defection and Dhankar's invasion, the esteem the Guardians currently possessed would dwindle to little more than a flickering flame at the end of a spent candle. The path of the Guardian would only become far more difficult.

All she could do now was prepare Vincent and the others, if they so chose, for the challenges ahead. From the moment they reached their home in Sylva until her part in their journey was over, she would train them—teach them everything she knew to keep them alive. She had ten years to turn them into seasoned warriors, but was it enough? Then again, was any amount of time enough?

CHAPTER 1

HE clash of swords rang through the cool summer air as the sun rose to its peak. Two of Fira's children were exchanging blows with swift and precise movements in a training yard surrounded by wooden houses, shops, and stables that all rested atop lush green grass. A refreshing breeze swam through the air, gliding across the droplets of sweat on their brows before vanishing into dense trees full of vibrant leaves that longed to graze the cotton clouds above. Gardeners tilled small yards that yielded a motley array of colorful weeds and flowers, while children ran and giggled through the roads, stumbling about. Shopkeepers remained steadfast in the face of haggling customers searching for a more preferable price. Guards clad in brown leather took their spears for a leisurely walk adjacent to the tall and pointed wooden pillars that lined the perimeter of Sylva, the city buried deep within the eastern woods.

Fira watched the sparring match from just outside an oak fence that acted as the boundary line for the training arena. She scanned over every one of their moves, ready to critique them on even the smallest of errors. Only a few minutes into the match, after they both had exchanged a series of attacks, Fira already had words of criticism for each of them. She leaned slightly to her left without taking her eyes off the battle before her.

"Vincent, tell me what Vera is doing wrong right now."

Vincent was leaning over the fence with his arms folded on top of each other. He analyzed the fight in front of him for a moment. His green eyes paid no mind to the loose strands of golden-brown hair in front of them as they searched for the answer his mother was looking for.

"Barrik has the reach on her," he answered. "She's letting him keep too much space between them."

Fira nodded. "And what about Barrik, Alexandra?"

Alexandra stood beside Fira, mimicking her firm posture. Her fierce dark blue eyes were locked onto the fight. Her arms were crossed in front of her leather breastplate, and a dark leather glove covered her left hand. A chestnut-colored ponytail split into three thick braids—one on either side of her head and one down the middle. She allowed the gap of silence to linger in the air while she watched the battle. Her eyes narrowed as she focused on the larger of the two combatants. At first, she found no blatant mistakes in his actions. It was not until both of their swords collided that she realized his fault.

"Well?" Fira prodded.

"She may be giving him the reach, but he's not taking advantage of it, or anything else. He pulls back when he should have attacked, and he's not using anywhere close to his full strength. I think he's too worried he's going to hurt her."

A smirk grew across Vincent's face. "Well, he did all but put you in the stars with one punch the other day," he said without turning around.

"And I'm about to do the same to you as soon as they're finished," she fired back.

Fira disregarded their squabble and began to shout. "Get closer, Vera! He's bigger than you! And Barrik, if she does, show her your full strength!" She paused as a smile snuck across her face. "Otherwise... Vince will be cooking your dinner again!"

"It wasn't *that* bad," Vincent said, trying to defend himself.

"Ehh, I'm pretty sure it quacked at me," Alexandra retorted.

Vera's golden cherry hair bounced with every one of her steps. While each curl barely made it past her chin, two skinny braids twisted down to the center of her back.

Barrik stood perfectly still on the balls of his feet, monstrously tall and broad-shouldered, analyzing the girl half his size as she rushed toward him. In order to even come close to hitting her, he needed to swing his sword at a downward angle. Still, she was too quick of a target. She ducked beneath his sparring sword, but before she was able to attack, Barrik launched his shoulder into her, forcing her into the ground. Dust burst into the air as she slammed into the dirt. She lay on the ground, gasping for air. As soon as Barrik lowered his sword to claim his victory, Vera launched her foot high into his groin and quickly lifted her sword to his neck. With both of them indicating a killing blow, Fira ended the match.

"That's enough," Fira called over to them.

Both Vera and Barrik lowered their weapons and took a moment to catch their breath.

"You okay?" Vera asked from her spot on the ground.

Barrik held up a single finger for a moment before he answered her. He let out a long, deep breath of discomfort. "I'll be fine in a minute or two. You?"

Vera groaned. "It feels like Nexella threw me off the saddle into a tree at full speed."

Barrik extended a meaty palm and pulled Vera up to her feet as if she weighed less than nothing. Both of them took their time hobbling back to the training yard gate to Fira and the other two. As soon as they stood in front of her, she began her lecture. No matter how well they performed, she always found something to critique.

"Vera, you're small, so fight small. Don't allow your opponent the opportunity to take advantage of your stature. Blend your strengths and weaknesses together, so there won't be any part of you to exploit. Understood?"

Vera nodded and watched as Fira turned and began to speak to Barrik. The sun shone brightly behind her, giving her a golden, ethereal silhouette. Although the top of her head only rose to his chin, she still seemed taller than him somehow. She was the only one capable of making him appear smaller than he actually was.

"Having restraint is okay, but don't expect anyone to reciprocate it. Pulling one too many punches could be a fatal mistake. Anyone out to kill you will surely take advantage of that should they notice." Fira rested a hand high up on Barrik's shoulder. "Don't allow your kindness to become your demise."

"I won't," Barrik said softly.

"I don't know, Bear," Vincent said, poking him in the side. "You might be a little too soft for the Guardian lifestyle."

Barrik swatted away Vincent's prodding fingers. "Knock it off," he said. "Here." Barrik forcefully handed his sparring sword to Vincent, pushing him away.

"All right, all right, I take it back. The bear has a growl to him as well." Vincent turned and started to whistle cheerfully as he walked toward the center of the training yard.

Barrik shook his head and turned to Alexandra. "Would you take him down a notch for me?"

"I'll see what I can do," she said happily.

Barrik plopped his arms down on the fence, causing the oak plank to bow underneath his weight. "You think she'll take it easy on him this time?"

With hands on her hips, Fira confidently shook her head. "I don't believe there is anything under the stars she loves more than to put that boy's arrogance in check. And if I had to guess, I'd say it being his birthday will only increase her enjoyment."

As Vera stood silently next to Barrik, a mischievous grin grew across her face. His side was stretched out, vulnerable. With two fingers, she jabbed him in the midsection. Caught off guard, he jumped, and she started to laugh.

"Why?" Barrik asked, mildly irritated.

"You should have seen how high you got!"

"I'm gonna—"

"Knock it off and pay attention," Fira said firmly, not letting him finish.

Both of them quickly silenced themselves and turned their attention to the center of the training yard.

Vincent and Alexandra stood a few paces apart from each other, silent. Both of them were about the same height, clad in their leather armor, sparring swords at their sides, knees slightly bent, grips tightened, eyes locked.

"I've got you this time," Vincent said confidently.

"Only in your dreams," Alexandra responded.

In that moment—the silent second before the battle commenced—to them, everything faded. There was nothing else around them, nobody to see, no sounds to be heard. Time slowed to a near halt as the breeze drifted across the vacant ground between them. As if they had become permanent fixtures in a painting, motionless, they waited.

"Begin," Fira shouted from the fence.

Her voice met their ears, and as if her words carried some unknown power, their environment returned to normal. In a rush, everything raced back to real time. They charged.

Alexandra thrust her sword forward at Vincent's midsection. He swatted it away with ease. Using the momentum, she spun around and swept at his legs. Vincent fell to the ground and rolled away quickly. He rose to his feet, frustrated.

"Always with the same move," he complained.

Pleased with his reaction, Alexandra smirked. "Stop falling for it, and I'll stop doing it."

He gritted his teeth and launched toward her with a salvo of slashes. She blocked and dodged, remaining on the defensive until she found a chance to counter.

Vincent raised his hands above his head, ready to bring his sword down on her. There it was—he had left himself wide open.

She motioned to slash at his stomach. Vincent smiled; it was a feint. He sidestepped her slash and brought his sword down hard against hers, knocking it from her hands. He followed it up with a kick to her chest that sent her flying.

He leaned over, picked up her sword, and twirled it in his hand. "I'm going to borrow this."

Alexandra climbed to her feet and glared at him under a furrowed brow. Slowly, as her enemy approached her, she raised her fists. His attacks came with speed and control, but not one of them found its mark. Much to Vincent's dismay, she continued to dodge and sidestep away from danger. While his opponent was unarmed, she was still in control of the fight.

Annoyed with his inability to land a hit, Vincent threw one of the swords and dashed behind it. Alexandra ducked beneath the projectile and met him sooner than he expected. She maneuvered around to his rear flank, wrapped her arms around his waist, lifted him over her shoulders, and slammed him into the ground behind her. All three of their spectators winced at the sight of him hitting the dirt.

"That is definitely taking him down a notch," Barrik said with satisfaction.

"Several notches," Vera corrected.

When Vincent finally made it back on his feet, Alexandra was already in front of him. His sword had tumbled to the side from the impact. With him no longer armed, the battle was even once again.

Two jabs came quickly for Vincent's head. Despite his daze, he managed to slip them both. However, he failed to see the left cross that followed. A leather glove connected with his cheek, creating a small cut. He hopped back to make space, and while he managed to buy himself a brief moment to shake off the hit, Alexandra did not let up. She threw punch after punch at her target, but nothing landed. Vincent twisted his torso to duck beneath an incoming fist and launched an uppercut straight into her side. The counter was beautiful, but he mistakenly followed it with an overreaching hook. Alexandra snatched his arm, threw her hips back into him, and pulled him over her down to the ground once more. This time, there would be no letting him up. She threw herself on top of him and unleashed a storm of closed hands. Vincent quickly threw his arms up to guard.

"You can yield whenever you're ready, Vince," Alexandra said confidently.

Vincent was under a barrage of knuckles. He had to act quickly. He leaned to his left to avoid her next hit. As soon as it flew past him, he launched his head forward, smashing into the bridge of her nose. She fell back with both hands covering her face. With Alexandra disoriented, he scrambled for the nearby sword and swung it down on her. Down on one knee, Alexandra caught the blunt blade in her left hand and yanked it from him, pulling his stomach right into her other fist. Vincent instantly dropped to his knees.

Alexandra stood up and lowered the weapon to Vincent's neck. She stared down the length of the sword in her right hand, victorious.

Vincent hung his head before looking back up at her. She lowered the sword and reached out with her left hand to help him to his feet.

"Just once, you couldn't let me win?"

"Maybe next time," she said with a wink.

Vincent pointed to her already swollen nose, which was pouring blood out of both nostrils. "You got a little, uh…"

She forcefully handed the sword to Vincent as she pinched her nose with two gentle fingers and tilted her head back.

He started to chuckle. "I think I still kinda won."

His comment earned him an extra slug in the arm. Together, they started to return to the others, Vincent rubbing his arm, and Alexandra attempting to slow the blood loss from her nose.

Once they reached the fence, Fira squeezed a wet cloth into a bucket on the ground next to her and held it to Alexandra's nose. After a moment, she took it away and inspected the injury. She placed her hand gently underneath Alexandra's chin and tilted her head back. "Let me see." She poked the bridge of her nose, making her twinge. "Well, it's not broken. Just keep that there, and you'll be fine."

Barrik rested his hand on Vincent's shoulder. "Yet another loss to Alex."

Vincent quickly brushed away his hand. "I'll get her next time. After all, I basically won this time."

"I don't know about that, bud. She may look worse, but tomorrow you're going to *feel* worse for sure."

"I'll be fine."

Vera laughed. "Yeah, right. She slammed you so hard into the ground that *my* bones cracked."

"Barely felt it," Vincent said as he looked away.

Barrik patted him on the back. "Yeah, okay, bud."

"Regardless of who looks worse and who feels worse," Fira said as she began their evaluation, "Alex won. Almost isn't going to count in a real battle. And Vince, in comparison to Alex, your hand-to-hand is horseshit."

"So, you're saying it's gotten better?" he joked.

Fira ignored him and continued. "How many times have I told you to stay on your feet? You're as good as dead on the ground. As for you, Alex, you're going to have bigger problems than Vincent's head if you continue to get too confident."

"I don't think there's anything bigger than Vince's head," Alexandra teased, her voice slightly muffled behind the wet cloth.

Vincent crossed his arms and glared at her, unamused.

Fira turned to face all of them. "You have all come a long way, and I'd feel confident with any one of you by my side in a battle, but you're not without faults. None of us are. What's important is that you recognize them and actively try to fix them. You may leave tomorrow, but your training is far from over. Every rising sun is accompanied by an opportunity for improvement. Don't forget that."

"We won't," Alexandra said.

"Well, *you* might, if you take any more hits from Vince's thick head," Vera said jokingly.

Everyone laughed as Vincent reached up to his forehead with his palm. "Is it really that big?"

Fira, still smiling, walked over to him. "You are most certainly thick-headed, just like your father. But we love you for it anyway." She planted a motherly kiss on top of his head.

"Henry's looking a little troubled today," Alexandra suddenly said.

A younger guard, with a worried look, was running right for them.

"What could he possibly want this time?" Barrik questioned.

Fira stepped forward to receive the boy.

The guard slowed to a halt and hunched over with his hands on his knees as he spoke between ragged breaths. "M'lady... The soldiers... They're here. And they're makin' a terrible ruckus."

"Where?"

"They're at the pub. Sam's pub."

"Okay, thank you, Henry. We'll handle it."

Fira motioned for them to follow. Without hesitation, they hurried down the gravel trail until they came to the corner of the main road that ran through the center of Sylva.

Suddenly, there was a loud crash, followed by several people scrambling out of a wood-and-stone building. Above the porch, a plaque gently swayed in the breeze, carved with a bubbly mug of ale.

They walked inside the pub to find a group of soldiers clad in bright silver armor spread throughout the room, each with a longsword belted to their hips. A woman with a long chocolate braid was casually leaning against the bar while an older man behind the counter poured his own ale. The other two soldiers slowly walked around the room, meticulously inspecting the few patrons sitting down.

"Don't make this difficult for us, and nobody will get hurt," the soldier behind the bar said before sipping from his mug. He had a thick head of gray hair and a goatee to match. The wrinkles on his forehead and around his eyes hinted at his age. "We're only here to deliver a message, and for some ale to quench our thirst." He took another gulp and slammed the empty mug down.

Vincent noticed the same tree from his mother's old armor engraved into the center of the man's breastplate. These were

Meditas soldiers, and it was no coincidence that they were here on his birthday.

One of the soldiers patrolling the room, a younger boy with a pointed nose too big for his face, suddenly snatched a middle-aged man from his seat. Two lines were carved into the man's right cheek, identical to Fira's.

"Look, Captain! We've caught ourselves a Rogue," the big-nosed soldier said.

The soldier behind the bar, the captain, scoffed and spat on the floor. "You know what we do with their kind. Get some rope."

"I'd put him down if I were you," Fira interjected firmly, drawing everyone's attention.

"Aww, how cute," said the woman leaning against the bar. "Another one has come to the rescue."

The captain laughed. "Why don't you run along before we give you the rope as well?"

In the corner of the room, Vincent caught a glimpse of a man dressed entirely in black, a cloak with a raised hood, and a mask covering his entire face. All of his clothes were dark enough to blend in with the shadows. Vincent could only see him in the first place thanks to a beam of sunlight that crept in from the window slightly above the man.

Fira crossed her arms and leaned up against the wall. "If I'm here to rescue anyone, it isn't him, I assure you. That man in your hands there, soldier, is known as the Blue Flame."

The soldier with the pointed nose raised an eyebrow and looked at the harmless-looking man in his clutches.

Fira continued, "That Rogue's scar on his cheek proves he was once a Guardian of Meditas. You're probably too young to know, but we Guardians used to love our nicknames. Can you guess why he's called the Blue Flame?"

The soldier looked back down at the man, who was now smiling. Both of his hands were engulfed in ocean-blue flames that were breathing calmly. The soldier quickly dropped him and backed away.

The captain smiled nastily and walked around to the front of the bar. "All of you Rogues and your neat little tricks. More like freaks, if you ask me. The Guardians too. But I must admit, I'm now curious; what name did the freaks give you?"

Fira returned the captain's nasty smile, but did not answer his question. "And I'm curious as to why you're harassing my people, and what exactly I need to do to get you out of my city."

The captain scoffed. "We'll leave when we're damn good and ready. I don't take orders from Rogue scum. You're no better than rats." He spat on the floor. "But then again, rats can sometimes be useful. Maybe you can help us. We're looking for someone—the son of that traitorous Victor Raine."

Fira's eyes darted to Vincent as if to ask, *"Are you ready?"*

He was—or at least, he thought he was. He took a few steps forward. "My name is Vincent, son of Victor Raine."

The captain approached Vincent and inspected him thoroughly, invading his personal space. "You?" he asked doubtfully. "You're the son of the once revered Victor Raine?"

"What? You don't see the resemblance?" Vincent snarked.

"All I see is a disappointment."

The captain's words sent a jolt of anger through Vincent's bones. "What do you want?" he asked with narrowed eyes.

"What I want," the captain started, "is for you to take what is owed to your father."

The captain threw his fist into Vincent's mouth and ripped him to the ground. Before he could throw a second punch, Alexandra launched forward and kicked him in the side of the face with the heel of her boot. Nobody else was able to make another move; the other three soldiers had quickly drawn their swords. The big-nosed soldier was sure to keep Fira at the tip of his blade, while the other soldier, a man with a shining head, kept maneuvering his sword back and forth from Vera to Barrik. The woman with the chocolate braid restrained Alexandra and pressed the edge of her sharpened steel against her neck. A small drop of blood slid down beneath Alexandra's tunic.

"You'll hang for that!" the woman shouted.

The captain climbed to his feet, marched over to Alexandra, and hurled his fist into her stomach. She immediately fell to her knees, coughing and fighting the urge to vomit.

"Leave them alone!" Barrik called out.

"Quiet! Or it'll be your turn next," the captain threatened before looking back to Alexandra. "I should take your head," he said as he spat on the floor beside her. "Don't get back up, and maybe I'll let you keep it."

He turned and walked back over to Vincent, who was still lying on the floor. The captain dropped his knee into Vincent's chest and continued to apply pressure. "Pay attention, scum. You're about to come into *my* city to disgrace *my* people with your traitorous blood. The reason why King Sentis wants you anyway is lost on me. I'd rather have you rot far away from me and my people."

"I bet…" Vincent coughed, forcing the words out. "A lot of things are lost on you."

The captain slammed his metal fist into Vincent's mouth again, this time splitting open his lower lip. "Keep your mouth shut! If it were up to me, we'd hang you from the nearest tree and sip some ale by your dangling corpse until it was time for the horrors to feed. But as you can see, unlike your father, I follow my king's orders."

The captain finally stood up, but continued looking down at Vincent. "You are to meet us at the western gates of the Cayland ruins in two weeks' time. From there, we will escort you directly to the king. And for your own sake, boy, hope that the king finds no semblance of your father in you, because even mentioning Victor's name is enough to fill him with rage."

Vincent spat out a mouthful of blood. "And what if I said I'm just like him?"

The captain flared his nasty smile, revealing a few blackened teeth. "Then you'll lose your head—just like him."

"Hey! What are you doing? What's over there?" the soldier in front of Fira suddenly yelled at her.

Vincent followed her line of sight to where he had seen the dark-clothed man sitting—but he was no longer there. All he saw was a wispy black trail that looked like smoke.

"Lower your swords. It's time we get out of this rat's nest," the captain said. "But first, give them a taste of what will happen if the boy fails to meet us." He spat again. "Burn it."

The soldiers shoved their captives aside and returned their swords to their scabbards—a mistake. They had only managed to flip over a single table before it happened.

"Just don't kill them," Fira said.

"Don't tell us what to do!" the big-nosed soldier fired back.

Fira chuckled. "I wasn't talking to you."

All of a sudden, the dark-cloaked man appeared next to the soldier and slammed his palm into his big nose. He disappeared in an instant, leaving behind the wispy black trail. He reappeared in front of the bald soldier and elbowed him in the temple, knocking him unconscious. The woman quickly drew her sword and slashed. All she hit was the black smoke. The man appeared behind her, kicked her behind the knee, wrapped her long braid around his arm, and yanked her head back to punch her several times in the face. By the time the captain drew his sword, one was already pressing against his neck. He felt the blade scrape against the lump in his throat as he swallowed nervously. Vincent tracked the wavy steel at the captain's neck to the hooded man, almost entirely blending in with the shadows.

Vera and Barrik stepped over the unconscious soldier and helped Vincent to his feet.

"I am a captain to the soldiers of the great nation of Meditas, serving your king! You wouldn't dare harm me!" the captain howled shakily.

"He is no king of mine," the man in the shadows said coldly. His voice was rough and muffled behind his mask.

"Put it down, Ghost," Fira commanded.

Ghost's hand tightened around the hilt of his blade. Although clearly reluctant, he lowered his weapon.

The captain started laughing nervously. "Nothing more than a chained dog, I see."

Fira started slowly walking toward the captain with a storm of rage in her eyes. "You threaten my people, insult my husband, strike two of my children, and hold the other two at the end of a blade. What do you think would be an appropriate way for me to respond to these transgressions?"

"I—I—I," the captain stammered.

Fira nodded. "That's what I think too. So, allow me to make myself perfectly clear." She walked closer, forcing the captain to take several steps away until his back touched the bar. "My children will meet you when and where they are supposed to. However, should any harm come to them—should you lay hands on them again, or even if I learn that you spoke to them with disrespect—my 'dog' here will find you, no matter where you hide, and bring you to me." She placed her index finger against his forehead and glared menacingly into his petrified eyes. "Where I will then proceed to rip you apart limb from limb with no more than a single finger."

Vincent felt a chill run down his spine. He had never seen his mother like this before. He was terrified. He had only seen her use her Favor a few times before, during hunting trips—and even then, only with horrors. He had never seen her use it on a human, but he had a vivid imagination. He knew very well that she could instantly turn the captain's head into a red mist if she wanted to.

Fira removed her finger and moved close to the captain's face, forcing him to lean back even farther. "Unless you'd like an example of how I would do that, I suggest you get the hell out of my city."

The captain and his soldiers quickly gathered their unconscious comrade and scurried out of the pub. Once they were long gone and the pub was restored to relative order, Alexandra walked over to the man dressed in shadows.

"You're the Ghost?" she asked.

He returned his wavy sword to its sheath. "What gave me away?"

She paid no mind to his sarcastic remark and extended her hand. "All of it was so long ago… It's all just a blur to us now, but Mom told us that we were brought to her by a ghost—a man who lives in the shadows. I'm guessing that was you. So, thank you."

The moment he accepted Alexandra's hand, Vera crashed into his side, wrapping her arms around him.

"Thanks, Mr. Ghost!" she exclaimed.

Barrik's meaty palm suddenly landed on his shoulder. "Yes, thank you."

Fira started to laugh. "You may not be able to see his face right now, but I can promise you, he is extremely uncomfortable. Save the rest of your pleasantries for dinner."

"Fira, I can't stay," Ghost protested.

"Ghost, I know how you live. When was the last time you had an actual meal? Or a bath, for that matter? What kind of pet owner would I be if I didn't throw my dog a bone?"

Ghost grunted behind his dark mask in defeat.

"Apologies for the trouble, Sam," Fira said to the short, round barkeep hiding behind a barrel in the corner of the room. "After the kids leave tomorrow, Charlie and I will come by to help with any repairs."

"Thank you, M'lady," Sam replied, wiping the sweat from his brow.

Fira turned to her children. "Speaking of Charlie, he mentioned wanting to give you all a parting gift before dinner. Why don't you head over there while Ghost and I have a little chat?"

Vera's eyes lit up with excitement. "Oh, I think I know what the parting gift is," she said, cheerfully stepping out of the pub.

Vincent followed behind the others and caught a small snippet of Fira and Ghost's conversation. He could not quite make out the words, but heard something that sounded like, "...only if it's life or death."

Outside, Vera jumped in front of the group and started walking backward down the road. "Did you see his Favor?! He was all, I'm here, now I'm over here, now I'm over there... How do you think it works?"

"Mom said he moves with the shadows, so it's some sort of relocation Favor, I guess," Alexandra replied.

Vera jumped back in line with everyone and tensed up with enthusiasm. "I can't wait to get ours!"

"I just hope the fountain doesn't kill us," Barrik said.

"Or turn us into anything dark and twisted," Vincent added, still pondering the words he might or might not have heard.

Alexandra remained silent as she held her left hand closer to herself, anxiously imagining what could happen once she drank from a second fountain.

The sun slowly continued to fall, casting the city in golden afternoon light as they traveled on. Birds used the cool breeze to glide between the wooden rooftops of stone houses, while cooped-up chickens watched in envy from below. Locals gave the group a friendly wave as they passed by before they returned to their daily chores—mostly the tilling of gardens full of brightly colored fruits and vegetables and the chopping of wood. As they drew closer to the crossroads in the center of the village, the sound of metal against an anvil grew louder and louder, filling the air with a rhythmic clang.

A shop with no front or side walls rested on the opposite corner from where they stood. Thick wooden pillars acted as supports for the ceiling, leaving the innards exposed. Above them dangled a wooden sign with the image of a hammer and an anvil. From one side to the other, the stony interior was decorated with a wide variety of armor pieces and weapons. Just a few feet away from the fiery forge stood a boy hammering away on a blade of no magnificence. Vincent and the others ducked beneath the weapons on display as they entered. Before they had fully made it into the shop, they were ambushed.

"Vince!" the young boy shouted.

They turned to see Rucker, a twelve-year-old boy with messy blonde hair full of ash and soot. Wide brown eyes and plump cheeks covered in sweat and dirt were launched into Vincent's chest with a familiar force of endearment.

"What happened to your face?" the boy asked as he pulled away, noting the gash in Vincent's lower lip.

"Ah, it's nothing," Vincent answered. "What are you working on over there?"

"I'm getting out the kinks in my brother's sword. I almost beat him the last time we sparred! You should have seen it! I made him fall over, just like Alex showed me! Oh, oh, and also, Charlie's gonna show me the fortification sign tomorrow! Look! He already taught me how to do the fingers for it."

The boy stood up straight, closed his eyes, and held his first two fingers up to his lips while leaving the other three closed tightly against his palm.

Vincent chuckled and placed his hand on Rucker's shoulder. "You're going to be running this place for Gramps in no time."

"And then I'll be able to beat you, too!"

"I wouldn't go that far. You see Alex's nose? Wouldn't want to end up like her, now, would you?"

Rucker cringed when he saw her red and swollen nose.

"You lost," Alexandra said, defending herself.

"If you say so," Vincent said with a shrug.

Alexandra rolled her eyes. "We're going to slip into the back, Ruck. Is the old man in?"

The boy nodded. "Yup, he's in there, but I need to see your hands before you go!"

"Just mine?"

"All of you. Just hold them out in front of you, and spread your fingers like this."

The four of them did as the young boy requested and stood still, confused, as he carefully examined them.

"Okay, that'll do! I'll see you later!" Rucker chirped before he returned to the anvil.

"Strange kid," Vera said plainly.

"You would know," Vincent joked.

The four of them walked to the back corner of the room through a doorway blocked by a black curtain. The large room inside was chaotically filled with open books, scrolls, and old parchment. Prototypes of weapons and armor pieces, sketched in charcoal, hung all over the gray stone walls. In the center was a wide, ovular table carved grotesquely from dark wood. Burned into the glossy tabletop was a map of the continent.

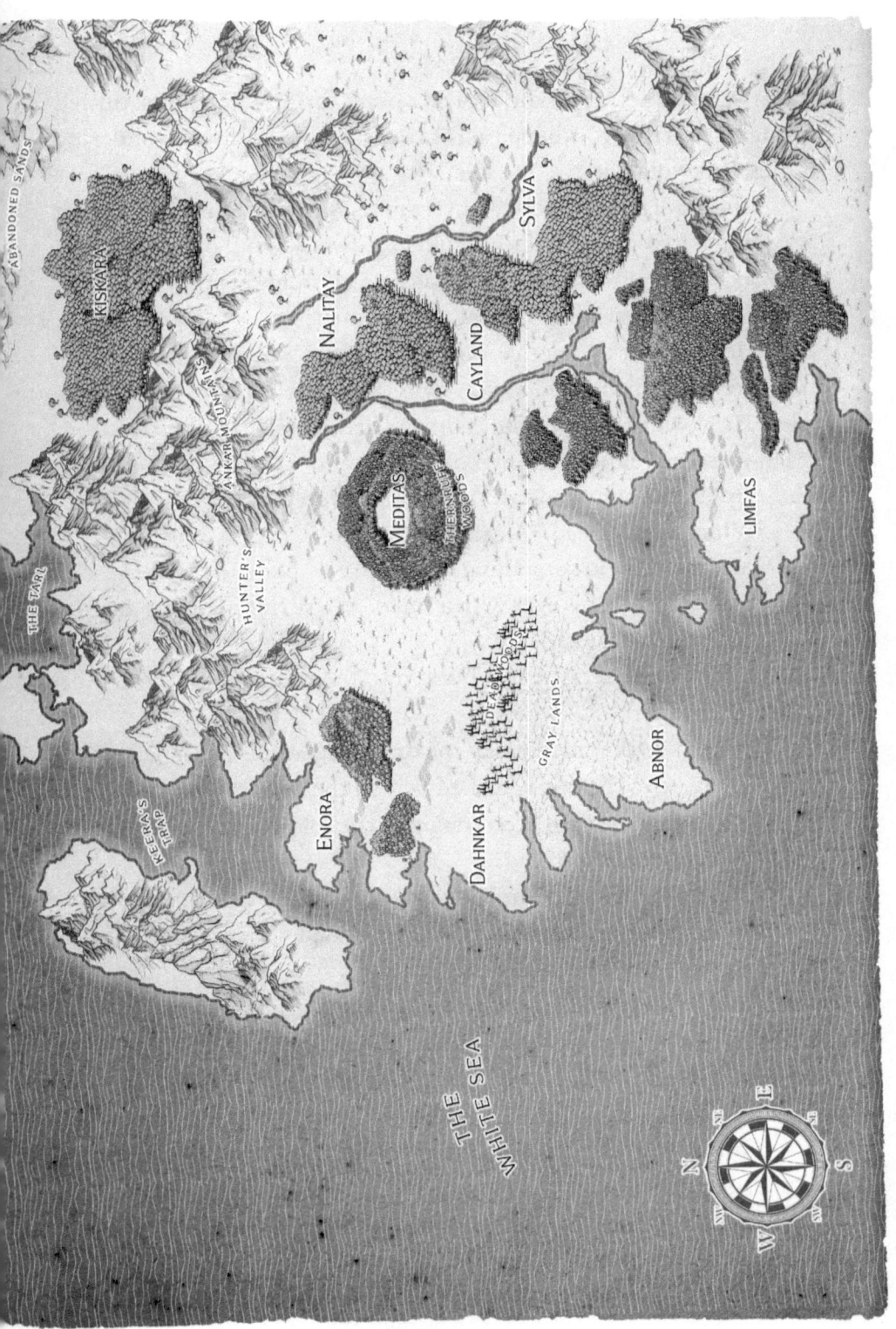

Charlie, an older man who looked young for his later years, turned around from the workbench across the room. "Ahh, I was wondering when you would arrive," he said.

The sunlight that flooded in from the glass window behind him gave his soft and scruffy face a golden glow. Eyes full of wisdom and the occasional silver strand that peeked through his otherwise jet-black hair were the only indicators of his true age.

He was quick to notice Vincent's lip and Alexandra's nose. "By the stars, what happened to you two?" he asked as he rushed to their side. His voice was powerfully soft and gentle, with a calm inflection, each word traveling at its own pace.

"Soldiers from Meditas," Vincent answered.

"Vincent's fat head," Alexandra teased.

"Let me get you something for that."

Vincent rolled his eyes with a smile. "We're fine, Gramps, really."

"Nonsense. Rucker!"

A moment later, the boy burst into the room from beyond the curtain. "Yes, sir?"

"Would you mind fetching me one of the water pails, please?"

"Okay, sir." The boy vanished behind the curtain again.

"Your mother wasn't too rough on the soldiers, was she?" Charlie asked, concerned.

"No, Ghost handled the roughing-up part," Alexandra said.

"Although she was terrifying," Vera added with a shiver.

"Agreed," Vincent remembered.

Rucker waddled back into the room, struggling to carry the pail of water any higher than his ankles. Water splashed out of the sides with every step. Barrik quickly rushed over to relieve him of the heavy load, making it look weightless, and set it down next to Charlie.

"Thank you, lad. Rucker, finish up quickly, and you can hurry home, okay?"

Rucker nodded and quickly disappeared once more.

"Is that Ghost still here?" Charlie asked.

"Mom is forcing him to stay for dinner," Barrik said.

"I see." He tore a piece of cloth in half, dipped both halves in the bucket, and wrung them out, letting the last few drops splash back into the water before he handed the torn pieces to Alexandra. "Hold these for me, would ya, dear?"

"I take it you don't care for him?" she guessed as she took the wet cloth.

"He's far from my favorite person beneath the stars."

Charlie placed an open palm slightly above the water. With his free hand, he formed a circle with curled fingers gently pressed into his thumb. Just a few seconds later, a soft blue light radiated from beneath his open palm, and the water in the pail slowly began to freeze. When the entire bucket was frozen solid, he removed his hands and walked to his workbench.

"I shouldn't have said that. It's just... while I'd like to believe he has the best intentions, his methods sometimes make me question how much he should be trusted." He returned to the bucket with a hammer and chisel, chipped out two small pieces of ice from the bucket, then wrapped the two pieces of cloth around them. "Here, hold these to your injuries for a bit."

Vincent winced when the icy cloth touched his lip.

Alexandra smiled softly. "Thanks, Gramps. You didn't have to do all that, though."

"Of course I did. Now then, I didn't call you all here for sly talk or short rumors. I have a gift for each of you."

From underneath his workbench, he pulled out four oak chests varying in size, one for each of them. After each was placed on the table in front of its designated recipient, he reached behind him for a silver hammer covered in Sanorian runes, symbols consisting only of lines depicting images rather than actual letters.

"Weapon chests!" Vera exclaimed with a large grin on her face. "I knew it."

"Ah, don't get ahead of me, now. Open them up, if you would, but don't remove the contents quite yet. Inside, you will find a star stone in the center of all your weapons, wherever the blade meets the grip. Except for yours, Barrik—yours is in the pommel. Now, cover the stones with your palms and close your eyes."

Sure enough, just as he said, embedded in each of their new weapons was a stone shining brighter than any regular jewel, almost as if each one had a tiny lantern inside to cast its ocean hue more vibrantly.

Once all their palms were placed and their eyes had fallen shut, Charlie made several signs with his left hand while resting the hammer on the table. When he was finished, the runes engraved on the hammer glowed a bright blue. He lifted the hammer high up in the air and quickly slammed it down.

The air in the room began to stir. Parchment drifted around with nowhere to go. Books flew open and began to levitate. The prototype designs on the walls fluttered and flailed as if they wanted to be freed. A warm wind from an unknown source gusted through everyone's hair. A moment went by until the blue runes began to steam. Everything dropped into its place. The wind vanished, the air became a steady flow, and the room returned to its chaotic norm.

"All right, now, you may remove them."

With Charlie's permission, they reached into the wooden chests and carefully inspected their gifts. They quickly noticed the color change in the star stones.

Vera lifted two short daggers, narrowly angled and without cross guards, it was as if she were holding the tip of a spear. The steel blades ran the length of her forearm to a black leather grip that fit perfectly in her palm. The pommel was a hollow ring just big enough for her finger. The star stones embedded in the base of the blade appeared to create a small red circle in the air as she spun them both around. She tossed one up and snatched it on its way back down with a large smile across her face.

Barrik hoisted up a double-bladed great axe with an ashy wooden shaft. Bright and silvery edges curved from the heel of the blade to the toe. Long, dark grains stretched from a jagged pommel to a pointed tip that rose several inches above the blades. Inside the pommel, he noticed his stone now shone a bright yellow.

Alexandra traced her fingers across a sword hilt barely big enough for both her hands. The wooden grip was glossy and dark, like it had been carved out of the very table in front of her. It already felt familiar beneath her palm. The cross guard, silver encased in a golden trim, reached out long and sturdy. She circled the rigid blue stone at the center with her right thumb.

Vincent raised one of the two identical blades out of the chest. The only difference between his swords and Alexandra's was a gentle curve in the handle that continued on into the blade itself, and the star stones embedded in the center of his crossguard shone an emerald green. He took a step back and twirled it in his hands.

"Well? What do you think?" Charlie asked, putting an end to the silence.

Vera placed her daggers back in the chest and threw her arms around Charlie. "I love them! Thanks, Gramps!"

"You're welcome, pumpkin," he said with a chuckle.

Barrik lifted his axe up and down like a newborn child. "It's unbelievably light."

"Your work never ceases to amaze me, old man," Alexandra said gently as she looked up at him. "Thank you."

He looked into her eyes with a smile and gave her a soft nod before divulging the details of his work.

"The sign I just performed was a bonding type. Only you four may wield these weapons, as they only respond to your energy. To you, they are extremely light, yet remain well balanced. However, should anyone else try to wield them... Well, let's just say they'd find it an easier feat lifting Mr. Barrik over there."

They shared a small laugh at the thought before Charlie continued.

"Also, at the base of your blades near the edge, you will see the four Sanorian runes for earth, water, air, and fire. All of your weapons are enchanted with each effect, so you won't need to sign for them in battle anymore. Keep them sharp, and they'll be an excellent ally for any situation you may find yourself in."

"So, they'll do just fine against ghouls, is what you're saying?" Vincent asked.

Barrik laughed. "Still can't get that out of your head, Vince?"

Vincent shuddered at the thought of his last interaction with a ghoul. "Those things give me the creeps."

Vera teased him from across the table by wiggling her fingers whilst making ghost noises. He sneered at her in response.

"Yes, my boy," Charlie said with a smile. "They'll do just fine with any horror, for that matter. Now, why don't you all head home for dinner, and I'll meet you there shortly?"

They said their goodbyes and expressed their gratitude before exiting Charlie's shop. By now, the sun had set beyond the western treetops, shading the sky in deep oranges and reds. Its light stretched their shadows long and thin in the middle of the road as they journeyed home.

Chapter 2

VERYONE was gathered around a dinner table covered with a wide variety of foods. Plates filled with berries, cheeses, slices of bread, and meats were spread out all over, leaving barely any room left for their ale, but make room they did.

While the rest of the group was dressed in their evening tunics, Ghost refused to remove his cloak, as he insisted he would not be staying long. However, once the sun had completely fallen to darkness, he removed his mask and hood. Hard features and a sharp chin full of scruff made up a face just as rugged as his voice. He was not a man of many words, but the deep blue eyes hiding behind his long black hair suggested there was much to be heard within them.

With everyone else lost in their conversations, Vincent took a silent leave into the sitting room, where the fire was dying down. He lifted a fresh piece of wood from the pile beside it and poked around in the ashes. The flames hissed at him as he rearranged the burning kindling. Embers leapt from their fiery confinement with a pop and a crack, drifting into the air above. They only had a brief moment of ascension before they vanished beneath a black banded necklace that hung just above the mantelpiece.

Vincent left his eyes to linger on the accessory. It bore a star stone, now damaged and faded; it no longer contained its ethereal illumination. He longed for a clear memory of the man who once wore it, even if it were just a brief image or the sound of his voice. Yet even in the deepest parts of his mind, he found nothing more than blurred silhouettes and fragmented noises, like echoes in a dream—a dream that had become more of an idea, a code of ethics for Vincent to uphold, a legacy for him to carry on. Strange, he thought, that he desired to emulate someone he barely remembered.

"If you're watching me from the stars, Father," he whispered to himself, "I hope I make you proud."

No birthday candle, no falling star, no fountain or Favor could ever bring him what he truly wished for, but he had accepted that long ago. Acceptance, however, was not a remedy for the want; it was merely a tonic to help him choke down the rough truths of reality. He found himself lost deeply in thought when a voice from the dining room called him back.

"Vince, come on back in here for a moment," Charlie requested from the dining room. Even with a raised voice, his tone lost none of its gentleness.

When Vincent returned, he stopped just beneath the archway separating the two rooms to see everyone looking at him with a full mug in their hand. Fira was standing behind his chair, gesturing toward it with an open hand.

"Come sit," she said.

With him seated, she raised her mug. "A toast to Vince."

She looked into his eyes for a moment. There was an endless list inside her head of things she wanted to say, but in the end, "Happy birthday" was all she said. A soft flicker in his eyes suggested that he understood the words unspoken.

"Happy Birthday, Vince," everyone followed.

They all raised their mugs in the air, then tapped them to the table before finally bringing them to their lips. As Fira sat back down, Ghost lifted a small leather pouch shaped like a pear from his pocket and took a swig.

"Here, Vince," Ghost said as he tossed the pouch to him.

Vincent caught the projectile and inspected it carefully. It looked like a smaller version of any normal water skin, but when he popped the cork and took a sniff of what was inside, he was revolted and looked back at him with a horrid expression. "What is it?"

"Tastes better than it smells. Have a drink. Pass it around."

Hesitantly, he brought it to his lips and took a small taste. Again, he was revolted.

"Did you mean *worse* than it smells?" he said with a cough.

"Enjoy it. That's a rarity only familiar to the king of Limfas and his guards."

"Then how'd you get it?" Alexandra asked as she took the mystery liquid from Vincent.

"The King. Couple sips of that is the same as several ales."

She choked down her sip and handed it to Barrik. "You know King Lian?"

"Never met him."

Barrik squirmed as soon as it touched his tongue. "Why does it burn?"

"So, you stole it?" Vera asked as she sniffed the pouch several times.

"He unwillingly relinquished it from his possession."

"You stole it," she said with a smirk before taking a second sip.

Alexandra leaned in, curious. "You used your Favor to steal from a king?"

In an instant, before Vera could take her third gulp from the pouch, Ghost appeared behind her and snatched it from her hand. All that remained in his seat was a wispy black trail. He looked at Alexandra and took a swig before appearing back in his seat, answering her question with silence.

Vera's mouth was left wide open with amazement. "How does your Favor work?" she finally asked, barely able to contain herself.

Ghost handed the pouch to Fira, who then passed it on to Charlie.

"I can relocate to any nearby shadow," he said, pointing to Vera's shadow on the floor.

"See, I told you, V," Alexandra said.

"You didn't kill anyone today, did you?" Charlie questioned.

"Unfortunately, no."

Charlie seemed genuinely surprised. "Well, that's a first."

Vincent started to imagine the many bloody ways in which the encounter with the soldiers could have ended differently.

"Killing them before they returned to Meditas would have only given Sentis a reason to bring his army to our doorstep," Fira said. "And we don't need to give these four any more trouble than they've already bargained for."

Ghost leaned back in his chair. "Trouble only Vince is required to deal with," he said, looking at Vera, Barrik, and Alexandra. "You three would be wise to stay here."

Alexandra, put off by his comment, crossed her arms and spoke conclusively. "Mom has taught us many lessons over the last ten years, and no matter how difficult they were, how bad we struggled, or how much our bodies ached, it was always easier to do with one another. Whatever challenges one of us faces, we'll face them the same way we always have. Together. As a team."

Vincent nodded gratefully to her before she turned back to Ghost.

"We're going," Alexandra said definitively.

"Yeah!" Vera chimed in. "I can't become the most fearsome Guardian in all of Sanora by sitting here in Sylva."

Barrik set down his mug of ale and wiped the foam from his mouth. "Guardians aren't supposed to be feared, V. We're protectors."

"Pffft." Vera waved away his words. "Besides, Vincey probably couldn't even find his way there without us, anyway."

"Not true," Vincent disagreed defensively.

Vera grinned and narrowed her eyes at him. "Okay, then, which direction out of Cayland do you go to Meditas?"

"West, just like the captain said."

Alexandra shook her head. "No. You go north."

Vera rocked back in her chair and crossed her feet up on the edge of the table. "Ha! Told you!"

Fira glared at her, rivaling the look she had given the captain. Vera promptly returned her feet to the floor.

Barrik placed his hand on Vincent's shoulder. "You get lost easy, bud."

"Why did he tell us to meet at the western gates, then?" Vincent asked, brushing away Barrik's palm.

"That I don't know," Alexandra admitted.

"Because it's the safest route," Ghost answered. "Normally, you'd head to the northern gates. But those parts of the ruins lead you to the southeastern corner of Thernruff Woods. Both places are overrun with bandits. The western side of the ruins, however, is littered with horrors. Bandits avoid it like the star plague. I'd rather you avoid Cayland altogether, but you don't have that kind of time. Together or not, it's no place for children."

"We're not little kids anymore," Alexandra said firmly.

Fira laid a platonically reassuring hand on Ghost's arm and looked into his eyes. "They're going to be fine. Besides, they almost killed you when they were barely waist-high." She smiled proudly. "They're a little better now."

Ghost grunted and rolled his eyes.

"We almost killed you?" Alexandra asked, surprised.

"Well, to be specific, it was Vera," Fira said. "Go on, show them."

Reluctantly, Ghost pulled back his dark hair on the left side of his head, revealing a deep scar that ran from the front of his ear to the nape of his neck.

Vera's eyes widened in amazement as she leaned closer across the table. "I did that?"

Charlie laughed. "A craftsman should always recognize their own handiwork."

Vera fell back in her seat. "It was so long ago, I don't remember it. I'm sorry."

"You should be honored, not sorry," Fira said. "Only twice has someone brought Ghost here close to death, and one of them was you, a tiny little girl." She laughed.

Ghost grunted.

Vincent suddenly noticed that while Ghost bore the grotesque scar from Vera on the left side of his face, the trademark cuts of a rogue were absent from his right. He did not understand how he had overlooked this before, but now his curiosity was piqued.

"Why don't you have the...?" Vincent asked, gesturing to his right cheek.

"The Rogue's scar?" Ghost scoffed. "I wasn't about to sit around and let someone cut me up. Besides, I never made it back to Meditas. I was a little busy with three strange kids." He turned his attention to Alexandra and gestured to her left hand. "How is your... condition?"

Alexandra self-consciously laid her right hand over the linen glove covering her left, as if to conceal it further. "It's slowly spreading," she answered nervously.

"Does it hurt?"

She shook her head.

"And she hasn't shown any sign of a Favor?" he asked, looking at Fira.

"Not one," she replied. "Even after all the mental and physical stress I put them through."

"Lucky."

"How is that lucky?" Vera asked. "She could've ended up with two Favors!"

"No," Ghost responded firmly. "You only ever get one. I've seen what happens to those who try for another."

"What happened to them?" Vincent wondered.

Silence and the solemn faces of Fira and Charlie were the only answers he received.

"I'll be fine," Alexandra stated.

Even though her tone suggested confidence, Vincent knew how she felt. She was drowning in worries; they all were. Her mutated arm had long shrouded them in mystery, and now, as the day approached where she would drink from a second fountain, the imagined potential consequences covered them all in a cloud of fear.

"I hope so," Ghost said as he stood up from the table. "You're still better off staying behind."

Fira rose from her seat to embrace him. "They're going to be fine," she reassured him.

He did not respond—at least, not verbally. Vincent watched Ghost's eyes leave Fira's and linger on the necklace hanging above the fireplace momentarily before they returned. Fira gave him a nod, and with it, he threw on his mask and hood.

Vera rushed over and threw her arms around him. "Thanks, Uncle Ghost! We're going to miss you!"

Ghost stood still, frozen with confusion. Vera turned back around and headed to her seat with a mischievous grin on her face. His eyes were hidden, yet they all felt them as he looked back at the table. "Thanks for the meal," he said just before he vanished. All that was left was the black, wispy trail that dissipated into the air.

"Well, he was pleasant," Vincent joked.

"Ghost may not be the sweetest of berries, but he means well," Fira said, sitting back down.

Charlie crossed his arms. "If you say so."

"Even *you* would become a bit coarse if you spent as much time alone in the wild as he does."

"Why doesn't he just stay here then?" Barrik asked.

Fira sighed. "He'll never come out and say it, but I'm sure half of the reason he never stays in one place is because he feels responsible."

"Responsible for what?"

"His Favor allows him to go into the kind of places where people wish not to be seen or heard. Places you might hear the underlying truth within rumors or the whispers of war. And with the shield of night, his Favor allows him to travel twice as fast as any horse. Makes for a great messenger. He can inform those necessary of potential dangers, or remove them before they become a larger issue. But if he didn't and let things unfold however they may, then he'd blame himself."

"Sounds like a lot of weight to carry," Barrik said.

"Much lighter than the weight of lost lives you might have been able to save. And being surrounded by that much chaos makes the return to a normal life far from easy."

"What do you mean?" Alexandra questioned curiously.

Fira paused for a moment and took a breath. She turned and gazed into the fire in the sitting room. As the flames began to pull her in slowly, her voice softened.

"Being exposed to that kind of darkness changes the way you see the world. It's like an abrupt awakening from a beautiful dream. And no matter how hard you try, there's no falling back into it. Now you're awake, and you see everything in a new, unwelcoming light. Sleep is no longer your friend, no matter the warmth of your bed. Noise becomes a comfort, while silence is deafening. Anything that nears a sense of peace can only be a lie. No matter how bright the sky, all you can see are the shadows."

Charlie gently placed his hand over Fira's. She turned to him, almost startled, and wiped a tear from her eye.

"Mom, are you okay?" Vincent asked gently.

"I'm fine, love. Let's get all this cleaned up and get ready for bed."

Everyone did their part in returning the dining room back to normal, and once everything was finally back in its proper place, Charlie said his goodbyes for the night. Fira closed the door behind him and turned around to see Vera lifting the water skin pouch to her lips. Like a deer that had just been spotted, she froze. Fira gave her an expression of slight disapproval and shook her head.

"Well, you might as well hand it over," Fira said to her.

Vera quickly took a sip and handed her the pouch.

"I can't believe you actually enjoy that stuff," Barrik said.

"Yeah, it's terrible," Vincent agreed. "However, I don't think I'm going to be able to sleep tonight, so…" He held out his hand until the pouch was placed in his palm. He took a sip, instantly shivered, and then handed it back to Vera.

"Reading usually puts you all right to sleep," Fira suggested.

"It's been a long time since you read anything to us," Vincent choked out through a tightened throat. "Do something we've read a hundred times, so I don't have to do any thinking."

"In that case, it doesn't matter what I pick," she teased.

He sneered as everyone else laughed.

Vera plopped herself down on the sofa, while Barrik sprawled out on a rug made from bear fur with his hands crossed behind his head. Vincent positioned himself next to the fireplace as Alexandra sat down with her back propped up against the sofa. Fira ran her fingers along a bookshelf in the corner of the room, searching for something to read.

"Any requests?" she asked.

"Since we have to go to Cayland," Alexandra suggested, "what about *The Battle for Sanora?*"

"Yes!" Vera exclaimed, practically jumping out of her seat. "I'm so excited to see the statues of the Four!"

"*The Battle for Sanora* it is, then." Fira reached for a large maroon novel with worn corners and weathered edges. Dust floated into the air as she lifted it from the shelf. The title was stitched in gold letters on the front cover, with the author's name, *Gram Saybin,* underneath. She took a seat in a wooden rocking chair with an olive-colored cushion just to the left of the fireplace. She cleared her throat as she opened the novel to the first page. Silence fell over the room as she began to read.

"Peace—a strange concept. Something we all desperately desire to the point that we are willing to wage war for it. Yet once we have it, we grow restless. The Sanorians did not rule over mankind poorly—at least, not at first. Beings of similar nature to us, but standing over a foot taller than the largest of men with—'"

"Oh, Bear, maybe you're part Sanorian!" Vera interrupted.

He shook his head gently with his eyes closed as Fira continued.

"'...with abilities beyond those of mortal men. Perhaps we were jealous of their powers, or simply feared what they could do with them if they so chose. Whatever the reason, a change was desired. When the stars rained from the dark sky above, the end of the Sanorian's reign had begun. At first, they seemed like marvelous jewels in the sky, like gods descending to our land to grace our eyes with their beauty. But there was nothing graceful about them.'"

As Fira turned the page, Alexandra patted Vera on the leg and held her hand out for the pouch. She handed it down from the sofa before repositioning herself to lie on her back, with one of her legs dangling off. She started to swing her foot as Fira read on.

"'Four bright burning stars crashed into the ground with a miraculous blast, ending any form of life for miles. Man and Sanorian alike were instantly turned to ashes with the rest of the land, and soon after the stars' arrival, an illness befell the Sanorians. The star plague, they called it. There had been a change in the atmosphere that had affected only them. We humans, and the rest of our life, remained unaffected. They believed the planet was dying, entering its final stages. So, in an attempt to heal it, four of the Sanorians' strongest warriors were chosen to use their power at each of the star sites.'"

Alexandra suddenly whipped around and smacked Vera's swaying leg. "V, if you kick me one more time, I swear to the stars I'm going to rip your foot off and throw it in the fire."

Vera looked down at her with warm red cheeks and a sly grin. Fira shot her a look before she could act on her mischievous thoughts. When she turned to Vincent, he was sitting straight up next to the fireplace with his eyes closed and his head slowly drifting to the side. Barrik remained perfectly still, his chest slowly rising and falling with each breath.

Fira turned the page. "'Their power was as impressive as it was beautiful to witness, but it was not without its downside. As amazing as it was, using that much power cost all four of them their lives. Yet with their sacrifice, life returned, stronger than before—and with it, something strange. Shortly after, the land reverted to its former state, but at each of the four sites, a natural spring of raw energy formed. Some believed these springs to be the manifestation of the souls that were sacrificed. Due to this belief, the springs became sacred, and cities were built around them to protect their divinity, with monuments erected all over Sanora to commemorate the four who were lost.

"'While their efforts brought life back to the land, they did nothing for the star plague. The sickness continued to ravage the Sanorians, and as they failed to find a cure, humanity saw an opportunity. Rumors spread of the sacred water's ability to grant powers similar to those of the Sanorians with just a drop—if one could survive it. Driven by desperation or lust for power, men and women from all nations drank from the springs, and those who survived did indeed gain exceptional abilities. With these new powers, and with the star plague weakening the Sanorians, mankind soon took over. No longer would we be looked down upon or seen as lesser beings. We would fight for a new kind of peace—a peace of our own making, a peace of man. And thus, the battle for Sanora began.'"

Fira looked up to see everyone's eyes closed except for Alexandra's and she smiled. "Whenever we read this at night, you're the only one to ever make it through the prologue."

"How many nights did it take us to finish that one for the first time?" Alexandra asked.

Fira turned and looked at Vincent. "To this day, I don't think he knows how it ends."

Alexandra laughed. She looked over her shoulder to see Vera passed out with her mouth hanging wide open. The pouch was still gripped beneath her palm. She gently snuck it out from under her and went to take a sip, but found it was already empty. When she held it upside down, not even a drop came out.

"Should I keep reading?" Fira asked.

"No, that's okay. You don't have to. Another chapter, and I'll end up like her." Alexandra gestured over her shoulder to Vera.

Fira smiled softly. "All right, then." She closed up the book and set it back on the shelf.

"Hey, wake up," Alexandra said as she shook Barrik's foot. He grunted.

"You're on Vince duty. Come on, grab him, and go to bed."

He grunted again and let another moment pass before he sat up and looked around the room to quickly remember where he was. When he rose to his feet, he walked over and scooped up Vincent gently in his arms.

"My hero," Vincent muttered in his half-awake state.

Barrik grunted with his eyes half open.

"Goodnight, boys," Fira said as she hugged him from the side. As they left the room, she turned to Alexandra. "You got her?"

"Yeah, I got her." Alexandra groaned as she picked Vera up in her arms. Aside from her breathing, she gave no signs of life.

Fira walked over and kissed Alexandra on the top of her head. She let out a soft laugh at Vera's condition. "Always a handful, she is."

"Vince and her both," Alexandra said with a toss of her eyes.

Fira laughed again. "And something tells me they always will be."

"Unfortunately, I agree."

She smiled. "Well, off to bed with ya, then. And try not to drop her this time."

Alexandra nodded with a grin and went back to her room with all of Vera's deadweight in her arms. Fira returned to her rocking chair and sat down. She slowly looked around the room—from the bookshelf, to the sofa, to the dining room, to the fireplace. It was quiet. And before tomorrow's sun had even reached its peak, the silence she presently sat in would become permanent. Her heart began to ache. The day she had been dreading for the last decade had finally come, and it had arrived much too soon. She closed her eyes, hoping that sleep would overtake her, but the gentle crackling of the fireplace never fully faded away.

Vincent awoke to the smell of bacon crisping in the kitchen. The day had finally come. For a while, it had seemed as if it never would, but now, it was here, and everything felt surreal. Knowing it would be a long time before he ever set foot back in his room again, he took his time getting dressed, savoring every moment he had left. When he finally walked out his bedroom door, he turned back around. Both his and Barrik's beds were neatly made for the dust to settle in their absence. Sunlight washed over the wooden floorboards, stopping just at his feet. He took a breath and shut the door.

Everyone, including Charlie, was already seated in the dining room. Fira was placing plates of eggs, fruits, bacon, and bread all across the table.

Charlie patted Vincent on the shoulder as he sat down next to him. "How'd you sleep, my boy?"

"No different than any other night, really." He turned to Barrik as he started to assemble food on a plate. "Surprised you beat me out of bed, though."

"Mom's breakfast is the only thing that will ever get him out of bed," Alexandra said.

Barrik grinned with a mouthful of food.

She shook her head and smiled. "I swear, you and Bear could sleep through another starfall."

Fira slathered a small piece of bread with butter. "Vince gets that from his father."

Vincent looked down the table to see Vera hovering over a cup of tea, letting all of the steam roll over her face and into her nose. Her eyes were half-open, and her hair was a frizzy, tangled mess.

"V, you feeling okay?" he asked with a chuckle.

She groaned and mumbled something under her breath.

"She'll be fine in an hour or two," Fira said. "Maybe now she'll have learned that stealing has its consequences."

Vera took a sip from her tea. "I didn't steal it."

"What do you call it, then?"

"… He unwillingly relinquished it from his possession."

Fira glared at her from across the table. "Eat the bread too. That'll help."

She groaned.

Barrik reached across the table to fill his plate again. He continued to pile food on top of it until it was practically spilling over the edges.

Alexandra stared at him, disgusted and slightly impressed. "What is that now, Bear? Your third plate?"

Barrik looked at her with his mouth stuffed full of food and held up four fingers.

"How?"

"I'm just really going to miss Mom's cooking," he said defensively.

Fira laughed. "While I appreciate that, you'll have plenty of delicious options to choose from in Meditas. Plenty of new dishes I could never make you here."

"Oh, yeah," Charlie added, "if that old pirate is still around, ask him for his beef stew. While he pours a terrible ale, the stew is a tender and salty perfection."

Barrik froze with his mouth half full. "Beef shtew?" he asked, as if his breakfast no longer satisfied him.

Everyone burst into laughter. They continued to eat and chat a bit longer, until Fira decided it was time for them to go. Everyone gathered their belongings and said their quiet goodbyes to their home.

Vincent panned around and watched all of his memories flash before him in an everlasting instant. Loud dinners full of shouts and playful arguments at the table, drinking competitions held in the sitting room, and peaceful nights by the fire, just like last night. He basked in the moment until a heavy hand fell upon his shoulder, telling him it was time to go. Barrik gave him a nod, and together, they stepped outside.

"All set?" Fira asked the group.

Everyone nodded in response.

"Good. We'll walk you to the gate."

"You don't want to walk us the whole way?" Vincent joked.

"While I would love to, if I am seen anywhere near Meditas, it would be the end of my days. Come on, now," she said as she turned and began to lead them through the village.

A somber cloud seemed to dwell over Sylva. For everyone else, it was nothing more than a normal day, yet it felt quieter. No birds were singing, no children were playing, and not even the breeze made a sound as it swept across them. Everyone was left to their thoughts until they reached the tall wooden gate to the city, where they were greeted by Rucker waving frantically. Vincent noticed a small brown pouch in his stationary hand.

Fira motioned to the two guards, who stood below with their spears, to open the doors. As the large gate slowly dragged across the ground, she turned around to give them their final lecture.

"I've taught you all everything I can. However, you'll soon find that a real battle is a teacher far better than I. You will get hurt, and you will recover, but for every scar, there is a lesson. Learn from it, and you'll grow even stronger. Fight only when you need to, and when you do, fight together, and if you run, run together. Fleeing from battle and retreating are two different things; do not confuse them. One is cowardly, and the other may be necessary. The foolish strength to stay and fight a battle clearly lost for no purpose other than your pride is no strength at all."

She looked over each one of them from head to toe. An olive-green cloak covered them from the neck down to the tops of their knees. Barrik's axe and Vincent's sabers could be seen hanging on their backs, while the hilt of Alexandra's sword on her hip peeked out from under her cloak. Vera kept her daggers in a small sheath on the lower part of her back beneath the olive cloak.

"Each one of you has become a fine warrior, and with your Favors, you'll be even stronger. I wish I could attend the ceremony with you and continue your energy training, but Kai will have to suffice. In truth, there is most likely no one better to do so anyway. Try not to give him too hard of a time." She looked from Vera to Vincent and back again. "Now, hold out your hands."

Charlie handed her a small drawstring pouch that rattled slightly as she put her hand inside. Fira handed each one of them a small colored stone from the pouch, similar to the one above the fireplace and in each of their weapons.

"Star stones?" Alexandra asked.

"Yes. Now close your hands tightly, and close your eyes."

They all did as they were told. Fira stepped to the side as Charlie went to each one of them and placed his hand over theirs. With his free hand, he made a sign. His first three fingers formed a circle, while his ring and pinky pointed straight into the sky. When he was finished, he stepped back, and Fira spoke again.

"Okay, you can open them," she said softly.

Now, each stone's original color had changed. Barrik's was now yellow, Vera's was red, Alexandra's was blue, and Vincent's was green, just like the stones in their weapons. Fira went down the line, taking each stone and handing them all back to Charlie.

From his pocket, he pulled a black banded necklace with a hollow silver raindrop suspended at the end. He placed each of the stones inside and wrapped his hand around it, weaving yet another sign with his other hand. When the sign was complete, he clasped both hands around the necklace tightly. From between the cracks of his fingers, they could all see a bright white light bursting out.

When he finally reopened his hands, the stones were all fused together inside the raindrop. He placed the necklace over Fira's head and let her examine it further. They could see each of their designated colors glowing brightly within the raindrop that now rested around her neck.

"There. Since these now respond to your energies, as long as you're okay, I'll know it. You have just under two weeks to reach the captain and his soldiers in Cayland. That gives you plenty of time to avoid any nighttime traveling, but I doubt they'll wait beyond the sunrise of the day you're expected, so it's best if you're early. Let's say our goodbyes and send you on your way."

Fira opened her arms. Vera rushed in to wrap herself around her and took a deep breath.

"You smell like sunshine and horses," Vera said softly, her face buried in Fira's long, sandy hair.

Fira smiled as she squeezed her. "Don't let those swift hands of yours get you into trouble."

A guilty smirk fell over Vera's face as she gave a final squeeze. "I won't."

Vera turned to Charlie and launched her arms around him. "I'm going to miss you, Gramps."

He was forced to take a slight backstep with a groan. "I'm going to miss you too, pumpkin."

She threw her arms around him once more before moving aside. Barrik wrapped his arms around Fira, practically making her disappear.

"I swear to the stars, boy," Fira started, "you get bigger every sunrise. If I didn't know any better, I'd say your father was an elder tree."

He smiled and moved to the side to make Charlie disappear next.

"Careful now, lad, I'm old. Squeeze me too hard, and I might turn to dust."

"No way. You're the strongest of all the steel, Gramps," Barrik said with a squeeze.

Alexandra rested her cheek on Fira's shoulder and gripped her tightly. "I don't think there is a scholar or writer in any corner of Sanora who has the words to tell you how grateful we are for you. Thank you. For everything."

"You don't have to thank me for anything," Fira said, glancing up at Vincent. "Just try to knock some sense into that one for me, would you?"

Alexandra laughed softly with tears in her eyes. "I will."

When she pulled away, Fira held her by the shoulders and shook her head. "I feel so guilty."

"For what?"

"A part of me wishes at least one of you would stay," she said with a smile and watery eyes.

Alexandra hugged her once more before letting go. She walked over to Charlie and embraced him gently. "I'll try not to turn you into dust, old man."

He smiled and pulled her close, the scruff of his face scraping against her cheek. "You take care, my dear. And of everyone else."

"Always."

Vincent stepped forward and held his mother as tightly as he could. He was excited to embark on the long-awaited journey, but the aching thought of never seeing home again made it hard to pull away.

"What's this? A hug with no fuss?" she asked as she squeezed him.

"Not this time," he said with a smile.

She held him close. Maybe, if she held him long enough, he would never leave. She squeezed harder. Tears fell down her cheeks. There were so many things she knew she would never find the words to say. "I'm so sorry, Vince."

He shook his head on her shoulder. "Don't be. I wanted to become a Guardian long before you told me I had to, remember?"

"I know, I know." She kissed the top of his head. "Your father would be so proud of you."

He held her tighter. "I hope so."

Fira pulled away to look him in the eyes. "I hope you know, there is nothing you could ever do to make any one of us feel otherwise."

An uncontrollable smile spread across his face. "Thanks, Mom."

"My boy," Charlie said as he embraced Vincent. "You've grown into a fine young man, but you'll always be my boy. No matter what."

Vincent pulled away, still smiling. "I can live with that."

"Good. Off you go," Charlie said, steadying himself.

Vincent took a step back and fell in line with the others.

"My turn! My turn!" Rucker demanded.

He rushed to the front of the group and rustled through his little pouch. "Okay. Hold out your hands. But spread your fingers!"

With all their hands laid out before him, Rucker placed a bright silver ring on each of their index fingers. When he got to Barrik, he realized his measurements were slightly off and he could only fit the ring on his pinky. Once it finally slid on, he exhaled a breath of relief.

"And I was worried it was too big," Rucker said.

Vincent carefully inspected the gift. It was a thin silver band, marked with clear hammer impressions, with a tiny blue star stone embedded on top, glistening in the sun. The design was simple, but something about the way the silver gleamed made him realize that, although the craftsmanship seemed amateur, the metal Rucker had used was far from easy to work with.

"Ruck, is this Sanorian silver?" Vincent asked.

The small boy nodded wildly with a large smile. "Yup! Do you like them?"

"I love it!" Vera exclaimed, holding her hand high in the air.

Charlie examined the rings with amazement. "This is incredible work, my young apprentice."

Rucker stood proudly.

"But I'm wondering," Charlie continued, "where exactly did you get this Sanorian silver?"

Rucker's eyes widened with panic. "I only used a little bit, I swear! I just couldn't let them leave without a gift to remember me by!"

Vincent knelt on one knee. "We could never forget you, Ruck. Even if we wanted to," he joked as he gently flicked his forehead.

"You mean it?" Rucker asked, rubbing the minor injury.

"Of course we do," Alexandra said, crouching with open arms.

Rucker flew into her embrace. "Come back soon!"

"As soon as we can," she replied.

Fira gently pulled Rucker back by the shoulders to stand with her and Charlie. "All right, everyone. It's time."

Fira looked over the four soon-to-be Guardians—her children—with proud eyes and an ache in her heart. After a moment of silence, she gave them a gentle nod and watched as they turned toward the gate. The guards all bowed their heads as the four of them passed beyond the city walls.

Charlie put his arm around Fira and watched the four of them disappear into the forest with the gates closing behind them.

CHAPTER 3

HE late summer days were gentle to them beneath the forest shade. With every setting sun, the breeze grew colder, bringing with it the call of autumn. Soon, the dense trees would hold up a colorful motley of leaves that would inevitably blanket the ground. The winding trail was full of roots and rocks, which the four new adventurers carefully avoided as they pressed on. While the road varied in width with every twist and turn, it never narrowed to less than the size of two full-grown horses standing side by side. Every few hundred feet or so, on either side of the road, were lanterns rested atop iron poles set deep into the ground. At one time, with Sanorian power, they had acted as a ward to the horrors, allowing travelers safe passage between the major cities. Now, however, they served as little more than a mere reminder of a past civilization.

When the long days finally turned to night, the moon sent an icy breath into the air. Their small fires brought them a friendly warmth, but the chill of the wind was only part of the reason they huddled close to the flames. As the curtain of darkness fell, the horrors of the night rose. Ghouls, wretches, and weren were just a few of the foul creatures that lurked under the light of the moon. While they were well equipped to deal with any one of them, they traveled only by day to minimize their chances of encounter.

As the days started to blend together and drag on, they mostly entertained themselves through jokes played on one another, little games taught to them by Fira and Charlie, or reminiscing in shared memories. It began to feel as though they were making little to no progress, until the forest finally broke, opening into a vast prairie full of hills and brush. Before they continued any farther, Alexandra stopped and looked at the dark, cloudy sky above. The sun had only just begun its descent.

"We're still a few days from the ruins," she started, "but if we want a fire tonight, we should probably stop here."

"Do we have time?" Vincent asked.

"We can spare half a day," Alexandra said. "Besides, I'm not eager to see those soldiers again. Even with Mom's threats, I doubt they'll be welcoming."

"Maybe the captain will punch Vincey in the upper lip this time and make him look like a duck," Vera said, contorting her lips.

The girls laughed as Vincent mocked them.

Barrik held up his hand. "I would love a fire."

"Great! Well, since you volunteered, you can get us the firewood," Alexandra commanded with a smile.

"Why do I always have to do it?"

"Because you can take a tree down with one swing."

"With your hand," Vera added.

Barrik hung his head. "Fine. Vince, you're coming with me."

"What? Why?"

"Because I might need some bait. Come on." He turned and walked into the woods.

Vincent pouted behind him, practically dragging his knuckles the whole way until they stopped just over a small hill out of sight of the trail. Barrik stopped beside a smaller tree, looked it up and down, and pushed it effortlessly. They both watched as it toppled gracefully to the ground.

Vincent looked over the tree as Barrik pulled out his axe. "You have the strength of several oxen."

Barrik turned to him. "Are you comparing me to a farm animal?"

"Well, you kinda smell like one, and you make chores easier."

He shook his head. "It was already dead," he said as he started to chop away.

"Sure it was." Vincent started to look around as Barrik created smaller pieces for them to burn. "Actually… a lot of these trees are dead."

"Probably just some sort of fungi in this area. Grab those there and some kindling. And hurry up, I have beans to cook."

Barrik trotted off over the hill with a few logs in his hands. Vincent walked over to one of the dead trees and placed his hand on it. He turned around to see if Barrik was still there. Once he knew the coast was clear, he pushed with all his might to try to force the tree over, but failed to move it an inch. He pulled back and ran into it with his shoulder. Finally, it broke loose.

The tree fell to the ground, taking Vincent with it. He rolled to the side and watched it fall the rest of the way before it came down with a rather quiet crash. Now resting on the ground, he could feel the heaviness of his breath. "Yeah, that's why you get the wood," he said to himself.

After lifting himself up, he wandered over to the pile of wood Barrik had left him and started gathering it in his arms. Just as he placed the last log on top, a high-pitched wail pierced his ears. He instantly hunched his shoulders in a failed attempt to nullify the noise. Although the sound came from a distance, he scanned the area before quickly scaling the hill.

When he returned to the trail, nobody was in sight. Barrik's woodpile was just out of the center of the road, so he knew he had not lost his way. They had to be hiding, he thought.

"Barrik? Vera? Alex?" he called out. "Not funny, guys." He panned around the area until something hit the ground behind him, and he whipped around.

"Rawwr!" Vera shouted, knocking him backward as he cried out in fear.

All of the firewood in his hands fell to the ground. Barrik and Alexandra emerged from behind a tree and joined Vera in laughter. Vincent remained on the ground for a moment, his heart racing.

"S-s-sorry, Vince," Vera managed to get out, hunched over from laughing so hard.

Barrik walked over with a helping hand, still chuckling. "Sorry, bud. We heard the ghoul scream and couldn't resist."

Vincent brushed himself off and gestured to all the wood on the ground. "I'm not picking any of this up."

"I wish you could have seen your face!" Alexandra said as she started collecting the wood.

Resting against a tree with his arms crossed, Vincent remained unamused. "Just wait. I'll get you all back when you least expect it."

"Sure you will."

As the fire started to crackle and the flames grew from a spark to a small dance, each of them inched as close as they could to its warmth. With a crackling fire and the calm of night, it was easy for them to drift away into sleep, but one of them was always left awake to be wary of potential dangers that might spring on them at any moment. Yet no matter what inhuman screams were heard in the distance or rustling in the bushes nearby, the only thing that greeted them was early morning beams of light.

With the forest finally behind them, they entered the territory of Cayland. Green hills and tall blades of grass were now at the forefront. While their day had started with clear skies and bright sunshine, clouds had slowly crept in from afar. The rest of their journey through the region was a never-ending fall of rain. The nights were even colder now, especially without the comfort of a fire to warm them from the wet and cold. While it began to feel like the chill in their bones and the chatter of Vincent's teeth would never end, a dry hope came into view once they reached the peak of a slippery hill.

"It's the ruins!" Vera shouted from beneath her hood.

The large remnants of a white-stoned city were about a mile away, although barely visible through the dark and pouring mist. Excited by the prospect of being dry for the first time in what felt like forever, Vera started to run, but slipped, fell on her backside, and slid the whole way to the bottom of the hill.

"V, wait!" Alexandra called to her from behind. She was either ignored, or Vera simply could not hear her. They chased after her, chopping their steps to minimize the chance of slipping.

By the time they caught up to her, she was stopped in her tracks with her head tilted back, unbothered by the rain splashing her face. They joined her in marveling at two massive white hands carved from stone with fingertips pressed together. Both were covered in moss and the cracks of time. The right middle finger had broken off some time ago and now lay on the ground in the tunnel that the other fingers created. Once, they had been little more than an entrance to the city, but now, with the vegetation on and around them, they appeared as though they had always been a part of the very land beneath them rather than something sculpted by the beings that once lived here.

"The book doesn't do them justice," Vera said, amazed.

"No, it doesn't," Alexandra agreed, looking on with amazement.

Vincent ran his hand along the large thumb to his right. The stone was smooth and wet beneath his fingertips, like he had pulled it from the bottom of a riverbed. Barrik walked under the finger tunnel and looked at the city ruins beyond. Tall grass covered every part of the crumbled debris on the ground and reached up as if it were trying to pull down what was left still standing.

"All right, let's find our lovely captain," Alexandra said.

Vincent rolled his eyes. "Can't wait."

They marveled at the ancient city as they searched for the western gates. Beyond the entrance, the ground beneath their feet turned to a road of stone and wet weeds guiding them through the remnants of a society long extinct. Barely anything was left intact. Houses and shops of the same smooth stone were crushed and crumbled, making up the rubble floor. What was once a city that shone brightly in the sun looked more like a graveyard for meticulous craftsmanship. Yet despite all the destruction and wet gloom from the dark clouds above, a melancholic beauty lingered between each blade of grass. It was inescapable, as if every splash of rain released waves of fresh tranquility into the air.

They came to a stop at a bridge that arched over a river, poised to overflow past the guard rail. At each of the bridge's four corners was a statue that stood over a foot taller than Barrik—life-sized sculptures of the Sanorians they represented.

"So, these are the Four who gave their lives to heal the planet," Vincent said, looking the statue on the left up and down, a tall, broad Sanorian man with a sword and shield resting beneath his palms.

"Amazing!" Vera exclaimed.

Alexandra looked up at the one on the right, a lady with long hair and a halberd raised across her shoulder. A few strands of her hair were swept across her face just above her eyes. Maybe it was the rain, or how she was carved, but Alexandra thought they seemed to bear a deep sadness.

They crossed over the bridge to find the other two heroes of stone, a Sanorian man and woman, both of whom had fallen to the ground. Now covered in wet moss and overgrown weeds, they appeared to be more of a natural landmark rather than the remnants of history.

"We should keep moving," Alexandra said, urging them all onward.

They tore their gazes from the figures of the past and continued their way westward. The sound of splashing footsteps and the steady patter of falling rain filled the streets as they drew closer to their destination. However, once an arched wooden gate at the end of the road came into their sights, something started to feel wrong.

"Those are the western gates, right?" Vera asked.

"They have to be," Alexandra ventured. "If we went any farther west, we'd be outside the city."

"Then where's the lovely captain?" Vincent questioned.

"I doubt they'd wait for us out in the rain. They're probably in one of those houses up ahead. Come on."

They peeked inside two of the crumbling homes, but found nothing except broken floorboards and more debris.

"Maybe they left for Meditas already," Barrik suggested.

Alexandra shook her head. "I don't think so. Why create such a fuss back in Sylva if they were going to leave us behind anyway?"

"I'm getting a bad feeling about all this," Vincent said.

"Me too," Alexandra agreed. "Let's check that one over there, and if we don't find them, we'll continue on ourselves."

"All right."

The four of them crossed the street to a two-story home that was still surprisingly intact compared to the others around it, save for a large hole big enough for a horse to fit through right next to the doorway. As soon as they stepped inside, a horrid stench hit their noses.

"What is that?" Vera asked, covering her mouth and nose.

Vincent walked around to the back of the house, just past the steps leading to the upper floor, where he unfortunately found the source of the smell. He coughed and gagged not only at the smell's intensity, but at the sight.

"Guys…" he croaked out.

The others rounded the corner and recoiled in a similar fashion. Blood was splattered all over the wooden floors. The captain and his three subordinates were spread throughout the room in pieces—an arm here, a leg there. They had been ripped apart in a peculiar fashion. Although at first, it appeared as if they had been brutally dismembered and murdered, all of them suffered an identical fate. All of the soldiers' breastplates were peeled apart or caved in, as if a dog had frantically dug a hole into their chests. Upon further inspection, they also noticed that the top half of each fallen soldier's head was missing.

"V..." Alexandra started, desperately trying not to vomit. "Can you check their..." Failing to finish her sentence, she gestured to her head.

Vera nodded and knelt beside the woman who once had a long braid. An expression of terror was still burned into her eyes.

"It's empty," Vera said, unable to remove her eyes from the bloody and hollow skull.

"Something ate all of their brains..." Vincent muttered in realization.

"And searched through their chest for something else," Barrik added, disgusted.

"What kind of horrors did Ghost say this area is overrun with?" Vera questioned nervously.

"He didn't," Alexandra answered. "But there's only one horror Mom told us about that goes for the brain."

"A nidbahk," Vincent whispered.

A loud thump on the floor above let them know they were not alone. Something started slowly making its way down the wooden steps. Nobody dared to move, paralyzed with fear as a horror with a thick body of ash-like skin and a head with only a few strands of rotted hair stood only a few feet away from them. A hunched back and long arms allowed its claws to hang so low they were dragging against the steps—a nidbahk.

Vincent's stomach turned. He knew the creatures were practically blind, but their sense of hearing was impeccable, and their ability to smell was not far behind. Not only that, but once they located a target, they moved faster than a hunting hound.

A low, guttural growl followed by several slow clicking sounds drew everyone's attention. Another one had made its way inside behind them. When they turned back to the first nidbahk, it was gone. Vera slowly raised a finger to the ceiling. Vincent looked up to see the horror slowly crawling around, twitching its head suddenly every step or two, listening. Another few clicks came from the second nidbahk, and this time, the first one responded. They were communicating.

Alexandra put her finger to her lips and motioned for everyone to crouch. She pointed toward the hole in the wall—their exit. They started to move as silently as possible, practically holding their breath. Desperately trying to avoid detection, they took their time, evading whatever obstacles were on the floor, but what they could not maneuver around was the floor itself. A wooden plank creaked from beneath Vincent's foot.

There was no time to react; the nidbahks charged. One ran right into Vincent, knocking him backward into a bookshelf.

"Vince!" Alexandra shouted, drawing her sword. Just as her blade rang out of its scabbard, the other nidbahk collided with her. Both of them tumbled through the large hole in the wall out into the rain. Vera followed quickly behind.

Vincent looked up from the ground into a mouth of drooling fangs. Barrik quickly bashed the horror in the face, stunning it long enough for Vincent to scramble out from under it. Before the beast could recover, Barrik swiftly dropped his axe on its neck. Its decapitated corpse twitched on the ground as dark blood spilled onto the floor. With one of the horrors eliminated, Vincent and Barrik ran outside to aid the others.

Alexandra hopped back and slashed upward, her sword slicing through drops of rain until the tip of the blade created a deep cut in the nidbahk's chest. The horror shrieked, stepped back on its hind legs, and lifted its head.

"Don't let it howl!" Alexandra shouted.

Vera quickly hurled one of her daggers through the air, sinking it into the nidbahk's throat, but it did not seem to bother the horror in any way. Its jaw opened wide and released an ear-piercing scream that forced all of them to wince in pain.

Vincent leapt into the air from a full sprint and slashed through the horror's neck with both of his sabers. Although the horror's howl had been cut short, it had served its purpose. From somewhere close by, they could hear another ear-piercing scream.

"We need to get out of here!" Barrik said in a hurry.

"Agreed," Alexandra replied, sheathing her sword.

Just as they all started toward the western gate, another nidbahk crashed through one of the broken homes into the center of the road, blocking their path. Then came another—and another. The nidbahks started sniffing around, growling and clicking with twitching heads.

Alexandra brought them all to a sudden halt and rushed into an alleyway.

"Now what?" Vincent asked in a hushed voice.

Alexandra peered around the corner to keep her eyes on the horrors. "The rain might cover our footsteps at a distance, but they'll hear us up close. And there's no telling how many more of them there are," she whispered.

"So, what are you thinking?" Barrik asked.

"I think it's safer to head north."

"But I—" Vera started before being hushed by everyone else. She quickly dropped her voice. "But I thought north was bandit territory?"

"With the captain and his squad dead, I think it would be wise to get to Meditas as fast as possible, which means we go north. Besides, we'll have a better chance sneaking past bandits than nidbahks."

"Yeah, way to go, Vince," Vera teased quietly.

Vincent rolled his eyes. "As if I could tell which floorboards were creaky."

"None of us stepped on it," Vera said with a shrug. "Just saying."

"Knock it off," Alexandra demanded. "Keep quiet until we're out of the city, and watch your steps. Let's go."

The four of them made their way through the city as silently as they could, checking behind every corner and down every alley for more nidbahks. Luckily, the only ones they found were out of audible range and preoccupied with whatever animal they were feasting on.

Once the northern gates were in sight, their shared tension faded. Even if they were entering another enemy's territory, at least the bandits were human. Strangely enough, however, there was no sign that anyone had been in the area for a long time—no leftover campfires or shelters large enough to house a tribe of bandits. There was nothing but more rubble and overgrown weeds.

"I don't see any bandits," Vincent said, looking around.

"We're not out yet. Bear, help me with the door," Alexandra commanded.

Vincent and Vera stood guard behind them as they removed the wooden crossbar and slowly pushed open the gate just wide enough for them to pass through. Once everyone was on the other side and out of the city, Alexandra surveyed the road behind them one last time before shutting the gate.

"Well," Vera started as they walked away, "as excited as I was to see Cayland, I am thrilled it's behind us."

"Me too," Vincent agreed. "Never wanted to see a nidbahk that closely."

Barrik chuckled. "Finally find something more frightening than ghouls?"

Vincent shuddered. "I still prefer the nidbahk."

Alexandra waved her hand at a bug buzzing around her. "I'd prefer if we were in Meditas already. I'm sick of these bugs and this rain," she said as she smacked the side of her neck.

"Sounds like someone's a little grumpy," Vincent teased.

"Shut up, Vince," Alexandra snapped.

With the city ruins behind them, their journey was soon at its end. It was only a few days through the rest of Cayland until they neared the edge of a dense forest. Thernruff Woods surrounded Meditas, and once they were under its canopy, it would only be a couple of hours to the gates. The sight of the trees brought a breath of relief. Pictures of warm beds, hot baths, and hot meals began to flood their minds. However, next to no light and bodies teeming with exhaustion meant they would need to spend one last night outdoors before the images in their minds could be realized.

Eager as they were to receive the wishes in their imaginations, their pace quickened to arrive under the forest as soon as possible.

By the time they breached the tree line, the sun had given way to the moon, but at least the rain had finally stopped in what seemed like weeks. They put together a small fire, removed their boots to dry, and huddled close to the warmth of the flames.

Barrik was rummaging through his bag, searching through what food they had left. Alexandra was leaning on one elbow, twiddling a blade of grass between her fingers. Vera clicked her feet together while gently swaying her head back and forth as if there were music heard only to her. Vincent lay on his back with his arms behind his head, slowly drifting away into sleep. None of them had any idea they were being surrounded.

Without warning, an arrow hissed through the air and sank into the ground next to the fire, startling each of them. Just as they scrambled to draw their weapons, a commanding voice stalled their movements.

"Don't move!" a woman shouted. "And keep your hands up where I can see them!"

As the four reluctantly raised their hands, several people slowly emerged from behind the trees. Each one was dressed in mismatched pieces of armor and cloth masks covering the lower half of their faces—bandits.

"What do you want?" Alexandra demanded.

Vincent started to feel a wave of regret flood his stomach. They had been aware that bandits were potentially in the area, yet were still foolish enough to let themselves be surrounded. He could practically hear his mother's voice shouting her judgment.

One of the bandits, a tall and skinny man with a mouth of fangs painted on his mask, started walking up to her. He carried a butcher's cleaver in his right hand. Vincent moved to step forward. He had barely lifted his foot before an arrow sank into the ground next to it.

"I said, don't move!" the woman shouted again.

"Don't think she'll warn you again, kid," said the man with the fanged mask. "To your question," he said, lifting his cleaver to Alexandra's neck. "You traveled into our territory, so really, we should be asking what it is *you* want?"

Alexandra narrowed her eyes at him, unafraid. "This isn't your territory. It's under Meditas's rule. You can't just go around claiming land."

"Why not? That's how it's always been done. Kill and take, take and kill. That's all life really is. Now, answer my question."

Vincent looked around as the tension grew. By his count, they were outnumbered two to one.

"We're traveling to Meditas," Alexandra said.

"She's lying!" the woman exclaimed, pulling back her bowstring.

"Why would we lie?"

"Just let us go," Vincent added.

"He sent them to kill us, Jay!" she said with a panicked voice. "Just look at them! They're armed to the teeth."

The fang mask whipped back around to the archer. "Be quiet, Cass!" Jay commanded.

Something had the bandits on edge. Even though they had surrounded Vincent and the others, *they* seemed to be the most frightened.

"Nobody sent us to kill you," Alexandra said. "Look, we just need to get to Meditas."

Jay examined them intently, paying close attention to each of their weapons. "You don't bear the crest of Meditas on your armor, so you're not soldiers. Not carrying any goods or wares either, so you can't be merchants—not good ones, anyway. So, if you're truly only going to Meditas and not looking to cash in on our bounty, why are you so well armed?"

Vincent shot Alexandra a look of uncertainty. "We're on a mission from King Sentis."

She quickly followed his idea. "Exactly, so if you do anything to us, there will be even more people looking for you."

"Oh, really?" Jay questioned suspiciously.

"Yup!" Vera said, lifting her chin proudly. "We have to become Guardians."

The bandits roared with laughter.

Alexandra glared over her shoulder at Vera with a look of disapproval. Vera immediately understood she had said too much.

"Now we *know* you're lying," Jay said.

"She's telling the truth," Barrik added.

"Yeah, and Cass over there is Sanorian," Jay responded sarcastically.

Alexandra looked at Vincent nervously. They had tried to avoid divulging their identities but were beginning to feel backed into a corner.

Jay noticed the glances exchanged between Vincent and Alexandra and immediately grew angry. "All right, I've had enough of this." He launched his knee into Alexandra's stomach. She hunched over, clutching her abdomen.

"Alex!" Vincent exclaimed. An arrow hissed by, inches from his face before he realized he had taken a step toward her.

Jay looked into Vincent's eyes as he lowered his cleaver to the back of Alexandra's neck. "Last chance. Tell us what you're doing here."

Vincent felt helpless. He desperately searched for a way out. He shook his head, unsure of what to say.

With no response to his demands, Jay lost his patience. "Fine." He raised his cleaver high in the air.

"Wait!" Vincent shouted in a panic.

Jay lowered his cleaver to his side. "Oh? Ready to talk now, are we?"

Vincent took a deep breath and swallowed the lump in his throat. "Look, we were telling the truth. We really are on a mission from King Sentis to become Guardians."

"Why would the king demand that four brats join a cult of freaks nobody has cared about since Victor's war got them all exiled or killed?"

"Because of a soul oath my father made with him ten years ago."

Jay stepped in front of Vincent. "You realize the soul oath is a pot of shit, right?" He looked Vincent up and down. "Even still, if your father made one with the king himself, he must be some kinda big shot. What's his name?"

Vincent hesitated. He painfully remembered what had happened when he told the captain he was Victor's son.

"Well?" Jay pressured.

"Victor Raine," Vincent finally answered.

A hush seemed to fall over the bandits.

Jay took a step back. "You're telling me you're the son of Victor Raine?"

Vincent slowly nodded.

"You?" Jay scoffed. "You look a little too pathetic to be his son, if you ask me."

Vincent clenched his jaw as if it helped to suppress the rage he felt from Jay's insult.

"Hmm..." Jay thought to himself for a moment. He quickly turned and went to Cass's side to communicate with her in hushed voices. The whole time, she never lowered her bow.

"You think that was smart?" Alexandra whispered to Vincent.

He shrugged defensively. "Was I supposed to let him chop your head off?"

Alexandra slightly turned her head to whisper over her shoulder. "V, can you make the throw?" Her eyes gestured toward the archer.

"Yeah, but I don't know how fast."

"Doesn't matter. Just—"

"Stop talking!" Cass suddenly shouted with an angry and troubled voice.

A moment later, Jay made his way back to the group. "So, we've come to a decision, and I have some good news. We won't be killing you today."

Everyone sighed a breath of relief—relief that was short-lived.

"However," Jay continued, "you won't be traveling to Meditas either. Instead, you'll be coming with us back to Enora."

"And why would we do that?" Alexandra asked with narrowed eyes.

"Well... you don't have a choice," Jay said with a nasty grin that could be felt from beneath his mask.

"We're not just going to let you take us," Vincent protested.

Jay lifted his cleaver to Vincent's neck. "Don't do anything stupid, kid—you're only Victor's son, not Victor himself." Jay lowered his weapon and took a step back. "Bind their hands, boys. Make 'em extra tight on the big guy."

As the other bandits moved in to follow their leader's command, Vincent looked at Alexandra, awaiting her signal. His heart started to thump against his chest.

As soon as the man behind her grabbed Alexandra's wrists, she threw her head back, breaking his nose.

"Vera!" she shouted.

Vera quickly launched one of her daggers from the sheath on her lower back. The blade raced through the air toward the archer. As fast and accurate as Vera was with her attack, it was not quick enough. Just before Vera's blade pierced Cass's neck, she released an arrow. The sharpened stone sank into Alexandra just below her right shoulder, forcing all of the air out of her lungs. She dropped to her knees, gasping for breath.

Vincent rushed to Alexandra's side just in time to block a slash aimed right at her head. At the sight of Alexandra injured on the ground, Barrik's blood boiled. His vision narrowed. His heart raced. A war cry full of a ferocious need to protect burst from his lungs. The bandits approaching him stopped in their tracks at the sudden fear rattling their bones. However, they were already too close. Barrik split one of their heads in two as if it were a piece of wood. In a bout of courage, one of the bandits charged at the beast that stood in front of him with a spear. Much nimbler than the man had anticipated, Barrik hopped to the side, snatched up the spear, and thrust it through the bandit's chest. The third attacker stood with his hands frozen and his legs shaking. His head looked small in the center of Barrik's meaty palms. With one quick motion, he snapped the bandit's neck as if it were a small twig.

Vera ducked, dodged, and danced around the chaotic onslaught of swings from a large woman holding two short-handed battle axes. She continued to scan for an opening in the woman's attacks, but saw no opportunities. What she did see was Barrik storming toward them from behind her enemy, his eyes fierce and wet with anger.

Vera took a quick step back. Before the woman was able to sense the imminent danger approaching, Barrik picked her up and slammed her back down on his knee. She instantly let go of her weapons and cried out in pain—pain that would not end there. Barrik grabbed her by the ankle and whipped her body against a nearby tree. There was a splatter of blood and several loud cracks. She dropped to the ground, motionless. Barrik turned to Vera, who had a hint of fear in her eyes.

"Are you okay?" he asked.

"I'm fine," she answered.

Vincent, trading blows with the bandit in front of him, heard rapid footsteps closing in from behind. He ducked beneath an attack and pivoted with a slash to end both enemies simultaneously. The first bandit fell to his side, blood spilling out of his midsection. The second, who tried to attack Vincent from behind, met a much swifter end.

Vincent's eyes widened in horror when he saw the body of a young boy lying at his feet, while his head lay several feet away. The boy's soft, round cheeks and bright brown eyes still stared up at him with innocence. His heart sank into the depths of his stomach. The world around him faded away. He no longer saw anything but the boy's face.

Tears streamed down Jay's face and disappeared beneath his mask of painted fangs as he gently set down Cass's head and picked up her bow. "What did you do?!" he shouted, aiming at the injured Alexandra once more.

"Vince!" Vera exclaimed, trying to get his attention.

No response. Jay pulled back the bowstring. Vera and Barrik scrambled to reach Alexandra, but they were too far away and not fast enough. Jay fired. The arrow soared through the air, and just as it was about to reach its target, it vanished. A wispy black trail slowly dissipated right before Alexandra's face.

Ghost suddenly appeared in front of Jay with the arrow in his hand and forced it through his shoulder exactly where Alexandra had been hit, forcing the bandit to his knees.

"Where did you come from?!" Jay cried out in pain.

Ghost snatched the bow from Jay's hands and threw it into the darkness of the woods. The silver of his wavy blade shone like a star in the dark sky as he drew it from the scabbard on his hip and lifted it to Jay's neck.

"Answer my questions, and I'll kill you quickly," Ghost said plainly.

"If you're going to kill me anyway, why does it matter what I do?"

"If you don't, I'll cut off both of your legs and toss you into the forest, where your best hope will be to bleed out before something catches a scent of your blood. Why were you trying to take them back to Enora?"

Jay coughed, groaning with pain. He hesitated for a moment before he answered. "There's a man in Enora who's been collecting people."

"Collecting people?"

"People of interest to him, I guess. Guardians, Rogues, advisors. Doesn't seem to matter. Pays so well, we thought it was better not to ask questions."

"He's paying you to kidnap these people?"

"Not anymore. We failed to come through one too many times, and he said if we failed him again, he'd kill us all. But we couldn't even locate the person he told us to, so we stayed in this area, thinking we'd never go back there."

"Until you thought the son of Victor Raine would restore his faith in you."

Jay nodded, guilty.

"Well done," Ghost said, looking around at all the bodies. "The person you failed to find—do you have a name?"

"Udurim was the only name we were given. Said he lives in Meditas, wears a blindfold, and wields a fiery sword. Sounds hard to miss, but we never found him."

Ghost lowered his blade, and although nobody could see behind his dark mask, he smiled. "Be grateful you didn't," he said, stepping back. "Now, make your peace."

Jay looked at the shadowy figure in front of him and only now truly understood that he had been speaking to his executioner. Silently, he lowered his head and closed his eyes—forever.

Once Ghost's sword was back in its scabbard, he returned to the others.

Barrik stood beside Alexandra, trying to find a way to painlessly remove the arrow stuck in her shoulder.

"May I?" Ghost offered.

Barrik moved away to let Ghost inspect her wound. Sweat poured down her face as she looked back at him.

"What are you doing here?" she asked softly.

"I've been with you since you left Sylva," Ghost answered, examining the bloodied arrowhead. "It's not poisoned. You'll be fine."

In one quick motion, he snapped off the arrow and ripped the shaft out of her shoulder. She groaned in pain and reached up to clutch the wound. "You could have warned me!" she exclaimed angrily through gritted teeth.

Ghost ignored her and looked over to Vera, who was still trying to get Vincent to come to his senses. Ghost stormed over to them, snatched Vincent by the neck, and pinned him against a tree.

"Woah! What are you doing?!" Vera cried.

Ghost disregarded her and spoke only to Vincent. "Your hesitation would have gotten her killed if I wasn't here! Do you get that?! Why did you stop?"

Vincent's eyes fell to the young boy's head on the ground. He opened his mouth, but found no voice to answer with. His eyes welled with tears.

Ghost dragged Vincent by his neck and held him above the boy, forcing him to look at what he had done.

"Let him go!" Barrik demanded.

Ghost gave him no acknowledgment. "Look at him! Don't you dare cry for the mercy you gave him. He died quickly and with less pain than he would have suffered in life. And what was the alternative? Let him kill you? Would you rather it be you?"

Vincent shook his head frantically. "I-I-I... I don't know. No. I just... It's just, he was only a kid. He couldn't have been any older than Rucker."

Ghost let go of Vincent's neck. "Killing him was a kindness."

"How can you say that?"

"Do you think he lived a good life? Roaming the darker places of Sanora with a band of mercenaries and thieves who didn't care about anyone but themselves? Young, old, sick—they have no sympathy for anyone as long as their bellies are full. He was most likely beaten, starved, and only valued for his size to get into small places the rest of them couldn't—the same life those three would have been subjected to if Fira hadn't taken them in. You sent his soul to the stars. Maybe he'll finally find peace among them."

"Is that supposed to make me feel better about it?"

"No."

Vincent closed his eyes tightly. His body was trembling. "Why couldn't they just let us go?" he said, almost to himself.

"Someone in Enora seems to be collecting people of particular interest," Ghost answered. "And being Victor's son puts a giant target on your back."

Barrik leaned in with a puzzled look on his face. "Did you say collecting people? Why would someone do that?"

"Yeah, why not just kill them?" Vera added.

"I don't know," Ghost replied, grabbing a log of burning wood for them to use as a torch in the darkness. "You all go on up ahead. I'll burn the bodies before something picks up the scent from all of this, if it hasn't already. I'll catch up once I'm done here."

"You're coming with us?" Vera asked, confused.

"He's been with us," Alexandra corrected. "Said he's been with us since we left Sylva."

Vera was now seething with rage. "What?! You've been with us this whole time, and only *now* decided to help? Not back in Cayland, with the nidbahks? Or maybe *before* Alex took an arrow to the chest?"

"My orders were only to intervene if I *had* to," Ghost answered.

"Wait—whose orders?" Barrik demanded.

"Who do you think?"

Alexandra shook her head in disbelief. "There's no way Mom told you that."

"I think he's telling the truth," Vincent said softly. "I heard her say something like, 'only if it's life or death' as we were leaving Sam's pub."

"Fira gave this order so you could have your first real battle without the true threat of death. There's a mass grave of men and women who didn't make it past their first fight. Grow up. Don't blame me for not stepping in sooner; blame yourselves for your own mistakes. You knew you were in dangerous territory, and you still lit a fire and paid no mind to your surroundings. You three chose this life. If you don't like it, then turn around and go home. I'll take Vince the rest of the way myself."

Vera snatched the burning log out of Ghost's hand. "Thanks for your words of wisdom. You've been a real peach, but we're not going anywhere without Vince."

Ghost watched as the four of them gathered their things in silence and marched down the trail. He waited until the lambent light of the burning log faded before he started gathering the bodies into a pile. The young boy was the heaviest of them all.

He watched as the pile of bodies burned in front of him. While he was lost in the deepest valleys of his mind, something rustled in the darkness behind him. With a sigh, he drew his sword.

CHAPTER 4

VINCENT watched the trail of smoke as it swam up from the fire into the canopy above. Soft rays of sunlight crept between the leafy treetops, flowing onto the forest floor. He pressed his back against a tree as he watched the others sleep. The sound of footsteps approached from his right, but a familiar voice called out before he fully stood up.

"Relax, it's only me," Ghost said quietly.

Vincent sat back down and remained silent.

"Did you sleep?" Ghost asked, taking a seat beside him.

Vincent left his eyes on the fire and shook his head.

From behind his dark mask, Ghost followed Vincent's line of sight to the fire's embers. He allowed the silence to grow momentarily as he searched for words that might pass as wisdom.

"Vince, I know you don't have a choice, but why do you *want* to be a Guardian?" Ghost questioned quietly.

Vincent tried to answer, but found his words buried beneath his tightened chest. He took a few deep breaths to fully break out of his dissociation. "I want to help people," he finally answered.

"That's it? Healers help people. Craftsmen help people. Hell, even dogs help people."

Vincent sighed. "I... I don't remember much about my father. But I do remember how people saw him. I remember villagers coming to him when something was wrong, knowing he could do something about it. People in Sylva would always tell me what a good and capable man he was, and that I was lucky to be his son. I want to be strong like he was so I can help people the same way he did. No matter what the issue is, I want to be able to fix it. To protect people and make them feel like they can rely on me for anything."

"You want to be the kind of man Victor was?"

Vincent nodded.

"Easier said than done," Ghost said plainly.

"I know that."

"No, I don't think you do."

Vincent tried to defend himself. "I have to train and get stronger. I have to learn how to use my Favor once I get it. I know it's not going to be easy."

"That's not what I'm talking about."

"Then what do you mean?"

"How many children do you think grew up without a parent because of your father? How many husbands, mothers, sons, and daughters were led to the stars at the end of Victor's blade? Do you think those people would see him as a good man—as a protector rather than an executioner?"

"But he was only doing what he had to!" Vincent exclaimed, growing frustrated.

"Which is exactly what you did when you removed that boy's head. Does that make it any easier?"

Vincent looked away from Ghost and fell silent.

"I think you've made your point," Alexandra said, sitting up painfully.

"Look," Ghost began, rising to his feet, "all I'm trying to say is, protecting people, fighting battles, and slaying horrors are all deeds glorified through stories and songs. But there's nothing poetic about them. You hurt people. You lose friends. You change. If you want to become someone like Victor, then you're going to have to give up a part of yourself."

Curious, Vincent turned back around to face him. "Which part?"

From behind his mask, Ghost stared into the fire's embers. "The only part that matters," he answered.

Vera suddenly rolled over with a loud groan. "You know, maybe if you didn't dress in all black, you wouldn't have to be so dark all the time."

Ghost grunted, giving her no further acknowledgment. "Grab your things. We can reach Meditas by midday if we start moving."

Without waiting for a response, Ghost started making his way down the trail.

"Just a beaming ball of sunshine, that guy," Vera said sarcastically.

Vincent scoffed. "No kidding."

"He's right, though," Alexandra said, solemnly looking at the ground.

Vincent looked at her, surprised. "About what?"

"If we were more prepared, then maybe you wouldn't have had to…" She trailed off, not wanting to say what they already knew she was talking about. "But we can't fix that now, and if we let all our mistakes hold us back, then we'll never get any better."

"You're starting to sound a little too much like Mom," Vera said before hopping to her feet. She crossed her arms and altered her voice to give her best impression of Fira. "Every rising sun is accompanied by an opportunity for improvement."

Alexandra smiled softly at Vera's antics before returning to Vincent. "Vince, I know it was your blade, but still, we'll carry this burden together, just like everything else. Okay?"

Vincent held Alexandra's gaze as the thoughts raged throughout his mind. She was right. It was *his* blade that had ended that boy's life—nobody else's. Claiming the fault was all of theirs as opposed to only his felt wrong somehow—almost like he was failing to accept responsibility for his actions. But as he looked behind her blue eyes, he knew Alexandra felt just as responsible as he did. And there was no doubt that Vera and Barrik did too. So again, she was right. This was yet another challenge for them to overcome, and they would do it together, like everything else.

"Okay," Vincent said softly, his spirits somewhat restored.

The corners of Alexandra's lips turned up ever so slightly. "Good. Now, let's wake up the big guy and catch up to Ghost before he gets even grumpier."

"Ugh, is that even possible?" Vera wondered aloud.

Alexandra grimaced at the throbbing pain in her shoulder as she stood up. "I'd rather not wait around to find out."

Once Barrik was finally awake, they gathered their things and set off for the final stretch of their journey. Despite the sun shining through the trees, a somber cloud seemed to hover over them all, which Vera attributed to Ghost's looming presence. But as they steadily marched on in silence, each step slowly felt a bit lighter until the trees began to thin, and they found themselves at the edge of Thernruff Woods.

The forest's edge circled the entirety of a vast and shallow pit, now the only evidence of the star that had collided here many years ago. The ground was covered in bright green grass with dandelions, weeds, and flowers all reaching for the sun. And there, in the center of the pit, rested the capital city of Meditas. High circular stone walls covered in roots and vines rose from the ground to a battlement that ran the entire perimeter, with a guard tower every few hundred feet. While the city was as marvelous to them as they had read about, what made them all forget their words was a tree that grew so tall that the leaves befriended the clouds. Strong limbs, big enough to be trees themselves, all connected to a broad bole that ran down into the heart of the city. With the sight of Meditas in front of them, the troubles of their journey seemed to vanish momentarily.

"I imagine you can find your way from here," Ghost said.

"Where are you going?" Barrik asked.

"Somewhere dark and unpleasant." Ghost walked over and stopped right in front of Vera. Still angered at his lack of aid throughout their travels, she crossed her arms and stuck up her chin.

"Don't ever steal from me again," he said threateningly.

Vera's eyes widened and darted to the ground, guilty.

Alexandra stepped forward to Vera's side, looking through Ghost's mask and into his unseen eyes. "Thank you," she said.

He gave her a nod and vanished a moment later, leaving behind the smoke-like trail once again.

With him gone, they made their way to the gates of the city. By the time they reached them, the sun had just begun its descent into the early afternoon hours. There were two younger guards in bright silver armor standing behind tall iron bars in an archway. One of them was tall and frail-looking with a bushy upper lip, while the other was a tad shorter, but much rounder, as if he had been eating all the food the skinnier one left on his plate.

"State your business in Meditas," the skinny soldier said with a lackadaisical tone.

Vera placed her hands on her hips proudly. "We're here to become Guardians!"

Similar to the bandits, the two soldiers exchanged a look and burst out in laughter.

Vera hung her head. "Why does everyone laugh when I say that?"

"Why do you feel the need to keep telling people?" Alexandra scolded.

Vera shrugged. "I'm excited."

"Someone gots ta be pullin' our chain, Bolk," the round soldier said.

The skinny man, referred to as Bolk, leaned against the iron bars for support as he laughed deeply. "They gotta be, Skohl! There ain't no way there's even more of 'em!"

"What does he mean, 'more of them?'" Barrik asked, confused.

Alexandra shrugged her shoulders, equally confused.

Skohl pointed at Vera through the gate. "Say, girl, yer messin' about with us, ain't ya?"

"No, I'm not 'messin' about with ya,'" Vera mocked. "We're really here to become Guardians."

"Watch yer tone, girl!" Bolk snapped. "We're soldiers of Meditas, which means we can put y'all in irons fer disrespectin' us."

"You'll do no such thing." A man's voice seemed to come from nowhere, startling the guards.

"Kai?!" Skohl squealed. "When did you get here?"

A middle-aged man whom nobody had noticed before was leaning up against the wall, his foot planted against it for support, with an open novel in his hand. He wore a piece of black cloth wrapped around his head, holding back silver hair that draped down to the center of his neck.

"These four say they're here ta—"

"I know who they are. I know why they're here. Open the gate," Kai fired back firmly before Bolk could finish his sentence.

The two soldiers hurriedly moved to the gate's wooden winch and began to turn the handles, raising the iron bars. Kai flipped the page of his novel, patiently waiting to greet the four newcomers.

Once the party was finally inside the city walls, Kai closed his book and faced them. "Come with me. I'll take you to your quarters."

The four of them exchanged a look of uncertainty and did as instructed.

The farther Kai led them all through the city, the more the sky became blocked out by the tree above. Massive roots snaked their way through the city streets, climbing up and over the moss-covered stone walls when they needed to. Leafy vines overgrown with an array of multicolored flowers wrapped their way around the thick and spidery roots, giving a brilliant contrast to the chestnut bark beneath. Weeds and flowers alike forced their way through wherever there was a small crack or gap in the stones, whether it was the walls or the ground beneath their feet.

They all followed him in silent awe, dodging the people scattering about the streets, until they came to a pair of arched wooden doors with two torches needlessly burning in the daylight on either side. Straight ahead, they could see the southern gate entrance, identical to the eastern one they had entered. To its left was a fenced-in training yard, where a group of soldiers with halberds was following commands shouted by their superiors. Kai threw open the doors and gestured for them to walk in first.

Beyond the doors was a large gathering hall with a long red rug in the middle of the room that led to a crackling fireplace. On both sides of the room were stairs leading up to a second level with a high guard rail of dark rock. Soldiers out of their armor, dressed in regular tunics and trousers, lingered on wooden chairs and sofas cushioned with feather pillows all around the room. Some mingled with one another, while others were quietly reading to themselves. Lanterns lit on the walls and support pillars became the primary light source once the doors were closed behind them.

"Vincent, let Barrik take your things up to your room. I need you to come with me," Kai said.

"Where are we going?" he asked, handing Barrik his pack.

"To see the king."

"Where are our rooms?" Barrik asked.

"Yours are up the stairs to the left and down the hall, first door on the right. Vera and Alexandra, yours are up the stairs to the right, the second door on your left."

Surprised, Alexandra turned to Kai. "How do you know all of our names? We haven't introduced ourselves yet."

Kai reached into a pocket and handed her an open envelope. In the center of the flap was a blue wax seal in the shape of a raindrop that no longer performed its duty. She looked back up at him. "Our mother sent you a letter?"

He nodded. "Told me all about the four of you. I'm Kai. It's nice to finally meet you."

Alexandra handed him back the envelope. "She's told us a little about you as well. It's nice to meet you too."

"Your ceremony isn't for another few days, so I suggest you all take this time to recover from your little skirmish last night. Make sure you clean your wounds well."

Alexandra narrowed her eyes at him. "That letter wouldn't have mentioned anything about the bandits, so how do you know about them?"

Kai looked at her with calm blue eyes and relaxed his posture. "Skeptical, and not quick to trust. That you sure are."

Feeling slightly attacked, Alexandra grew rigid.

"Relax, it's a good thing. It means you can't be easily manipulated. I know about the bandits because…" He leaned in closer and softened his voice. "…sometimes when I find myself alone in the shadows, I hear the whispers of a Ghost," he said with a wink. "Which is also how I know what happened to the captain and his team—which is unfortunately going to complicate things a bit, I'm afraid." He turned back to the wooden doors and swung them open, allowing a sliver of sunlight to sneak into the room. "Let's go, Vince."

"Guess I'll see you guys later, then," Vincent said to the others before he stepped outside. Once the doors were closed and they were gone, the rest of them found their way to their rooms.

Vera and Alexandra stepped into their chambers and were delightfully greeted by rays of evening sun spilling onto the wooden floor through a window in the center of the dark stone wall across from them. Three neatly made beds were spread out across the room, each with a large storage chest at the foot. In the corner of the room was a long mirror with a golden frame that stretched three-quarters of the way to the ceiling from the floorboards.

Vera dropped her pack at the edge of one of the beds and let herself fall down face first into the pillow, "…ss'at… mm… talkin' 'bout…" Her words were slow and muffled as she spoke into the bed.

Alexandra placed her things on the floor and sat down on the empty bed next to Vera's. She took a deep breath and let her head fall into her palms. Between the gaps of her fingers, she could see a stick of chalk and a piece of parchment on the bed across from her. The longer she remained still with her head in her hands, the harder it was to fight her exhaustion. She leaned back on the bed and groaned from the pain in her shoulder. Her head sank into the soft and fluffy pillow, and before long, she was pulled away into a deep sleep.

Not a moment after Barrik opened the mahogany door to their own room, a shrill voice punctured his ears.

"By the stars!" shouted an over-eager boy with freckles and messy red hair as he leaped from his bed and hurried to Barrik's side. "How did you get so tall?"

Barrik sighed. Tired and weak from the night before, he had no energy to deal with introductions, but the kindness of his heart allowed him to power through.

"I'm Barrik. Looks like my brother and I are going to be your roommates," he said with an outstretched hand.

The boy shook it firmly. "My name is really long and hard to say. Only my mom calls me by that name, so just call me Toran." The boy's smile was wide and profound, and his words leapt from his mouth with such speed that it was almost like they would be in danger if they lingered in his mind any longer.

Barrik looked around the room and saw two empty beds neatly made. "I take it those are ours?"

"Yeah, yeah, yeah, make yourself comfortable. Is your brother just as big as you? You guys might need another bed just so you can fit." Toran laughed at himself.

Barrik tossed Vincent's things onto the bed in the middle of the room and sat down on the one farthest from Toran's. "No, my brother is not as big as I am."

"Oh, so you're the taller one, but not by much, I imagine?"

"He's about your height, maybe a bit taller."

"No way, that can't be! How could you be brothers?"

Barrik lay down on his back and closed his eyes. "We have different parents."

Toran's face grew a look of confusion. "I don't think you quite understand what brothers are... but that's okay. I have two. They're younger. One has blue eyes, and the other has green. We're not sure where he got those because my dad…"

Toran rambled on and on, answering his own questions whenever he asked them. To Barrik, his voice quickly became a nuisance, preventing him from sleep, and he was only able to drift in and out of a slight slumber.

Kai led Vincent through the city until they came before a set of stone stairs that rose high to a pair of large wooden doors blocked by three guards. One stood in the middle, with the other two on either side. All of them were dressed in silver armor with the Meditas crest engraved on the breastplate. They each bore a long halberd with a green ribbon tied just beneath the blade.

Kai stopped at the base of the steps and spoke over his shoulder. "He *will* try to provoke you. Do not let him. He will also likely blame you for what happened to the captain, so be prepared for that. I'll help you where I can, but mostly, I'm afraid you're on your own past these doors. I can't let on that I know any more than what you would have told me yourself. Just remember, when surrounded by high walls and gold chalices, words become powerful weapons. Your silence is a tool that can act as the strongest of shields and the sharpest of swords simultaneously. Speak as little as possible, but when you do, take great care in what you say. One wrong word, and you'll be beyond the little aid I can offer. Understood?"

Vincent nodded nervously. Kai's words sent a sudden rush of anxiety through his bones. Previously, he had given no thought to meeting the king, outside of his appearance. Now, as they both started up the stairs, he was slightly frightened, as if he had done something wrong and was about to receive his punishment.

The guards barely acknowledged them as they passed through creaking doors into a vast, empty banquet hall of chairs and tables. Sunlight filtered through stained glass, casting colorful hues across the stone floor. A lavender rug stretched from the entrance to a small staircase, where King Sentis sat upon a throne, modest except for its unnecessarily tall back, cushioned in matching lavender. Beside him stood a lone guard, motionless as a statue, clad in black and scaly armor with a greatsword on his back and a sharp, unwavering gaze.

"News of Gala's return, have you, Kai?" King Sentis asked as they reached the middle of the room.

"Not yet, Your Majesty. However, I do expect their return soon."

"Well then, what about Captain Sans and his team? Have they brought the traitor's son back yet? I'm eager to meet him."

Being referred to as the "traitor's son" made Vincent's blood bubble with anger.

Kai stepped to the side and gestured openly to Vincent. "This is him, Your Majesty."

The king leaned forward, interested. "Is that so? Come closer, boy. Let us see if the same traitorous blood flows through you." His voice was slow and soft, with remnants of strength from days long past.

Kai urged Vincent forward with a nod of the head and stepped to the side. As Vincent drew closer to King Sentis, his years became more apparent. The thick fur on his face matched his head's particular shade of snow. He bore a golden crown with multicolored jewels all around the band and a deep blue-and-white robe that draped onto the floor. Vincent stopped just at the bottom of the steps.

King Sentis looked Vincent up and down. "Would you not kneel before a king?"

Vincent gently fell to one knee and bowed his head.

"Hmm…" The king eyed Vincent and began to wonder, "Kai, can you explain why you were the one to bring me the boy, and not Captain Sans?"

"I'm afraid Captain Sans and his team never returned, Your Majesty," Kai said, taking a bow to show his respects.

"I see… So, tell me, what misfortune has befallen my dear captain?"

"I will leave the fate of Captain Sans's team to young Vincent to divulge."

Vincent watched nervously as Kai stepped to the side, effectively signaling that he was now on his own with the king.

"Well then, boy, don't keep me waiting. Tell me what happened," the king demanded.

Vincent tried to clear the lump from his throat. "We were supposed to meet them in Cayland, Your Majesty. However, when we arrived, we found the captain and his team dead. They were killed by nidbahks."

"Nidbahks? How can you be sure?" the king questioned.

"I saw them firsthand, Your Majesty."

"Oh? And how closely did you see these horrors?"

"We killed two of them, Your Majesty. But western Cayland is overrun with them, and there were plenty more."

"'We'?" the king asked curiously.

Vincent knew it was best not to refer to the others as his siblings in front of the king, for then they might be subject to the same scrutiny as himself. "Three others from Sylva who traveled with me to become Guardians as well, Your Majesty."

"I see. So, you expect me to believe that my most distinguished captain and his hand-selected soldiers fell victim to a couple of horrors, yet four inexperienced children were able to best them without issue? What do you think about that, Rayahan?"

"Sounds like a cover story, Your Majesty," the guard behind the king replied.

"My thoughts as well. Seems more likely that you and your friends slit the captain and his soldiers' throats in the middle of the night while they slept."

Vincent was astonished. Kai had warned him that the king would blame him for the captain's death, and he had expected to be treated poorly, but this was a wild accusation. "Your Majesty, I swear to the stars I'm telling the truth," he responded in a panic, rising to his feet.

"The king never told you to rise, boy!" Rayahan barked.

Vincent quickly dropped back to his knee.

"You swear to the stars, you say? Do you have any evidence to prove your claim?" King Sentis inquired.

Vincent shook his head slowly. "No, Your Majesty. All I have is my word."

"Your word? Tell me, what is the value of the word from the mouth of an oath breaker's son?"

Vincent's eyes fell to the floor. He felt defeated, as if any moment now they would take him away and throw him in a dark cell.

"Not one sunset behind my city walls, and already am I suspicious of you. I don't trust a single breath uttered from your lungs. Luckily for you, however, that's what Rayahan is here for. You see, he has the eyes of a hawk and the nose of a bloodhound. He can smell deceit and see through lies. Why don't you give him an inspection, Rayahan? See if what he says is true."

"With pleasure, Your Majesty," Rayahan answered.

Rayahan's dark armor clinked with every footfall as he approached Vincent, his sword barely missing each step as he walked down them. His neatly groomed black hair was slicked behind his ears, not a strand out of place. Rayahan walked right up to Vincent, invading his personal space, and scanned over him intensely with light brown eyes.

Leaning against one of the rigid support columns, Kai listened intently, but only occasionally glanced up from his book.

"Stand up, boy," Rayahan commanded as he looked him up and down.

Vincent could feel the man's warm breath against his face. His voice was powerful, making the king's feel like little more than a whisper.

Rayahan circled Vincent slowly, thoroughly examining him as if he were a horse for auction.

"Have you ever killed a man?" he asked.

Vincent's thoughts strayed to the night before and the unfortunate boy at the end of his blade. He clenched his jaw and swallowed the feelings that came with the image of the child's face.

"I asked you a question," Rayahan said aggressively.

"Yes. I have killed a man," Vincent answered with eyes forward.

"Did you like it?" Rayahan whispered with a grin.

Vincent scrunched his face in disgust at Rayahan's question. "No, of course not. I only did what I had to do."

Rayahan scoffed. "Pity," he said, taking a step back. "Well, Your Majesty, he doesn't have the eyes of a killer. Definitely not the eyes of someone to kill the captain in cold blood. I can't say if his story is without lies, but at the very least, I don't believe the captain's death was his doing."

Vincent felt his shoulders relax as he sighed a breath of relief.

"Well, that is good to hear," King Sentis said as he leaned back on his throne.

Rayahan continued looking at Vincent with an arrogant smirk and ever so slightly narrowed eyes. His expression alone was enough to give rise to Vincent's impatience.

"You know, boy," Sentis continued, "your father and I were once good friends. Good friends we were. Perhaps you and I can undo the damage to your family name I so graciously gave him. Although that will take some time, indeed. You see, I still don't trust you, and my trust will not be so easily won. Please do not give me a reason to force Rayahan out of retirement. I doubt he even remembers how to swing that sword of his."

Rayahan swiftly pulled his sword off his back and maneuvered it around expertly. The blade stretched much longer than a typical sword and whooshed through the air with every one of his swings. Despite its monstrous length, it still seemed to retain its balance, or the wielder had simply become used to its disproportionate weight distribution.

"I still remember," Rayahan said, lowering his blade.

"Poetic as it would be, young Vincent..." Sentis started.

Rayahan quickly raised his blade to Vincent's neck.

"...I would hate for you to meet your end at the same blade as Victor," Sentis finished.

Vincent stared down the blade into Rayahan's devilish eyes. *This* was the man who had robbed him of a father? The smug look on the man's face gave birth to a rage unlike any he had ever felt before. He had never thought he would stand face to face with his father's murderer.

Rayahan's entire expression dripped with arrogance. He knew precisely why Vincent was eyeing him so ferociously. He bore the title of Victor's executioner without a shred of regret; if anything, he seemed proud of it. In fact, Vincent was certain he was.

Vincent's jaw clenched, hands tightening into fists that he remained smart enough to hide behind his back. His breaths began to mimic his quickened heart rate. He saw Rayahan's lips move and felt the vibration of his voice, but he heard none of the words uttered. But he *did* hear when the king said, "It was a true shame that he couldn't send that whore mother of yours to the grave as well."

Vincent's eyes widened, logic and reason fleeing his consciousness. His fists drew forward, and just as he began to take a step, Kai slammed his book shut, drawing everyone's attention and ultimately staying Vincent's movements.

"Will that be all, Your Majesty? I need the boy well rested for the ceremony in a few days if he is to be of any use to me."

The king looked at Kai for a moment before he eventually motioned for Rayahan to return to him. Vincent eyed the man fiercely with emerald balls of abhorrent fury as he walked away from him.

"I believe my point was clear," the king replied. "Yes, that will be all."

Kai bowed his head before he collected Vincent. With a hand on his shoulder, Kai led him back out of the royal hall.

Once outside, Vincent stormed down the stairs, ignoring Kai as he called after him. Teeming with rage, he failed to notice the man walking past, and as they bumped into each other, he reacted. Vincent threw all of his rage into his hands and shoved the man to the ground, but no sooner did the man fall than Vincent's anger twisted into an immense regret.

"I'm so sorry. Are you okay?" he asked as he reached down to help the man.

The man looked up at him, full of confusion and frustration. He refused Vincent's hand, pushed himself to his feet, and brushed the dirt from his white trousers. "First, you throw me to the ground, then offer to pick me back up. What gives?" the man asked with a fiery tone.

Vincent averted his eyes. "I'm sorry."

Kai stepped to the man's side and placed a hand on his shoulder. "Please forgive the boy, good sir. Are you all right?"

The man nodded. "Perhaps you should teach 'em some manners."

"Manners he has. However, control over his emotions he does not, and that is what has caused you harm. Such will be his lesson today. I apologize that you were a casualty in his learning. He is my responsibility, so if you would accept this as a token of our apology…?" Kai handed the man three copper coins from his pocket. "For a drink on me. May you enjoy the rest of your day."

The man accepted the coins and continued down the street, mumbling and grunting away. As he drew farther out of sight, Vincent slumped against the stone wall behind him. With his mind torn asunder by a raging storm of emotions and no way for him to release them, his eyes welled up with tears. He clenched his jaw in a failed attempt to hold them back. Kai observed his struggle momentarily before he sat down on the ground next to him.

"Do you believe the things they said back there?" Kai asked.

"No, of course not," Vincent choked out.

"Then why allow the words of unfamiliar men to anger you?"

"Because they're wrong! My father was a good man who saved thousands of lives, and so did my mother."

"Victor was indeed a good man, and Fira is far from deserving of their disrespect."

"How would you know?" Vincent snapped. "You're not marked as a Rogue, and the king clearly sees you as an ally, so you obviously didn't choose to fight alongside them in the war. My mother spoke kindly of you, but after you just let them insult her, and my father's memory, I can't understand why." His words were sharp and harsh. The anger within him snuck out in his voice, whether he was aware of it or not.

Kai gently scoffed and hung his head silently for a moment before he responded. "Regretfully, you are correct. However, that does not change the fact that your parents only care about how *you* see them. As long as you know who they truly are, the false words and fallacies spoken by others should hold no weight against you, no matter the chair they sit on."

Vincent let his head fall into his lap and allowed a small silence to fill the air for a few moments before he spoke again. "I don't know what happened. I was so angry, I could barely see. I didn't even know that man was there until I was already shoving him to the ground. I didn't mean to hurt him."

"I know. But take what will become a forgotten memory to that man in but a few weeks and learn a crucial lesson. Much like your words, your emotions can also be used against you as danger-ous weapons."

"So, what am I supposed to do? Never feel anything ever again?"

Kai's eyes wandered to the white clouds above. "If only that were a possible solution. You will never escape feeling your most fervid emotions, nor should you try. Pain, happiness, love, and anger will flow through you as easily as the wind brushes against your skin. Any one of them can be a beautiful wonder to behold, or an ocean to drown in. Experiencing them is a part of life—something everyone must do. Something that makes us human. But *act* on any of them free of analysis, and you'll often find much more harm than good. In some cases, it may even get you killed."

"How would an emotion get me killed?"

"All feelings of the soul have the capacity to cloud your judgment and lead to rash actions. When you let your emotions take control, logic and reason quickly fade."

"I've just... I've never felt like that before. All I wanted to do was hit Rayahan as hard as I could over and over again until that stupid smile on his face was gone. How do I just pretend like I don't feel something like that when I can barely even hear myself think?"

"Controlling your emotions is a skill like any other; it takes practice. You'll learn to refuse admittance to what would anger most and become nonreactive to what seeps through. It's an undervalued ability—arguably more powerful than any Favor from the fountains." Kai looked into Vincent's eyes and spoke with gentle grace. "The beasts of our world take many forms. Some lurk in shadows with twisted faces and a thirst for blood; others wear robes and crowns, hungering for power. But the worst monster of them all will always be the one inside of yourself that you failed to tame."

Kai watched as Vincent took in his words and fell silent. After a moment, he slowly rose to his feet and extended a helping hand to the slouched boy at his side. "Come on. Dwelling in the past will bring you nothing more than depression and sickness. Take the next few days to rest and explore the city. Once the ceremony is over, your days will be much busier, so enjoy it while it lasts. I trust you can find the way back on your own."

"I think I can figure it out."

"Good. I'll leave you to it, then."

Kai turned away and disappeared down the road. Vincent spun around a time or two, trying to remember which way to go, until he finally picked a route and made his way back to the barracks in a silent reflection.

Chapter 5

LEXANDRA awoke slowly to a rhythmic humming and a scratching sound. As she blinked away the remnant blurs of sleep, she could see a girl of a similar age with auburn hair sitting on the bed across from her, legs crossed, drawing in a brown leather-bound book with some charcoal. With a pained groan, Alexandra sat up and swung her legs off the bed to the floor.

The humming stopped. "Did I wake you? I'm so sorry!" the girl exclaimed.

Alexandra waved her worries away with one hand and held her head with the other. "No, no, don't worry about it. My name's Alex," she said, extending her left hand—still hidden beneath her leather glove.

The girl set aside her things and leaned closer to accept her greeting. "Rinna," she said with a smile.

"Nice to meet you, Rinna. Whatcha drawing?"

Rinna looked over her shoulder at her unfinished artwork. "It's supposed to be a portrait of my mother, but I just can't seem to get her eyes right. Or at least, not the way I remember them."

"May I?" Alexandra asked, gesturing toward the portrait.

"Sure," Rinna said as she handed over the book to her. She sounded slightly surprised that Alexandra was interested.

Alexandra scanned over the black-and-white image in her hands, a woman with long hair kept behind her ears by a ribbon. Her chin was tilted slightly, pointed toward an unseen light reflected in her soft eyes that held a subtly strong sense of pride.

"She's beautiful," Alexandra said as she returned it to Rinna.

"Thanks," Rinna said, smiling softly. "She used to wear her hair in braids kind of like yours when she was younger."

"How long has it been since you've seen her?"

"She died a few years ago."

"Oh. I'm sorry. I shouldn't have—"

"It's okay," Rinna quickly responded, shaking away Alexandra's apology. "It's always going to hurt, but I think being okay to talk about it sometimes makes it a little easier."

Alexandra quickly scanned for something to say as an awkward silence rapidly began to take over the room. "Are you here for the ceremony?"

Rinna nodded. "Yup. Trying to become a Guardian, just like she was. Following in her footsteps, I suppose. What about you?"

"The same. As well as my sister behind me, who..." Alexandra turned around to see Vera snoring away with her mouth wide open. She grabbed a pillow from her bed and whipped it at Vera's head, groaning from pain as she did so. Vera quickly jolted awake and sat straight up. The other two laughed.

"Vera, this is Rinna; come introduce yourself."

Vera blinked several times as Alexandra's words took a moment to register. When she finally realized what she had said, she sluggishly maneuvered over to Alexandra's bed, plopped herself down, and crossed her legs.

"Nice to… meet you," Vera said with a yawn. Alexandra shook her head.

"Likewise. How long have you both been on the road?"

"Too long," Vera said, still waking up. "We had a run-in with some bandits too."

"Bandits?! I'm guessing that's where you got that, then." Rinna pointed to the bloodied bandages around Alexandra's shoulder.

"Yeah. An archer got me pretty good. Knocked the wind right out of me."

"That sounds awful. But otherwise, you're okay?"

"Yeah, we'll live. We left Sylva about three weeks ago, and it is so nice being back in an actual bed."

"Oh, I can imagine. I've always wanted to go to Sylva. I've heard so much about the forest—how the leaves fall differently, the beautiful color of the trees, even that the morning birds have a special song for the Sylvan woods."

Alexandra laughed. "I don't know about all of that, but the trees are definitely different from the ones here. Did you grow up in Meditas?"

Rinna shook her head. "No, I've only been here for a few weeks. Probably arrived around the time you were leaving. I left sooner than I had to, but I was getting a little tired of the snow. Needed a change of scenery, you know?"

"Snow? Are you from Nalitay, then?" Alexandra assumed.

"Yup. The one and only."

"Nalitay?!" Vera all but shouted.

"Now she's awake," Alexandra said with a grin.

"I want to go so badly! To walk alongside the mountains. To see snow that reaches your chest. And the energy rays—they're real, right?" Vera inquired enthusiastically.

Rinna laughed. "Yup. That sounds like Nalitay, all right. And yes, the energy rays are very real."

"V has wanted to go ever since she read about them in a book when we were kids."

"I just can't imagine seeing them up close!" Vera began to speak as if reciting something she had read in a novel: "Shades of greens, blues, and yellows swim through the night sky, as if you are far beneath a river's dancing current."

Rinna stood up without saying anything and walked over to her wooden chest. After a moment or two of rummaging around, she pulled out a sketchbook similar to the one currently on her bed and flipped through it. Once she finally settled on a page, she handed it over to Vera. As soon as her eyes landed on the image in her hands, an uncontrollable smile spread across her cheeks as her face lit up. Tall snow-capped mountains looked like rocks in a riverbed beneath several streams of color that stretched across the page. She had no words.

Alexandra looked over the image, then back to Vera, and found herself shocked. "Wow. I don't think I've ever seen her speechless."

"I promise they look much better in person," Rinna said reassuringly.

"These are wonderful," Vera said, still amazed.

Rinna smiled softly. Vera's reaction to a drawing she was not entirely confident in brought a comforting warmth to her heart. "Have you had the chance to eat yet? I know a place with some good food, although the company isn't exactly the nicest."

"Good food is my only concern," Vera said as she relinquished Rinna's picture back to her.

"Yeah, and I'm sure Bear is starving for something other than rationed stale bread," Alexandra joked.

"Bear?" Rinna asked, confused.

"He's one of our brothers."

"One of them? How many of you are there?"

Alexandra laughed and then grimaced at the ache in her shoulder. "Just four. Barrik is his actual name, but we call him Bear."

"You'll see why," Vera whispered.

"Vincent is a royal pain in the ass, but he grows on you."

"Does he, though?" Vera teased.

Alexandra gave Vera a gentle shove. "All right, Rinna, where are we headed?"

In the common quarters, Vincent sat alone with his thoughts, paying no mind to those who wandered around him, as they paid no mind to him. His thoughts screamed at him as he replayed the events of the last two days over and over again—the boy in the woods, Ghost's poor version of advice, his meeting with the king, and his actions that followed. He was overwhelmed trying to process everything all at once. He watched the crackling flames dance in the fireplace, enveloped by his silence, until Alexandra's voice saved him from the dangers in his mind.

"There you are, Vince. How was the king?"

"Pleasant. Extremely welcoming. Great guy. Wish you could have been there," Vincent said sarcastically as he turned around.

"That bad, huh?"

"Yeah, I could use an ale and some food."

"Well, that's just perfect," Vera said, throwing her arm around Rinna. "Rinna here was about to treat us to a meal and some ale. Sounds like that will lift your spirits. Whadaya say, Vincey, care to join?"

"I don't think I mentioned any treating," Rinna said, scrunched up in Vera's clutches.

Vincent chuckled. "Don't be fooled by any of V's tricks. Otherwise, you'll find your words twisted and your pockets empty," he teased as he stuck out his hand. "I'm Vincent."

"Nice to meet you, Vincent. I'll try to keep that in mind."

As she took his hand, her icy palm sent a warm sensation coursing through his arm. His eyes lingered over the details of her face. Brown eyes hid beneath her dark eyebrows, contrasting with her bright smile. A purple ribbon that he thought suited her nicely was tied in a bow just behind the top of her head to keep her hair pulled back.

"How did you get stuck with these two, anyway?" he asked.

"We're roommates," she answered.

"Oh… That is unfortunate."

"Shut up, already, Vince," Alexandra said with a roll of her eyes. "Do you want to come with or not?"

"Yes, I'm coming. Did you speak to the big man yet?" he asked.

Alexandra shook her head. "No. We haven't seen him since you left."

"All right, I'll go get him."

Vincent marched up the stairs and was only gone for a few moments before he came back with Barrik. Following close behind them, saying something inaudible, was Toran, with a red scarf lightly wrapped around his neck.

"Who's that with them?" Alexandra asked out loud.

Rinna leaned in closer to them to whisper. "That's Toran. One of the other boys who came to join the Guardians as well. He's as sweet as he is talkative."

"… So then, he got stuck with his hand inside the wheel of cheese, but he couldn't—"

Barrik quickly cut off Toran's story to introduce him to the others. Vincent stood behind them, found Alexandra's eyes, and stared blankly at her with his eyes wide open and his mouth half agape in shock after gesturing to Toran. She tried to hide her smile.

After shaking Barrik's hand, Rinna leaned closer to Vera and whispered, "You were right. 'Bear' makes more sense now."

Vera laughed.

Toran shook Alexandra's hand. "Oh, wow, firm grip!" He laughed. "Hiya, Rinna! Great to see you again. Have you been well?"

"I have, yes. You?"

"I'm great. Can never be too happy, my dad always says. Although I think he means it ironically, because he's always miserable."

Vera held out her hand to greet Toran. "Nice to meet you, Toran. I'm Vera."

He seemed to shrink when he was face to face with Vera. Suddenly, he was less talkative. "Nice to meet you too," he said quickly before shying away. His cheeks turned bright red beneath his freckles.

Vera shook off his strange change of character and turned to Barrik, who was hunched over, staring at the floor with heavy eyes. "You look exhausted, Bear," she said.

"No sleep. Need food."

Alexandra laughed as she patted him on the arm. "All right, big guy, we're going."

Vincent held the door open and slapped his thigh repetitively as he looked at Barrik. "Come here, boy. Come on. Chow time."

Barrik barely looked at him as he placed his hand on his shoulder, and despite his own exhausted state, threw him to the ground with ease. The others laughed as Vincent climbed back to his feet.

The shades of orange and yellow in the distant sky continued to dim as Rinna led them through the city. Soldiers traveled the streets, lighting lanterns suspended on the stone walls. Since most of the shops were already closed for the day, the city was rather quiet, unlike before. Fewer and fewer people wandered the streets, but muffled laughter and shouting could still be heard beyond the closed doors of homes and pubs.

"All right, it's just on the other side of the market," Rinna said as they rounded a corner. She took a few steps before she sensed she was no longer in everyone's company. When she turned around, everyone except for Toran was frozen, eyes fixed on what was right in front of them. Toran, however, found more interest in another subject.

In the center of the market were giant roots covered in flowers, stretching from the base of a tree beyond the size of anything they had ever seen before. The roots grew far past the market and disappeared down streets and alleys, or up and over the walls to somewhere else in the city. Where the tree connected with the ground was the only place not covered with cobblestones. Instead, there was a garden with neatly trimmed grass and the same colorful flowers that had taken over the vines and roots, protected by a small wrought-iron fence.

"It's beautiful!" Alexandra said with a wide smile.

Rinna drew their attention to a winding set of wooden steps that wrapped around the tree. "Up there is the fountain, although we're not allowed up yet."

When Barrik finally had no desire to loiter any longer, he gently urged everyone on with a nudge on their backs. "How much further, Rinna?" he asked impatiently.

As if in answer to his question, a door just ahead—past the edge of the market—flung open, and a man was thrown to the ground from inside. He coughed several times.

"Don't be showing ya face around if ya got the Ash! Ya gonna give it to someone else, to ya selfish bastard!" The man standing in the doorway spat on the ground before turning back inside.

Toran quickly rushed ahead to aid the man on the ground. "Are you all right, sir?"

The man coughed a few more times before he answered, "He's right, lad. Don't touch me, lest you be wanting ma illness too." He shoved Toran away weakly and fell back to his knees.

Toran turned back to the group. "We should take him to Master Darion."

"Uh, who?" Vincent asked, confused.

"Master Darion is the healer. He's been serving Meditas since before the war," Rinna answered. "You guys go on ahead. I can help Toran," she said, kneeling beside him.

"No, no, no, Rinna, that's okay. I can take him. Besides, I already ate; I was just enjoying everyone's company."

"Are you sure, Toran? It's halfway to the other side of the city from here."

"It's no problem at all. They probably won't be able to get a seat without you anyway. Besides, I sat around for most of the day. My body could probably use the extra steps. I'll catch up with you all tomorrow."

Toran knelt down and put the man's arm around his shoulder. Soft yellow light from inside the pub he had been thrown from illuminated his hand, revealing blackened fingers, as if they had been left in the snow and long forgotten.

"Ya got a death wish er somethin', do ya, lad?" the man softly asked Toran.

"Not at all, sir. You just seem like you could use some help."

"Oughta just let me here ta die."

Toran laughed. "You sound just like my father. He's as stubborn as an ox too. I'm sure you'd get along just great. Actually, this reminds me of this time we went hunting…"

Everyone turned to head inside as Toran's words faded down the street. A wooden plaque with a golden engraving of a broken broom hung just above the door. Rinna pushed it open just a sliver before she turned back to the group with a grin and said, "Well, everyone, welcome to The Wicked Broom."

She flung the door open to reveal a crowd of people that stretched from wall to wall, leaving next to no room for the servers to deliver their food and drink. The patrons who had overindulged and could barely stand made their jobs even harder. Lanterns of lambent orange light ran the wall higher above, safe from any foolish misfortune. A young bard dressed in blues and greens plucked the strings of his lute as he melodically recited tales of a distant past. Vincent thought he had a certain elegance about him, and whether it be his attire or his eloquent lyrics, he thought the bard seemed a tad out of place, as if he would otherwise never be seen anywhere near such debauchery.

Alexandra leaned close to Rinna to be heard above the din. "How do you suppose we find somewhere to sit?"

"Oh, that won't be a problem," Rinna answered confidently.

"Why's that?" Vera asked.

A playful grin spread across Rinna's face. "Just watch."

She started to work her way through the crowd—or rather, the crowd worked their way around her once she was spotted. Everyone stepped out of her way with some form of respectful acknowledgment: a hand on their chest, or a smile and nod of their head.

Just as they were passing a table that sat beneath a window, a man leaped from his seat. "Miss Rinna, are you in need of a place for you and your friends?"

"Oh, hey, Mr. Skally. How are you this evening?"

"I'm mighty fine, thank you for asking. Would you care to sit? My company and I are quite all right to mingle amongst the crowd. Probably should be headin' on outta here soon anyway."

"We would greatly appreciate that, Mr. Skally. Thank you so much!"

The three men at the table gently rose from their seats and took their mugs with them, but not before they parted with an overly friendly but not uncomfortable goodbye. Everyone sat down at the table, shocked.

"Okay, what was all that about?" Alexandra asked. "They all seemed either excited or frightened when they saw you."

"Yeah, are you some kind of a princess?" Vera asked.

Rinna laughed. "No, no, nothing like that. My first night in Meditas, I stumbled into this place, but when I walked in, everyone was drunk and treated me rather harshly—that is, until Mancho stepped in." She changed her voice to sound as if she lived on the seas. "He said, 'Now, that ain't the way ta treat a lady, is it?'" She laughed a little at herself, which forced the corners of Vincent's lips to curl upward. Rinna continued, "Then I think he threatened them in some way I didn't quite understand, because ever since then, everyone in here goes out of their way with kindness."

"How did he threaten them?" Vincent asked.

"Well, he didn't say anything else. He just sorta looked around the room with his hand on my shoulder."

As soon as she finished her sentence, five mugs of ale slammed down onto the table. They all turned to see a large, burly man with a furry mustache that traced his cheeks all the way to his ears. Broad-shouldered, with his arms practically bursting out of his shirt sleeves, he rivaled Barrik in size.

"Aye, there be mystery behind the eyes. Ye give 'em a look and let their mind do the rest," the man said with the voice of a sailor.

"Hey there, Mancho," Rinna said graciously.

Mancho leaned over to her and gave her a gentle side hug. "Brought some friends in with ye tonight, aye?"

"Yup. Got a hungry one over there too," she said, pointing to Barrik.

"Aye, by the looks of 'im, I'd say he always be hungry."

Barrik nodded with a guilty smile. "Pretty much."

As Mancho scanned over the group until his eyes landed on Vincent. "'ang on a minute..." He leaned closer over the table, making everyone slightly uncomfortable. "Yer Victor's boy, ain't ye?"

Before Vincent had the chance to answer, Mancho shot his hand across the table. "It be the mightiest o' pleasures ta finally meetcha!"

Vincent's hand disappeared in Mancho's. "Vincent. It's a pleasure to meet you too, sir."

Mancho stood back with his hands on his hips, shaking his head as if he could not believe his eyes. "Ye look just like the ol' rascal. Pains me heart dearly for what happened. How 'bout I bring ye all a little o' everything?"

He quickly strode away, making it apparent that his question was rhetorical.

"You guys didn't mention that Vincent is famous," Rinna said.

"Oh, yeah, he's a princess too," Vera joked.

He glared at her. "And because of that, you must obey all of my royal commands."

Vera scoffed. "Pfft. I'd rather be thrown in the dungeon."

"Here ye's go," Mancho said as he set down two full-roasted chickens. Everyone was shocked at the speed of his return. Two other workers continued to set down several other items as he pointed them out. "Ye got some mutton over here, crispy taters, a bit o' lamb, and some freshly baked bread for... Oh, 'ang on a minute." He disappeared for a moment before he promptly returned with a bowl of hot stew that he placed right in front of Barrik. "'at beef stew right there was one o' yer father's favorites, Vince. Him and 'at old man Charlie."

Steam rolled from the stew into Barrik's nose, lighting up his eyes. "So, you're the old pirate Gramps told us about."

Mancho laughed. "Aye, that'd be me, although me days on the sea are far behind."

Rinna looked at all of the food in front of them, amazed. "Thanks, Mancho, but this is a lot of food."

"Oh, don't ye worry, dear." He pulled up a chair, sat down with a thud, and poured himself an ale. "I'm gonna help." He turned to see Barrik already halfway through the stew. "Not that ye need it. Vinnie boy, how is yer mum doin' these days? Get ye in fightin' shape, did she?"

"She's great. And yeah, I think we're all pretty capable."

"'We'?" Mancho asked, confused.

Vincent gestured to everyone else. "This is Vera, Alexandra, and the big guy is Barrik."

"Nice to meet ya, Mr. Mancho, sir," Vera said.

"Thank you so much for this feast," Alexandra added.

"Mmm, yah, sahr gerd," Barrik said with a mouthful of food. The steam spilled out of his mouth as he spoke.

Mancho laughed. "Ahh, it's me pleasure, but ye don't need yer formalities wit me, girl. What makes ye three wanna join the dwindlin' force o' special protectors?"

They all exchanged a look before Alexandra answered. "For as long as I can remember, Vince has been going on and on about being a Guardian just like Victor was, so it was already an obvious choice for us. But then shortly after Fira took us in, she told us that he *had* to become a Guardian, no matter what he wanted. She never asked us to go with and reassured us countless times that we didn't have to do anything we didn't want to." She looked to Vera and Barrik before she continued, "But I think we all knew what we were going to do, even before she told us."

"Yeah, he's a massive migraine, but we couldn't let him go alone," Vera teased with a slight elbow into Vincent's arm.

"Always did everything together, and we always will," Barrik added, only removing his eyes from his food briefly.

"Fira took ye's in, ye say?"

"Yup. Brought us all the way from Abnor to Sylva," Vera said.

Mancho leaned in against the table. "Really, now? Found ye's on the battlefield, did she?"

"Yup."

Mancho laughed. "Ten years gone by, and she still be surprising me."

"What do you mean?" Vincent asked.

"I mean, in order fer her ta sneak all of 'em in and outta the city wit out me knowin is quite impressive. Ye see, Vinnie boy, nothin' happens in Meditas witout ol' Mancho hearin' 'bout it."

"How come?"

"If ye keep yer eyes an' ears open, an' yer mouth closed, people spill all sorts o' stuff. Especially once they've had an ale or two."

Vera looked at him with disbelief. "You can't possibly learn that much just from listening to a bunch of drunken fools."

"Ye'd be surprised what the fools say when they let the ale do all their talkin'. But o' course, I have me other ways too. Eyes an' ears all over the city."

Alexandra turned to Mancho inquisitively. "Say, Mancho?"

"Aye?"

"You said Mom 'snuck' us through the city. Why would she need to keep us a secret?"

"Well, I'm afraid because if the king were ta have found ye three, he woulda had ye's killed. Wee lads er not."

Barrik looked up from his food, shocked. "Why would he do that? We weren't even a part of the war!"

"Aye, but that would matter not ta the king. He'da seen ye's little more than prisoners ta be made an example of, so she woulda had ta be extra careful. Which terns me mind not, knowin' how she did it. How much do ye's remember?"

Alexandra shook her head. "It was so long ago, so unfortunately, not much. Most of it's a blur."

"I remember walking... a lot!" Vera said.

Barrik pondered for a moment as he cycled through his memories. "I don't remember a city at all—at least, not one that wasn't on fire."

"Same here," Alexandra agreed. "I remember walking through the woods with someone in a cloak, but I can't make out their face—which I suppose was Ghost. And I remember being scared, not knowing what was going to happen to us."

"I'm sure Fira took good care o' ye's."

"She did," Alexandra said with a smile.

Rinna looked across the table at Vincent curiously. "Vince, can I ask you something?"

"Of course."

"Why do you *have* to join the Guardians?"

The fear of how she would react upon learning his truth forced him to hesitate for a moment before he answered. "The king ordered my service to the Guardians as one of the punishments for my father's actions."

Rinna's eyes widened as she came to the realization. "So, when Mancho said you're Victor's son, he meant Victor Raine?"

Vincent nodded slowly. "Yup. You're not going to insult me or throw your ale in my face now, are you?"

Rinna chuckled as she shook her head. "No, no, I would never do any of that. My mother always used to say he was a good man, despite the opinions of everyone else."

Vincent let out a small breath of relief.

"Aye, that he was," Mancho agreed. "Lotsa good stories bout 'im too, if ya ever wanna hear one." He leaned in closer as if to whisper. "An' I won't spare ye all the details that yer mother would."

Vincent laughed. "I'd like that."

"Wait 'til ye hear the one about 'im and 'is wolf."

Vera laughed. "Oh, we've heard that one a time or two already. One of my personal favorites, actually."

"Well, I have plenty more than just that ol' one, but..." Mancho stood up and pushed in his chair. "We'll save the stories fer another time. I'll leave ye's be. Make sure ye come back soon."

"We will," said Rinna.

"And Vince?"

"Yeah, Mancho?"

"I know ye didn't exactly have a choice ta be here, but it be great ta have ye."

Vincent let his words resonate for a moment before he showed his gratitude. "Thanks, Mancho."

With a nod of his head, the man disappeared beyond the crowd of people that seemed to have somehow increased in size.

Barrik leaned back in his seat with his hands on his stomach and started to groan. "I don't think I've ever been this stuffed."

Vera looked at him, shocked. "I don't think I've ever heard you say you were stuffed."

"And yet he'll be hungry again by the time we get back to our rooms," Alexandra joked.

Barrik smiled. "Yeah, probably."

Vera looked over the remaining food on the table and wondered. "You guys think Toran would want some if we brought it back for him?"

"Oh, I'm sure he'd love that," Rinna agreed.

Alexandra snickered. "I'm sure he'd especially love it if you delivered it yourself, V."

"What's that supposed to mean?"

"She's saying Toran has taken a special liking to you," Vincent said. "Poor boy."

"At least I'm capable of being liked."

"Hey, it's not my fault I'm so intimidating to everyone else. The life of a princess is a pretty hard one, ya know?"

Rinna laughed. "So, this is what having siblings is like?"

"Pretty much," Barrik said plainly. "Constant bickering, and there's never any peace and quiet."

"Or enough food to go around," Vera added. Barrik grinned guiltily.

Alexandra poured herself another ale from the pitcher on the table. "What was wrong with that guy, anyway?"

"What guy?" Vincent asked.

"The one Toran helped outside. His fingers were all black, and he looked like he hadn't eaten in a few weeks."

"'The Ash', I think the one guy called it," Vincent said.

Rinna placed both of her hands around her mug and looked at her reflection in the tiny golden pond as she spoke. "I don't know much about it, but from what I've heard, there's no cure."

Barrik grew concerned. "Is Toran going to be okay, then? That man was practically coughing all over him."

"Although that's still gross, I don't think it spreads that way. It just makes people uncomfortable because they don't want to get it. He should be fine. I imagine he'll be back soon, if you want to meet him there."

"Yeah, that sounds like a good idea," Alexandra agreed.

They gathered up a little bit of everything leftover to bring back for Toran. Once they arrived back in their quarters, Toran was elated to learn that they had thought of him. He accepted the food from Vera with a thankful bow of his head, which doubled as a smokescreen for his bright red cheeks.

CHAPTER 6

INALLY, the morning of the Guardian ceremony had arrived, and along with it came all the anxiety of potential unfortunate possibilities. The fountain's water could kill any one of them, and while they had always known it to be possible, now they *felt* it.

Alexandra sat in front of her wardrobe mirror as she attempted to put her hair into braids. With each frizzy mess of a result, she grew more and more frustrated.

"You're going to make us late," Vera said.

"Well, then go without me," Alexandra fired back.

"You could always just cut it off."

"V, I'm not cutting off my hair. I like my braids."

Vera laughed. "What braids?"

Alexandra glared at her with molten lava bubbling in her eyes.

Rinna set down the book she was drawing in. "Would you like me to help?"

"You know how to do it?"

"I think I could figure it out."

"Can't do any worse than her," Vera teased.

Defeated, Alexandra sank into her seat with a sigh. "She's not wrong."

Rinna laughed. "Okay, hang on." She stood behind Alexandra, gathered several groupings of her hair, separated them between her fingers, and started to hum. She twisted, flipped, and pulled her hair as tight as she could.

"Ow!" Alexandra cried out.

"Sorry, hon, but they have to be tight if you want them to stay in."

Rinna continued to hum along for several more minutes as she worked her magic. When the humming stopped, Rinna finally took a step back. Alexandra could see tears in the eyes of Rinna's reflection.

"Okay, how's that?" Rinna asked with a sniffle.

"Are you okay?" Alexandra asked before looking at herself in the mirror.

Rinna smiled and nodded her head as she gathered her words. "Yeah. I'm okay, thank you. How did I do?"

Alexandra tilted her head at various angles to see as much of her hair as possible, and much to her surprise and relief, she was unable to find a single strand out of place. Three thick braids atop her head, two on either side just above her ears, and one in the center, all pulled back into a ponytail, just the way she liked. She was amazed.

"It's just as good as when our mother would do it! Where did you learn?"

Rinna pointed to the purple ribbon in her hair. "I used to do my mom's hair every morning for her."

Alexandra stood up and gave Rinna a consoling hug. "It's perfect. Thank you, Rinna."

Rinna welcomed Alexandra's embrace. "You're welcome."

"Although I think you almost snapped my neck a few times," Alexandra joked as she pulled away.

"Oh, don't be such a baby."

The three of them stood in front of the mirror silently, each individually preparing to accept all of the fountain's possibilities.

"Well, are we ready?" Alexandra finally asked.

Vera nodded.

"Let's do it," Rinna said.

The girls made their way to the main room, where the boys were already gathered, along with two new faces they were unfamiliar with. One of the other boys was short with broad shoulders, a shiny bald head, and a poorly grown goatee. The other was dark-haired, tall, and skinny. He had a fluffy mustache as dark as his head with cheeks of shadowy stubble.

Vincent launched from his seat when he saw them come down the steps. "What took you so long?"

"The rat's nest on Alex's head was giving her trouble," Vera joked.

"I hate rats," Toran said with a shiver.

Everyone began to laugh until Kai suddenly demanded all of their attention. "Right, then," he said firmly. He stood in front of the double doors with his arms crossed and a katana sheathed on his hip. Tall and strong, with a fierce look in his blue eyes, he appeared as if he were about to give a pre-battle speech to rally his troops, but instead, all he said was, "Follow me." And with a turn, he headed out the doors.

All eight of them followed Kai through the city as they listened to the chorus of the early morning birds. Their songs filled the cool air as the group passed through gentle rays of sunlight, piercing the gaps in the clouds above as they stepped over the roots that seemed to encompass every street.

Toran followed close behind Vera, searching his mind for something to say. No matter how hard he tried, he felt a loss for words, something he had never struggled with before. While he was searching through the depths of his mind, Vera had fallen back to his side without him noticing.

"Hey, Toran, you feeling okay?"

He looked up from the ground, slightly startled. "Hey, Vera. Yeah, I'm okay. Why do you ask?"

"You're just quieter than your usual self. Feeling a little nervous?"

He was, but not for the reason she was referring to. "A little, yeah."

"That's okay, me too. Don't worry, though; I'm sure you won't turn into some sort of horror with fangs and bad breath. But if you do, I'll make sure you don't hurt anybody."

He looked at her, horrified, now nervous for another reason, thanks to her imagery.

As they rounded a corner to see the market, the sight of the stairs winding up the tree in the center made his stomach turn.

Although it was still in the early hours of the morning, the market was already buzzing with people, many of whom were lining up in front of shopkeepers who had yet to fully set up, eager to begin haggling for the goods they wanted. The sound of a hammer against an anvil provided the birds' songs with a rhythmic clang of metal. However, all of the commotion abruptly stopped once they were noticed. Everyone turned to get a good look at the new Guardians. Some of the people sneered and turned up their noses, while only a few elders bowed their heads.

"Not much of a ceremony," Vera said.

Toran looked around. "My mom said when she was younger, the whole city used to come and watch. They would shout and throw flowers, scream and holler. Soldiers had to form a perimeter just so they wouldn't all charge the steps."

"See, now that sounds like a ceremony."

"This way," Kai said, urging them to ignore everyone else and keep moving.

The once-forbidden wooden steps winding all the way up the tree were crafted to appear as if they were part of the tree rather than added on. A twisting vine covered in colorful petals that acted as a guardrail only added to the staircase's natural appearance. The higher they stepped, the more the people below started to shrink in size, and the sounds of the market grew muffled and distant. They could see far beyond the city walls, and while they enjoyed the view, the staircase began to feel never-ending. Each step forced Vincent further into his mind, as if he were climbing into the very depths of his consciousness.

The day was finally here. Ten years suddenly felt as if they had passed by in an instant. Years that all blended together as if they were part of one big dream—a dream that he now believed he might have taken for granted. For ten years, he had been excited, eager to follow in his father's footsteps, stand where he stood, recite the words of the Guardian's oath, and drink the fountain's water, but now that the time had come, all he felt was nervous, as if he was knowingly doing something wrong. The urge to turn and run back down the stairs gripped him by the spine.

"You okay?" Alexandra asked, pulling him out of his mind.

Vincent shrugged, unsure of how to respond. "I don't know. I thought now that we're finally here, I'd be more excited. But I just have this—"

"Bad feeling in your stomach?" Alexandra said, finishing his sentence.

Vincent nodded with a soft smile. "Yeah."

"I think there's a lot of that going around," she replied with a gesture behind them.

Vincent looked over his shoulder to see everyone silently watching each step, clearly lost in their own concerns.

"We'll be fine," Alexandra continued, "no matter how the fountain changes us." She glanced at the dark leather glove on her left hand, filling her with anxiety.

"I know. You're right. I think I'm just ready to get this part over with."

"Me too."

"I also wasn't expecting there to be so many stairs," he joked, trying to lighten the mood.

Alexandra chuckled softly and rolled her eyes.

"Hey, Bear!" Vincent called out.

"Yeah?"

"What would you say to—"

"No." Barrik already knew what he was going to ask. "I will not carry you the rest of the way."

"Well, how about on the way down, then?"

"I'll give you a little push while we're at the top; how about that?"

"Yikes. You don't have to get nasty."

"Fine. If you carry me up the rest of the way, I'll carry you back down."

Vincent scoffed. "If I try to carry you, the only way we're going is down."

The thought of Vincent trying to lift the monstrous boy threw Vera and Alexandra into a fit of laughter.

As the group finally reached the end of the winding staircase, two guards clad in bright silver armor stood beneath an archway of thick roots. The crest on their breastplate, which resembled the very tree they were climbing, shone with a bright magnificence in the sunlight. Their posture was so firm and fixed that they could almost be mistaken for statues. Neither one of them spared anyone other than Kai a glance as they passed between their spears.

Vincent looked up to see the treetop much closer now. Branches split off in several directions, twisting and turning as they tangled themselves together to disappear amongst the leaves. The ground softened beneath his feet as he was greeted by green grass once he stepped off of the wooden steps. Five chestnut bark-covered spidery fingers reached all the way to the edge of the small patch of land they stood on, and beneath each archway they created was another statue-like guard with silver armor. He thought it looked as though they were on top of a mushroom cap, and the branches were all trying to pull it back closer to its body.

Straight ahead of them, where the grass met the base of the tree, stood a woman in a wispy golden white dress. Each strand of her hair flowed like an amber river of silk, kept at bay by the circlet of flowers atop her head. Behind her rested a pool of glimmering water—the Meditas fountain.

"Is this all of them?" the woman asked as they approached. Her voice brushed their ears with a wispy grace, not unlike her dress. They all heard her words as if they *were* the wind.

"It is," Kai answered.

"Only eight, I see. The numbers grow smaller every year, Kai," she said softly.

"I know. It is a tragedy."

"Is there any new knowledge of Gala and the others?"

Kai shook his head. "Afraid not. If there is no word soon, I may have to continue where they left off."

The woman caressed Kai's cheek with the back of her fingers as she looked into his eyes. "Prepare yourself for the worst, but do not let go of hope. Should the time come for you to pick up where they may have failed," she said, turning back to the rest of the group, "may you be in grand company."

Kai's emotionless expression did not change, but when her hand finally fell to her side, he bowed his head respectfully. "Thank you for your words, Tahara," he replied.

"The fountains thank you, child, for your service to our world. Gala is one of the finest Guardians I have come to know. I do not know of a foe with the power to defeat her. She will return with her party."

Kai took another bow before he leaned against one of the nearby roots and rested both hands on the hilt of his katana.

With the water behind her, Tahara looked over each of them intently as they stood shoulder to shoulder. Even with the growing silence, she continued, worry-free of how uncomfortable they might be with the prolonged inspection. Her eyes lingered on Vincent much longer than the others. A gentle smile grew across her face as a tear fell from her eye.

"I possess a great deal of respect for your father, Vincent Raine. Our world misses him dearly," she said delicately.

Her words dealt an unexpected blow to the part of Vincent's stomach that held his feelings. "I don't think you know our world very well," he said softly.

"Some of those who inhabit our world may not carry his well-deserved appreciation, but such is their right. Regardless of the mistruths they may spread and swear upon, in the end, Victor Raine fought to uphold the balance of energy and the preservation of life. For that, the fountains are ever grateful to him and his kin."

As she bowed her head, Barrik elbowed Vincent in the side to reciprocate the action.

Tahara began to pace slowly up and down the line of soon-to-be Guardians as she spoke. "The water you all see before you, that we know as the Fountain of Meditas, was a gift from the stars to help us in the war against the Sanorians. By giving humans abilities to rival the power of our former masters, the fountains created the necessary balance needed to sustain our world. Today, we live in a time of great peace, but before the time when humans were granted Favors from the fountains, Sanora was cursed with illness, starvation, war, and anarchy. We have continued to accept these Favors to assist our mission in upholding this balance. Should the fountains ever become compromised in any way, our world would fall back into chaos, and it would be the end of Sanora as we know it. This is your oath. By drinking this water, you swear to live the rest of your days fighting for the balance of Sanora.

"Your reasons for standing here in front of me today matter not. Whether it be for power, to protect those you love, or even…" She stole a glance in Vincent's direction. "…an unavoidable destiny laid before you. The only thing that matters now is your sacred promise. I must warn you: do not take this lightly. To break an oath is to tarnish the soul. However, if you are sure of your desire to adhere to this life, you need only repeat these words…" She paused for a moment. "'I am the darkness.'"

Everyone repeated the words in unison: "I am the darkness."

"'I am the light.'"

"*I am the light.*"

"'In one hand lies the moon.'"

"*In one hand lies the moon.*"

"'In the other rests the sun.'"

"*In the other rests the sun.*"

"'Before me stands the night…'"

"Before me stands the night."

"'…while behind me creeps the day.'"

"While behind me creeps the day."

"'And if I must be the dealer of death…'"

"And if I must be the dealer of death."

"'…may it be for the preservation of life.'"

"May it be for the preservation of life."

"'Forgive me for that which I may not…'"

"Forgive me for that which I may not."

"'…until I find my peace among the stars.'"

"Until I find my peace among the stars."

As soon as the last words of the oath were uttered, Tahara walked over to one of the guards to retrieve a small bowl. She knelt down and carefully dipped the edge in the water, allowing only a few drops inside. When she turned back to the group, she cupped the bowl with both of her hands.

"Think of this water as though you are taking a small sip directly from the soul of Sanora. It is pure energy. Drinking but a little can grant you Favors of miraculous ability. Powerful as they may be, should you receive no Favor, this is the ultimate blessing, for the fountain believes there to be enough power within you already."

"What nonsense! Better give me two bowls full, just in case!" the shorter boy exclaimed as he elbowed the taller one in the side. "Maybe even three! Right, Dortha?"

He laughed while the skinny boy he called Dortha seemed to shrivel in size. "I guess so."

"That will not be a possibility, Bjorn," Tahara said firmly.

"And why is that?" he questioned.

"To take in more than what the fountain offers would surely lead to your undoing. The few drops I have here in this bowl alone have the potential to kill everyone here."

Alexandra reached down to her left arm. The knot in her stomach leaped from a slight nervousness to an infectious petrification.

Suddenly, the air on the back of her neck felt invasively torrid as it spread throughout her skin. *Maybe this was a terrible idea after all,* she thought.

"So, no swimming, then?" Vincent asked jokingly.

Vera snickered, while Barrik smacked the back of his head.

Tahara shook her head. "Even touching the water can cause severe harm."

"If it's so dangerous, why even bother guarding it, then?" Vera asked.

"Are you stupid?" Bjorn asked aggressively.

Vera turned toward him with a raised eyebrow.

"Don't speak to her like that!" Toran exclaimed.

"Ya know, Toran, I think you're long overdue for the lesson on when to shut your mouth," Bjorn fired back. "Maybe after this, I'll teach ya."

"Sure. Then maybe afterward, I can teach *you* how to read. We can start with some children's picture books."

Vera bit her lip to muffle her laughter. Bjorn's cheeks warmed with red frustration as he gritted his teeth. "Maybe we should just start now." He only managed to take one step before Dortha held up his arm as a barricade.

"Gentlemen, please," Tahara called out calmly.

Toran turned away from Bjorn and looked to the ground with a small, triumphant smile.

Tahara turned her attention back to Vera. "There are no stupid questions, child. Shortly after the fountains were created, before their power was understood, animals would mistake the water for a natural spring. It mutated their poor souls into the horrors we now depend on people like you to protect us from."

"So, if that's where horrors come from," Dortha began to ask timidly, "and all of the fountains have been guarded for hundreds of years, how have they not gone extinct?"

Tahara smiled. "Beautiful are the mysteries of our world, aren't they?"

Dortha stared at her with eyes full of confusion.

She turned back to Bjorn, and with the bowl in her hands, she asked him, "Are you ready? Once you drink, there will be no turning back."

"Why would I want to turn back?" he asked as he took the bowl from her hands. He lifted it to his lips and tossed it back without any hesitation. Everyone kept their eyes on him, waiting to see any changes, but nothing happened.

Tahara bowed her head as she retrieved the bowl from him. "The fountains welcome you, Bjorn."

He stood proudly as she returned to the water's edge and refilled the drops in the bowl. Dortha took it from her hands and paused. Silence grew as his indecisiveness became clear.

"You do not have to drink, my child," Tahara assured him with a hand on his shoulder. "You may still join the soldiers of Meditas with your pride intact. The fountains do not call to everyone."

Dortha waited another moment until he made his decision. Slowly, he began to lift the bowl—but just before it touched his lips, Bjorn fell to his hands and knees. Terror flooded everyone's veins as he coughed, wretched, and heaved puddles of dark blood that splashed onto the ground. His screams of agony quickly filled the air as his arms and legs started to twist and bend, beginning to take on a new structure. Tahara stepped away from the boy with a gentle nod to Kai. He unsheathed his katana. His footsteps were quick, but not rushed. There was a slight pause deep in his bones before his blade was positioned, but once his mind was set, his blade fell.

"Stop!" Alexandra yelled.

Too late. The boy's cries came to an abrupt halt. Silence fell over everyone as the now yellowed eyes of Bjorn lifelessly gazed at them all from the grass.

Tahara looked at everyone's aghast expressions and waved for two guards to remove the body. Kai cleaned what he could off his blade and reassumed his position against the root, his hands once again folded over the hilt.

"…Why?" was all Barrik could bring himself to say.

"What you just witnessed was the tragic transformation from man into horror," Tahara said plainly.

"Why didn't you help him?" Rinna demanded.

"The fountain's wishes are beyond our aid. The only deed we may grant him is a swift end to the painful misery he had begun to undergo."

"Brutal," Vera muttered to herself.

Tahara brought everyone's attention back to Dortha, as if nothing had happened. "Now, child, as you were."

Dortha's eyes were still wide with horror, his face frozen in shock. His decision was already made; he just no longer had the power to move his body. Tahara gently placed her hands over his and whispered something in his ear. His face fell into an expression of peace. He seemed more at ease now than ever before, and with a gentle nod of his head, he returned the bowl to her. She placed a soft kiss on his forehead and took it from him. "Do not permit the fountain's wishes to cause you any inner turmoil, child. There is still a mighty strength in you."

As he took a bow, she gently smiled and turned toward the water. Rinna's stomach began to flip as she watched Tahara gracefully pour out what was intended for Dortha—and refill it for her.

"Remember, child, you do not have to drink," Tahara said placidly as she handed Rinna the bowl.

Rinna's gaze briefly lingered over the few drops of water before she took a deep breath and put the bowl to her lips. Her eyes were shut tightly in anticipation as she handed the bowl back to Tahara. Rinna could feel everyone's worried eyes on her.

After a few moments, Vera placed her hand on Rinna's shoulder. "You still in there?"

Rinna slowly opened her eyes and looked at everyone else. "I think so. At least, I don't feel any different."

"The fountains welcome you," Tahara said with a gentle nod.

There was a mass sigh of relief. However, their anxiety quickly returned as Tahara walked back from the water. It was Vera's turn.

She looked at the bowl in Tahara's hands, snatched it, tossed it back, and returned it to her in one motion. Her eyes darted across her body as she inspected it for any immediate changes.

"V?" Vincent urged.

She hopped up and down before she looked at him and shrugged.

His eyes widened. "You got a little..." he said with a circular gesture around his face.

Vera tapped her upper lip with two fingers, finding them dyed red from the blood streaming out of her nose. She went to tilt her head back in order to slow the bleeding, but the rest of her body seemed to forget not to lean with her head. Rinna quickly caught her before she fell to the ground.

"Maybe you should sit down, hon," Rinna said with Vera in her arms.

"Sitting sounds nice," she agreed mildly.

Rinna helped her to the ground gently, where, this time, she successfully tilted her head back.

"Are you okay, child?" Tahara asked.

"I'm wonderful. Never better. Definitely no need to call him over here," Vera said with a gesture to Kai.

"Then the fountains welcome you," Tahara said with a bow before she turned away.

As Vera's spirits rose, Alexandra's stomach plummeted. There was a lifetime between every one of Tahara's steps to and from the water. The closer she grew, the faster Alexandra's heart pounded in her chest, up until the very moment she stood right in front of her; then, time stopped. All she could hear was the intensely rapid beat of her heart.

With the bowl in her hands, she stared into the water and watched all of the daunting possibilities pass by in each tiny ripple. She looked at Kai, who was still leaning against the root, his silver hair kept back by the dark band of cloth wrapped around his head. His hands rested calmly on his weapon, his eyes firm and dangerous—the eyes of an executioner.

Whispers of War

"Are you ready?" Tahara's words pulled Alexandra out of her mind, but offered no peace for her worries.

At last, Alexandra accepted whatever would come next and lifted the bowl to her lips. The icy water chilled her entire chest as it went down. She dropped. The bowl rolled away to one of the nearby soldiers.

Barrik knelt down beside her, his hand on her shoulder. "Alex, hey, what is it? What's wrong?"

She gave no response, her right hand tightly grasping her left as she gritted her teeth.

"Come on, talk to me!"

"… My arm… feels like… it's on fire," she said in between deep gasps of pain.

With her eyes clamped shut, flashes of a cloaked figure flew across her mind. No details could be made out from the images, but she did hear a woman's voice, deeper than Tahara's, yet just as ethereal. Her words echoed through Alexandra's inner mind repeatedly as if she stood right in front of her: *"You have already been chosen."*

Tahara leaned down to her and reached for her arm. "Let me see, child. Perhaps I may ease your pain."

Alexandra quickly recoiled. She moved her right hand over the leather glove covering her left and looked at Barrik with panicked eyes.

"Don't worry, child," Tahara said reassuringly.

Alexandra's eyes darted between Barrik and Vincent as if to ask what she should do, but they were just as unsure as she was. With a desperate desire for the pain to end, she reluctantly relinquished her left hand to Tahara and anxiously watched as she started to remove the glove. She pulled finger by finger until the leather no longer concealed the hand beneath it.

Once she saw what Alexandra was so intent on concealing, Tahara's one and only reaction was a step back. Kai pushed off of his root. Again, his steps were quick, but not rushed. Alexandra's panic doubled as her heart raced. She pulled her left hand close to her body to conceal it once more. Just as Kai was about to reach her, Vincent positioned himself in between.

"Stand aside, Vincent," Kai said sternly.

"Make me." Vincent's head was slightly tilted downward. He looked into Kai's blue eyes through furrowed brows, his feet planted firmly.

"Kai, you don't understand," Barrik said in a hurry as he looked up from the pain-stricken Alexandra. "Alex's arm has looked like this for a long time; this didn't just happen. It's why she wears the glove. Our mother told her to keep it hidden, I swear! Please, don't…" He trailed off.

"May I see?" Kai asked softly, never removing his eyes from Vincent's stare.

"Let him through, Vince," Barrik said.

Vincent hesitated before slightly turning his body to allow Kai to walk past him. He crouched next to Barrik and Alexandra and paid no mind to her arm; he looked only into her eyes, two worried oceans filled with pain and fear. He lingered for a moment with no words before he stood up and walked away, leaving her alone to deal with the pain. Only once he leaned back against the root did his hands touch the hilt of his blade.

Quickly becoming overwhelmed with helplessness, Barrik turned to Tahara. "Can you help her?"

Tahara handed Alexandra's glove to Barrik as she knelt beside them and looked over Alexandra. She was clutching her arm tightly to her chest, rocking back and forth as sweat poured down her head.

"Roll up your sleeve," Tahara commanded.

Barrik helped Alexandra pull the sleeve of her tunic all the way up just past her elbow. Tahara looked on with horrified amazement as she slowly started to reach toward Alexandra's arm. "This isn't new?" she asked, surprised.

Alexandra frantically shook her head. The pain was too much for her to answer with words.

"What happened?"

Concerned about whether they should tell her the truth, Barrik glanced at Alexandra for approval before he spoke. "We… don't really know. It's been this way for as long as she can remember."

Tahara's fingers gently followed the deep crevices on Alexandra's blackened arm that turned and split apart like veins or cracks in the side of an ancient stone wall. The dark, jagged texture surrounding them mimicked the armored skin of a dragon and felt rough beneath her palm.

As she turned over the girl's arm to view the underside, she was greeted by a soft, faint white glow from her wrist to her palm, almost as if there were no surface at all, only an endless void of white light. Tahara's curiosity grew even further at the sight of Alexandra's fingers; each one came to a sharpened tip where her nails would have been, forming claws that seemed to be meticulously forged to slice through even the toughest of materials.

"This is a darkness far beyond anything I have ever witnessed," Tahara said, full of bewilderment. "Perhaps if I…" She delicately clasped Alexandra's hand in both of hers and closed her eyes.

The white glow on Alexandra's palm peeked through the gaps of Tahara's fingers as it slowly grew brighter and brighter. The gleam of light, previously confined to the underside of her hand, raced up through the crevices of her arm like a river flowing upstream. Everyone was stunned at both the appearance of Alexandra's arm and Tahara's mysterious abilities. Alexandra was the most amazed of all, as after only a few moments, her pain had almost entirely vanished.

Entranced, Alexandra watched as the light coursed up each little path on her arm and disappeared behind her rolled-up sleeve. Once all of the crevices were illuminated, Tahara let go of her hand and opened her eyes.

"How do you feel?"

"… Great. Really great!" Alexandra answered with a smile of relief as she maneuvered her arm around. "I just…" The pain was gone entirely, but the voice she had heard left an eerie feeling deep in her bones.

"What is it, child?" Tahara asked.

"Do the fountains ever speak?"

"The fountains operate in mysterious ways. Some people remember past lives, some people hear voices, and some people even have hallucinations. Rarely are these experiences anything more than a minor side effect of taking in such pure energy. What did you hear?"

She hesitated, still frightened to tell Tahara the truth. "I only heard a voice. I couldn't make out what was said," she lied.

"Well then, there's no sense in paying any extra mind to it. All that's important is that the fountains welcome you," Tahara said with a bow.

"Thank you for your help," Alexandra responded gratefully with a bow of her own.

"Wonderful!" Vincent said as he snatched the glove from Barrik's hand. "Now, throw that back on before you frighten all of Meditas."

"We'd better get a sack for your face, then," Alexandra teased.

Barrik chuckled. "Definitely feeling better, I see."

Alexandra was about to cover up her arm once more when...

"Hey, Alex?" Rinna said.

"Yeah?"

"Forgive me if this is strange, but may I get a closer look?" she asked, gesturing to her arm.

"Uh, yeah, sure," she responded, surprised.

Rinna gracefully took her outstretched arm into her hands and moved it all around with a smile from ear to ear. "It's beautiful. Why do you hide it?" she asked as she let go.

"Our mother always told me to keep it hidden. Only because it would draw a lot of attention, which is something she tries to avoid."

From behind them, they could hear Tahara's words. "The fountains welcome you."

They turned to see Toran handing her back the bowl with a bow. Alexandra slid her hand back into the glove and let the sleeve of her tunic fall back over it, concealing her arm again.

"Mr. Barrik," Tahara said as she stood before him, "are you ready to accept the fountains?"

"I am," he said confidently.

The bowl seemed to shrink once it entered his hands. He tilted it all the way back until every last drop was gone.

"How do you feel, big guy?" Vincent asked as soon as Tahara took the bowl.

He shrugged. "I don't know. I'm a little hungry."

Vera and Rinna laughed.

Alexandra rolled her eyes. "Of course you are."

"What? It's not like we had breakfast."

Vincent shook his head. "I meant, do you feel any different than normal?"

"Nothing yet."

"Maybe for someone your size, you need an extra sip," Vincent joked.

"Neither your physique nor any physical quality has any role to play in the fountain's blessings upon you," Tahara said as she approached Vincent.

"I know, I know."

"Vincent Raine." She paused. "I cannot help but wonder if your destiny began with your father's defection or perhaps there is something more yet to be revealed." She handed him the bowl. "Whatever the origins of your destiny or where it leads you, may the fountains bless you."

Vincent held the bowl in his hands for a few moments. Both his mother and his father had stood right here. They had climbed the winding steps, sworn the same oath, and drunk from the same fountain. Now it was his turn to do just as they had done before, and hopefully, he would make them proud.

Slightly nervous, he tossed his tongue around his cheek. "Welp, here's to destiny, I guess."

As soon as he swallowed the water, he fell to the ground, no longer able to feel his legs, as if they had completely disappeared.

"Vince!" Barrik exclaimed.

He tried to answer, but failed to speak. All of the air had been ripped from his lungs, and no matter how many breaths he took, it would not return. He reached out for Barrik as tears flooded down his cheeks, but it was only seconds before he lost control of the rest of his body.

Vincent could see everyone huddled around him with their mouths moving, but there was no sound; in fact, now, he felt nothing at all. Barrik held his shoulders down as his body started to convulse. Alexandra looked to be begging for Tahara to help in any way she could. His mind began to race, but his heart, while its beats were fierce, started to slow. Dark blood poured out of his nose. His world spun faster and faster as his mouth began to foam. His vision blurred... His eyes grew heavy... The world darkened.

The last thing he heard before the void he was falling into had completely overtaken him was a voice. A woman's voice. An ethereal whisper in his ears.

"Finally."

CHAPTER 7

AKE up."

The soft whisper echoed through Vincent's mind. Slowly, he rose to his feet to behold a new environment entirely unfamiliar to him. Fluffy white clouds drifted across the bright blue sky above him, yet no matter where he turned, the sun could not be found, nor any source of light, for that matter. The ground beneath his feet reflected everything above like the clearest mirror he had ever seen, yet every one of his steps sent small ripples to dance away in every direction. Everywhere he turned, everything was the same for as far as he could see. It was peaceful, calming to his heart, a much different state of mind than the one he remembered before he got here.

"Where am I?" he said to himself.

"Now, that is the question, isn't it?" a gentle voice answered from behind him.

He whipped around to see a figure in a midnight-black cloak far in the distance.

"Who are you?!" Vincent shouted.

"Now, that's two questions," the same voice answered, but it came from behind him again. When he whirled around, the figure was only inches away from his face. Startled, he fell backward, sending ripples throughout the glassy surface. He looked over his shoulder back to where they were only a moment ago, and sure enough, nobody was there. When he climbed back to his feet, he took another look around.

"Am I dead?" he asked.

"No, you are not dead," the figure answered firmly.

"Then where am I?"

"You are somewhere beyond the physical realm."

"Oh, yay, riddles."

"No riddles. We are within the depths of your soul while your vessel remains in Meditas."

"My vessel? Do you mean my body?"

"Correct."

Vincent struggled to understand what was going on. His shoulders and hands raised as his expression tensed. "Okay, so if I'm inside *my* soul, how are *you* here?"

"We have a very strong connection."

Vincent leaned over to peek underneath the hood, but he found nothing but darkness. It was as if there were no face at all, just a robe resting over the body of an endless shadow.

"And you are...?" he asked.

"I believe your people refer to us as fountains, but you may call me Larissa," she said. Her words swam through his ears like a gentle stream.

"'Us'?"

"I am one of four."

"One of four fountains—like the one that just killed me?"

"Again, you did not perish."

"Sure felt like it."

Vincent took a moment to try to make sense of his situation.

"I drank the water. Your water? And then you tried to kill me, and now I'm... dreaming?"

"Your people's use of the term 'dreaming' implies that whatever you've experienced was little more than a mere hallucination. And I did not try to kill you."

"Well, you don't have a face, and I'm standing on water that isn't wet, so..."

"Just because you do not fully understand the experience does not necessarily mean it is any less *real*. Your kind perpetually makes the mistake of believing anything outside of the physical world is delusion, with the only exception being whatever they decide is the power of whichever deity holds their faith. All of this simply due to the lack of an explanation."

"Well, if you have any explanation for all of this, I would love to hear it, Larissa, all-wise and knowing fountain of death."

Despite the blatant sarcasm in Vincent's tone, Larissa's voice retained the same delicate affection as when he first heard it. "*You are not confined to the same restrictions as your vessel. While soul and body are connected, they are not attached. The soul possesses the luxurious freedom to wander to places your body may not physically travel. In sleep, you can revisit memories, venture to faraway lands, or even speak to loved ones who have long since passed. And when it comes time for your soul to return to the stars, the energy that was once inside it will sprout new life, creating the cycle of balance we strive to protect.*"

Vincent's eyes narrowed as he pieced together her words. "Okay... but I still don't understand why you're here. No offense."

"When you drank the water, our souls touched, forging this connection."

"I *touched* your soul?"

"Think of it like this: when someone absorbs the water, it's as if you have thrown a stone against a wall; the souls briefly come into contact. Most times, this causes a change of some kind, which you refer to as 'Favors.' Sometimes, there is little to no harm besides that, while for others, there is irreparable damage. Neither the soul nor the human body, for that matter, are able to withstand overexposure to an excess amount of energy; otherwise, they become twisted and deformed until they no longer resemble their prior self."

Vincent's thoughts strayed to the forever-ingrained image of Bjorn's unfortunate transformation.

Larissa continued, "For you and me, however, it's as if you have cast your stone into the ocean."

"Last time I threw a rock into the water, it sank to the bottom." The more he began to understand, the more his worries grew. "If I'm not dead, then what's going to happen to me?"

"While there's no way of knowing exactly how you'll be affected, your soul contains the potential for an enormous amount of energy—much more than I have seen in a long time. Which is why there is something I must ask of you—a favor, if you will."

"What kind of favor?"

"The worst kind. I'm afraid someone has found a way to harness our power for their own treacherous agenda."

"I thought you give out your power willingly?"

"A small sample of our power is given to assist in the preservation of our world's balance. But they seek all of our power only to satiate their greed."

Vincent cocked an eyebrow. "And you want me to…?"

Larissa answered before he was able to finish his thought. "Dispose of them and return my brethren's power back to its rightful owner, restoring the balance. The longer they are left unchallenged, the further Sanora will descend into darkness. Clouds will dry up, soils will lose fertility, and pestilence will wreak havoc upon not only the vegetation, but your people as well."

Flashes of the man with blackened, ashy fingers from that first night they had all entered The Wicked broom flew across Vincent's mind.

"The dangers I speak of will be much worse the closer you are to where the power was stolen," Larissa added.

"The Gray Lands," Vincent whispered.

"The what?"

"The Gray Lands. It sounds like what you're talking about, but there's no fountain there. The closest one would be..."

His thoughts led him to a heart-crushing conclusion. Beginning to feel heavy, he sat down on the rippling floor of glassy water. "They lost," he said to himself.

"Who lost?"

"Ten years ago, my father took a small army to protect the city of Abnor and their fountain, but shortly after the war ended, the surrounding environment started to die—so much so that the color seemed to fade from existence. Even the sun stopped shining there, which allowed horrors to roam freely in the daytime. Everyone who lived there was forced to move away."

"Then it has already begun."

Vincent looked to the ground and nodded his head slowly. "Could that also be why horrors are growing in numbers every-where else?"

"There is no limit to what the darkness of unbalance may bring. If left unchecked, it may spell the end of Sanora entirely."

"How do I find this person?"

"They have the powers of my kin, and now that our souls have connected in this way, you now carry a part of me. You'll be drawn to each other. If you don't find them, they will find you."

Vincent huffed a laugh. "Well, at least they're gonna make it easy for me."

"Do not submit to such a foolish thought. This task will be far from trivial. Presently, you do not possess even a fraction of the power necessary to defeat them. However, *if* you accept, I can give it to you."

"And what happens if I don't?"

"Then I will continue to wait."

"For what?"

"Another connection as strong as ours. Although, there's no telling how long that will take, or what could happen during the time in between. But I would not force you to see this through, nor fault you should you decline."

Confused, Vincent raised his eyebrow and asked, "Why would I decline?"

"Because the power I offer you does not come without a cost. Those who have wielded it before paid dearly for it, and you may be subjected to the same fate as they."

Her words launched an ominous anxiety through his mind as he wondered what could have happened to those before him.

"What is this power?" he asked.

"The power lies within a sword buried at the back of the tomb beneath the city. She rests between two blue flames."

Without warning, Larissa vanished. Vincent stood up quickly and whipped around in search of her, but could see nothing in any direction.

"Larissa?" he called out. Several moments of silence passed until she reappeared right in front of him once more, knocking him back to the ground.

"I am sorry, Vincent. Our time together is fading. Despite the strength of our connection, it is not indefinite. You must decide."

Vincent already knew what his decision would be, but something stayed his response. Maybe he only needed to work up the courage to say the words aloud, or just wished for the ability to talk to someone close to him first. He turned away from Larissa as if to grant himself a moment of privacy, and she respected the gesture.

Memories of Sylva began to take over the environment as he wandered through some of the cherished moments of his past. Like a visitor to his own history, he watched different scenes come and go. Days in the bright and sunny training yard with Fira shouting her criticism from beyond the wooden fence. Rucker jumping up and down, overjoyed with the new sign Charlie had taught him that day. The dinner table, crowded with wide smiles and full bellies. Everyone, much younger than they were now, gathered around the fireplace in the sitting room as Fira read whatever story had been chosen to lull them all to sleep that evening. It had only been a few weeks since they left Sylva, but already he had begun to miss her dearly. The soft tone of her voice filled him with endless warmth.

When her image faded, he strayed into another memory that lingered much longer than the others. He stood right in front of the fireplace, just like he was back at home. His father's necklace hung just above the mantelpiece. But now, unlike the one he had grown up knowing, the star stone encompassed by silver contained a green illumination that shone brightly in his eyes. He reached out to try to touch it, but his hand went right through it as if nothing was ever there. The longer he looked at the glowing necklace, the more it felt like a message from his father—a message of reassurance and guidance. A message that said, *"I'll be right beside you."* If he were to be the kind of man his father was, the kind of son his parents could be proud of, he knew what he had to do.

When Vincent finally turned back around, he was ready.

"I'll do it."

"Hold out your hands," Larissa said plainly.

Vincent lifted his hands to the height of his chest, palms down. Larissa drew closer, and her hands emerged from the shadowy depths of her sleeves. The rest of her arms above the wrist disappeared behind a veil of darkness, as if her hands came from an entirely different plane of existence. She turned his palms upward and gently laid hers on top.

"This will give you, and only you, the ability to wield the sword. Touch the wall in the back of the tomb, and it will fade away, but I must offer you one last warning to heed: do not use the sword for anything other than this purpose. Its power will take a toll on not only your vessel, but also your soul." She paused for a moment before she asked him, "Are you ready?"

Vincent nodded slowly.

"This is going to hurt."

At first, her hands were icy to the touch, but slowly, they began to heat up. Vincent's skin grew hotter and hotter until it felt as though he had shoved them both directly into the fires of a forge. Larissa began to steam and slowly fade from sight. The pain grew unbearable. His eyes clamped shut. He screamed in agony until he finally fell to his knees.

Larissa was gone. Smoke rolled off of his hands. He fell to his side. Lying on the watery ground, he looked into the reflection of the sky. Like the curtain of night, his heavy lids draped over his eyes, shrouding him in darkness.

When Vincent finally started to open his eyes again, he found himself in another entirely new environment. He sat up slowly from the uncomfortable bed beneath him. Through the barrier of iron bars in front of him, he scanned the room. Green moss peeked between each gap and crack of the dark stone walls. The only light crept in from the few barred windows where the wall met the ceiling. Judging by the color of the sunlight that spilled onto the damp floor, it was around midday, he figured. He swung his legs to the floor, anchoring himself to the earth, and leaned over with his pounding head in his hands.

"You're awake!" someone exclaimed.

Startled, Vincent quickly looked up at a man leaning against the other side of the iron bars between them. He wore only a pair of black, weathered trousers, ripped and torn at the cuffs. Thick brown hair full of knots and dirt fell to the nape of his neck. The repulsive scars of deep cuts, slashes, and burns that covered his lean torso left Vincent wondering where each one came from. Narrowed hazel eyes rested above the corners of a grin that sent a message other than what the expression usually suggested. It felt mischievous and full of tricks, like a wolf ready to bear its fangs hidden beneath the skin of a smile.

"I have been dying to talk to you," the man said as he slumped against the bars. His voice sounded like an intricate dance of soft steps and elongated movements. Every word felt like a dramatic partner in a game of deception.

"And who are you, exactly?" Vincent asked with exhaustion in his tone.

"A friend and ally to your daddy, the King of Rain," the man said with a bow. "See?" He pointed to the Rogue's scar on his right cheek, identical to Fira's.

"What do you mean by 'the King of Rain'?" Vincent asked, confused.

"Yup. If there was rain on the battlefield, you knew Victor was somewhere nearby. So, I guess that makes you a prince. Oh, how fun!" The man stuck his arm through the iron bars with an open hand. "So, from one prince to another, it is an absolute honor to meet you. Name's Faux."

Vincent remained on his bed, confused.

"Uh, hello? Fira taught you manners, didn't she?" Faux asked as he waved his outstretched hand.

Vincent softly shook his head in disbelief before he got up and walked closer to the bars.

"So, what are you prince of? The dungeon?" Vincent asked as he accepted his hand.

Faux glared at him for a moment before yanking him forward. Vincent smacked his head on the bars and fell to his knees, clutching his forehead as the sound of vibrating iron bounced off the stone walls.

With his hands on his hips, Faux mocked, "No, I'm not 'prince of the dungeon.' I'm *the* prince. Faux Kasura, son of the rat bastard King Sentis himself. So, I guess technically also prince of the dungeon, but the way you said it was degrading."

Vincent slowly got back to his feet, still rubbing his head. He chuckled to himself. "Right. So, they just locked up the prince of Meditas, the only heir to the throne, for so long that I didn't even know you existed. And you don't even share the same surname."

Faux gasped in shock. "Well, first off, rude. Surely, Fira told you all about me. And second, I abandoned the Sentis surname for my mother's."

"Well, either way, I've never heard of any fake princes," Vincent said as he massaged his temples.

Faux held the bars in both his hands and pressed his forehead against them. "That is so disappointing to hear." He slid down the bars until he was slumped against the floor, pouting.

Vincent walked over to the cell entrance and tried to open the gate. Locked.

"Why would they throw me in the dungeon?" he asked himself. Defeated, he returned to his bed, where curiosity overtook him. "Even if you really were the prince, why would they lock you up down here?"

A devilish grin snuck across Faux's face. "I killed the queen."

Vincent had no idea how to respond. Faux returned to his own bed, where he lay on his back and crossed his arms behind his head. Lost in thought, Vincent fiddled with the ring on his finger that Rucker had gifted them. His thumb slid across the silver band, finding each subtle imperfection.

"Oh, good, you're awake," Kai suddenly said to him from the other side of the gate.

"Kai?! Oh, thank the stars! Let me out, already. I'm starving," Vincent begged.

"Not yet."

"Wait—what? Why?! What do you mean, not yet?" Vincent asked as he drew closer to the bars.

"Back up."

Vincent stopped in his tracks, shocked. "What's going on, Kai?"

Kai pulled a stool over to the bars and sat down. Steam rolled out of a clay cup in his hands. "I just need to make sure it's safe to let you out, that's all."

"Why wouldn't it be?"

From the other side of the room, Faux hissed and clawed at the air before laughing to himself. Kai did not acknowledge him.

"You want to make sure I'm not a horror?" Vincent said in realization.

"Something like that. Take this." Kai held the cup just beyond the bars. Vincent nervously watched Kai as he slowly reached for the cup.

"What is it?" Vincent asked as he peered into it.

"Tea."

"Some kind of horror-killing tea?"

"Just tea."

Vincent smelled the cup before bringing it to his lips and taking a sip.

"Have a seat, Vince."

Vincent plopped himself back down on the edge of his bed with the cup held close to his nose. The tea's heat was refreshing and numbed the pain in his head. He took another sip.

"How do you feel?" Kai asked.

"I'm starving. I'm exhausted. My head feels like Barrik was kicking it over and over again. I have no idea why I'm in a dungeon. And I was having weird dreams that maybe weren't dreams... I'm confused, and I don't know if I've mentioned this, but I'm starving."

"I don't know, Kai," Faux chimed in. "I wouldn't trust him. I say let your fancy sword have her way with him."

Again, Kai paid him no attention.

"Kai, seriously, this is ridiculous," Vincent protested.

"What do you mean, 'dreams that maybe weren't dreams'?" Kai asked him.

Vincent hesitated to respond. He was unsure whether or not to tell him everything that had happened with Larissa. After all, he still did not fully believe it himself. Ultimately, he thought it was either just a dream and did not matter, or it was real, in which case Kai ought to know. So, he told him everything in as much detail as he could, and much to his surprise, he seemed to remember it all with such clarity that not a single word was left out.

"Do you think I'm crazy?" Vincent asked after his recount.

"Did you finish your tea?" Kai prompted.

Vincent looked into the cup. "Yeah."

Kai held out his hand for Vincent to give it back to him. He pointed to a window above Vincent's bed. "Put your hand in the sunlight."

Vincent stood up on his bed and placed his hand in the beam of sun spilling into the cell, as directed, and looked back to Kai with a shrug.

"Okay, sit down," Kai said before taking a deep breath. "So, someone managed to harness the power of Abnor's fountain after all..."

Vincent felt an uncomfortable knot tighten in his stomach. "You're saying all of that *was* real?"

"I am."

Vincent lowered his head in thought. "So, what do we do?"

"Did she give you any information on this mystery person?"

"No. Only that I would be drawn to them, or them to me."

"Then there's nothing we can do without more information. Right now, we just need to be cautious and keep our ears to the ground. While the other fountains are still guarded, they no longer partake in the ceremony. With all the disappearances throughout the last several years and no new Guardians to replace them, our strength is severely weakened."

"I'd love to help, but ya know..." Faux waved his hand around the room. "You'd have to let me out."

"Vince, you said this... *Larissa* gave you some kind of sword?" Kai asked.

"She told me about a sword I should only use to defeat whoever this mystery thief is. It's behind a wall between two blue flames at the back of the tomb under the city."

"I don't know of any blue flames, but I can take you to the tomb. But first, let's get you out of here."

Vincent hopped from the bed to his feet, ecstatic. "Finally!"

Kai disappeared down the hallway briefly before he came back with a ring of jangling keys. He tried several before he found the correct fit for Vincent's gate.

"Kai?" Vincent started as he stepped out of the gate. "I've been thinking…"

"What is it?"

"Why didn't you go with? To fight in Abnor, I mean."

Kai fell silent. His eyes remained on Vincent's as he searched for his answer.

Faux jumped up from his bed and stuck his face between the iron bars. "Dearest Daddy didn't allow him to go—poor boy. But *I* was there. Side by side with Mommy Fira and that cranky Ghost, who at least comes and visits sometime—unlike you, Kai. Maybe I was closer with them after all."

"Shut your mouth," Kai responded without looking at him. The frustration in his tone was clear.

"Well, it's about time you gave me some attention! I was beginning to think we weren't friends anymore, Kai. That would make me just oh so sad," he said as he hunched against the bars.

"Kai, what's he talking about?" Vincent asked.

Kai exhaled a deep breath before responding. "It's not that I didn't want to go. Victor ordered me to remain back here, and despite my barrage of protests, he wouldn't budge."

"Oh," Vincent said as his eyes darted to the floor. Guilt suddenly welled up in his stomach as he remembered his harsh words to Kai outside of the king's throne room.

"Come. Everyone else has just finished training, and I believe there was some mention of The Wicked Broom. I'll walk you."

As they started their way down the dimly lit hallway, Faux called after him, "Perhaps Victor just couldn't trust you, Kai. It's not like you haven't lost control before, ya know."

Kai snapped around with no words, only an expression of fury upon his face. A glint of crimson rage burned in his blue eyes.

A wide, victorious smile slowly spread across Faux's face. "There *she* is."

Kai opened the door to The Wicked Broom and led Vincent to their usual corner table beneath the window, where everyone except for Toran was gathered around plates of food.

"Kai? What are you doing here?" Vera asked, surprised to see him.

"I'm just here to drop something off." He turned to the side, allowing Vincent to step forward.

"Vince!" everyone exclaimed in unison.

Alexandra jolted up from the table and threw her arms around him. "Thanks for not dying!"

"Although you look like you did," Vera pointed out.

"Smell like it too," Alexandra added as she pulled away with a scrunched-up nose.

"Thank you, V. Thank you, Alex."

Barrik held out a mug of ale for Vincent as he sat down. "Here, Vince, have a drink."

"Well, I'll leave you to it, then," Kai said as he started to walk away.

"What? You're leaving?" Alexandra asked with disapproval in her voice.

"Yeah, come on, Kai, have a drink with us for once," Rinna insisted.

Kai shook his head. "Never going to happen. There are things I need to see to. Where is Mancho?"

Barrik pointed back toward the kitchen.

"Thanks. Vince, you're way behind everyone else on your training, so we'll start first thing in the morning."

"What about the tomb?"

"That can wait until tomorrow as well. So, eat up, and get your rest."

Once Kai disappeared into the back of the tavern in search of Mancho, that was the last they saw of him for the day.

"What does he mean, I'm way behind the rest of you?" Vincent asked, confused.

Barrik placed his hand on Vincent's shoulder. "It's not your fault, bud. We've just had more time than you to work on our Favors; that's all."

"More time? Hang on—how long have I been down there for?"

A hush fell over the table. Everyone looked around at one another to see who would deliver the news, until Alexandra finally spoke up.

"Two weeks and three days."

Vincent's eyes widened, then fell to his pint. "Kai failed to mention that part."

"Yeah, you gave us quite the scare there for a while," Barrik said softly.

"But we're glad that you're back," Rinna said with a gentle smile.

Vincent shook his head in an attempt to rid himself of the shock. "Thanks, Rinna. Well then, uh, what did I miss? Did you all figure out what your Favors are?"

"Well," Alexandra started, "Toran can strike his target twice with a single swing. Barrik can conjure up this barricade of energy that our swords can't even break through, and V is able to—"

"Wait, wait, wait!" she interrupted. "Let me show him!"

"All right, all right, go ahead."

Vera pulled out one of her daggers with a twirl of excitement and stabbed it down into the table. Vincent watched with anticipation as she got up out of her seat and walked out of the tavern. A few moments passed by before he started to grow impatient.

"Okay, what am I—"

Before he could finish his question, Vera reappeared back in her seat.

"Woah!" Vincent cried out, slightly startled. "A relocation Favor?" he assumed.

With another twirl, Vera returned her dagger to the sheath on her lower back. "Yup. I can instantly move to one of my daggers, no matter how far away they are, and anything that's on me or in my hands seems to come with."

"How'd you figure that one out?"

Rinna snickered. "She dove for one of them and ended up with a face full of dirt."

Vera shrank in her seat. "I got there much quicker than I thought I was going to."

Vincent laughed. "Wish I could have seen it."

Vera sneered at him.

"Show him yours too, Rinna," Alexandra urged.

Rinna set down her pint and cleared her throat. "Okay," she said, resting her elbows on the table with her hands up. Vincent waited patiently for the next magic trick to begin. Sure enough, a moment later, like a reflected image on the surface of a pond quickly erased by the splash of a rock, both of her hands started to blur away until they could no longer be seen.

"Woah!" Vincent leaned in closer to try to find any sign of them. "Just your hands?"

First, she smiled—then she vanished.

"It also works on anything I touch." Other than her voice, the only other indication she was still with them was the mug in front of her, which also vanished just as quickly.

"That's amazing," Vincent said, astounded.

Rinna reappeared with her mug in hand. "The bigger something is, though, the harder it is to do, and I get sleepy pretty quickly."

"She almost scared Alex to death when she did it the first time," Vera said with a chuckle.

"Well, yeah, how was I supposed to know *that* was going to happen?"

"What did you do?" Vincent asked.

Vera started to laugh. "She tried to spook Rinna as she was coming back into our room, but as soon as Rinna got scared, she went *poof!*"

"I thought I killed her."

Rinna and Vera were both laughing now.

"You thought you *killed* her?" Vincent asked.

"Well, what was I supposed to think? She was there one moment, and then she wasn't. It was supposed to be a silly prank, but I ended up being more scared than she was."

"You guys did get Kai pretty good with that one, though," Barrik chimed in.

"Oh, yeah!" Rinna remembered. "I snuck right up next to him the next morning while he was reading."

"Oh, man! I wish I could have seen that too," Vincent said, disappointed.

"I don't recommend trying to pull any more tricks like that on him, though."

"Why not?"

"While him throwing his book up into the air was pretty funny, he almost drew his weapon."

"Yikes. I'll keep that in mind. What about you, Alex?"

"You kind of already saw mine."

Vincent searched through his memories. "When?"

"When Tahara was holding my hand during the ceremony. I can take in energy with my left arm and then use it later on. Although it doesn't work if I have the glove on. I need to be able to *feel* the energy, I guess."

"So, why don't you just stop hiding it?"

"That's what I keep telling her!" Rinna agreed.

"Come on, you've seen the way people react once they see it. They freak out like I'm some kind of horror ready to eat them."

"Yeah. And suck out their eyes like they're those little sweets from the market," Vera added with a noise like she was slurping up the final noodle in a bowl of soup.

Barrik recoiled in his seat. "Eww, V. Gross. Really gross."

"Yeah, hon, we might have to limit your nighttime reading," Rinna suggested.

Vera gave an exaggerated gasp. "You wouldn't dare!"

Rinna pointed at her with her index finger as if to warn her.

"You'll be fine, Alex," Barrik said confidently.

"Yeah, besides..." Vera leaned back against the wall and crossed her arms. "People already hate Vincey the moment they figure out who his father is. I doubt it would be any worse for you."

Vincent rolled his eyes. "Gee, thanks, V."

Alexandra looked over her left hand, still hidden beneath the leather glove. "I don't know. Mom always said too much unnecessary attention can lead to an early grave."

"Speaking of graves," Barrik wondered aloud, "Vince, why were you and Kai talking about the tomb?"

"Oh, right," Vincent said, realizing he had momentarily forgotten about everything that had happened with Larissa. "I'll fill you guys in, I promise, but let me eat first. In the meantime, that can't be all that happened while I was out."

Each of them took turns recounting all the events that had occurred while Vincent was absent, sharing as much detail as they could remember. But no matter what story was being told or how hard they laughed together, the anxiety bestowed upon him by Larissa never fully left.

CHAPTER 8

HE sweat on Vincent's brow glistened in the early autumn sunlight. Each one of his quick breaths delivered a cool blast of refreshing air to his lungs. His muscles shook with fatigue from a restless night of tossing and turning. His encounter with Larissa had birthed a cacophony of thoughts in his mind that refused to be silenced. Was any of it even real? Kai seemed to think so. If the power truly was stolen from the Abnor fountain, then did that mean his father had sacrificed everything in vain? And how was he supposed to defeat this mystery person? How would he succeed where his father had failed? If Victor Raine, the renowned commander of the Meditas Guardians, with all of his experience and loyal followers, had still been unable to protect the Abnor fountain, how was he, Vincent, the son of an oathbreaker, supposed to do any better?

As he stood in the training yard, weighed down by exhaustion and a mind full of questions, Vincent realized just how much he had taken sleep for granted—and how he feared peaceful nights might now be a thing of the past. Even as he eyed his opponent, Larissa's words hung heavily over him, weighing his body down with worries about an inevitable threat—or rather, an inevitable failure.

"I need you to focus, Vince," Kai shouted.

Kai stood perfectly still as if he were a permanent fixture of the training yard. None of Vincent's half-hearted attacks had any effect on him. From what he could tell, Kai had yet to expend even a hint of effort.

Like a predator preparing to devour its prey, Kai slowly began to circle him. "Listen to your body, Vince. Don't ignore even the slightest differences you feel. Stop thinking of how to defeat me at the moment; that is not your goal. We're only trying to place you under stress."

"Believe me, I'm stressed," Vincent said in between breaths.

Kai dashed in close, sidestepped Vincent's attack, and cracked the back of his leg. "Then focus."

Vincent stopped and rubbed the point of impact on the backside of his thigh. Although they were only using wooden staves, which were little more than glorified sticks, each hit still packed a wallop.

"How am I supposed to focus right now?" Vincent yelled. "Aren't there other things we should be doing instead of smacking each other with sticks? Like going to the tomb to see if I'm crazy or not?"

"After," Kai responded firmly.

Vincent growled. "I can't even hear myself think right now."

"Good. Do you think you'll have the opportunity to think in a real battle? You need to be able to calm your mind and focus on the task at hand. This is good practice. Control your breaths, control your mind, and focus."

Frustrated, Vincent charged.

Barrik and Alexandra sat together on a pile of wooden crates underneath the shade of an apple tree along the outer perimeter of the training yard. Barrik reached above his head and plucked one of the reddish-orange fruits from a branch. "Did you notice anything different?"

"Get me one," she demanded.

Barrik handed over the apple he had picked for himself before retrieving another.

"He's slower than usual," Alexandra said with a crunch.

"Well, he's probably pretty beat. And all of that Larissa stuff is obviously weighing on his mind too."

"Yeah, but also, they've been at this for a while now, and he hasn't run himself out yet."

"What's your point?"

"I just feel like…" She took another crunch of her apple and continued with her mouth full. "…he should have burnt out by now."

Barrik tossed the core of his apple behind his head. "He's always been stubborn."

"That's true. But I don't know. This seems different. It's almost like every time he's at his breaking point, he finds a small second wind."

Kai swatted away Vincent's slash and countered with a sweep to his legs. Vincent crashed into the ground hard and lay still, flat on his back. His throat burned with exhaustion, his heart raced against his chest, and every one of his muscles begged for rest. He tried to lift himself, but his body had become too heavy. For now, the ground was his home.

"*Now* he's done," Barrik said.

Kai peered down at Vincent from above. "Anything?"

He weakly shook his head. "Nothing."

"Well then, we're not done yet. On your feet."

Vincent closed his eyes for a moment and let his fingers dig into the soil beneath him. The soft and cool touch of the earth felt calming to him, as if the very ground he lay on told him he had nothing to worry about. Everything would be okay. Slowly, he started to relax. The smell of fall slipped into his nose as the breeze swept across his face. With each deep breath he savored, his exhaustion slowly withered away. The weight of his muscles faded as gardens of peaceful silence rose in his mind. He felt as though he could lie there forever with not a care in the world. Everything that once ailed him had almost entirely vanished.

"Come on, Vince, on your feet. This isn't the time to be sleeping!" Kai shouted.

"Right," Vincent said. He pulled his legs up to his chest and quickly launched himself to his feet, ready to go again.

Alexandra hopped down off of her crate. "What did I tell you? Right there, he was done, but now he takes a few seconds on the ground, and he's good to go again?"

"Okay, I see what you mean now," Barrik agreed.

"Kai!" Alexandra shouted. He responded with nothing more than a quick nod of his head.

She sat back down. "He sees it too."

"What exactly is he doing?" Barrik asked, trying to follow.

"I'm not sure, but just watch."

"All right, Vince. I know you're probably pretty exhausted at the moment, so let's wrap this up for the day," Kai said.

"Actually, I feel pretty good."

"Good. Then come at me with everything you have left. Don't worry about exposing yourself; I won't counter. I just want you to go all out."

"Are you sure? I don't want to hurt you, old man," Vincent said with a smirk.

Kai twirled the staff in his hands. "I *want* you to try."

Vincent exploded toward him. Dust flew into the air behind him as he closed the distance. With a salvo of slashes, he attacked.

Kai did as he said he would and left his guard up, choosing not to counter a single one of Vincent's actions, no matter how wild they were.

"I thought I told you to go all out," Kai began to instigate.

Over and over, Vincent thrust forward, slashed, poked, and prodded with all of his strength.

"All out, and this is all you got?"

Alexandra and Barrik unknowingly drew closer to the fight. Both of them were being silently pulled in, as if they were afraid they would miss something.

"This isn't even a fraction of your father's strength."

Vincent gritted his teeth in frustration. While Kai was not attacking physically, his verbal jabs were finding their mark, strategically uprooting the peace he had just established in his mind. Kai could feel every one of Vincent's blows gaining power.

"Looks like Fira's training was worthless."

Each one of Vincent's connections began to force Kai farther backward.

"Worthless. If this is your strength, then all you're ever going to be is the lingering remains of a traitorous fool."

In a bout of anger, Vincent twirled his staff, torqued back his hips, and let go. As if he were trying to take down a large tree in one stroke, he chopped at Kai's midsection. Vincent's staff connected with the center of Kai's and broke clean through it, hitting him in the chest. As he went soaring several feet back, a shock wave of dust flew into the air in every direction. Barrik and Alexandra put up their hands to brace themselves. Vincent dropped to his knees, panting once again.

Kai shook off the hit as he slowly climbed back to his feet with his staff, which was now cloven in two. Curious, he looked up into the sky above. The sun radiated through the bright blue void, unobstructed by any clouds save for the few directly above them.

"That was quite the hit, Vince," Kai said as he walked over to him.

Barrik and Alexandra rushed over to their side.

"Kai, are you okay?" Alexandra asked.

"I'm fine. Apologies, Vincent, they were merely words to provoke an emotional response, not my true beliefs."

Too exhausted to respond, Vincent waved away Kai's apology as he continued to take quick breaths of recovery.

Alexandra knelt down beside him. "How'd you do that?"

Vincent shook his head. "I don't know. I just hit him as hard as I could."

Kai dropped the pieces of his broken staff in front of him. "That was more than just raw strength. Looks to me like you're gathering energy from somewhere, similar to Alexandra's Favor."

"Vince, how were you recovering so quickly?" Alexandra asked.

"What do you mean?"

"Every time you seemed spent, you bounced right back with little to no rest."

"Vince," Kai started, "tell me what went through your mind when I put you on the ground the last time."

Vincent crossed his legs and placed his hands behind him on the ground as he rummaged through his memories. "Well, for a moment, I thought there was no way I was getting back up. Everything was killing me, and I couldn't stop thinking about Larissa."

"Then what?"

"I don't know, exactly. I just started to feel calm. With the breeze on my face and the dirt on my hands, I felt like I could've fallen into the best sleep of my life." As another wisp of wind wandered between them all, Vincent leaned his head back and closed his eyes. "Kind of like right now," he said as he pulled in a deep breath through his nose.

With a finger placed against his lips, Kai urged Alexandra and Barrik to be silent. "Vince, keep your eyes closed and look through your mind right now. Tell me what you see."

"I don't *see* anything."

Alexandra nudged Barrik with a smile on her face. "Nothing *to* see," she whispered.

Vincent continued, "It's all just black. Darkness and... Do you guys hear that?"

"Hear what?" Kai asked.

"It sounds like flowing water."

"Can you see it?"

Vincent started to shake his head. "No, I... Wait... Yes, yeah, I can see it."

"Tell me about it."

"It looks like a spring. The water is crystal clear and sparkling in the..." He stopped.

"What is it?"

"Someone's coming," Vincent said as he opened his eyes.

Kai turned around to see a soldier quickly approaching them from across the training yard. As he drew closer, the clang of his armor grew louder and louder until he stood right in front of them with a strong salute and a familiar face.

"Kai, sir!" Dortha stood tall and strong, seemingly carrying a newfound confidence in himself.

"What is it?"

"King Sentis would like to speak with you, sir, and I am to inform you that it is a matter of urgency."

Kai stood in silent thought for a moment. "All right," he said at last, turning back to his subordinates. "While I'm gone, I want you three to go to the tomb and see what you can find. If the guard gives you any trouble, just tell them you have Mancho's permission. Afterward, gather everyone and meet me in the sitting room later tonight. We're going to have a lot to discuss."

The three of them exchanged a look of confusion.

"Why Mancho?" Barrik asked.

"Because Mancho is probably the one person in Meditas other than the king himself, that you don't want to upset."

Kai turned away with Dortha, and together, they quickly disappeared into the city.

"What do you think that was all about?" Alexandra asked.

"I have no idea, but I'm more concerned with my new fear of Mancho," Barrik said as he pulled Vincent to his feet. "How are you feeling?"

Vincent started rolling his shoulder in a circle. "I'm fine. Could use something to eat, though."

"Me too."

Alexandra shook her head. "You're both ridiculous. Grab yourself some apples, and let's head over to the tomb. We can get something to eat after that."

Vincent sighed in defeat. "I don't even know where the tomb is."

Alexandra pinched the bridge of her nose. "Unbelievable. Years of Mom constantly telling us to pay attention everywhere we went, and you still can't find your way around."

Vincent shrugged.

She groaned. "This way."

Barrik chuckled and patted Vincent on the back. "Told you you're not good with directions, bud."

"Yeah, yeah, shut up."

The three of them soon came to a stone archway lined with flowers of white and yellow, guarded by two soldiers.

"There it is," Alexandra said. The two soldiers crossed their spears as they drew near the entrance, preventing them from passing into the shadowy corridor. One of them wore a helmet that seemed a little too big for his head, while the other seemed too young to be already losing his dark hair.

"State your business," the balding soldier said firmly.

Vincent quickly stepped to the front of the group and cleared his throat. "Forgive our intrusion, gentlemen. My dear friend here has a passion for the dead," he said as he placed his hand on Alexandra's shoulder. "It is a rather creepy passion, I do admit. Nevertheless, she would like to visit the resting place of the men and women who once walked these very streets a long time ago."

The guards exchanged a look before the one with the tiny helmet spoke. "This tomb is reserved only for the royal families, not just random peasant folk like yourselves."

Vincent threw his hands up as if he were welcoming someone into his home. "What a wonderful surprise! We get to experience a walk through royal history."

The balding guard leaned in closer. "No, you do not. Piss off."

"Gentlemen, I assure you, I have absolutely no interest in venturing into those shadowy depths. However, my big fellow here and

I did promise Mancho we would personally escort her... and I would hate to disappoint him."

At the mention of Mancho's name, both soldiers instantly straightened their postures and uncrossed their spears.

"My deepest apologies, sir; please forgive our behavior," the balding one said with a bow.

The other held out his hand, guiding them toward the entrance. "Right this way, m'lady."

"Thanks," Alexandra said plainly as she walked between them.

Vincent clasped his hands together to show his gratitude before entering a dark, winding stairwell lit only by lanterns and what little afternoon sun peeked down the steps.

Once they were out of earshot of the guards, Alexandra turned around. "What was the point of that? You could have just mentioned Mancho's name at the beginning."

Vincent shrugged. "I don't know. I thought it was funny. Right, Bear?"

"Meh. I could take it or leave it."

"See, he thought it was funny."

Alexandra shook her head and continued on down the steps. "What is it with Mancho, anyway?"

"Beats me," Barrik said.

When they finally reached the bottom of the stairwell, they found themselves in a wide-open room with a narrow walkway lit by lanterns atop tall iron poles. The path split away down several different avenues, all leading somewhere unknown. Every few feet on either side of the walkway rested a coffin with a statue behind it, depicting the royal person entombed there.

"Woah!" Barrik was stunned. "How far do you think this continues on?"

"I have no idea," Alexandra answered as she walked up to one of the nearby statues. A woman carved from a copper-colored stone was clad in light armor rather than an elegant gown, or dress with a small banded crown that held back her long hair. Her hands were folded over the hilt of a sword that barely reached the floor. She stood tall and powerful with unrivaled confidence.

Barrik peered down one of the avenues to see a very similar setting: coffins, statues, and lantern poles evenly spaced apart. He turned around to look down another hallway and again found the same. He began to wonder. "What happens when they run out of space?"

"Huh?" Alexandra asked, confused.

"This place can't go on forever, so what happens when it's full and there are more royal family members to bury?"

She pondered the question for a moment before raising her eyebrows at him. "That's a good question."

"Guys…" Vincent's voice echoed off the stone walls. Barrik and Alexandra hurried over to him. He was staring at the back of the room. They tried to follow his eyes, but found nothing of interest other than a plain wall flanked by two torches.

"What is it?" Barrik asked.

Vincent pointed to the arched wall and said, "That's it."

"I thought you said it was in between two blue torches?" Alexandra asked.

Vincent looked at her, confused. "What? You don't see the two blue torches right there?"

"Nope."

"Bear?"

"Sorry, bud, I don't see any blue either. Just plain ol' torches. You're the only one who spoke to Larissa, so maybe only you can see it."

Vincent started to walk closer to the wall. "Only one way to find out, I guess."

He took a deep breath before he placed his hands against the wall. As soon as his palms contacted the stone, a large gust of air rushed through the room, extinguishing every lantern and torch, leaving them all in darkness. Vincent took a few steps back from the wall.

"Ow!" Alexandra cried out.

Vincent chuckled. "My bad."

"Now what?" Barrik asked.

"I'm not sure. I guess we just—"

Before Vincent could finish his sentence, the bottom of the wall burst into deep blue flames. The fire spread from the floor to the ceiling between the two torches that no longer burned.

"Now *those* are blue," Alexandra said.

They watched as the wall behind the ocean of fire began to fade away, slowly revealing a small hidden chamber behind it. Once the dance of incineration had reached its end, the flames blew into the room, lighting several torches suspended on the walls. Waves of blue fire now breathed calmly, casting an eerie illumination on a stone coffin that lay in the center of the floor.

Each of them walked around the coffin to inspect it carefully. It appeared as if it had just been placed. There was no sign of age on the stone, nor a single speck of dust, despite the ancient appearance of the rest of the room.

Alexandra knelt and traced the edge of the lid with her fingers. "Vince, check this out."

Inscriptions were found all around the lid, similar to those on their weapons, with deep lines that seemed to depict images rather than words, except these ones were unfamiliar to them.

"Sanorian runes?" Vincent guessed.

"That's what I would assume, but I've never seen these any-where before."

"There's more on the top," Barrik pointed out.

Both of them rose to investigate the surface of the lid, and sure enough, there were four large runes carved in a vertical column that ran the length of the coffin. While each one was unique, they still were unable to decipher their meaning.

"Try to remember what they look like," Alexandra suggested.

"Right," Vincent said, lowering his fingers to the lid. Just as he started to trace a rune with his finger, all of those along the sides began to glow a faint white. Each of them quickly took a step back.

"What did you do?" Barrik demanded.

Vincent shook his head. "Nothing. I just touched it."

"Maybe you should stop touching things."

"Shut up and help me open it."

Approaching the coffin again, they could see that only the first rune on the top gave off the same glow, while the others showed no change. All three of them placed their hands against the lid and bent their knees as Vincent began to count down.

"Okay, ready? On three: one… two… *three!*"

Each of them shoved with all of their might, which they quickly found to be unnecessary; the lid easily slid right off the top, like it weighed nothing at all. It crashed onto the stone floor, revealing the person inside—a woman who, much to their shock, exhibited no signs of death whatsoever. With warm red cheeks and silky blonde hair that lay across a gleaming white dress, she appeared to simply be asleep. Her hands were folded over her chest, her fingers gently wrapped around the hilt of a sword tucked away in its scabbard.

"Is she dead?" Barrik whispered.

Vincent slowly reached toward her face with a finger, which Alexandra quickly swatted away. "Do *not* poke her."

"Well, how else are we supposed to know?"

"She's lying in a coffin! What more proof do you need? Let's just get the sword and get out of here."

Taking a deep breath, they gently removed the woman's hands from the hilt and lifted the sword from the coffin. Thankfully, she gave no reaction. Vincent held it flat in his hands as they looked it over. The scabbard and the hilt were dark as night except for a bright silver trim that caught the blue light from the torches, resembling the ring on each of their fingers—Sanorian silver. The cross guard took the form of a crow's wings, spread wide and curving gently upward on both sides, each tip bearing a colorless star stone set in a diamond-shaped frame, forged from the same gleaming metal. On the pommel, Vincent spotted another star stone—faded, and framed just the same.

Alexandra reached out to touch the hilt of the sword with her right hand. "It's beautiful," she murmured.

As soon as her fingers made contact, there was the hiss of steam, and she quickly recoiled in pain.

"Are you okay?" Vincent asked.

"Yeah." She inspected her fingertips, which were now bright red. "It just burns," she said with a wince.

"Well, Larissa did say I'm the only one who can wield it." Hesitantly, Vincent wrapped his hand around the grip and drew the sword to reveal a shadowy blade void of light. Its tip was armored in a spear-shaped cap of the ancient silver the Sanorians seemed to adore.

"A little bigger than your typical sword," Barrik pointed out.

"Yeah, but it's just as light as one of my sabers," Vincent said in wonder, twirling it around.

As he did so, the same runes from the coffin began to appear from the base of the blade to the tip. As they slowly began to glow, the air in the room started to swirl. Dust rose from the floor, cobwebs fluttered, and the blue flames waved back and forth. Vincent dropped to his knees.

"Vince! What's wrong?" Barrik asked, concerned.

He could not answer, only cry out in pain. The power coursing through every part of his body forced his hands to clench tightly, locking the hilt in his fists. Images flashed across his mind. A woman... A man... A family... Nothing he was able to make any sense of.

Alexandra quickly snatched the scabbard from the floor. "Bear, hold his arms still!"

Barrik got behind Vincent and grabbed his forearms to steady them. Then he cried out as he too began to feel the sword's pain.

Alexandra tried to line up the opening of the scabbard with the tip of the sword. "Hold him steady, Bear!"

"I'm... trying!" he shouted.

Finally, once she was able to return the blade to its home, Vincent threw the sword to the ground, both he and Barrik breathing heavily.

"How'd you know that would work?" Vincent asked.

Alexandra shrugged. "I didn't."

"No wonder she told you to use it carefully," Barrik muttered.

"Yeah, no kidding," Vincent agreed. "You okay?"

Barrik nodded. "All good."

"Thanks, guys."

Alexandra pulled him back to his feet. "Don't mention it."

Vincent stared at the sword for a moment before he regained the courage to pick it back up. "Can we get out of here now?"

"Yeah, I'm starving," Barrik agreed.

Alexandra shook her head. "Come on, let's go."

As soon as they left the room, another rush of wind flew through the tomb, relighting all of the lanterns and torches. When Vincent turned back around, the torches were burning their normal fiery hues, and the arched wall had returned, as if nothing had ever happened.

Vera and Rinna walked through the barracks door into the sitting room, where Alexandra, Vincent, Barrik, and Toran were gathered by the fire.

"What's this? Trying to party without us?" Vera asked with narrowed eyes.

"Wouldn't dream of it, V," Alexandra said.

Vincent threw his legs up on the table and rested his head on his hand. "We're all supposed to sit here and wait for Kai to get back."

"How come?" Rinna asked as she took a seat.

"We don't know yet," Alexandra answered. "He was summoned by the king earlier today, and that was the last we saw of him."

Toran turned to Vera as she plopped down on the sofa. "Hey, Vera! How was your watch at the fountain?"

"It was so much fun! We fought dragons and horrors of all kinds. Me and Rinna barely made it out alive."

"Really?" Toran asked, surprised.

Vera sank into her seat. "No. We just stood around and talked to Tahara the whole time. It was so boring."

Rinna laughed. "That's not entirely true. They showed us how to fire the warning signal."

Vera sat forward. "Oh, yeah! The arrows up there have a small rope thingy attached to the arrowhead, and you light that on fire and shoot it into the sky, and *boom*!" She mimed the explosion with her hands.

"What makes them explode?" Vincent asked.

"The arrowheads are hollowed out and filled with dye and flash powder, so once the fire touches it, you get a pretty red cloud."

"Did you get to shoot one?" Alexandra asked.

Vera sank back in her seat again. "No."

"Although she was going to!" Rinna said with a scolding look at Vera.

Guilty, she sank further into her seat. "I just wanted to see what it looked like."

"I don't even know what it looks like," Kai said as he seemed to materialize from thin air.

"When did you get here?" Barrik asked.

"Never mind that. Vince, what did you find?"

Vincent stood up and placed the sword from the tomb on the table. Everyone gathered around to see it.

"Woah! Is that Sanorian silver?" Vera asked as she reached for the handle.

"V, wait!"

"Ow!" Vera waved her hand around in the air to shake off the fiery pain in her fingertips.

"Are you okay, Vera?!" Toran asked, overly concerned.

"Yeah, I'm fine. But what the hell, Vince? You could have warned me."

"You didn't give me a chance to."

"So, what, it burns whoever touches it?"

"Anyone who isn't me."

"Oh, so kind of like our weapons?"

"Pretty much, yeah."

Toran looked confused. "What happens if someone touches your weapons?"

Vera pulled out her dagger and laid it on the table. The star stone in the center of the steel blade continued to glow bright red. "Pick it up."

Toran looked at her suspiciously.

"It's not going to hurt, I promise."

He leaned over and tried to lift the dagger with one hand. As soon as he touched the grip, the color faded from the star stone, and after a moment, he failed. With two hands, he pulled with all his might, but could barely lift it an inch from the table. Finally, he gave up. As soon as Vera picked up her dagger, the star stone illuminated bright red once again. She stuck her finger in the open pommel and twirled it before returning it to the sheath on her lower back. "See?"

"How'd you get it to do that?" Rinna asked.

"Our grandfather is a blacksmith."

"A mighty good one, at that," Kai added before he turned back to Vincent. "What else did you find?"

"Not really anything, except that the coffin we opened, as well as the blade, are covered in what look like Sanorian runes, but like none we've ever seen before."

"Can you show me?"

"When we left, the torches next to the wall weren't blue anymore, so I don't think I'll be able to get back inside."

"What about on the sword?"

"Well, I can't exactly wield it without feeling like I'm dying, so I'd rather not."

"Doesn't seem like a very useful weapon, then, does it? Do you at least remember what they look like?"

Alexandra nodded. "We can draw them for you."

"Good. Make sure you do that before we leave, and I will take them to the Lorekeeper once we return."

"Leave?" Barrik asked, confused. "Where are we going?"

"I have your first mission."

Vera psyched herself up. "Finally, some real action!"

"Before you get too excited, there are a few conditions you must all agree to before I approve your departure."

Vera sat back down as Kai continued, "As you know, now that you all belong to the Guardians, you need permission from the king before you are able to leave the city limits, and it took a lot of pleading from me for him to grant you all that permission."

"If you've been assigned a mission, why would he not want us to go with you?" Rinna questioned.

"Two reasons, the first being that Guardians operate in units of four, so three of you would have been left behind. However, I explained that I would like to utilize this opportunity to give each of you real experience as opposed to dancing around in the training yard."

"What about the second reason?" Alexandra asked.

"Despite the king's words, and even some of his actions, he still believes in the importance of Guardians, even if it's only confined to his subconscious. And everyone in this room is most likely one of the last remaining Guardians of Meditas."

Toran furrowed his brow in thought. "But wasn't there a team sent to investigate a northern village? Or at least, that's what Tahara said. She said they were some of the finest she had ever seen. Gala, I think she mentioned, is their captain."

Kai nodded. "Correct. Except they left before you all arrived and still have yet to return. That village they went to investigate is only a few days away."

"So, we're going to find out what happened to them?" Barrik guessed.

"Not exactly. We've been reassigned their original mission of investigating the village, and that is to be all. However, I have every intention of finding them as well. Gala is a dear friend, and despite her strengths, enough time has passed that I fear she has finally found her match. I want to ensure that she and her team have found their peace."

"All right then, Kai," Alexandra said. "What are your conditions?"

"To start, I will need you all to give your word that there will be no contestation of my orders. You will follow them with absolutely no deviation or complaints. The idea is to work as one complete unit, which we cannot do if there is a consistent lack of respect for authority. So, I ask for your unwavering trust in my experience, so that I, in return, may give you mine. With that being said, if you have an idea that you believe to be better than the one I lay before you, tell me, and we can discuss it. But once we've decided, it is final. A poor plan that we all fully commit to will prove more successful than a brilliant plan with divided forces."

"Yeah, Vince," Vera teased.

He did not respond. His eyes were locked on the sword before him; he was lost inside his mind.

"I would like a verbal confirmation that you all agree to this. Do I have your word?" Kai asked, looking around the room.

Everyone responded with a firm indication that they would place their trust in Kai and his experience, until he awaited Vincent's response.

Vincent sat in a room full of people, alone in his head, their muffled voices becoming ambient noise. It was true. Whatever he had experienced with Larissa was more than just a dream, and the proof was right in front of him. He felt surreal, lost, confused—and overwhelmed with anxiety. How was he supposed to defeat some unknown person who held the power of a fountain with a sword he could barely touch? He wished he was able to speak with her again, ask her his many questions. Already, he was beginning to feel like he had agreed to a task he was incapable of seeing through.

"Vincent," Kai said, clearly not for the first time.

Vincent looked up, his composure momentarily fractured as he returned to reality. "Sorry, what were you saying?"

"Do I have your word?" Kai asked again.

"Oh, yes, you have my word."

Kai nodded gratefully. "Very well. I would also like you all to choose one person who will lead in my stead should anything happen to me."

"Alex," Vincent answered without hesitation.

Alexandra looked surprised. "Wait—*me*? Why me?"

"Agreed," Barrik eagerly added.

"No arguments over here," Rinna said with a soft smile.

"You seemed to me to have plenty of experience during our training," Toran quickly pointed out. "So, you have my vote as well."

"Yup, yup, yup. Has to be Alex," Vera said while enthusiastically nodding her head.

Alexandra looked panicked. "Hang on, don't *I* get a say in this?"

"Do you disagree with them?" Kai questioned.

"I don't know... I guess not. I just..." Her eyes darted to the floor.

"You just what?"

"I don't feel ready to lead anybody."

"You already do," Vincent stated. "You navigated us safely through Cayland, didn't you?"

"Yeah, directly into some bandits."

"And you came up with a plan to deal with them as best you could."

"I took an arrow in my shoulder!" she exclaimed.

"Well, we survived, didn't we?" Vincent pointed out.

"Barely..."

"You've always taken the lead, ever since we were kids. Don't get all nervous about it now just because we pointed it out."

"Yeah," Vera interjected. "You haven't gotten us killed yet."

Alexandra rolled her eyes. "Very reassuring, V. Thank you."

A playful grin spread across Vincent's face. "I'd say I would do it, but we all know I couldn't even lead us out of the city."

Alexandra softly chuckled and turned to Kai, reluctantly ready to accept the responsibility bestowed upon her. "All right, I'll do it. Just don't go dying on us, so I don't have to."

Kai smiled gently. "I won't. Now, off to bed with you all. We leave first thing in the morning."

Vera threw herself against Alexandra. "Oh, my fearless leader, please guide me up the stairs to our room!"

Rinna laughed as Alexandra slugged Vera in the arm. "Shut up, V."

"Ow..." Vera rubbed her arm. "Some captain you're shaping up to be."

As everyone took off to their rooms, Kai put a hand on Vincent's shoulder before he could walk away. "May I have a minute?" he asked gently.

"Yeah, sure," Vincent answered as he sat down on the sofa.

Kai looked over the sword on the table briefly before he began to speak. "I wanted to apologize for being pulled away before we could finish discussing your training today."

"It's not a big deal, don't worry about it."

"Earlier, when you were gathering energy, you were pulling from the sources near you— the soil, the air, even myself."

"I was taking it from *you?*"

"Well, it would be more accurate to say I was giving it to you in order to test the theory, but yes."

"I still don't even know how I did it."

"In time, you will start to recognize the feeling, but for now, it will act as another function of your body you're not always consciously performing. But I would like to extend a warning for when you do get a feel for it."

"A warning?"

"While pulling in energy like that can be useful, it can also be problematic. Take in too much, and your body may not be able to handle it all. And depending on *where* you take it from, you may be better off without it."

"Well, that's not ominous at all..." Vincent muttered.

"What I mean is for you to be wary of the energy you take in. Not all of it is good. Sometimes, it can be negative, especially in places where a great tragedy has occurred."

"Like in the Gray Lands?"

"Exactly. If you were to feel the energy in those lands, you would also experience all of its pain. Take in the negative energy around you, and you may find your mind shrouded in an inescapable ocean of darkness. You must be careful not to permit its entry."

Vincent thought to himself for a moment. "What about Alex? She can take in energy too."

"Yes, but much differently than you. Hers only comes directly from her opponent, which could also have similar effects, but not to the same degree. If you were to strike her whilst thinking about the death of your father, then she may get a sudden rush of sadness with the energy she took from you, whereas if you take in energy from the aftermath of a large battle, you'd likely be overwhelmed with despair."

Vincent's eyes fell to the sword in front of him. He remembered the images that flashed through his mind while it was in his hands, and he parted his lips to speak, but no words came out.

"What is it?" Kai asked.

"There was something else that happened when I held the sword."

Kai waited patiently for Vincent to continue.

"The power was too much to bear, but as I was trying to let go, I saw..." His eyes moved across the table as he pulled the memories from his mind. "...a woman. Then there was this man with a darkness all around him. And a family I've never seen before."

"And you didn't recognize any of them?"

Vincent shook his head. "No. It was all so fast that I couldn't even tell you what color their hair was. None of it made any sense."

Kai took a deep breath. "I don't know what to make of it yet either," he admitted, standing up and placing a reassuring hand on Vincent's shoulder. "But I promise you I will help you every step of the way."

Vincent returned Kai's words with a gentle smile and a nod of the head.

"Now, go get some sleep."

Vincent grabbed the sword from the table and took the stairs up to his room. Toran was miraculously sound asleep as Barrik practically rattled the walls with each snore. Vincent laid his head down on the feather pillow and bundled up in the warmth of his bed covers. Yet despite all the comfort and his best efforts, he could not quiet his mind. Toss after toss and turn after turn, he knew his earlier suspicions to be true: peaceful sleep was now just another piece of his past. There would be no more true rest for him.

CHAPTER 9

HE next morning, the seven Guardians approached the northern gates of Meditas just as the sun began to peek above the horizon. Kai motioned for the guards to raise the gate, then turned around to face everyone. Each of them was clad in brown leather armor that had the fountain's tree burned into the breastplate, while a gray cloak was draped over their back. Vincent had his new sword sheathed at his hip, while his other two sabers were strapped across his back, their hilts jutting out from behind his head. Vera eagerly hopped up and down, jabbing Barrik in his side to fully wake him up. Toran carried a circular shield of light metal with a one-handed sword belted to his hip and his cherry-red scarf tied loosely around his neck. Rinna held a metal staff with a long, curved blade at the tip, while Alexandra had the left sleeve of her tunic rolled up to her elbow.

"Are you ready?" Kai asked the group.

Everyone nodded with impenetrable confidence in their eyes.

"I don't know, Kai," one of the guards shouted from the battlement. "Taking that traitor's son with you might be a bad idea. You might end up with a knife in your back."

"Or eaten by that freak," another one added, pointing at Alexandra. Both of the guards started to laugh.

Alexandra grew slightly rigid, but she did not try to conceal her arm.

Rinna leaned in closer to Vincent and Alexandra, gesturing to her weapon. "I can throw this at one of them if you want," she whispered.

Vincent smirked. "No, that's all right. I have a better idea."

Rinna looked at him, momentarily confused.

Vincent pointed at one of the guards. "What is your name, good sir?"

"My name is Lucarious the Third, and you'd better not forget it."

"I wouldn't dare. I'll be sure to pass on to my good friend Mancho just how helpful you've been today. Thank you!"

Silence befell the battlement. Even from down below on the ground, everyone could see the panic in the guards' eyes.

As they all passed beyond the gate, Kai looked over his shoulder. "So, you've just decided to weaponize Mancho's name now, have you?"

Vincent shrugged with a proud expression. "Only when necessary."

"Why is everyone so afraid of Mancho, anyway?" Alexandra asked.

"Information is an extremely powerful weapon," Kai started, "and when it comes to acquiring it, Mancho is the best. So, everyone assumes he knows all that they don't want known to the public. That's part of it, at least."

"What's the other part?" Barrik asked.

A small smile crept onto Kai's face, but he did not divulge why.

Kai led them all beyond the grassy pit that surrounded Meditas and into the tall trees of Thernruff Woods. As the sun rose higher throughout the morning, its warm golden rays snuck between leaves that had only just begun to show autumn's colorful hues. While the forest's shade possessed a nostalgic coolness, their footsteps lingered wherever there was a puddle of sunlight on the road.

Alexandra took a deep breath of the forest air. "Feels great to be out here again."

"Yeah, it's tough being cooped up in the city all the time," Barrik added.

"Why don't you guys sign up for a patrol shift?" Toran asked.

They looked at him, confused.

"He's right," Kai said over his shoulder. "The soldiers need help with more than just guarding the fountain. Bounties, patrols, hunting missions, all sorts of things for you to do to stay busy and earn some money as well."

"Why didn't you tell us this sooner?" Alexandra asked.

"I didn't realize I had to teach you *everything*."

Barrik noticed Vera's narrowed eyes rapidly scanning the trees. "V, what are you looking for?"

"...Bandits," she whispered.

"Relax, Vera," Kai called from up front. "There are no Bandits nearby."

"How do you know?"

"I would be able to detect their energies if they were."

"Oh." Vera's shoulders released their tension. "Is that how your Favor works?"

"Part of it. I can also erase the presence of someone's energy."

"Like Rinna's Favor?"

"Not quite. Rinna uses her energy to cloak herself and whatever she touches, but her energy is still present. While I wouldn't be able to see her, I would still know where she is. Mine, however, completely erases your presence. So, unless you already know where I am, or see me in direct line of sight, you'd find it quite the challenge to detect me."

"Is that how you seem to appear out of thin air all the time?" Barrik asked.

"Yes. Rarely do I walk into a room without first using my Favor."

While everyone was conversing with one another up at the front of the pack, Rinna noticed Vincent lagging behind and paused until he caught up.

"Hey there, slowpoke," she said to him.

Entirely dissociated from the world around him, he failed to register her words. She waved her hand in front of his face. "Are you in there?"

"Oh—hey, Rinna," he said as he snapped out of his stupor. "Yeah, sorry, I'm feeling a little out of it. I didn't get any sleep last night."

"You should have said something! I could have made you a tea that my mom used to make. Smells wonderful and always puts me right to bed."

"Well, I hope you brought some with. You might need it to sleep through all of Barrik's snoring."

"I'm used to that sort of thing already. My dad is louder than a thunderstorm when he sleeps," she said with a laugh.

Vincent smiled softly. Her laughter filled him with an unfamiliar warmth not even the summer sun could provide. The more they talked, the more he began to notice the details of her appearance that he had not previously realized. Patches of tiny freckles that matched the reddish brown of her hair huddled together just above her cheekbones. A glint of golden amber peeked through the irises of her eyes every time she passed through a curtain of sunlight, reminding him of almonds and honey. As he continued to admire the subtle features of her face, he started to feel as though she were an embodiment of everything he loved about the season to come. Yet despite the brightness of her smile and the comfort of her laugh, he could sense something underneath it all.

A concealed visceral sadness slowly seeped into the depths of his heart. It was as if she were a bouquet of vibrant flowers hugged by the dying comforts of a cracked vase. Her pain leaked through every one of the deep fissures in her fortress. Not only could he see beyond the bright colors of her petals and into the puddle of anguish that pooled around them, he could *feel* it.

By the time the forest broke, the sun had slipped into the late hours of the afternoon. Gentle shades of peaches and plums filled the cloudy sky above a rolling thicket of wild shrubs that now lay before them. Kai's pace seemed to quicken with every question Toran fired away, as if he were trying to outrun the obligation to answer each and every one of them—a subtle hint that was lost on Toran.

When the light had whittled down too far to continue on, Kai brought them to a halt under a small patch of thin trees. "We can rest here tonight."

Vera dropped to the ground. "Thank the stars! My feet are killing me."

Kai wandered in a circle as he peered out beyond the trees in every direction.

"Do you see anything?" Alexandra asked.

"No. But that doesn't mean something isn't out there."

"Wouldn't you be able to know if there was?"

"If it were human, yes. Horrors, however, I can detect only as well as you can. You all get your sleep; I'll take the first watch."

Everyone found a spot to make themselves as comfortable as possible to gather what rest they could. Bundled up underneath their cloaks, they waited eagerly for their dreams to overtake them.

Soft light from the sun lifted Vincent out of his slumber and into an unfamiliar environment. He stood alone on the bank of a lake with water as clear as the sky above. Pine trees grew tall all around and calmly waved at him as they swayed back and forth in the breeze. The air was quiet and drifted into his nose with an earthy bliss, while each ripple in the water next to him rolled across the surface of the lake with a shimmer as they caught the sunlight.

He took in his newly defined sense of peace with a deep breath and looked around.

"Another dream?" he asked himself.

Next to the water, he lowered himself to his knees and looked into his reflection. From each strand of earthy gold on his messy head to the small scar on his left eyebrow, every detail was as he remembered, except for something in his emerald eyes. With an age foreign to his present self, they looked on him fiercely as if they were ready for battle—or rather, yet another one. He reached toward his reflection with his fingers and instantly recoiled at its ice-cold temperature.

No sooner did the first drop of water fall from his skin than a sudden gust of wind rushed across the lake. Day fell to night. The trees turned bare. Every sparkle from the water's surface transitioned to the reflection of a lambent star in the dark sky. Vincent rose to his feet before he looked back down at the water. A woman behind him stood just beside his reflection, peering down over his shoulder. Startled, he tumbled to the ground beside her. For as long as his eyes remained locked onto her, she never moved. Slowly, he climbed back to his feet. Frightening as her sudden appearance was, he sensed no threat from her. Instead, he felt nothing more than a calming aura of familiarity.

She stood beneath the grace of the moon, motionless in a white dress dusted with gold that flowed like a river of moonlight from her neck to the dew-soaked grass. Thousands of shimmers, each no bigger than a grain of sand, beamed from the dress's depths with a mesmerizing radiance rivaled only by her silken blonde hair.

"Hello," he said softly.

There was no response, nor any indication that she had heard him at all, for that matter. He followed her gaze to her reflection in the water, where her eyes quickly darted to his.

"Vincent Raine," she said quietly.

He turned back to the woman who now faced him. Finally, he recognized her. "You're the woman from the tomb. How do you know my name?"

Blood from the center of her chest began to spread throughout her dress. She held a sword in her right hand and looked at him with eyes of sorrow. His heart began to race as she lifted the blade. It was dark as night with silver trim—the same sword from the tomb, he realized. Except the star stone in the pommel of this one shone blue, while all of the stones in his version were faded and without color. He tried to back away, but his feet were locked to the ground.

Her palm gently fell to his shoulder as her lips glided to his ear. She whispered, "I am the first."

"The first wha—"

Without warning, she drove the sword through his heart, all the way up to the winged cross guard, and took a step back. As the air left his body, he watched a tear fall from her eye. Another gust of wind blew over the lake and swept her away with it. Other than the sword in his chest, there was no trace of her.

He fell to his knees. With all his strength, he tried to pull the sword out of his body, but it would not budge. His lids grew heavy, and he dropped to his side. Afraid to close his eyes, he desperately fought to keep them open. Weakly, he watched as his vision blurred and the lake in front of him turned a dark crimson.

Vincent jolted awake, clutching at his chest. There was nothing there. It was just a dream.

"Shhhh," Kai hushed him with his finger pressed against his lips.

Vincent looked down at his feet and slowly regained control of his breathing before he repositioned himself next to Kai.

"You wanna talk about it?" Kai whispered.

Vincent looked at him, confused. "Talk about what?"

"Your nightmare."

"... How'd you—"

"You weren't exactly sleeping peacefully."

Vincent looked to the ground and hesitated. "It felt so real... Just like with Larissa. Which *did* turn out to be real... At least, kind of."

"What did you see?"

"I was standing by a lake when all of a sudden, the woman from the tomb appeared with this sword in her hand, except the star stone in the pommel..." He gestured to the sword on his hip. "...this one was glowing blue."

"Did she say anything to you?"

"Yeah. She said, 'I am the first'—right before she stabbed me through the heart. Nice lady, you really oughtta meet her."

"'I am the first,'" Kai repeated to himself.

"Any idea what she meant?"

"Your guess is as good as mine."

Both of them slipped behind the curtain of thought for a while as they allowed the buzzing and chirping of the local insects to be the only sound. Vincent rummaged through the events of the last few weeks in his mind, until he fell on his meeting with the king and what had occurred shortly after. Guilt bubbled up inside of him. His throat twisted as he tried to find the right words.

"Hey, Kai..." he finally said nervously.

"What is it?"

"I... I just wanted to apologize for what I said to you outside of the throne room. I shouted at you and just assumed you were on their side, with everything they said without knowing the truth, and I'm sorry."

"It's all right," Kai said softly. "Anyone in your position would have thought the same thing." He leaned back and looked between the leaves above at the rolling clouds in the night sky. "It truly is a shame."

"That my dad didn't allow you to go with them?"

"Well, that too. But I was referring to how King Sentis now views your father."

"You mean, he didn't always hate him?"

"At one time, it was quite the opposite. When we were younger, they were the closest of friends. I think even until your father's death, Sentis still looked at him as a friend."

"Now that you mention it, I do remember him saying he used to be friends with my father." Vincent scoffed. "A public execution is some display of friendship."

"Well, he had to take some form of action against Victor to dismantle any prospect of war against Meditas."

"He tried to save a nation and its fountain. Why would anyone start a war over that?"

"How do you think it looks if a king cannot control his own subjects and allows them to wander beyond borders without consequence? Actions like that cause people to ask questions. 'Was this an act of war by Sentis? What is he planning? Who will he go after next...?' All these questions circulate until the public grows weary. General unrest spreads between your walls, and eventually, you will have chaos. People demand answers, even if they are fabricated fragments of reality."

"But he was trying to *help* Abnor, not invade their territory."

"Unfortunately, when generally referring to the world, appearances are all that matter. Truth becomes an outdated relic no one cares to listen to. All that is is what is seen. Rarely do people ever dig beneath the surface. So, Victor helped Sentis prevent a war he knew his actions could have started. They made a deal: his life as an example of punishment for disobedience, the banishment of those who followed, to illustrate the king's mercy, and then you—a strong soldier to replace the one previously punished, hopefully not to repeat his mistakes. Although I think that was a malicious part of the deal that Sentis made out of pure rage."

"I still don't understand. If that were the case, why would the king speak about my father the way he does? He showed no signs of love in his words whatsoever."

"Like I said, they were friends. And when your father went against his orders, he betrayed that friendship. The king was hurt. And while he was vulnerable, Rayahan took to his side and fed him a potion of lies about things Victor had never actually said or done. The king allowed Rayahan to plant a seed of doubt that has now grown throughout his mind."

Something suddenly rustled in the bushes nearby. Kai quickly brought his finger to his lips. Vincent scanned the area for any potential threats before his eyes landed on two horrors with a thick hide of ashen skin, slowly walking on four emaciated limbs with hunched backs. Just above their tails were spikes of bone that protruded from their lower backs all the way to long snouts on their faces with blood-red eyes. Hooked talons adorned their paws. They sniffed around the perimeter of their campsite.

Kai crouched down next to Vincent. "They're just urberaks. Ever fought one?"

Vincent shook his head.

"They're no tougher than ghouls, but if we're careful, we can sneak up beside them. You see the fourth spike back from its snout?"

"Yeah."

"Bring your blade down hard and fast right behind that one. Hit it just right, and its head will come clean off."

"All right, I can handle that."

"I'll take the one on the left, but don't attack until I give the signal. We'll try to get them at the same time. And don't draw your weapon until you're going to swing."

"Okay."

"Ready?"

Vincent nodded. Both of them stayed low to the ground as they snuck behind the tall grass and shrubs to get into position. Vincent positioned himself just behind a jagged bush right next to one of the urberaks. He could hear it sifting through the dirt with its snout. The rapid sniffs sounded to him no different than those of a curious dog. He could see Kai sneaking around his target just a few feet away and held still until Kai locked eyes with him.

He held up three fingers for Vincent to see his silent countdown. One finger fell, and Vincent readied himself. The second finger dropped, and Vincent's hand lightly grasped the hilt of his saber behind his head. His heart started to thump faster against his chest. Then down came the third. In one swift and silent synchronized movement, both of them drew their weapons and sliced down through their targets' necks. The two felled horrors dropped to the ground with a thud. They returned their weapons to their sheaths and retreated beneath the patch of trees.

"Nice job, Vince," Kai said. "First encounter with an urberak, and you killed it with one swing? Fira did teach you something after all."

"Thanks," Vincent responded proudly.

He waited until his heartbeat returned to a normal pace to pick up their conversation.

"Kai, something still confuses me about Sentis."

"Go on."

"If he and my father were so close, why would he believe the things Rayahan said about him?"

"If I had to guess? Because he wants to. He could either accept that he was betrayed by a friend, or believe he was misled by an enemy. Most people will choose to ignore their own reality because lies often taste better than the truth. And the king is no exception."

"So, he despises everything that has to do with my father, including me, because it's easier?"

"Essentially."

"*That* makes sense," Vincent said sarcastically.

Kai chuckled and slowly rose to his feet. "I trust you can take over for me?"

"Yeah, I got this. Go get some sleep, old man."

"If anything else decides to lurk about, and there's more than one, or you don't know how to kill it, wake me up."

"I will."

"All right, then. Goodnight, Prince of Rain."

Kai positioned himself against a nearby tree, crossed his arms, and drifted off to sleep. Vincent let his thoughts roam as his eyes and ears wandered through the dwindling darkness. He wondered just how different his life would be if the king had celebrated his father for his deeds rather than had him executed. Would they all be together in Meditas, or back home in Sylva? Would he have still wanted to become a Guardian if his father were still alive? These were all questions he knew he would never have the answer to, yet they circled his mind anyway.

The sun's first rays of morning light finally peeked over the horizon, signaling that it was time for them to continue on. Alexandra stood up with a stretch of her arms and lightly delivered a kick to Vera's leg. Vera launched upright instantly and mumbled something inaudible. She blinked the sleep away from her eyes to see Toran still sound asleep with his head lying against his folded-up red scarf. She grew a mischievous grin and snuck over to him.

"TORAN!" she shouted right in front of his face.

Toran frantically scrambled to his feet while Vera held her sides as she laughed.

"Why are we yelling already this morning?" Rinna asked with a yawn.

"Because Vera decided to choose chaos for breakfast," Alexandra said with a glare.

"What? It was only a little fun," Vera said with a shrug of her shoulders.

Kai placed his hand on Toran's shoulder, who stood perfectly still with his eyes half closed. "Someone get Barrik up. We need to start moving."

"Sounds like a job for Vera," Vincent said.

"Why me?"

"Because you decided to scare Toran half to death before he even saw first light," Alexandra scolded.

Vera pouted her way over to the snoring Barrik. "So, now I get punished. Wonderful." She kicked him in the side. "Wake up, ya big oaf."

He gave no response, not even a little movement. She tried again. Nothing. She pushed, shoved, kicked, and nudged, and still, nothing seemed to work.

"Does he always sleep that heavily?" Rinna asked curiously.

"Oh, yeah. Unless he can smell our mother's breakfast," Vincent said with a nod of his head. "It's quite the spectacle."

"No kidding."

Vera lightly slapped Barrik in the cheeks. "Hibernation isn't for another few weeks. Wake up!"

Still, he did not move. Defeated, she groaned and rooted through her things before she pulled out a loaf of bread wrapped in cloth. She unwrapped it and waved the bread in front of Barrik's nose. Not a moment later, Barrik's nose started to twitch until his eyes shot wide open.

"Finally," she said as she put the bread back into her bag.

"You're just going to tease me with it?" Barrik asked with a little disappointment in his voice.

"You have your own! Plus, I don't need you trying to bite off one of my fingers again."

Alexandra saw the confusion grow on Rinna's face and affirmed her suspicions. "Yes, he bites."

Kai urged them all to gather their things to start the day's journey. They traversed through the shrub thicket for a few hours before it finally broke into an open field of hills and large moss-covered rocks. Far in the distance, they could see a forest resting at the bottom of a cliffside, and at the top stood a structure of stone and wood, too far away to make out any details.

"Is that the village?" Toran asked.

"No," Kai answered. "It's an old Sanorian outpost, but that *is* where we will make camp tonight."

With the sun entering its descent, Kai quickened their pace. They passed over the hills and through the forest until they finally reached the bottom of the rocky cliff that rose just above the treetops.

Kai started to walk back and forth along the side of the cliff.

"How are we going to get up there, Kai?" Alexandra asked.

"During the war for Sanora, a group of Guardians carved out a route to climb up this backside here while another group attacked from the front." Kai placed his palm on the rocky wall and looked up to the outpost. He started to count his steps as he walked forward until he finally came to a stop. "Here we go." He turned back to everyone. "Watch where I place my hands and feet, and make the same moves. Go slow, and make sure you have your footing before you press on."

"We're going to climb?" Toran asked nervously.

"It's not *that* high," Kai said.

Everyone looked to the top of the cliff, which now seemed to grow even taller.

Toran began to panic. "But what if we fall?"

"Don't," Kai said plainly.

Vera started to measure the height with her eyes and unsheathed one of her daggers. She took a step back before hurling it high in the air. They all watched as it soared up and beyond the trees until it disappeared behind the top of the cliff. She vanished. A moment later, she appeared at the top of the ledge, waving down at them all with a big smile.

"That's cheating!" Rinna cried.

Kai looked at her, slightly surprised. "Smart use of your Favor, Vera. Just keep a lookout until we get up there," he shouted up to her.

"You got it!" she replied with a salute.

One by one, everyone else followed Kai carefully up the side of the cliff, meticulously placing each hand and foot exactly where his went.

"You guys should look down!" Vera shouted once they all reached the midway point.

"Shut up, V," Vincent yelled back at her.

Once they neared the top, Vera helped to pull everyone up the rest of the way. When everyone finally cleared the summit and was back on their feet, Vincent turned around to peer down over the edge. Alexandra snuck up from behind him and quickly grabbed him by the shoulders. Panicked, Vincent flailed his arms frantically in fear of falling over the edge. He whipped around to find her laughing hysterically.

"Think that's funny, do you?"

She broke her laughter for only a moment. "Obviously."

Barrik patted him on the back consolingly. "It's probably not high enough to kill you, bud."

Vincent stared blankly ahead. "Thanks, Bear."

As the day's light faded, Kai urged everyone inside. While the walls were crafted of a perfectly smooth stone that showed the damages of war and time, the interior was made entirely of wood that remained decently intact. A stairwell at the back of the room wrapped its way around to the tertiary level, where the watchtower was positioned. As they all investigated the rooms on each floor, Kai opened a wooden door to one of the bedrooms, where his gaze settled upon three wooden logs with charred edges inside a cast-iron fire pit. There he lingered for a moment as a sudden birth of unease took root in his mind.

"All right," he drew everyone's attention, "we're nearing the village. We should reach it within the next two days. I'll take the first watch again, but when it's your turn, keep your eyes and ears open. If there is anything suspicious at all, from the rustling of a bush to a knot in your stomach, I want to know about it. Understood?"

Once he had everyone's confirmation, he moved himself to the third-floor watchtower while the rest of the group drifted off into sleep.

An angry rush of sand and dirt blasting against Vincent's face forced him awake. He coughed away the foreign invaders in his lungs as he stood up. With a hand covering his eyes as he looked around, he had no words for the new world around him.

A barren wasteland sprawled before him, littered with butchered soldiers and horses. The sky was a smoky brown continuation of the ground beneath his feet. Bodies lay everywhere he looked. He had found himself at the center of a large battle's bloodied remains.

Gory and brutal, these fallen soldiers had been slaughtered without mercy. He could not believe his eyes, and once the smell hit his nose, his stomach pulled him to his knees to force out everything inside. Hunched over with his hands on the ground, he retched again at all the maggots worming through the dismembered bodies next to him. This was nothing like the epic battle stories Fira used to read them as kids. Those were glorious; people fought valiantly and died with honor. But here… There was no honor here. This was far from a battle. This was a massacre.

"Vincent Raine!" a man's voice rang out.

Vincent quickly turned to see a man in the distance. His heart started to pound against his chest. His breaths grew faster. Sweat poured down his head. Panic had set in.

He scrambled to his feet and started to run. But no matter how fast he ran, it quickly became clear there was no escape from the ocean of corpses beneath his feet. Trapped in an endless sea of terror and torment, he begged to get out. He closed his eyes. *It's just a dream*, he thought. *Just a dream.*

He was wrong. It was a nightmare.

Lightning cracked the sky as the man now appeared in front of him. Vincent stumbled to a halt.

"Who are you?!" he shouted in a panic.

There was no answer. Lighting flashed across the sky again.

The man silently walked closer. His cloak, dyed with the blood of his victims, rested upon sharp black armor. A sword, held tightly in one of his golden gauntlets, dripped blood with each step. His eyes were hidden beneath his hood, yet somehow Vincent felt them on him—*in* him, as if the man were staring into the depths of his soul.

Vincent's breaths quickened as the fear rattled his bones. He started to back away, but only took one step before he hit something behind him—a tall wooden column that had not previously been there.

The man raised his sword to Vincent's neck, the cold steel biting into his skin. Beneath the blade's murderous intent, something about it seemed familiar. Then, in the time it took to blink, ropes coiled around his wrists and ankles, binding him to the post. He squirmed to break free, but with no luck; nothing would loosen.

The man lowered his hood to reveal long, black, messy hair that fell over a face carved with deep scars. Everything about him was menacing—except his eyes. Heavy lids rested above dark brown wells of eternal sorrow, stirring a strange sense of pity in Vincent.

As the man slowly raised his sword in the air, Vincent realized why it felt familiar—it was the blade from the tomb again. Only now, another one of the star stones glowed while the others slept. A red light pulsed from the star stone nestled in the left wing of the cross guard.

The man brought the dark blade down across Vincent's chest. The icy steel sent a burning pain lancing through his body. He tried to scream away the agony, but no sound escaped his lungs.

The man raised the sword again. Vincent clenched his eyes shut, bracing for the next strike. Over and over again, the blade carved searing pain into his body as his flesh was torn open. How much time had passed? Hours? Days? Weeks? Months? There was no way for him to know. No markers. No end. Just pain. Was this even a dream… or was it his new reality?

He hung limp, still bound to the post as blood seeped from his many wounds. "Please," he whispered. "Please stop."

The man gently pressed the tip of the blade beneath Vincent's chin and slowly lifted it until their eyes met. Vincent stared into the man's sorrowful gaze—eyes that now mirrored his own. The man nodded slowly, as if sadly admiring a finished painting.

"I am the second." He lowered the sword, and the world fell away as Vincent slipped into darkness.

CHAPTER 10

INCENT jolted awake with a gasp and frantically looked beneath his tunic at his chest. There was nothing there. He fell back down on his back, relieved. Once he was fully sure he was safely outside of his nightmare, he started to calm down. He knew there would be no sleep left for him tonight, so once his breathing returned to normal, he rose to his feet to relieve whomever was on watch.

He snuck his way up to the tower to find Rinna leaning up against the wooden guard rail, looking out into the distance as she hummed a soft melody to herself. The moonlight that peeked between the clouds above trickled down the back of her hair and over the purple ribbon tied around her ponytail. His foot lifted from the top step with a creak in the floorboards that suddenly caused her to turn around.

"Hey, Vince," she said quietly.

"I'm probably not going to be able to sleep anymore, if you want to catch some more rest."

"Wow. No 'hi,' no 'how are you doing,' just trying to get rid of me right away, huh?"

"No, no, I'm sorry, I didn't—"

She laughed. "I'm only joking."

Vincent leaned against the railing beside her and looked out into the field beyond. Short, flat ground covered in rocks and bushes led up to a tree line he could not see past without the aid of light.

"Besides," Rinna continued, "I don't think I'll be able to get any more sleep tonight either."

As her chin seemed to tilt lower toward the ground, Vincent felt the same twinge of sadness as when they were walking through the forest together.

"How come? Something bothering you?" he asked.

"I…" She hesitated for a moment. "Do you ever question whether or not you made the right choice in coming here?"

"On this mission?"

"No, no, I mean joining the Guardians."

Vincent thought about her question briefly. Even though he never really had a choice, he had always wanted to be a Guardian just like his father. Maybe that would be different if his father were alive, but even now, as anxious about the future as he was, his desire was the same. "Honestly, I've always wanted to be a Guardian for as long as I can remember. But even if I didn't want to, I never had a choice."

Rinna suddenly realized her mistake and looked up, panicked. "I am so sorry. I forgot that you… That was silly of me. I'm sorry."

Vincent smiled softly. "It's all right. But what are you saying? That you regret your decision to join?"

She shook her head. "No, not that I regret it, I just…" She sighed. "Sometimes I just feel guilty."

"For what?"

"Leaving my dad behind, I guess. He's been a shell of himself ever since my mom died, and I just left him in Nalitay, alone."

"I'm sure he understands. Besides, you have your own life to live, right?"

"I guess," Rinna said as she rested her chin on top of her folded hands.

"What made you want to become a Guardian in the first place?"

A gentle smile of remembrance grew across Rinna's cheeks. "My mom did. She always looked so strong and proud, even after she was exiled from Meditas."

Vincent quickly connected the dots. "Your mother fought in Abnor?"

She nodded. "She followed your father into battle and faced the same punishment as everyone else."

Vincent felt a sense of secondhand guilt rush through his body.

"Once we got back to Nalitay, it was fine for some time. We cooked together, she taught me how to fight and how to hunt, and every night, she would read by the fire while my dad showed me how to draw and paint on parchment."

"That sounds nice."

"It was... at first."

"What happened?"

She took a deep breath. "Soon, with all the talk of Guardians being worthless and traitorous liars, Nalitay started to ridicule everyone who had returned from the war, including my mother. It started with a simple nasty comment in the market or while walking through the square, but over time, it grew worse. People eventually tried to pick fights and started throwing things at her every time they saw her, so she stopped leaving the house. That's when she slowly grew quieter and quieter and just seemed sad all the time. She just couldn't handle being pent up inside all the time like that."

"Why didn't you leave? Sylva always welcomed Rogues with open arms as long as they were civil. My mother gladly would have found somewhere for you all to stay."

"All the other Guardians who were in Nalitay eventually did leave, but for some reason, we stayed. Truthfully, I don't know why. I brought it up several times, but was only met with lectures about how I was too young to understand anything." Rinna shook her head, unsure. "Maybe she just didn't want to leave 'home,' even though it was hard to call it that anymore. I tried to stay, for my father's sake, but after what they did to her, I knew I had to leave."

"What who did? The city?"

She nodded slowly. "One night, while my father was on his way home, he was ambushed by a bunch of lowlifes. It was a miracle they didn't kill him. Ribs cracked, bones broken—he could hardly breathe, and it was all just for 'marrying that traitorous freak,' they said to him. My mother was furious. She couldn't take any more of it, and she snapped. She left him in my care and went hunting for them. I don't even know if she found the ones who did it. All I know is she made three children fatherless that night."

Vincent could see the tears welling in her eyes and felt a tightness in his chest. He gently placed a hand on her shoulder, unsure what else to offer.

"The next day, practically the whole city was outside our door, ready to give her the punishment they'd wanted to since she returned. They hung her in the town square for everyone to see, and from that point on, my dad confined himself to the local tavern every night." A small laugh of sadness escaped her. "Honestly, he's probably there right now. He stopped drawing and painting and barely even looked at me anymore. I tried to stay, just for him, but there was nothing left for me there."

Vincent looked to the ground. "That's terrible, Rin. And all just because she followed my dad. I'm... I'm so sorry."

She wiped her eyes. "Thanks, but it's not your fault. *They* turned her into the monster they thought she was from the start. No matter what happened, though, she never regretted her decision. No matter how dark things were or how far gone her mind may have been, she always said Victor Raine was a great leader. Even if you could ask her today, I'm sure she'd say the same. So, I'm glad I'm able to stand side by side with his son, and I think she would be too." She gave him a soft smile.

"Thank you," he said gently. The lump in his throat prevented him from saying anything else.

Rinna blinked the remaining tears away from her eyes. "Sorry for all of that."

"No, don't be. I can't imagine dealing with all of that alone."

"Well, I'm sure having everyone judge you just because of who your father is isn't easy either."

"Yeah, but I can always just sic Barrik on someone anytime I want."

Rinna laughed. "I have to admit, I'm a bit envious. I've always wanted siblings, but you four seem to be especially close."

Vincent nodded with a smile. "We are. Sure, we can work on one another's nerves from time to time, but that's mostly intentional."

"Since you grew up together, I imagine you've accumulated a novel's worth of stories?"

"I've got a few," he said with a smirk.

She looked at him with a playfully curious expression on her face. "Well, then?"

Underneath the vanishing light of the moon, Vincent shared as many of his tales from their days in Sylva as he could remember. Before they knew it, early morning sunlight had slipped past them as a welcome intruder that crept through every window and crack in the wall. As everyone began to gather their things and the fragments of slumber's fatigue faded away, they huddled around the only member of their group who had not risen with the sun's alarm.

Kai peered down at Barrik and shook his head, amazed he was still asleep. "If Enora's coliseum ever hosted a sport in the art of sleeping, I'd doubt he'd have any competition. Nevertheless, we must continue."

Kai grabbed Barrik's hand and shoved two of his fingers into his nose. Barrik jolted awake and quickly removed his fingers, confused about how they had gotten there. The others laughed.

"Nice of you to join us," Kai said cheerfully. "Time to go."

Beyond the outpost, they traveled across the open field to the edge of another dense forest full of tall trees and vegetation. With no trail or road on the route Kai had led them, fallen trunks and moss-covered boulders became obstacles for them to clamber over or duck beneath as they pressed through.

"We aren't much farther now. Once we reach the river bend, we will stop for the day," Kai said.

"How much farther is that?" Vera asked.

"A bit."

She groaned.

Barrik laughed. "Tired of walking already, V?"

"I was tired of walking yesterday. Kai moves too fast."

"I was wondering, actually," Toran started, "if we're trying to get there quickly, how come we didn't take horses?"

"You don't have much experience with horses, do you, Toran?" Alexandra asked as she stepped beneath a low-hanging branch.

"My mom used to be a great rider. She showed me how a few times, but that was some time ago now, although I'm sure I could figure it out again no problem."

"Even if you did, they still need a lot of care and tons of water," Alexandra explained. "They frighten easily, they're temperamental, and sometimes they try to toss you off for what seems like no reason. Very smart and beautiful creatures, but it's typically not as easy as just hopping on and going."

"There is also a stealth factor to our mission," Kai added. "Concealing seven horses would be quite the feat."

Vera hunched her shoulders and glared ahead. "So, we walk."

Vera's sore feet still managed to carry her through the rest of the day until they finally stopped near a bend in a small river. As everyone enjoyed the gentle sound of flowing water while they had their evening bite, Kai decided to take another course of action instead.

"We're only a few hours from the village," he said. "I'm going on ahead alone to have a look before we all move in together. There won't be much light beneath these trees, so you can build a fire, but keep it small. Alex, you're in charge while I'm gone."

Once his orders had been issued, he gave no time for anyone to respond before he took off.

Alexandra began to think out loud. "If we're allowed a fire, then..." She exchanged a mischievous look with Vincent and Vera before all three of them looked at Barrik with a big smile.

He sighed. "I'll get the wood."

The crackle of the small fire and the flow of the river's water nearby made up a complementary ambient sound to the calm beneath the darkened canopy. Easy as it was for most of them to fall asleep quickly, Vincent had volunteered for the first watch to draw himself even closer to exhaustion. Or maybe it was in fear of yet another dream rivaling the feel of reality. He watched and waited in the darkness for Kai's return. Unsure as to whether every sound he heard was friend or foe, he felt anxiety rush through his bones with even the smallest rustle of leaves. When it came time for Barrik to relieve him of his duty, Vincent still felt unready for sleep, despite all of his fatigue. Even so, he lay up against a boulder and watched the dying dance of flames before him until he could hold up his eyelids no longer.

Vincent opened his eyes to see a small home of large oak planks set ablaze by a cacophony of angry flames. Unwillingly, he started for the door. He had no control over his movements, and when he caught his fiery reflection in the glass window in the door, he realized his body was not his own. He looked into the tormented eyes of a middle-aged man with unkempt black-and-gray hair on his head and face.

He drew a sword and entered the burning home. He could feel the heat against the surface of a skin that did not belong to him, smell the smoking oak burning the man's nose with every inhale. It might not have been Vincent who entered the building, but he would experience everything that was about to happen as if it were.

Heartbroken screams of fear mingled with the ash in the air. A mother and her son cowered in the corner of the sitting room—two people Vincent had never seen before, yet he loved them both dearly. It was as if all of their memories together had been burnt away by the embers of time, but the connection to them, the emotions—the love—were all everlasting.

"Please! This isn't you!" the woman shouted in a desperate panic. She held the boy tightly against herself to shield both his body and his eyes from the monster in front of her.

Vincent knew what was about to happen. He tried with all of his might to turn around, to scream, to stop, to wake up. The woman's eyes widened at his raised sword. A tear fell from her eye. There was nothing Vincent could do. He was little more than a voiceless passenger forced to watch the slaughter of the nameless innocent before him he cared so fiercely for.

There in the corner, he now sat, cradling the two bodies on the floor as guilt and regret flooded throughout every part of his mind and body until the fiery fate around him came to fruition. He felt a pain unlike any other. No blade or arrow could hold a torch to the agony that now plagued his soul. He pulled them close to his chest. Tears fell fast to the burning floor as he held them with blood-soaked hands. Oak planks from the ceiling began to crash into the floor with an explosion of embers and ash. Smoke rapidly started to engulf his lungs with the message that *his* time had come.

"Vincent Raine," the man said with a nasty cough.

His vision grew blurry, his body lost its strength, and as he fell to his side, the man said aloud weakly, "I am the third."

As soon as the words were spoken, the ceiling came crashing in as if the words were the signal for his home to give way. And just before his teary eyes went dark, he saw it.

There on the floor in front of him lay the sword from the tomb. The sword that had pierced his heart. The sword that had cut him open, over and over again. The sword he used to take the lives of those dearest to him.

Now it had become a sword sordid with the love of his loved ones. And at the right tip of the cross guard, a star stone shone a bright emerald green.

"Vince, wake up!"

Vincent opened his watery eyes to see Alexandra kneeling down in front of him.

"Are you okay?" she asked with a look of concern.

He wiped his eyes. "Yeah, fine. The sun is just really bright."

She looked at him suspiciously. He was sitting in the shade.

"Is Kai back yet?" he asked quickly before she could question him further.

"I'm right here," Kai answered as he stepped down from the boulder behind him.

"Well, what did you find?"

"Nothing but more questions."

"What does that mean?" Rinna asked.

"It means that whatever has occurred continues to elude me. It means we need to be careful. Come on."

Kai led them along beside the river until it dropped off a ledge and flowed to the small village ahead. He halted them all just behind the tree line.

A moss-covered wall that stood just out of reach acted as the barrier for a small town of several houses made of the same moss-ridden stone. Wooden fences protected backyards with a surplus of tools and a few empty chicken coops. Black smoke rolled out of one of the chimneys and dissipated into the sky above. They all watched for several moments, but saw nothing out of the ordinary. However, something *felt* wrong.

Outside of themselves, all other life seemed to fade into legend. There were no insects buzzing about, nor any animal tracks beneath their feet. The trees looked sickly with peeling bark and weak limbs. The heat from the sun was absent of its usual warmth, while its light shone dull. A foul energy drowned the surrounding area in apathy from a source they could not detect—an energy void of color or feeling that seemed to siphon the life from the world around them. A sense that they were unwelcome lingered in the stagnant air.

"Vince," Kai whispered.

"Yeah?"

"You remember the warning I gave you about pulling in energy?"

"This is one of those places?" he guessed.

"Potentially, yes. All right, everyone, stay low, and stay silent. Follow me."

Kai led them down the ledge and around the village wall, with the river to their side, until they reached the black smoking chimney. One by one, each of them climbed over the wall, and as they did, the air tightened around them as if they had just willingly climbed into a glass jar and sealed the lid.

Alexandra noticed that every yard she could see had a chicken coop, yet she had neither heard nor seen a single chicken.

"Did they just abandon this place?" she whispered to herself.

Kai opened the wooden gate to the backyard in front of them, when a strange noise began to fill their ears.

"Do you hear that?" Barrik asked.

"I think it's coming from inside," Toran said quietly.

As they approached the back door, the sound grew in intensity. Snaps and cracks coupled with wet squelches leaked from behind the door. It sounded as though someone inside were jumping up and down on a pile of branches lying in mud. Kai put his fingers to his lips and slowly opened the door. Vera stood up on a wooden crate and peered in through a window.

There, lying in the middle of the kitchen floor, was a horror as big as a bear—one none of them had ever seen before. Patches of black and brown fur full of mange and soaked with blood grew out of flaked skin all over its body. Three rows of fangs ripped pieces of skin from what was left of a middle-aged woman. Horrified, they watched as she caressed the head of the twisted creature.

"Shh, shh, shh… Good boy," she whispered. "It seems we have some unexpected visitors who will be joining us for dinner." There was no sign of distress in her voice. With the lower half of her body gone and the floorboards doused in her blood, there was no telling how she was still alive.

The creature purred.

She turned her head slightly to face them while the horror continued to savor every lick of her bones. "Please come in and join us. My boy will soon be done with his dinner." She smiled at them.

Rinna covered her mouth and nose. Alexandra ripped her eyes away from the woman and gagged. Vera continued to watch, amazed.

"By the stars…" Kai said in shock.

"Kai," Rinna said nervously.

"Right." He started to shut the door.

"NO!" The woman's voice turned to a growl as she slammed her fist against the floor. "You WILL stay!"

The horror stopped purring.

"No, no, no, my love, please, go back to your meal," the woman urged.

It stopped eating.

"Now look what you've done!" she snapped at them.

In one swift movement, the horror unhinged its jaw, clamped down on the woman's neck, and tore her head clean off her shoulders.

Kai tried to quickly shut the door, but the horror came bursting through and leaped on top of him, taking him to the ground. A foul mouthful of fresh blood and saliva dripped from the rows of fangs onto Kai's face as it snarled at him.

Barrik took a mighty swing with his axe at the creature's mid-section, launching it through the wooden fence and quickly pulling Kai to his feet.

"What the hell *is* that thing?!" Barrik cried.

Kai shook his head and wiped the pestilent liquid from his face. "I have no idea. I've never seen anything like it before."

In the neighboring yard, wooden planks fell to the ground as the beast rose to its feet and shook off Barrik's attack. From what they could tell, there had been no damage to the beast whatsoever. First, it growled, then it stood up on its hind legs and lifted its chin.

"It's gonna howl!" Vincent shouted.

Without hesitation, Vera hurled one of her daggers right into the horror's neck. Yet somehow, her attack failed to prevent it from bellowing an earth-shaking cry for reinforcements. Vera appeared with her dagger in her hand and her arms wrapped around the creature from behind. She stabbed it in the top of the head, but again, it showed no signs of pain. Doors and windows from nearby houses crashed open as more horrors heard the call to arms.

Still rearing on its hind legs, the monster thrashed beneath Vera, snapping, twitching, and bucking erratically. Its movements were too jarring for her to reach for her other dagger—all she could do was hang on.

"Somebody do something!" she shouted.

Toran charged into the creature with his shield high, launching both Vera and the horror to the ground. As it lay helpless on its back, he brought down his sword to its underside. A whimper of pain escaped its mouth as its life faded away. Toran held out his hand to help Vera to her feet.

"Are you okay?" he asked.

"Yeah, thanks," she said shakily.

"Seems like their belly is their weak spot," Toran said as he looked down at the lifeless beast at their feet.

Vincent unsheathed his sabers with a twirl. "Well then, at least this is going to be easy," he said sarcastically.

Several more of the creatures quickly approached from all directions. Vincent slashed at one in front of him, but the beast caught his blade and threw him down the side of the house into the center of the road. Right behind Vincent as he rolled on the ground, the beast pounced and soared through the air. Before it could land on top of him, Alexandra leaped from the side and tackled it to the ground. Vincent quickly hurried over and pierced its exposed stomach with both his blades. Alexandra hopped to her feet, and together, they stood back-to-back in the middle of the road as more of the horrors closed in on them.

"Kinda reminds you of that pack of weren we ran into last year, doesn't it?" Vincent asked.

"You mean the pack that almost tore you apart?"

He chuckled. "Yeah, that one."

With a push off each other, they charged.

Barrik stepped to the side to avoid a pair of incoming claws and brought his axe down hard on his attacker's neck. It hit the ground with a whimper. Before it could recover, he kicked it over and brought his axe down again to finish the job.

Rinna cloaked herself as one of the creatures lunged at her. No longer able to see its prey, it looked around, disoriented. She took advantage of its confusion, and with the blade at the end of her metal staff, she sliced at its legs. She continued to poke at the beast, but no matter what she did, it would not expose its underside. She revealed herself to it and continued to hit it from a distance with small jabs of her blade until it could take no more; it snatched the blade in its mouth and yanked her forward. She had no time to defend herself—its massive paw sliced through the air and slammed into her shoulder, sending her crashing into the wall of a village home. The horror pounced to finish the kill. Rinna quickly cloaked herself again and raised her weapon in the air. The creature fell on the blade, skewering itself right before her eyes. As soon as she stood up to dislodge her blade from its stomach, she could see another one slowly sneaking up behind Barrik. Under the veil of her Favor, she ran.

Two horrors slowly circled Toran and Vera. Sweat rolled down Toran's forehead as he anxiously waited for one of them to strike. Vera narrowed her eyes and lowered herself as if *she* were the one about to pounce. "Here, kitty, kitty..." The two predators locked eyes with one another and then charged. Vera tossed one of her daggers into the air above the rushing beast and vanished. From the air, she threw both daggers down into its back just below its neck and disappeared again.

Toran continued to bash away and block the horror's attacks while he searched for a way to expose its weakness. He was able to counter with a successful swing of his sword consistently, but every landed slash seemed to do little more than anger the beast. Behind his attacker, he spotted Vera clinging to her daggers, her body whipping with the monster's every violent spasm.

"Hang on, Vera!" he shouted.

"Why... would I... let go?!" she shouted back. For a moment, he could have sworn there was a smile on her face.

Kai slowly backed into a narrow alley between two homes with two horrors in front of him and one behind him. There was nowhere for him to run.

Dust flew into the air behind each of Rinna's unseen footfalls. Without even the slightest bit of her being visible, the horror she charged at never even bothered to look her way. From a full sprint, she planted the end of her staff in the ground and launched herself into its side with a forceful kick. Blindsided, it slammed into the grass and skidded away. She knew she would be unable to reach it before it climbed back to its feet. Quickly, she lined up the moving target and hurled her weapon like a spear. The blade sliced through the air until it sank into the horror's underside. Barrik whipped around at the sudden noise behind him to see Rinna unveil herself, and he gave her a nod of thanks.

Everyone kicked, bashed, and slashed away at what seemed to be a never-ending horde of these new horrors. And the longer they fought, the more the sky filled with clouds of gray, as if a storm were about to take root right above them.

Vincent and Alexandra pulled their weapons from a felled creature and saw Vera burst from behind the houses down the road, still hanging onto the horror's back.

"What is she doing?" Alexandra asked.

"Not helping," Vincent answered.

Alexandra cupped her hands around her mouth and shouted. "Vera! Bring it this way!"

"Uh, yeah, sure, okay." Vera leaned and tilted the handle of her daggers to try and direct the horror's rage. "This way, horsey!"

Not a moment later, Vera and her steed were charging down the road toward Alexandra and Vincent. Alexandra sheathed her sword.

Vincent looked at her, shocked. "What are you doing?"

"I got it, don't worry," she said as she planted her feet. The crevices in her left arm all radiated a strong white glow. She pulled back her hips and waited patiently for the beast to come in range. Vincent took a step back as it drew closer. "Uh, Alex..."

No longer aimlessly running, the horror had locked onto a new target: Alexandra. As it closed in, she exploded from her stance—her hips snapping forward, fist tearing through the air toward its head. The blow landed with such force that a shockwave rippled across the road, hurling a cloud of dirt and grass into the air as the creature was driven into the ground. Vera, like a projectile fired from a catapult, was launched off its back into the air.

But just before she crashed into the ground, she vanished—only to reappear crouched atop the motionless creature.

"That was awesome!" she shouted.

"Glad you're having fun. Now move over so I can make sure it's dead," Alexandra said.

A crimson light suddenly burst from between two of the homes as she removed her sword from the horror's belly.

"What was that?" Vincent asked.

A moment later, Kai emerged from the gap and cleaned off the blood from his katana. Not far behind him came Toran at a full sprint, relieved to see no more of the new abominations that would haunt his dreams.

Alexandra looked around. "Where's Bear and Rinna?"

Barrik fell flat on his back with a horror's jaw locked onto the shaft of his axe. He pulled his knees up to his chest and launched it behind him with his feet. Rinna sank her weapon deep into its chest to finish it off. Before she could make another move, another horror crashed through wooden shutters behind her and took her to the ground. Hovering over top of her, its jaw unhinged as it lunged for her neck, its fangs tearing through the air. Barrik quickly raised his hand. Suddenly, the snarling maw fell short of its target—just inches away. It lunged again. Nothing. It clawed, scratched, and snapped over and over again, but all were failed attempts to reach Rinna. Barrik had conjured an energy barrier between them just in time. What looked like a small white cloud of waves protected her from all its attacks.

Vera charged around the corner as the horror reared up on its hind legs, throwing one of her daggers. Just as it was about to fly right by it, she appeared and sank both of her blades into its stomach as she slid across the ground, slicing it open from one end to the other.

Too stunned to move, Rinna continued to lie on the ground until Vincent and Alexandra helped her to her feet. The moment she was upright again, Barrik rushed to her side. "Are you okay?" he asked in a hurry.

"Thanks to you, yeah, I think so."

He pulled her in close and squeezed her tightly. "Thank the stars!"

"O… kay… hon," she managed to croak out from beneath his constriction. When he finally let go, she exhaled a breath of relief.

"Looks like that's the last of them for now," Toran said.

Alexandra nudged the beast at her feet. "Good. I don't need Vera trying to keep one as a pet."

Vera looked around defensively. "What? I wouldn't do that… Do you actually think they can be tamed?"

"Somehow, I think you'd find a way."

Vera smiled proudly.

Kai walked over, knelt down next to the felled creature, and heavily inspected it.

Vincent lightly elbowed Barrik in the side. "A distant relative of yours?"

"Shut up."

"Do you think these things ate all the villagers?" Rinna asked.

"I'd say it's a possibility," Kai said grimly.

"That poor woman," Rinna said, remembering the horrid image of the half-eaten villager woman. "How was she even still alive?"

"And why was she *petting* it?" Alexandra added.

"She had to have been in so much pain," Toran said.

"Have you ever received an injury from any kind of horror?" Kai asked.

Toran shook his head. "No, thankfully not."

"While their claws burn hotter than the stars, their saliva can actually be rather soothing if you come in contact with enough of it."

Rinna suddenly felt sick. "… Did you say soothing?"

Kai nodded. "Even today, you can still find some merchants and traders who sell it as a sort of pain relief. But you're right, that doesn't explain how she was still alive. Or why she seemed to enjoy the experience."

"Could this be what happened to the other Guardians too?" Alexandra questioned.

"I doubt it. Gala and her team were more than capable. It would take much more than this to subdue them." Kai looked around the village. "If I'm not mistaken, there's an old Sanorian mine at the other end of the village. Let's check the houses to see what we can find before we move inside."

"What if we run into any more of Bear's cousins?" Vincent asked.

Barrik rolled his eyes.

"Then just run into the middle of the road and give us a howl," Kai said with a smile.

CHAPTER 11

VERYONE stood in front of the entrance to a cave void of all light. Not even the smallest sliver of sunlight snuck inside.

"How are we supposed to see anything in there?" Toran asked.

Kai looked at Alexandra. "Charlie taught you all the sign for fire, I imagine?"

"Of course," she answered.

"Good. Then I will leave you four in charge of our light."

Barrik, Vincent, Vera, and Alexandra all placed one of their hands flat against the blade of their weapon and weaved a sign with the hand they held their weapon with. Once it was complete, each of their blades ignited with an orange breath of flames.

Toran was amazed. "Woah!"

Rinna looked over Vincent's fiery blade, astonished. "You learned how to use a craftsman's sign to make your weapons into torches." She smiled. "Amazing!"

Once they had their light, Kai put them into formation. "Alex, up here with me. Vincent and Vera, take the sides with Rinna and Toran between you. Barrik, you're our rear."

Vincent snickered. "Always thought you were more of an ass than a bear."

Vera laughed while Alexandra tried to stifle her laughter. Barrik just shoved him from behind.

"Knock it off and quiet down," Kai demanded. "We don't know what may be waiting for us inside. Whenever you're ready, Alex."

By the light of the lambent flames, they traveled into the depths of the earth. The cave walls turned and twisted, leading them deeper through the surrounding darkness until they came to a small chamber full of mining equipment and several corridors that seemed to lead only to more darkness. Wooden crates and iron tools were spread out in different locations, not far from metal carts filled with ore and dirt. Tracks for the mining carts circled the room, as well as a wooden walkway above them. They spread out to look for anything of interest.

With his fingers, Barrik traced the impressions in the walls from the countless strikes of a pickaxe. The hard rock was cold and damp beneath his palm. His eyes wandered up to the ceiling, where in the distant shadows, he could see an abundance of stalactites hanging above them all.

While Vera and Toran moved up to the wooden walkway, Vincent and Rinna sifted through the contents of the metal carts. No matter how many handfuls of rocks and soil they picked up, they still found nothing worthwhile.

"What do you think they were looking for?" Rinna whispered.

Vincent maneuvered a rock in his hand before he let it fall back onto the pile. "Beats me."

A glint of light to Alexandra's side drew her attention. Something was embedded in the cave wall that reflected the light from the fire every time it passed over. She held her torch closer. When she reached out to inspect the item further, she heard something move down the corridor beside her. Just as she turned to shine her light down the dark hall, one of the horrors from the village leaped out on top of her and knocked her sword out of her hand. The flames on her blade vanished as soon as her palm left the hilt. Before anyone was able to run to her aid, the beast clamped down on her left arm and shook her from side to side like a dog trying to break the neck of a rodent, until it finally let go, sending her flying into the cave wall. Kai sliced the beast in the side, but once the horror saw it was outnumbered, it ran off into the dark corridor.

Kai knelt down next to Alexandra. "Are you okay?"

She groaned as she rose to her feet. "Yeah, I'm fine."

"I'll get the thing," Vincent said as he started down the corridor.

"No," Kai commanded. "We don't know where it went, and there's no point in chasing it around in the darkness. Besides, it could also be leading us somewhere."

"You think a horror is that smart?" Barrik asked.

"Normally, I would say no. But I have also never seen a horror retreat before. Alex, are you sure you're okay?"

She looked down at her left arm, which now radiated a strong white light in each of the deep crevices that spread all over it. "My head is a little rattled, but other than that, yeah, I'm fine." She picked up her sword and, with a quick sign, turned it into a torch once more.

"What'd you do to piss that thing off, anyway?" Vincent asked.

"Nothing. I just touched something shining in the wall, and then it jumped out at me."

"Maybe you should stop touching things."

"Something shining?" Kai questioned.

"Yeah, here." Alexandra walked back to the glint in the wall and pulled out a small amber stone with a firm yank of her fingers. She handed it over to Kai.

"It's a star stone. Most likely what they were mining here. Keep it." He handed it back to her. "Might fetch some fair coin at the market if you choose to sell it."

Rinna looked around the chamber, but could not find any more. "If that's what they were mining, it doesn't seem like they had much luck."

"Or..." Kai followed the iron tracks beneath their feet with his eyes until they disappeared down another corridor. "...it was mined dry and they continued on deeper."

With Alexandra at his side, Kai led the group farther down into the cave as they followed the tracks into the corridor. Their footsteps echoed off the cold stone walls as they traveled deeper and deeper. A chilled air swept across them all and brought with it the scent of wet rocks and soil. When the path finally opened up again, they found themselves at the head of what was left of a wooden bridge. Only a few planks remained on either side, and the broken tracks dipped off into the darkness below. Kai peered over the ledge, but could see nothing in the abyss below them. If they were to cross, they would have to jump.

"What should we call those things, anyway?" Vera asked suddenly.

"Call what?" Toran asked.

"The big bear horrors. Should we call them horror bears?"

"Horror bears? Really, V?" Alexandra muttered.

She shrugged. "Well, I don't know. I'm just—"

Just then, a deep, unsettling growl came from behind them. Everyone slowly turned around. As if beckoned by her call, one of the horrors Vera had just mentioned snuck out from the darkness. Then another. And another. Several of the beasts slowly crept toward them, all with fangs bared.

"You just *had* to name them," Vincent said.

"Yeah, name them, not *summon* them!" Vera exclaimed, defending herself.

"May as well have."

"Everyone across the bridge! Now!" Kai commanded.

Alexandra launched herself across the gap and caught the lip of one of the wooden planks. She hoisted herself up and turned around for the others. Vera came flying over the gap with ease and landed with a roll.

"Any day, guys!" Vincent shouted as he slashed at one of the horrors.

Toran ran as fast as he could, but just as he jumped, his foot caught one of the iron tracks. As he stumbled through the air, it was obvious he was not going to make it. Before he could fall beyond their aid, Kai snatched him out of the air and thrust his katana into the wood. There, above the bottomless void, they dangled.

Rinna, Vincent, and Barrik continued to hold off the horde while Alexandra and Vera helped pull Toran and Kai up to safety.

One of the horrors spun around and kicked Vincent in the chest with its hind legs, forcing him into the rocky wall.

"Vince!" Barrik shouted.

Two horrors took advantage of Barrik's momentary distraction and pounced on him. One sank its jaws into his shoulder, while the other gnawed on his arm. They were only gifted with a brief taste of his flesh before each of them found a dagger in their skulls. Vera appeared and knocked both of them back away from him.

"Bear, get across!" she shouted.

"Not without you guys," he groaned.

Vera whipped one of her daggers across the gap and into one of the wooden planks of the bridge on the other side. "We'll be right behind you. Go!"

Barrik winced with every footfall as he sprinted to the edge. Even though he had remarkable speed for his size, it was not enough to clear the gap. He pulled back his axe just as he started his descent and slammed it down hard into the other ledge. He groaned in pain from the impact.

A set of claws swiped across Rinna's chest and knocked her to the ground. Vincent rushed to her aid, but was tackled away by another horror and rolled toward the edge of the bridge. Just before he went tumbling off, Vera snatched his hand. As she started to pull him back up, one of the horrors latched onto Rinna's leg and tossed her through the air.

"Lookout!" Vincent shouted.

Too late. Before Vera had time to turn around, Rinna slammed into her back.

As if her arm had suddenly developed an infinite reach, Alexandra threw herself at the edge with an outstretched hand. But still, all she could do—all any of them could do—was watch in horror as the three of them plummeted into darkness.

The horrors on the other side of the broken bridge growled and snapped at the prey no longer within reach. Too scared to jump across, they slowly gave up the hunt and backed away.

Barrik sank along with his heart against the wall. His wounds no longer ailed him now that a new, much stronger pain had taken hold of him. Toran stared silently into the dark abyss. Alexandra lay motionless, her eyes wide with shock.

Kai gently grabbed her by the shoulders to lift her to her feet.

"No, no, no, no, no..." Her voice was full of panic and disbelief. "We have to help them! We—we have to go after them!"

Kai had to tighten his grip on her as she tried to pull away toward the edge. "We can't, Alex. They fell."

Her eyes started to water. "We have to do something..." Her voice grew weaker.

"Right now, all we can do is press on," Kai said softly.

"Press on? Press *on*?" Now she grew angry. In a teary-eyed fury, she turned on Kai. "How can you say that? Now they're just a couple more lost Guardians to you? How can you expect me—expect *us*—to just carry on? How can *you* just carry on? How?!"

Kai looked into her eyes—blue wells teeming with a storm of emotions. "Because I *have* to."

Barrik leaned over the edge of the bridge and pulled Vera's dagger out of the wooden plank it was stuck into. His eyes lingered over the blade in his hands and watched as the star stone slowly changed from glowing red to yellow to match his energy. The sight of the color change turned his stomach, as if it signaled something he would rather not consider.

"We need to keep moving," Kai insisted.

Alexandra's eyes fell to the ground. Barrik placed his hand on her shoulder and mustered up a soft smile. "They'll be all right."

"You don't know that."

As the three of them started to continue into the cave, they realized Toran lagged behind them.

"Toran," Kai called.

"Hang on. Do you hear that?" He dropped to his hands and knees and lowered his head over the cliff's edge.

"Hear what?"

"Listen."

Everyone fell silent as they searched for the mystery sound that drew his attention. With a moment of focus, they could hear the distant flow of water from below them.

Alexandra's eyes widened with hope. "Water!" She jumped to her feet and started to move on. "Come on, we have to hurry!"

"Alex, wait!" Kai called after her.

She whipped around. "We don't have time to wait! We have to help them!"

"And if we can, we will. But blindly charging ahead when we don't know what lurks around the corner is far from our best course of action. We don't even know where they are, and even if we did, we don't know how to get there. For now, focus on what you *can* do, and trust in their capabilities. We'll find them. But until we do, we need to keep a level head."

Even though Alexandra knew he was right, time did not seem like something they had an abundance of. She took a deep breath and clenched her fists in an attempt to stifle her anxiety and desperate desire for haste.

A deafening silence followed them all as they continued on with a quickened pace. Shrouded in fears and hope-nots, they felt the cloud of gloom that hovered above them grow larger with every step.

Although he also possessed an equal amount of concern for their comrades, a different seed of unease began to sprout in the back of Kai's mind. The deeper into the cave they traveled, the more he felt something familiar, like the horrid scent of a distant memory he could not quite place, and something told him to turn back. To abandon those who had already been lost. To forget this place ever existed. To run.

Their path led them to a small chamber with multiple corridors. Even after briefly investigating each outlet by illuminating it with the light of their torches, they were still unsure which one to take.

"Great. Now what do we do?" Alexandra asked, her frustration clear.

Kai shook his head. "I'm not sure. Maybe if we—"

Vera suddenly appeared next to Barrik. "Give me back my dagger, you thief!"

"Vera!" Alexandra shouted.

"Helllooooo."

Alexandra rushed over and threw her arms around her. "Are you okay? Where are the others?"

Vera started to laugh. "We got all wet." Her voice carried an unusual bounce to it.

Toran noticed a cut across the side of Vera's thigh. "Vera, you're hurt!"

She looked down at her leg. "Yeah. It's just a scratch, though. I'm okay, see? Watch." She started to hop up and down joyously.

Alexandra and Barrik looked at each other suspiciously.

"Vera, are you feeling okay?" Barrik asked.

"I feel wonderful," she said with a smile that never faded from her face.

Underneath the light of the flames, Kai could see that Vera's eyes were glossy, and her pupils were the size of a silver coin. He looked at the wound on her leg.

"Vera, that had to come from a blade. What exactly cut you?" he asked.

She giggled. "He was just a little guy. Don't worry, though; we handled them all." She smiled widely and gave two thumbs-up.

"Did the little guy look like an evil garden gnome?"

She laughed. "Yeah, that's him. Angry little fellas."

"Ah, fuck..." There was a residue of panic in Kai's voice.

"What's wrong? What's she talking about, Kai?" Barrik asked.

"Imps," he said quickly. "Vera, what color were their eyes?"

Her eyes widened. "Ooooooh, they were so pretty! They sparkled brighter than any star stone I've ever seen."

"What color were they, Vera?" His voice was hurried.

Her eyes rose to the ceiling in blissful remembrance. "They were more beautiful than rubies."

"So, they were red." Kai let out a breath of relief. "Okay. That's manageable."

"What does it mean if they have red eyes?" Toran asked.

"Red-eyed imps aren't the worst ones you can encounter, but certainly not ideal either. They run in packs and can easily overwhelm you with their numbers. And like I mentioned before, horror saliva has strange properties, and imps are aware of this, so they coat their blades with it. That way, when one of them cuts you, you find yourself almost instantly enamored with their eyes and in a borderline delirious state—" He gestured to Vera. "—while you bleed faster than normal. Luckily, though, her wound is minor."

"...They coat their blades with *saliva?*" Alexandra asked uncomfortably.

"Imps always lick their blades before going into battle."

Vera quickly jumped up at Barrik and licked his cheek, imitating the creatures' battle ritual.

"Eww, Vera," Barrik complained as he wiped his face.

She laughed.

Alexandra looked at her with a raised eyebrow. "As if she wasn't weird enough already."

"Heyyy, that's not nice," Vera said defensively.

"Will she be okay?" Toran asked.

Kai inspected her wound for a final assessment. "Yes, she'll be okay. The effects should start to fade in a few minutes. It doesn't last long, but then again, in most cases, it doesn't need to. Vera, did anyone else get cut, or just you?"

She shook her head back and forth rapidly. "Just me. Vincey and Rinny told me to come find you, so we can then find each other. But he took my other dagger too." She started to pout.

"Well, how else would you get back to them?" Barrik asked her.

"Oh, yeah!" She chuckled. "Also…" She looked to her left and then to her right before she waved them all closer to her. She put her hand around her mouth once they leaned in to further conceal her words. "I think Vincey has taken quite the liking to Miss Rinny." She giggled again with her mouth hidden behind her hand.

"Uh, yeah, *obviously*," Alexandra said with a joking smile. "Every other girl our age he's met so far either beats up on him or sees him as the son of a traitor." She turned to Kai. "What do we do now?"

"I have an idea, but I think it would be best to wait for Vera to return to normal—or at least, her version of normal."

"So, we just have to sit around and wait until then?" Barrik asked.

"Unfortunately, yes."

Vera slowly looked from Barrik's feet all the way up to the top of his head. "You're big," she said as she started to laugh again.

A small smile came across Barrik's face as he nodded slowly. "Thanks, V."

Kai looked at Vera and thought for a moment. "Getting her to focus on something might speed up the process a bit. Vera, do you think you can tell us everything that happened since you fell? That might also give us a way of figuring out where to go."

She stopped laughing as her eyes lit up. She started to clap and hop up and down with excitement. "Oooooh, yisss! Story time!" She plopped on the ground and crossed her legs. "Okay, so there we were…"

CHAPTER 12

INCENT, Vera, and Rinna fell through darkness until they splashed into the unseen river beneath them. Trapped in its current, they flailed around to try to gain some sort of control despite being no more than passengers to be dumped out wherever this watery journey was taking them. Just as Vincent burst above the river's surface, gasping for air, he was thrown into a rock and cracked the side of his skull.

Rinna's hands frantically searched for something to latch onto, but all she found were the jagged edges of the rocks around her, which served no purpose other than tearing open her palms.

Vera struggled to surface and catch a breath. None of her desperate tactics proved successful, but just when she thought she could no longer hold her breath, they were all thrown off the side of yet another ledge into a large underground lake. She coughed and sputtered until her breath finally returned to her.

"Vince! Rinna!" she yelled out as she looked around.

A moment later, both of them popped up not far in front of her, gasping for air.

"Are you guys okay?" Vincent asked.

Before anyone could answer him, Vera could see movement in the distant water behind Vincent and Rinna. She slowly raised her finger to direct their attention to it. "Uhh, guys…"

Vincent never even turned around. "Out out out out out!" he stammered as they all swam as fast as they could to the bank of the lake. Two disfigured fins quickly closed the distance behind them. Vera appeared on the bank, and with her dagger in hand, she aimed just in front of the fins behind Vincent and Rinna.

"Hurry up!" she shouted.

Just as they were about to be in range of whatever lurked under the water, Vincent and Rinna crawled out onto the cave floor and sprinted as far away from the edge of the lake as possible before they hunched over to catch their breath. Vera left her eyes on the two fins until they turned away and sank beneath the surface.

"Ha ha… Not today, spooky fish," Vincent said through his labored breaths. He eyed the dark lake and shivered at what else could potentially be hiding in the water, just waiting for defenseless prey. "I hate the water," he muttered.

"Just the kind that holds monster fish that want to eat you," Rinna said.

"Yeah, so, all water."

Vera smirked. "Vince is terrified of any water that rises above your ankles. He's barely brave enough to stand in a puddle after it rains."

"Really?" Rinna asked, surprised.

He shrugged. "I guess it would depend on the size of the puddle."

"No, not that—although that's a little crazy. Why are you so terrified?"

Vincent looked at her, confused. "Uh, hello?" He pointed back to the lake they had just barely escaped from.

"Okay, fair point. But it's not like the rivers above ground have creatures like those."

"You don't *know* that. And besides…" He gestured to himself. "Land creature."

"Yeah, he doesn't swim very well," Vera added.

Vincent pointed at her. "There's that too."

Rinna chuckled. "All right. Well, what do we do now?"

The three of them scanned the area and found themselves in a vast open chamber. Moonlight snuck in through several small holes in the rocky ceiling above. Large stone pillars that ran the perimeter of the lake were carved with smooth curves and intricate engravings. Across the water, several lantern poles illuminated the entrances to more corridors, as well as a stairwell that led up to a set of arched stone doors.

"Those lanterns are still lit," Vincent pointed out.

"You think someone's here?" Rinna asked quietly.

"I don't know. Kai said it was an old Sanorian mine, so it could be Sanorian magic that still works down here."

"Like the lanterns on the main roads between the cities?" Rinna asked.

"Yeah, maybe. Either way, V, you should get back to the others, so we can figure out what to do. And also let them know we're not dead."

"Wait, Vera—if you could have relocated at any point, why did you fall with us in the first place?" Rinna asked.

"Well, I couldn't let you guys hog all the glory of a heroic death," she said with a playful smirk. "Besides, we do everything together, right?"

Vincent glared at her. "We were almost fish candies while you were safe on land. So, obviously not everything."

Vera shrugged. "I have to draw the line somewhere. I also had you covered; you were fine."

Vincent rolled his eyes. "Just give me your dagger and get out of here, already."

"Oooh, eager for some alone time with Rinna, eh?"

"Vera!" Vincent shouted with warm cheeks.

Rinna tried to hide her laughter as Vera started to hand over her weapon to him.

"All right, all right, settle down, cranky. I'll be right ba—"

A high-pitched snarl suddenly echoed throughout the chamber.

As the three of them looked around for the source of the noise, Vera slowly took her dagger back into her possession. "On second thought, I'm going to hang onto this for a little longer."

"Yeah, you do that," Vincent agreed.

The three of them crept around with their weapons at the ready until another snarl soared through the air. Then another. And another. Each one sounded like a rabid wolf cub trying to intimidate its prey.

Rinna suddenly demanded their attention. "Look! Across the lake!"

On the other side of the water, in one of the corridor entrances, stood a group of dark-fleshed creatures no taller than a young child. Each of them hid its body beneath a black cloak and pointed hood. Had there been no light, they would have easily blended into the shadows. In every one of their hands was a rusted sickle that looked way too big a weapon for their size.

"Are those goblins?" Rinna asked.

"No, they're too short. Not fat enough either," Vincent answered.

Vera squinted to try to see them more clearly. "They're kinda cute."

Astounded, the other two stared at her blankly.

Vincent relaxed his guard. "They're all the way on the other side of the lake. Who cares what they are?"

As if they took his words personally, all of the little horrors started to snarl and chirp simultaneously while they smacked their blades against the ground. With the metallic echo behind their feral sounds, it was a rallying call that sounded like a flock of birds and a pack of wolves had teamed up against a common enemy. Then all of a sudden, they fell silent.

"You think the silence is a good thing, or…?" Vincent asked.

Then the horrors all stepped to the side to make way for another to come forth. From the back of the pack emerged a horror that looked identical to the rest, save for the extra sickle in its hand and its slightly larger height. It came to a halt at the front of the pack and raised one of its sickles at the three humans across the lake, and with an ear-piercing shriek, they charged.

"Bad, definitely bad," Vera said quickly.

Vincent chuckled as the pack approached the water's edge.

"What's so funny, Vince?!" Rinna demanded.

"Well, what are they going to do? Swim over here? Good luck with that one. Mr. Spooky Fish is about to have a nice buffet on his hands. Or his fins… whatever."

When the group of charging creatures reached the water, they did not stop, nor did they start to swim. They sprinted across the surface of the lake without ever slipping under.

"What?!" Vincent exclaimed with wide eyes.

"How are they doing that?!" Rinna asked in shock.

Vera readied herself. "Vince, I really wish you'd learn when to shut your mouth."

He sighed. "Yeah, me too. But look on the bright side, V."

"Cannot wait to hear what you think that could be."

"We haven't had a competition in a little while; I'd say we're about due for one, don't ya think?"

A smirk grew across Vera's face. "Okay, now we're talking. It's not really fair, though, since I'm down a weapon."

"Fine, here," Vincent said as he tossed her one of his sabers. "But no excuses when you lose, then."

The emerald star stone in the saber's crossguard turned red the moment it touched Vera's hand. She grinned as she twirled his saber in one hand and her dagger in the other. "Nice."

The three of them readied themselves as they watched the pack draw closer to their side of the lake. The lizard-like feet of the creatures slapped against the water's surface, filling the air with chaotic splashes. As soon as they finally reached the bank, they stopped. Their bright red eyes were now visible beneath their hoods. Each opened their thin mouths and hissed as their long tongues split down the middle and scaled the sides of their sickles.

"Are they... licking their blades?" Rinna asked in disbelief.

"These things might be creepier than you, V," Vincent joked.

She narrowed her eyes. "Ya know..."

The pack hissed again and charged toward them, chirping even louder as they closed the distance. Then the three of them plunged into battle.

One of the horrors leaped into the air with his sickle aimed at Vincent's face. He ducked underneath and shoved his saber through its chest. The creature let out an ear-piercing shriek as it died, forcing Vincent and the others to wince in pain. Another one took advantage of his disoriented state and slashed at his legs. Just before the rusted metal cut him open, Vincent parried the blade to the side. "Get outta here, you little freak!" he shouted as he followed up with a kick that sent the beast flying backward toward the lake. "Go for their throats or their heads, so they can't whine again," he called out to the others.

Rinna kept her weapon cloaked with her Favor, and with its range, she prevented any of the oncoming horrors from getting too close, thrusting and slicing the end of her staff into the necks of her attackers where she could, and quick to silence those she could not. Some of them were too afraid to even move, confused by her ability to thin the herd with seemingly no weapon.

"They're quick, but not too smart!" she shouted.

Quick as they were, Vera was much quicker. She ducked, side-stepping their reckless swings with ease, and sliced at their necks as she worked her way through the horde.

"I've got seven, V!" Vincent yelled over to her.

Four of the creatures charged Vera all at once. One of them jumped high while the others remained grounded. She threw her dagger up into the air for it to find its mark in the head of the beast above. She evaded a slash from the first attacker and kicked the beast behind her, but did not bother to avoid the next one. The horror swung at her and missed. She was gone.

Confused, the three creatures, now in a line, looked around in search of her. A whistle from the skies above drew their attention.

By the time the middle horror saw the incoming blade, it was too late. The other two helplessly watched as the dagger sank into their comrade's skull. Vera reappeared a second later, and with a pirouette, removed both of their heads. More and more began to close in on her from all angles. She tossed her dagger up into the air and vanished.

Vincent charged at the horror in front of him, ready to thrust his blade through it. Just before he got the chance, Vera's dagger impaled the side of its head, forcing Vincent to an abrupt halt. She appeared with a roll to her feet as the horror hit the ground.

"That makes thirteen for me," she boasted with a smirk.

"No. No, that is absolute thievery and definitely doesn't count," he protested.

"Awww, don't be mad," she said just before she vanished again.

A line of horrors started to assemble in front of Rinna. She took a deep breath and stepped back. With her weapon still cloaked, she started to twirl it in her hands. She slowly moved toward them, all the while maintaining the momentum of her weapon. Her feet pivoted with her hips as they twisted, her body and her weapon moving together as a synchronized unit. Every horror that made it into her range met its end beneath the invisible windmill of death she wielded in her hands.

As he slashed through the shark-toothed devils, Vincent began to notice the same feeling he had while training with Kai. Slowly, it started to consume his entire body, and the longer he fought, the more he was able to latch onto the experience. The fatigue and pain from their fall had begun to wane.

All of his senses seemed heightened. He felt stronger, faster, so in tune with the battle that he could see the horrors' attacks better than before. At first, he thought it was as if time had slowed down, but it was more like he knew what they were going to do before they did it. Despite the barrage of sounds flooding into his ears, he found himself able to focus on any one of them with tremendous clarity. The sound of water dropping into the lake from a distant cave wall. Rinna's blade as it sliced through the air. Vera's controlled breaths as she danced around her enemies. He heard everything, everywhere, all at once, and not at all.

All of this energy worked its way through him until it swelled in every part of his body, to the point where he no longer felt like he could contain it. Like an emotion locked behind bars of reason and sense, something inside him wanted out. He needed to figure out how to release the excess energy he had picked up, because now it had begun to hurt. As if he had overworked every one of his muscles, he was engulfed by a burning sensation. He gritted his teeth to bear the pain as he fought on. He needed to rid himself of it—but how? There had to be a way.

His pain grew and grew until it evolved into anger and frustration. More and more of the creatures kept coming at him, which only led to more and more pain. He could bear it no longer.

With his next attack, Vincent slashed at the air with all of his strength and fury as he shouted, "Get away from me!" While his blade came nowhere close to any of the horrors in front of him, a green crescent light burst from the edge of his saber and raced toward them. Too slow to dodge the incoming danger, every horror that stood in front of him found themselves severed and burned wherever the green light touched them. As Vincent stood stunned at what had just happened, he realized the burning sensation in his muscles had suddenly vanished.

"Did you guys see that?!" he shouted.

"Little busy winning over here," Vera reported. She pulled her dagger from the throat of a dead horror by her feet and found her next opponent slowly approaching her. The larger one of the pack, wielding an extra sickle, pointed at her with one of its blades and snarled.

Sarcastically bashful, Vera dusted the ground with her foot. "Aww, thanks. I think you're pretty cute, too, ya know."

A sickle from one of the creature's fallen comrades lay on the ground next to its foot. Not amused with her antics, it kicked the weapon at Vera and charged behind it. She swatted it away and dodged the slash that came after. Fueled by a fiery fury birthed from the desire to avenge, the horror did not let up. This one was much quicker than the others, almost rivaling Vera in speed. Its chaotic swings made each attack harder to read and predict. She tossed her dagger up in the air to strike from above, but when she appeared in the air, the horror had jumped up to greet her. With a heavy downward stroke of both its sickles, it swung at her. She blocked the attack with Vincent's saber at the last second, but was launched into the ground.

"I guess this means you don't want to be my pet," Vera groaned as she rose to her feet.

The horror hunched over slightly and hissed at her. She hissed back. The two of them charged at each other once again. As they continued to exchange attacks, a wounded horror on the ground behind Vera suddenly reached out and latched onto her ankle with its teeth. Slightly immobile, the larger creature lunged at her with a swipe of its rusted blade. Vera quickly pivoted on her planted foot and watched as the weapon just barely missed her midsection, but ever so slightly cut open the side of her thigh. The horror's lunge, although it did land a hit, left it wide open. In one swift motion, Vera sank Vincent's saber through the side of its head and embedded her dagger in the head of the one latched onto her ankle. Both of the beasts fell limp. As she went to retrieve her weapons, a gleam from beneath the larger horror's hood demanded her attention.

There on the ground, staring right back at her, were two gorgeously captivating ruby-red eyes. Their divine radiance forced an uncontrollable smile onto her face. She heard an unspoken call to draw closer, as if each eye were its own voiceless entity. Vera let go of her weapons—and her guard—and knelt on the ground, eager for further admiration.

Her hands reached out to the dark leathery cheeks of the felled creature and pulled its head against her own to get as close as possible to her newfound obsession. Its pointed, leathery nose pressed up right against her chin. While the horror lay motionless and cold, the light from its eyes continued to warmly caress her soul. She refused to blink, as if missing even a second of the beauty in front of her would deal her a pain unfathomable. The longer she gazed into the two jewels teeming with glamor, the more her world faded away as she slipped into the one she now craved.

"Vera!" Rinna shouted again, trying to warn her of the incoming danger. However, once again, she failed to do so.

Vera heard Rinna's warning calls; she just did not possess the ability to care about them, or anything else, for that matter, other than what was right in front of her. Victim to her trance, she was an easy, motionless target for the two horrors running right at her.

Rinna knew there was no hope of reaching her in time. She took aim with her weapon as if it were a spear. Just as the two creatures leaped into the air, she pulled back.

Just before she released her projectile, she watched a green crescent blade of light sever both assailants in half. The bodies fell right next to Vera, but still, she did not move.

With the horde of horrors finally eliminated and the coast seemingly clear, Rinna and Vincent both hurried over to Vera.

"Vince, did *you* do that?" Rinna asked.

"Yeah, tell ya later."

Rinna gently placed her hand on Vera's shoulder. "Vera... Hey!" She gave her a gentle shove. No response. "What's wrong with her?" she asked.

"I don't know, but let's get her away from this thing," Vincent said as he tried to pull away the horror she clung to. He pulled and pulled again, but found more resistance in her than he had expected. "Rin, can you pull her back?"

"She too strong for you?"

Vincent glared at her.

"Just teasing," she said with a smile. Rinna got behind Vera, wrapped her arms around her waist, and started to pull, while Vincent pulled on the horror in her hands. Finally, she let go. Rinna fell backward with Vera in her arms.

Vera still stared straight ahead at the eyes on the ground until Vincent noticed her line of sight and rolled the body over. Vera blinked for the first time in several minutes. She looked around and then tilted her head back to see that she was lying in Rinna's lap. She smiled. "You're comfy."

Rinna chuckled softly. "Glad to see you're okay."

As Vincent helped them both to their feet, Vera looked at her, confused. "Well, of course I'm okay, silly. Why wouldn't I be?"

Vincent and Rinna exchanged a look before Vincent answered her. "V, you almost died because you were too busy having a staring contest with a dead horror."

Her eyes widened. "Their eyes!"

"What about them?"

"They're so pretty! Didn't you see them?"

"Uh, yeah, I saw them. Didn't think they were anything worth dying over. You, Rinna?"

"Nope."

Vera filled up with excitement. "Oh, you just didn't get a good look, then. Here, let me show you!" She hurried to turn over the body on the ground before Vincent stepped in front of her.

"No, no, that's okay. We believe you."

"Aww, but you'll love them! They're so breathtaking!" Vera looked at the back of the horror's head as if she could see the eyes through it.

"Their sickles were about to be taking *your* breath had we not done anything," Vincent joked.

Vera did not hear his words. "Do you think we could take one with us?" she asked. Wide eyes and an even wider smile darted from Vincent to Rinna and back as she anxiously awaited their approval.

Vincent looked at her strangely. "Uh, no, we're not taking one with us."

"Although they would make a decent ally if you could train one," Rinna thought out loud.

Vera whipped around to her, full of excitement.

Rinna snapped out of her momentary daze when she saw Vincent's horrified look of betrayal. "But no. We can't take one with us. Sorry, hon," she said in a hurry. She placed a consoling hand on Vera's shoulder when her head fell to the ground in disappointment.

"You need to get back to Kai and the others," Vincent said.

"Who?" Vera asked.

"You."

"Oh, well, lead the way, then!"

"What? No, you need to use your Favor to get back to them."

"Who owes me a favor?"

"What?" Dumbfounded, Vincent looked at her, concerned. "Seriously, V, what is your problem right now?"

She smiled widely. "I have no problems!"

Vincent started to talk slower. "You are going to give me your dagger, and then, you are going to relocate to your other dagger, which is with Bear or—"

"A bear has my dagger?!" Vera blurted out.

Vincent placed his fingers on his temples and let out a deep breath of frustration as he walked to retrieve his other saber from the ground.

Rinna placed her hands on Vera's shoulders. "Vera, honey."

"Helllooooo."

"You know how you can relocate to your daggers?"

"Yup, yup, yup. Wanna see me do it?!"

"No, no, that's okay. You only have one of your daggers right now, right?"

"Yeah, I lost the other one," Vera responded, pouting.

"That's okay, Alex or Barrik has it."

Vera gasped. "Did they steal it?!"

"Yes, they did. And you have to go get it back now."

Vera slammed her fist into her palm. "They're gonna get it!"

"But first, you have to let us borrow this dagger. Then you can come back to us once you have the other one, okay?"

"Okay!" Vera pulled out her dagger and held it out for her, but when Vincent went to take it instead, she pulled it back. "I'm not giving it to *you.*"

"Rinna can't hold it. You know this. Just give it to me already."

Vera clung to her weapon and looked at him suspiciously.

"It's okay, hon; he can hold it."

"Okay, if you say so." She handed it out to him, but once he went to take it again, she recoiled and started laughing. "Too slow!"

Vincent glared at her. "Give it," he said sternly.

"Oooooh, someone's grumpy," she whispered to Rinna. Vera leaned toward him with the blade in her hand and a smirk on her face.

"Vera, I swear to the stars, if you…"

As soon as Vincent took the dagger, Vera reached out with her other hand and pressed his nose like a button. "Boop."

Rinna curled her lips and quickly threw her hands up over her mouth to hide her smile. Vincent slowly exhaled his anger as he tucked the blade into his belt. "We'll be right here when you get back."

"Yes, sir!" she said with a salute. She snickered to herself and waved her hands in the air. "Poof!" she said—just before she vanished.

Vincent stood in silence and shook his head in disbelief for a moment before he looked over to Rinna, at a loss for words. She continued to hide her smile.

"Did she just boop me?" Vincent finally asked.

That was it. Rinna could conceal her enjoyment no longer. She burst out into laughter. At first, he was annoyed, but it was only a short time before the sound of her laughter entirely extinguished his embers of anger.

He could not help but smile. "Enjoying yourself, are you?"

As Rinna's laughter slowly came to a halt, she held up her index and thumb fingers close together. "Maybe a little."

With a gentle roll of his eyes, he sat down against a nearby column.

"Come on, it was a little funny," Rinna said as she sat down next to him.

"I guess. But why was she acting so weird? Weirder than normal, anyway. First, she's obsessed with that thing's eyes, then it's like I was talking to a child. Not to mention, she almost got herself killed."

"Maybe that bigger one cast a spell on her," Rinna said.

Vincent raised an eyebrow at her. "You think those things can wield Sanorian magic?"

She shrugged. "I don't know. It was just the first thing I thought of."

"Well, whatever it was, I hope it isn't permanent. She's rabid enough as it is."

Rinna shoved him gently. "Be nice."

"Relax, I'm only joking… mostly."

"So mean."

He shrugged.

"Well, what do we do now?" Rinna asked as she looked around the chamber.

"Hopefully, Kai has some sort of idea of how to regroup, but until Vera comes back, I guess we just wait here." Vincent crossed his arms and leaned his head back against the stone column with his eyes closed. "Maybe take a short nap until then."

As they grew silent, the ambient echoes of water flowing from the river and splashing into the lake swam throughout the vast space. Rinna's eyes followed another set of iron tracks on the other side of the lake around the chamber as if they were a distant tour guide illustrating various outlets, mining stations, and a rest area with wooden tables and benches. Beams of moonlight spilled through the holes above to shimmer on the lake's surface and reflect off all the grayish stone, making it appear to shine several shades brighter. When the tracks led her gaze to the stairs that rested at the bottom of the arched stone doors, her eyes lingered. Without the presence of danger, the more she observed their environment, the more she found it uniquely beautiful. She studied every little detail over and over again until she was certain the image would be forever clear in her mind.

"Hey, Vince," she said softly, breaking the silence.

His eyes remained closed. "Hmm?"

"Do you think you could teach me the fire sign?"

"The fire sign?" He opened his eyes and looked at her. "Why do you want to know?"

She shrugged. "Seems like it can be pretty useful."

"All right," he said with a yawn. "Do you know anything about how to use signs?"

"Not really. All I know is it's the only kind of Sanorian magic we are able to wield without drinking from the fountain. But I never understood why more people don't use them."

"Well, they take an incredible amount of focus to learn, and they aren't powerful enough to be used as an attack, which is why you only see crafters use them. As our gramps always said, 'Do not mistake these for weapons. They are tools. Use them as such.'"

"He's the blacksmith who made all your weapons, right?"

"Right." Vincent drew one of his sabers and set it flat on the ground in front of them. "Okay. First thing you want to do is take a few deep breaths. Then take your left hand, or your right, I guess—it doesn't matter, just whichever you want to use—and make a fist. Then, with your other hand, place it on whatever you're trying to ignite." Vincent placed the palm of his right hand on the blade of his weapon. "Then you lift your middle two fingers up. Now, put them down, making a fist again. Now raise your index finger and your pinky. Then make a fist again. Okay, good, now make a circle with your thumb and index finger while your other three fingers are up."

"Like this?" Rinna asked as she held up her fingers.

"Yup. You'll just have to practice the movement a bunch, because you have to do it all pretty quickly. So here, watch." Vincent ran through the hand motion much faster this time, and almost as soon as his fingers reached the final position, his blade began to breathe an orange flame.

Rinna looked on with amazement. "How long will it last?"

"Something like metal will only burn as long as I'm touching it somewhere. It needs a source of energy to continue to burn." He removed his hand, and she watched as the flames vanished without a trace, as if they had all been blown out by a rush of wind. "But if you use it on something like a tree, then the fire will act normally and burn until something puts it out. Give it a try."

"All right," Rinna said, placing her palm against the blade of his weapon. As soon as her skin felt the blade, she recoiled slightly. "It's cold."

"Since the blade doesn't burn, the flames only become *attached* to it. Once they're gone, so is their heat."

She closed her eyes and took a few deep breaths. When she opened them again, she made her fingers go through the same positions Vincent had shown her, but when she reached the final position, nothing happened.

"Did I do it right?" she asked, frowning.

"Yeah, you did; it just has to be a little faster. Once you get the finger movement down, you'll feel the warmth in the palms of your hands. Then you just kind of push it out. Actually, here, Gramps did this to us, and it helped us learn the feeling a little faster." Vincent laid his hand against the blade. "Place your hand on top of mine."

Although her palm felt ice cold against his skin, a rush of warmth washed over him. He cleared the lump from his throat and continued, "This should help you get a sense of what it feels like."

As Vincent ran his other hand through the movements, Rinna felt a wave of heat flow from beneath her hand, and once again, the blade lit up in flames.

"Okay, now, slowly slide your hand off of mine and onto the blade."

"It's not going to burn?"

"No." He laughed. "We are the source of the flames, so they won't hurt us."

She trusted his words and did as he said. "Now what?"

"Close your eyes."

Once he saw that her eyes were closed, Vincent removed his hand from the blade, only this time the flames remained.

Rinna's face lit up with a bright smile. "I can feel it now. It's like a calming breath of heat. What did you do?"

"Open your eyes."

When she opened her eyes, she saw his hand no longer there, and almost instantly, the flames vanished again.

Disappointment and confusion washed over her face. "What happened?"

Vincent smiled. "I started the flames, but had you maintain them. They vanished once you realized my hand was gone, because you thought they should. I told you it takes a lot of concentration."

"I never would have guessed signs to be so tricky."

"You'll get the hang of it for yourself; just be patient. It took me a few weeks just to move my fingers fast enough."

"Is that the only one you know?"

"Gramps taught us all the blacksmithing ones, but that's it."

"Was he also a Guardian?"

"Who, Gramps? No, he's a regular old blacksmith. Just our mother was a Guardian."

"In all of Sylva?" Rinna looked shocked.

"No, no, there are others. I just meant close to us."

"Do you miss them?"

"Of course." Vincent fell silent for a moment, a cloud of home-sickness settling over him. "I just wish I could talk with her about all of this." He gestured to the three-stoned sword on his hip.

"Your mom?"

Vincent nodded. "I don't know what she'd say exactly, but I know she would make me feel better about it all. She just has a way of making you feel like everything is going to be all right."

Rinna smiled warmly. "She sounds lovely."

"She is," Vincent said, his expression softening. "Without her, we wouldn't have lasted two days outside of Sylva."

"Well, I can't wait to meet her."

Vincent looked at her suspiciously. "You have plans to travel to Sylva sometime soon, do you?"

She nodded her head once, still smiling. "Yup. You're going to take me and show me all around."

He laughed at her demands. "Oh, am I, now?"

"Yup," she shrugged. "Sorry, but those are the rules."

He smiled softly. "Looks like I don't have much of a choice, then."

"So, you'll take me one day?"

"One day."

"You promise?"

"Yeah, I promise."

"All right, I'm going to hold you to that, you know?"

"Hey, I take sacred oaths such as these very seriously."

Rinna smiled. "Good."

As the two of them sat up against the column, awaiting Vera's return, Rinna's eyes became heavy and her head harder to keep upright. The more her consciousness dipped into her dreams, the more her head fell until it drifted all the way to Vincent's shoulder. There they waited, with warm silence wrapping around them like a worn blanket.

CHAPTER 13

ERA hopped up to her feet and moved around. With the imp's saliva no longer affecting her body, she found herself almost entirely back to normal, save for a few minor ailments.

"How do you feel?" Toran asked.

"The cut burns like crazy. I'm a little dizzy, and it feels like there's a troll in my head throwing a tantrum."

"Can you walk? Or better yet, run?" Kai asked.

"I'd rather not, but it won't kill me... I don't think."

"Good. I want you to go back to Vince and Rinna and look around the chamber for anything worth noting. Don't take any paths or pull any levers. All I'm looking for is a layout of what's down there. And try not to make any noise. We don't need any more unnecessary conflicts."

"That's it?"

"For now."

"All right." In the blink of an eye, she was gone again.

Everyone grew restless with no way of communicating, no way of telling just how much time had passed, and no way of knowing what was happening in Vera's absence.

Alexandra tried to pace away her impatience, with no success. "What's taking her so long?"

"You don't think they found more imps, do you? Or maybe something worse? What if this time they aren't so lucky?!" Toran worried out loud with a disturbed look on his face.

"I'm sure they're fine. Just be patient," Kai said. Although the knot in his stomach that continued to wind itself tighter suggested otherwise.

As more silence passed and their impatience reached its limit, suddenly, there was a noise from one of the nearby channels. Everyone's eyes turned to its entrance and remained fixed with their hands on their weapons. The sound drew closer, louder. Echoes of... voices?

Vincent popped his head around the corner. "You miss me?"

"Vince!" Barrik and Alexandra cried simultaneously, delightfully surprised. She rushed over and threw her arms around him. Vincent curled his lip and furrowed his brow, uncomfortable in her embrace. She reached up to inspect the wound on the side of his head, but he quickly swatted away her hand. "Stop touching me. I'm fine."

"You're such a baby. I'm glad you guys are okay," Alexandra said as she pulled Rinna in closely.

"Yeah, we're still in one piece. Vera seems like she's back to her usual self again too. She said the imp's saliva is what made her all loony?"

Alexandra recoiled slighlty. "Gross, right?"

Rinna turned up her nose. "Extremely."

"Well, if you think it's gross, how do you think *I* feel?" Vera complained.

"Unfortunately, though, it seems like the effects haven't entirely worn off," Kai said.

Vera looked at him, confused. "What do you mean?"

"Well, I specifically told you not to do anything besides give me a layout of the land. And since you would never deliberately disregard my instruction…" He glared at her. "…that could be the only possible explanation."

She scratched the back of her head with a nervous smile as Kai walked past her into the channel they had just come from.

"We're going back down?"

"Correct."

Vera's shoulders shrank. "Ugh."

As they reentered the vast chamber, Vincent welcomed them all with a wave of his hand as if it were his own home.

Kai carefully studied their new environment. "This place is… old," he said quietly to himself.

The newcomers looked around, astonished, as Vincent pointed out where everything had occurred.

"Over there is where the river dumped us out, which is also where Vera left us for fish food." He glared at her. She smiled widely in return as he continued. "Over there is where the imps came out, and as you can see from all the bodies over there, that's where I killed way more of them than Vera did."

Vera narrowed her eyes at him. "What was your final count?"

Vincent stood proudly. "Fourteen."

"You swear?"

Vincent placed his hand on his chest. "On our mother."

Vera smirked. "Seventeen."

"What?! You're still doped up on imp juice; there's no way you got seventeen! Are you counting the bigger one as two?"

Alexandra pretended to vomit. "Imp juice?"

Vera crossed her arms. "Nope. We've always agreed big ones only count as one. It's an honest and true seventeen. Face it, Vince, you lost."

"Well, my kills were more important," Vincent said.

"They were not."

"You'd be dead if I didn't kill those last two!"

Rinna thought back to the green beam of light that had raced past her. "Yeah, I almost forgot about that; how *did* you do that?"

"I don't know what I did, exactly; I just kind of did it."

Kai suddenly grew intrigued. "Did what?"

"I don't know how to describe it, exactly. It was like I was about to overflow, I guess. Everything burned, and I didn't know what to do to stop it, but when I slashed at the air, this green light came out from my saber and sliced a few of those things in half."

"You took in too much energy. Like I told you not to."

"I didn't do it on purpose!"

"I know. But you're going to need to learn how sooner than later. Your body can only handle so much energy at once. That's why it was burning you. But when you released it, you felt better, right?"

"Yeah."

"Good. Until you can learn to control it, whenever you get that feeling again, just let it go before it starts to burn again. I'll teach you more control when we get back to Meditas, but for now, we need to find a way to the other side."

Toran eagerly chimed in from the back of the group. "My great-grandfather used to be a miner in the lands beyond the Ankar Mountains. He always used to ramble on about levers or hidden stones that, when pushed, would open doors and secret pathways. Although I don't know why they would have such things. What's the point of hiding stuff? Sounds like more trouble than necessary, if you ask me."

Kai squinted and let his eyes wander over the far side of the lake for anything of interest. "Bandits, cave horrors, paranoia… There are all sorts of reasons to make it more difficult for any intruder to find their way to your precious gems and stones. It was their livelihood, after all." He turned to Vera. "You think you can make the throw?"

Vera glared at him, unhappy with the underlying doubt within his question. She easily launched one of her daggers to the other side of the lake and vanished. When she reappeared on the far bank, she took a bow.

Kai hung his head and sighed. "I didn't even tell her what to look for yet."

Alexandra consolingly patted Kai on the shoulder and looked around as Vera searched the far side.

Barrik nudged one of the imps with his foot and grimaced. "Creepy little things." He looked at Vincent and pointed to the creature on the ground. "Relative of yours?" he asked with a victorious smile.

"HA! Good one!" Vincent said with a toss of his eyes.

Toran picked up a pile of small rocks and began throwing them into the water to pass the time. Each splash gave life to tiny ripples that aimlessly wandered across the surface of the lake until their waves stretched too thin to continue their journey.

"At least you guys fell into water," Alexandra said as she watched one of Toran's rocks disappear beneath the lake's surface.

Barrik gently nudged Rinna with his elbow. "How bad did Vince freak out in the water?"

She laughed. "Like a child denied sweets at the market. But in his defense, there was something chasing us."

"Again," Vincent said, gesturing to himself, "land creature."

"How big was it?" Barrik asked.

"Oh, gee, Bear, ya know I forgot to ask for its weight. How silly of me! Why don't you go in for a little dip and find out?"

"I'm good, thanks."

With another splash from one of Toran's rocks, two grotesque dorsal fins emerged from the water briefly and dove back underneath. Toran dropped the rest of the rocks in his hands and slowly backed away from the water's edge. "Me too."

Vera suddenly appeared at his side as he continued to back away and crashed into him. Both of them rolled on the ground briefly before she hopped to her feet.

"Ya know, Toran, you really should watch where you're going," Vera said jokingly as she pulled him to his feet and brushed him off.

"What? You were way over there just a moment ago! How was I supposed to—"

"Did you find anything?" Kai asked as he interrupted Toran's complaints.

"I found some sort of wooden lever-looking thingy, but I thought I should ask before I pulled it."

"Okay, what's it—"

Kai stopped as the ground beneath their feet began to rumble.

Everyone looked around nervously, searching for the source of the tremors. A little way down the rocky shore, they could see a wide, arched walkway of wet stone that began to rise up from the depths of the lake. Water rushed off the sides of the bridge like small waterfalls and splashed into the lake until it finally came to a halt.

Kai turned to Vera. "I thought you said you thought you should ask before pulling the lever?"

"Yeah, I did. But I only thought that *after* I pulled it." She smiled widely at him.

He let out a deep breath and closed his eyes for a moment. "Let's go."

On the other side of the lake, Kai briefly peered down into the darkness of the other channels before he returned his focus to the two arched beige stone doors. As they all stood at the bottom of the stairs, they could see two intricate engravings carved into each of the doors. The one on the left was of a human skull with its jaw agape, as if it were screaming. Kai walked up the steps and traced over it with his fingers, so smooth against his skin; there was no sign of wear, age, or any imperfection at all. It was the same for the adjacent door: a rose, meticulously carved to perfectly resemble the flower commonly chosen to demonstrate one's affection. He took a step back with a puzzled look on his face as his thoughts wandered.

Barrik stepped up to the doors and pushed them. Nothing. He pushed again, harder this time, but still, they would not budge. Defeated, he took a few steps back.

Toran eyed the doors up and down curiously. "The Sanorians used to seal important things behind doors like this, didn't they? Maybe it's a riddle of some sort. Or they have a hidden key stashed away somewhere we have to find," he said, starting to look around the immediate area.

"I don't think it's a key; there's no place to insert it. It looks like an ordinary wall," Barrik said.

"Love and death," Kai whispered to himself.

Rinna could see him piecing together a potential solution in his mind. "What is it, Kai?"

"Toran's right."

Toran turned around, shocked. "I am?"

"Well, partly. It is a sort of riddle, and we do need a key, but not the one you're thinking of. The door is sealed with a spell, old Sanorian magic."

"So how do we open it, then?" Alexandra asked.

"The Sanorians were romantics. Lovers of poetry, metaphors, and symbolism. I think our 'key' is going to be something that can simultaneously represent both love and death."

"Like a kiss?" Vincent asked.

Alexandra looked at him with an eyebrow raised. "A kiss?"

He shrugged. "What? You never heard of the kiss of death?"

"Oh, you're right. Maybe that *is* the key. Why don't you lay one on the door, then, and see if it opens up?" A mischievous grin followed Alexandra's suggestion.

"Me? Why me?"

"Your idea, your duty."

"You did suggest it," Barrik added.

"There's no way I'm—"

Vera cut him off. "No time to argue. Pucker up, lover boy."

Barrik placed his hands on Vincent's shoulders and ushered him to the door before he could back away. As he now stood face to face with the sealed wall, he could feel everyone's eyes on him. He turned around. Kai was the only one not watching. He seemed to be lost in his own thoughts.

"Hurry up," Alexandra said with a chuckle.

Vincent turned back around. "This is ridiculous."

Everyone behind him snickered and chuckled as they made poor attempts to stifle their laughter.

"You guys are so cruel to each other," Rinna whispered with a smile.

Another moment of hesitation passed before finally, illuminated under the spotlight of embarrassment, Vincent shut his eyes tightly and pressed his lips to the wall. He pulled away quickly, his horrified expression only forcing everyone's laughter to new heights.

Alexandra clutched her side and found a moment between tufts of laughter to ask, "Hey, Vince, how's it feel knowing your first kiss was with a door?"

He glared at her. "Ha ha. Ya know, if I remember correctly, your first kiss was with Rucker's older brother."

"What's wrong with that? He's a cutie. Besides, at least it was with something that breathes."

"Yeah, mouth-breathes."

"Hey, I do that in my sleep," Toran unnecessarily added.

Barrik patted him on the back. "We know."

"If you all are done horsing around, I think I know what the actual answer is," Kai said, putting an end to all of the giggles. To everyone's surprise, he unsheathed his katana and sliced open his hand.

"What are you doing?!" Rinna asked in shock.

Kai placed his bloody hand against the door, and a moment later, the stone began to grind against the floor. He turned back to the others and held up the cut on his palm. "Blood."

Vera crossed her arms. "That's a lame answer."

Kai took a step away from the opening doors. "As I said, the Sanorians were romantics. A lot of their poems and stories contain some kind of duality. They loved the idea that one thing could represent multiple concepts."

As the doors opened further, a rush of air greeted them all with the soul-warming scent of sun-kissed flowers. Everyone closed their eyes and took a deep breath.

"What is that?" Alexandra asked before she took another breath.

Toran could not get enough of the aroma. "Smells like my mom's garden. She plants all kinds of flowers and stuff. She could grow anything anywhere, truly. Vegetables, trees, herbs, fruits, if it grows in the ground, she can do it."

Beyond the doors lay a great hall, its stone walls and pillars as dark as ash. At the far end, they could see a little pool of water gathered in a small pit beneath a toppled support pillar. Above, where the damaged column of stone used to touch the ceiling, was a large hole that invited the moon inside to cast its elegant illumination throughout the room. The remaining support pillars stretched to the ceiling from a floor covered by a sea of motley flowers that all contributed to the floral fragrance swimming in the air. An endless wave of colorful petals slept underneath the moon's blanket of soft white light. Everyone wandered inside and tiptoed around the garden under their feet.

A smile of disbelief washed over Rinna's face. "How did all of these grow down here? No sun, no water, yet they couldn't be in better health."

"Can your mother do *that*, Toran?" Vincent asked.

He stopped for a moment. "Probably."

Alexandra started to move slowly toward the pool of water at the far end of the hall. She felt almost entranced by the sight of the moon washing over the water below. Something drew her in. It called to her—something unseen, unheard, beyond her comprehension. Whether she knew it or not, she no longer moved of her own volition. She was being pulled.

"Hey, Kai," Barrik called to him. There was a softness in his voice—a softness that accompanied pity.

At the sound of his words, before he ever saw what Barrik wanted to show him, Kai knew what he had found. He had long known in his heart already, but now he walked toward the undesired confirmation. No longer could he hide under the covers of ignorance and disbelief.

Barrik and Toran stood in the corner of the room, where just in front of them slept the skeletal remains of someone clad in metal armor, two small axes still gripped tightly in their bony hands. On the breastplate, shining bright and true, was the engraving of the Meditas fountain. Vines overgrown with flowers snaked their way all around the bones, in and out of the armor. A rose rested in the left eye socket with a burst of bright red petals.

Kai knelt on the ground and took in a deep breath of acceptance. "Was this...?" Barrik started to ask.

Kai nodded slowly. "This is Gala." He smiled softly and gently placed his hand on Gala's cheek. His thumb rested just below the rose he now looked into as if she could still see him. "A dear friend." When he exhaled his grief, a single tear escaped his watery eyes—a tear that contained every one of the memories he cherished with the distant person so close to him now.

Barrik placed his hand on Kai's shoulder. "I'm sorry."

Alexandra stared into the tiny pond bordered by a perimeter of crushed stone. Just beyond her reflection in the shallow water slept a garden of the very flowers beneath her feet. Somehow thriving fully submerged in water, the flowers drank in the light of the moon and turned its illumination into their own. Each one radiated its own saturated iridescence that shimmered upon Alexandra's face. She had discovered a new treasure, and with it, an unwavering lust to have it. She *needed* it.

Barrik looked over Gala's remains and began to wonder. "Kai, I don't mean to be rude, but she wouldn't have been here all that long. At least, not long enough to—"

"To be nothing but bone," Kai said, finishing Barrik's thought. Something unnerved him. He had missed something somewhere. What was it? He backed away from Gala and studied her. His eyes fell to the rose in her eye socket, exploding with ethereal petals of ephemeral beauty—an image that closely resembled the engravings on the door. He turned around. The door had been resealed. Love and death. He turned back to Gala. She had found her end in the depths of the world, slain by the unknown, left to be forgotten, yet she appeared calm. She was at peace; a monument of nature; she was beautiful.

"A beautiful death," Kai whispered.

"What?" Barrik asked, confused.

Kai's eyes darted back and forth as he scavenged through his mind. The more he pieced everything together, the faster he spoke. "We got it wrong. The engravings weren't depicting love and death; it was a beautiful death."

Alexandra's knees dropped to the ground. She slowly reached out with her left hand to grace her fingers with the flowers' touch.

"But what about your blood?" Toran asked. "It still let us in. What does a beautiful death mean? What's going on, Kai?"

Kai shook his head. "Blood may still have been the answer, but that doesn't matter right now. We need to leave before it wakes up."

As soon as Alexandra's fingers breached the water's surface, a large gust of wind suddenly rushed across the room and started drawing all of the flowers in the chamber toward the water. Each one pulled through the air, carefully guided to their new location. Alexandra recoiled her hand and started to back away quickly, until something crunched under her feet. The bed of floral beauty that slept on the floor no longer concealed the horrid truth beneath. The fragrant curtain was forcefully removed to unveil a garden of bones. She stared down at the cracked skull under her leather boot, horrified.

Kai grabbed her by the shoulder, startling her. "Time to go."

As they rushed toward the exit, they could now see, just before the doors, three more bodies dressed in Meditas armor—the rest of Gala's team.

Kai placed the same bloodied hand against the sealed doors, and slowly, they opened.

Rinna's eyes locked onto one of the skeletons on the ground. Its arm was still stretched out, reaching for the door—reaching for life.

"What were they running from?" she whispered. "What are *we* running from?"

Kai turned back around to face them all. His eyes focused on the mound of flowers at the far end of the hall, piling on top of one another with purpose. They were building something.

"It's called a Soul Eater. Tell the king this is how the village and Gala's team met their end. Your mission is complete." He looked back at the incomplete structure of flowers. "Mine has just begun."

Rinna looked at Kai with sudden realization. "Wait—you're staying behind?"

"I am. This is something I must do, and I must do it alone."

"If you're going to stay and fight it, then let us help!" Alexandra exclaimed.

"You can't. One look into its eyes, and you'll end up like Gala and her team."

"We're not just going to leave you here!" Vincent protested.

"You said it yourself, you can't fight it!" Barrik shouted.

"I said *you* can't."

A wicked voice suddenly crawled through the air to invade their ears. Each word slithered through their minds with a bite of venomous fear in every one of their bones.

"Not a day goes by where I do not hunger."

Kai's eyes widened. "It's already awake," he whispered to himself. "You have to leave! Now!"

Alexandra could see that his entire demeanor had changed in an instant. His voice was panicked, face glistening with sweat, eyes full of terror. He was practically trembling. She realized he was not asking for them to leave, nor was he commanding them; he was begging. Her heart felt heavy.

"Everyone out!" she commanded.

Vera tried to argue, "You can't be—"

"Now!" Alexandra shouted fiercely.

In a reluctant hurry, everyone followed her orders and rushed out the doors.

Kai's hand briefly fell upon Alexandra's shoulder as she passed him by. His grip was firm, yet shaky. "Get them back safely," he whispered. The weight of his decision was clear in his eyes.

She gave him no words, but once she met his eyes, she was suddenly struck by the thought, *Is this goodbye?* With a quick nod of acknowledgment, she hurried to the front of the group.

The knot in Vincent's stomach twisted painfully, forcing him to stop. "This isn't right! Let us help you!" he shouted.

Kai closed the distance between them in a second and gently pulled Vincent's head close against his. With his palm softly laid against the back of Vincent's neck, the only thing Vincent could see were the oceans in Kai's eyes.

"Vince, how will I ever be able to find my peace in the stars alongside your father if you're there to greet him with me?"

Vincent's heart fell to the depths of his stomach. Leaving Kai behind felt like an indescribably visceral betrayal.

"Vince, come on, let's go!" Alexandra called after him.

Vincent clenched his jaw to dam the tears in his eyes. "You better be right behind us," he choked out, his words heavy with unspoken fears.

Kai smiled softly. "I will be."

Vincent ripped himself away and took off after the others. Alexandra looked over her shoulder and watched as the doors closed, with Kai inside. Her throat tightened as her eyes started to water.

"Goodbye," she whispered.

CHAPTER 14

AI let out a breath of relief. Now that the others were safe, his panic and fear quickly faded away. When he turned back to the flowers, he could see what they had been constructing. Now a chair with a high back and massive armrests sat on top of the water.

A throne.

He reached up to the piece of cloth holding back his silver hair and pulled it down tightly over his eyes. With his foot, he swept away the bones at his feet and positioned himself on the ground with his legs crossed and his katana gently laid across his lap. Each of his steady breaths was calm and deep.

"Your arrogance amazes me, human."

From the wall above the floral throne emerged a horror, large enough to touch the high ceiling, as if it were a ghost with no solid form. A thin layer of white emaciated skin pulled tautly across its bones hid underneath a soot-gray cloak tattered and torn all over. It floated down gracefully into its royal throne of vibrant flowers.

Kai was no longer able to see, but was far from blind. He could *feel* everything around him with incredible detail. His normal vision could hardly compare.

"You shield your eyes from me?" the Soul Eater asked, drawing out each and every one of its words. "You are aware of my kind, then. But do not think that will be your salvation." It raised its hand, and just like with the flowers before, all of the bones on the ground now flew through the air to their summoned location. The mass grave of human remains assembled into a scythe the size of an elder tree.

Kai tried to keep his heart from slamming against his chest.

The Soul Eater leaned forward in its seat and jerked its head to the side like a dog, observing Kai's actions. "It is folly for you to try and stifle your fear from me, human. It pours out of you, filling my throne room with the delicious aroma of your soul." It took a deep inhale. "Yours is quite… intriguing."

"Reconcile with your confusion, soul stealer. What you smell is far from fear." Kai picked up his katana and smiled viciously. "It's exhilaration."

Everyone's footsteps seemed to fall heavier and heavier the farther they ran away. Thoughts of helplessness and guilt twisted nauseating knots in each of their stomachs. While their escape was accompanied by a silent tension, their minds were beset with a barrage of questions.

Vincent felt his stomach twist and turn. With every step he took, he felt closer to throwing up. He hated the idea of leaving Kai behind to fend for himself. It felt like an unforgivable crime he would forever regret.

What would his father do in this situation? Just abandon Kai and continue on? Or would he find a way to help him? He was wracked with indecision. He started to think Ghost was right. Living up to his father's image was significantly more challenging than he had anticipated.

All he knew now was that he desperately wanted to turn around.

"This isn't right!" Vincent snapped, coming to an abrupt halt.

Everyone stopped in their tracks. Alexandra turned back around to him. "You heard what Kai said. This is our only option."

"Leaving him to die?!"

"We didn't leave him to die!" Alexandra insisted. "He said *we* can't fight it, which means he can, but there's no way we could have helped him. All we would do is get in his way."

"I just… I don't want to lose him," Vincent said softly.

"I don't either. But maybe this is the best way to ensure that we don't."

"But how is he supposed to win against something without seeing it?" Toran questioned.

Alexandra's eyes fell to the ground. "I don't know."

"He also said our mission is complete, but I don't understand anything," Vincent added.

"I guess whatever this Soul Eater thing is killed the entire village?" Barrik suggested.

Eyes still locked to the cave floor, Alexandra shook her head and repeated, "I don't know."

"If it killed the whole village, why did it take so long to show itself to us?" Rinna asked.

Alexandra clenched her fists tightly to suppress her emotions. "I don't know."

"What are we supposed to do if Kai doesn't come back?" Vera wondered.

There were too many questions, and Alexandra had no answers. Everyone had put their trust in her to take the lead in Kai's absence, but she quickly began to feel as though she was undeserving of the responsibility. Her eyes started to water. "I don't know. I don't know. I don't *know*, okay? I don't know if we'll ever see Kai again. I don't know what to make of any of this." The lump in her throat forced her to pause. "I don't know what's going to happen." She could feel everyone's silent gaze on her as she tightly closed her eyes, gathered herself, and took a deep breath before she continued, "All I do know is that we swore an oath to him before we started this mission, and as much as it hurts, and as wrong as it feels, I would like to keep my word. He put his faith in us; he deserves the same in return."

She looked around the group. "Right now, we just have to make it home."

Everyone remained silent for a moment.

With a soft smile, Rinna placed her hand on Alexandra's shoulder and said, "Lead the way."

Alexandra's teary gaze wandered from person to person until it finally drifted to Vincent.

She was right, he thought. As much as it hurt, they weren't abandoning Kai—they were honoring his choice. They had sworn an oath, not only to him, but as Guardians. And now, their mission was clear: get everyone back to Meditas.

The guilt still churned in his chest, but he forced himself to focus. His mind was scattered, full of uncertainty—but one thing he had always been sure of was his trust in Alexandra. He knew she shared his current feelings, yet still she maintained her composure. Without her leadership, they would likely falter. And in order for her to lead them, she needed his affirmation.

So, with a nod, he reaffirmed Rinna's words. "We chose you for a reason," he said with quiet confidence.

She responded with a gentle look of gratitude and turned to guide them all to safety.

Kai ducked beneath the Soul Eater's scythe and rolled behind one of the stone pillars. The creature sliced again, cutting the pillar in half. Stones and dust tumbled to the ground; Kai, however, was already gone. He dashed behind his foe and slashed at its pale ankles. The Soul Eater howled as it whipped around with its scythe low to the ground, but failed to find its target. Kai had slipped it again. The Soul Eater started to slowly walk down the center of the hall, carefully searching for its prey.

"Why do you draw out the inevitable?" the Soul Eater hissed. Each of its words crept their way through the air like a threatening whisper. There was no answer.

"You think *I* can be slain by anything crafted by you pathetic humans? I've felled Sanorian's twice your size and capability."

"And you'll fall to a pathetic human," Kai called out from behind a pillar.

The Soul Eater quickly moved to where Kai's words came from and slashed as he stepped around the pillar. Nothing. Kai dashed behind him again with another attack.

The Soul Eater turned around quickly. "I no longer find your arrogance amusing," it said as it started hunting Kai once again.

Kai sat in silence as he was stalked, waiting for the moment to slip from his cover of darkness to inflict another wound on his victim—*his* prey.

"There is a strange scent about you, human—a familiar scent I have yet to place. Perhaps I will not be able to completely recollect its origin until I devour you. You will find no peace in whichever afterworld you humans pray to. Your gods cannot help you. You will meet the same end as all those before you."

Kai fell from the air and sank his katana into the Soul Eater's back. Unfazed, the creature reached behind itself to tear off the intruder. Kai ripped his blade out with a twist and fell to the ground. He could hear the scythe of bones howl through the air above him. Quickly, he rolled to the side just as it slammed into the ground next to him. Again, he disappeared.

"Pathetic!" the Soul Eater shouted. "Your kind is nothing! Worthless! Insolent pests. No longer able to worship the Sanorians, you are left with no purpose. You are a plague on the world—a plague that will soon be cleansed."

"What are you talking about?" Kai's voice seemed to come from everywhere.

"Your kind has long been overdue for the extermination that is now upon you."

The Soul Eater glided across the floor of stone and crushed bones to where it had placed Kai's voice, but yet again, it was mistaken. Kai dashed out from the shadows to slice the horror once more. The Soul Eater took another frantic slash through the air.

"Enough of these games!" the Soul Eater growled in frustration.

"Not having any fun?" Kai called out.

"Show yourself!"

"You sound stressed. Maybe you should have a seat."

The creature quickly turned around to find Kai calmly sitting on the throne of flowers with his legs crossed and his katana lying across his lap. His eyes were still covered, but the Soul Eater could feel them on it—*in* it. Something stayed the horror's movements—something unfamiliar to it. A smile snuck across Kai's face below his blindfold.

"It is folly to try to stifle your fear from me."

The Soul Eater snapped from its daze and launched across the hall. It snatched Kai by the throat and lifted him into the air.

"So much arrogance," it hissed into Kai's ear.

Kai choked out a breath of laughter. Before his foe was able to make another move, he reached up and placed a bloodied palm on the creature's head. Instantly, it dropped him and backed away in pain. The handprint of blood began to steam as it branded itself into its skull. The Soul Eater growled in pain and frantically scratched at the brand on its head. However, its disoriented state was only brief. Before Kai could climb to his feet, the Soul Eater charged forward, pierced Kai's chest with something underneath its cloak, and hoisted him in the air.

"A blood seal?" the Soul Eater asked, surprised. "Impressive that you know such old Sanorian tricks, but I have allowed you to survive long enough." The Soul Eater squeezed Kai's throat and threw him far down the hall.

Kai crashed into the ground and rolled several times before he skidded to a halt. Still clutching his weapon's grip, he felt the steel scrape against the stone floor. As Kai slowly rose to his feet, he watched as the Soul Eater started to twitch and convulse. Its bones cracked and twisted, tearing through the cloak until the tattered pieces floated to the ground. No longer concealed underneath the curtain of soot was a bony rib cage full of razor-sharp pincers that extended outward, fluttering up and down as if they were desperately reaching for their victim.

The Soul Eater snatched its scythe up from the floor in its new form. "Now, the time has come for you to meet your end. Does it shame you to know you will die with no allies to fall beside you? All alone in the depths of the world, a forgotten piece of worthless history?"

"Maybe it would shame me if it were true. But you see, I'm never *truly* alone."

Kai reached up to the hole in his chest and covered two of his fingers in the blood that spilled out of it. He held his katana high above his head, and with a crescent motion, slid his bloodied fingers from the base of the blade to the tip. "My lady, lend me your light," he whispered.

As soon as he removed his fingers, a chaotic crimson flame burst into existence over the entirety of the blade. The fire was angry. Flames of rage and anguish now thrashed at his side.

Fearful of the monster in front of it, the Soul Eater hissed and crawled like a centipede up to the ceiling above its throne of flowers.

"Now for the fun part," Kai said to himself.

Everyone stood outside the cave entrance for a moment to catch their breath. The full moon shone brightly over the village in the clear night sky. The air around the village remained stagnant, giving each of them an eerie chill down to their bones. After a few moments, they began their reluctant journey back to Meditas.

As they all continued to press forward through the village, Vincent looked over his shoulder back toward the cave. In the midst of the battle of thoughts inside his mind, something within the shadows on the rooftops drew his attention. In the center of the village road, he stopped.

"Hang on a second," he said as quietly as he could to everyone.

Alexandra turned around. "We don't have time to waste, Vince; what is it?"

He paused for a moment before answering. His eyes searched for movement, but it was too dark to make anything out. There was nothing—no sound, no movement, no sign of anything other than them, except for a strange feeling—an uncomfortable feeling of invasion, a feeling of unwanted eyes. They were being watched.

"We're not alone," Vincent said as he drew his weapons.

Everyone followed his motion and put their backs to one another, forming a circle.

"What did you see?" Alexandra asked.

"Was it more of those bear things?" added Toran.

Vincent shook his head. "I didn't see anything, really. I just felt it. Look to the rooftops."

Everyone looked around, squinting their eyes carefully, searching for anything lurking in the darkness. Before any of them successfully spotted the hidden threat, a small needle-like metal projectile suddenly pierced the ground in the middle of them all. Before they could move or assess the object, a bright white explosion sent them all flying through the air in different directions.

Barrik collided with the corner of one of the nearby stone houses. Alexandra was blasted through a nearby wooden door to one of the village homes. Vera and Rinna landed just beyond the village entrance, while Vincent and Toran rolled farther back into the street.

Vera was the first to try to recover. She rolled over onto her back and tried to blink away the white dots in her blurred vision. Before the world around her could fully return to normal, someone stood over her. A cold metal hand wrapped around her neck and lifted her up. Quickly, she tossed a dagger into the air and vanished.

"Hmm, neat trick," the assailant said to himself.

Suspended in the air, Vera whipped her dagger down at the man. Even though his back was to her, he still managed to jump out of its path. She reappeared on the ground and rushed over to Rinna, who sluggishly attempted to get back on her feet.

Vera helped her upright. "You okay?"

Before she could respond, another needle sank into the ground right next to them.

"Move!" Rinna shouted as she shoved Vera away from her.

Another white flash launched Rinna through the air until she came crashing down on an empty chicken coop. Vera hit the ground with a thud right next to Barrik. The imminent danger pumping adrenaline through her veins negated any pain she normally would have felt. She scrambled to her feet and rushed to Barrik's side.

"Come on, big guy, wake up!"

Barrik felt a shrug against his shoulder. He opened his eyes slowly, his head pounding with a heartbeat of its own. All he could see was a blurred silhouette of Vera mouthing something inaudible over the ringing in his ears.

"Hey!" She gave him a gentle smack on the cheek. "You with me?"

He blinked his eyes faster as he realized the situation they were in and quickly rose to his feet.

"Are you okay?" he asked her in a hurry.

"I'm fine, but we gotta get the others."

"You get Alex and Rinna; I'll get the other two! And move quickly!"

"On it!"

Just as they went to move, another needle sank into the ground at their feet. Barrik quickly pulled Vera behind him and conjured one of his energy shields. They turned their heads away from the blinding light as the explosion went off.

"Go!" Barrik shouted. He hurried over to Vincent and Toran, who were both still on the ground. A few shakes of Vincent's shoulders were all it took for him to come to. Once he was conscious again, he reached up to find the wound on his head reopened and bloody. Toran weakly climbed to one knee to gather himself.

"Where are the others?" he asked.

"Vera's got them. Are you guys okay?"

"I'm good."

"Not dead yet," Vincent groaned.

The three girls ran into the middle of the street to regroup. The deep crevices in Alexandra's left arm were glowing brightly.

"Is everyone okay?" she asked.

"I think so," Barrik answered.

Just then, another needle pierced the ground. This time, however, Barrik was ready. He positioned himself in front of it and conjured his shield. The bright white blast had no effect on any member of the party.

"That's not going to work anymore!" Barrik shouted into the night.

From somewhere above, high-pitched laughter filled the air. Everyone quickly turned around to see two people standing on one of the rooftops illuminated by the full moon behind them. The first was a tall, bulky man clad in heavy silver armor from head to toe. His helmet bore a dark purple plume that fell down past his shoulders. In his right hand, he rested a long claymore on his shoulder. They were unable to see his eyes behind the narrow slit in his helmet, but they could *feel* them looking down on them.

"I don't know, Qruxy; without him, this might be easier than we thought," the voice of a young girl said. She sat on the edge of the roof, her bare feet dangling in the breeze. A broken shackle that jangled in the wind was locked around one of her ankles. The rest of her was entirely hidden beneath a white mask and a dark hooded cloak.

"Don't be too eager to underestimate them, Alice," the man known as Qrux said. His voice was hard and stern. He spoke in a steady cadence, as if every word needed to be meticulously placed.

"Who are you, and what do you want?" Barrik demanded.

"Now that *he's* gone, we're here to collect you," answered Alice. Her smile could be heard in every word.

"Now that who is gone?" Vera asked, confused.

"I think she's talking about Kai," Toran answered.

"Oh, so they're too scared to fight us all at once, I see!"

Qrux shook his head slowly. "Only a fool would willingly engage in battle with the Udurim with anything less than an army. Even then, I don't like those odds. I wouldn't be surprised if he managed to slay that horror down there."

They know about the Soul Eater, Vincent realized.

"Oh, come on, Qruxy, he can't be *that* good."

"Believe what you want. I've seen the Udurim in battle with my own eyes. If you continue to show a lack of respect for your enemies, Alice, I promise you'll meet your end sooner than you expect."

Alice shrugged her shoulders and continued to swing her feet back and forth carelessly. "If you say so."

"Udurim... Why does that sound familiar?" Vincent asked curiously.

Alice giggled. "They don't even know who *he* is. They really are just dumb kids."

"They're far older than you," Qrux retorted.

With Qrux and Alice distracted, Alexandra quickly whispered something to Toran and Rinna.

"So? I'm still much stronger than these so-called *Guardians,*" Alice replied.

"Come down here and prove it, then, cowards!" Vincent shouted.

Qrux started to walk toward the edge of the roof. "Confidently loud and impatient. If I were to guess, that one is the child of Victor Raine," he said as he leaped off the roof. The ground beneath his heavy feet moaned in agony as he landed. "He's all yours. But do not underestimate him; he is Raine's heir, after all."

Alice shot straight up and giggled as she clapped her hands together rapidly. "I'm so excited to finally make him pay!"

"Pay for what?" Vincent questioned. "I don't even know you!"

"Don't lie to me!" Alice screamed at him. "I'm going to torture you, just like your daddy tortured me!"

"I don't know what you're talking about! My father never tortured anyone!"

"Liar!" Alice screamed again.

Vincent had no idea what she was referring to, but one thing was certain: once again, he found himself confronted by the ghosts of his father's past.

"That's enough, Alice. We have a job to do," Qrux reminded her.

"Which prize are you going for, then, Qruxy?" she asked.

Qrux lifted his massive sword in one hand as if it weighed no more than a small twig. The tip of the blade was pointed directly at Vera. "That one."

Vera took a step forward with a smirk on her face, placed her finger through the ringed pommel of her dagger, and spun it continuously around. Barrik stepped to her side with his axe resting on his shoulder, his eyes narrowed on Qrux.

Vincent stood on Barrik's other side and gave his sabers a warm-up twirl. "If you're looking for the child of Victor Raine, you're in for a bit of a surprise."

"Hey! Where'd the other two go?" Alice questioned.

Qrux ignored her. "And what might that be?"

Alexandra placed her glowing left hand on Vincent's shoulder and smiled. With Toran and Rinna nowhere to be found, Vera, Barrik, Vincent, and Alexandra all stood together tall and proud with their eyes locked onto the enemy.

"We all belong to the house of Raine," Alexandra said firmly.

Blood spilled down Kai's arms and legs. While his wounds were not quite fatal, they did slow his movements. The flame on his katana still burned with a chaotic ferocity that cast him in a lambent crimson light.

The Soul Eater crawled around the room with horrific speed. Even if Kai were able to use his vision, tracking the creature with his eyes would prove to be an exceptional challenge. He only moved when he needed to, sure to make every single step or slight turn of his body necessary so as not to waste energy. He listened, smelled, *felt* its movements, and waited to strike. All he needed to do was pierce the seal on the horror's head, and everything would be over. But to do that, he first needed to slow it down.

The Soul Eater leaped off the wall from Kai's rear with its scythe aimed at his head. He could feel the creature soar through the air behind him. He ducked beneath the attack at the last moment and turned quickly with his blade pointed above him. Several of the horror's pincers fell to the stone floor. It hissed in pain and scrambled its way back onto the wall. Kai continued to patiently hold his position in the center of the hall, eager to strike again. His breaths were slow and controlled, his entire body burning with every inhale and cooling with every exhale. His focus was an immaculate armor impenetrable by even the sharpest of steel. His hands tightened around the hilt of his weapon as the Soul Eater circled to his side.

Kai turned toward his foe as soon as he felt it dive off the wall. He sliced through its underside once again as its pincers passed just inches above his head. Behind him now, the Soul Eater crashed into the ground and lay still. Slowly, Kai approached. He remained on his guard, for he knew the battle was far from over. There was no doubt in his mind that the horror still lived.

As soon as he was within arm's reach, in a flash, the Soul Eater hissed and slashed at him, sending him flying across the room. He crashed into the wall and dropped to the ground. Not willing to give him a chance to recover, the Soul Eater closed the distance between them in an instant. It snatched Kai by the neck and slammed him into the wall, forcing the katana from his hand. The moment the grip left Kai's touch, the crimson flame vanished.

Ice-cold air blew across Kai's face as the Soul Eater began to speak. "You have remarkable strength for a human." Its breath swarmed his face as if he were walking through a blizzard. "Strength, I'd say, that is not human at all. Yet…" It dug a claw into the wound in Kai's chest. "…you bleed just like the rest of them. So, where do you get this power, I wonder?"

The Soul Eater dug its claw further into Kai's chest and dragged it down, tearing him open. Kai gritted his teeth and breathed through the pain.

"Hush, human," the Soul Eater said just as it leaned in close to Kai's neck. Kai squirmed as the creature breathed him in.

"Your soul smells much different than your comrades before. Theirs were horrid, foul, and tasted equally so. Yours, however, smells of a rich sweetness subtly overshadowed by darkness… and of something I have not smelled in quite some time." It stole another whiff of its prey. "The scent of a Sanorian. First, there was *him,* and now you? How curious. I believed their kind to have been exterminated."

"What are you talking about?" Kai squirmed. "Sanorians are extinct."

"As a species, yes. But perhaps their energy has endured. I wonder if this lingering scent will affect your flavor."

The Soul Eater unhinged its jaw, and out of its mouth crawled a long, wormlike tongue with a tip sharp as a spear. Kai's cheek slowly split open as the worm tongue tasted his face. Kai continued his attempts to pull away from the creature's grasp as its tongue wriggled its way back into the Soul Eater's mouth.

"Delicious," the creature hissed. "Thankfully, it isn't you who has been touched by their energy. I can smell the Sanorian on you, yet you are entirely void of their unpleasant taste."

The Soul Eater reached for the cloth around Kai's eyes. He shut them tightly as the headband fell to the ground and whispered something inaudible to himself.

"Now, give me your soul!"

"As you wish!"

Kai's eyes shot wide open, and out burst a bright red light that blinded the Soul Eater and forced the seal on its head to burn once more. In a fit of rage, the Soul Eater whipped Kai across the hall and frantically scratched at its head, its howls of pain echoing throughout the hall. Kai crashed into a pillar and dropped to the floor. He could feel at least one of his ribs crack on impact. He was sure to tightly close his eyes again before he climbed to his feet.

"Insolent rodent! I tire of your tricks!" the Soul Eater growled just before it took off after him.

With his katana far out of reach, Kai had only one option. Quickly, he picked up one of the Soul Eater's blade-like legs and slid his blood-covered hand across it. Not a moment later, it burst into the same crimson flame.

As the Soul Eater raced through the air toward him, Kai jumped, planted both feet against the pillar behind him, and launched himself forward. With immense speed, the two of them collided. Both fell to the ground and skidded down the hall until they stopped just before the throne of flowers. Neither of them moved.

Moments passed, until finally, Kai struggled his way out from underneath the Soul Eater. As he climbed back to his feet, he removed the leg that stuck straight out of the Soul Eater's head to sever two of its other legs that had pierced his body. He reached down to pull them out of himself, but stopped short; less than eager to bleed out, he decided to leave them in.

The seal on the motionless Soul Eater began to sizzle and slowly disintegrated the felled creature's body to ash. Kai stood over it until there was nothing left but a pile of charcoal powder, out of which began to rise hundreds of multicolored orbs that all soared around in the air above him. Even though the coast was clear, he kept his eyes closed so he could watch with his Favor as all of the souls followed the guiding moonlight through the cracked ceiling above. One of them flew around him in a circle several times before hovering in front of him at eye level. Kai's lips trembled while tears welled behind his closed eyes. "I'm sorry I wasn't here," he whispered.

The orb remained briefly still before it responded by circling him once more, then floated above to join the others. A gentle gust of wind crept through the cracks in the ceiling and swept everything away, now nothing more than a remnant of Kai's memory. He looked up to the light of the moon and spoke as if he were not alone. "May you find your peace."

Kai turned and sluggishly made his way back to his katana. With it lying at his feet, he removed his leather jerkin and ripped out the two legs still stuck in his waist and thigh. Both of them turned to ash just as they hit the floor. Blood raced out of Kai's wounds like a never-ending waterfall. Quickly, he ignited his weapon and brought it to his body. His skin sizzled at the touch of the flame, yet he felt no pain from the fire. While it was chaotic and wild, it remained his ally. With his wounds cauterized, he sheathed his katana, threw on his armor, and limped over to Gala's remains. Too weak to move any further, he slid down the wall with a bloodied streak until he sat next to her and slowly succumbed to his fatigue.

CHAPTER 15

ALICE, separate them," Qrux demanded.

Two of Alice's needles sank into the ground between them all, too spaced out for Barrik to block anyone other than himself and Vincent. Alexandra and Vera dove forward out of the explosion's range, but straight into Qrux's. His claymore already sliced through the air with incredible speed. Alexandra had no time to dodge. She raised her sword to block the attack, but the inhuman force behind it launched her into the stone wall of one of the nearby homes. She struggled to get back up.

Barrik and Vincent charged forward to attack, but were quickly cut off by Alice's sudden appearance. She wielded a sword that looked like a sewing needle the size of her torso. She stabbed it into the ground and rocked back and forth on her heels as she waved her index finger in the air. "No, no, no, you heard Mr. Qruxy. You have to play with *me*."

Vincent could feel her eyes on him from behind her white mask. He looked at the thin blade she used as a support system. "You know that thing isn't a toy, right?"

Alice giggled. "Everything's a toy. And soon, *you'll* be my favorite toy."

She threw another needle and charged behind it.

Vera scrambled to her feet just in time to duck underneath the metal gauntlet aimed right at her head. She took a sloppy side slice at the gap in Qrux's armor right behind the knee. Qrux, however, was surprisingly light on his feet, despite all his heavy equipment. He quickly hopped away from the danger. Not about to let him gain the reach on her, Vera charged in to stay close. Qrux's claymore was practically useless at this proximity. Vera ducked and thrust her dagger at his chest. It bounced right off of the armor with a metallic *chink*. There was no way their weapons would get through his metal fortress. They had to focus their aim on the small areas that remained exposed.

Qrux followed her failed attack with a hard kick she was unprepared for. His metal foot sent her tumbling backward several feet before she could regain control of herself. He stood firm with his weapon in both hands and his feet planted, waiting for her next move. When she rose to her feet, she threw her daggers at the ground near him, one in front and one behind. Before Qrux could react, Vera reappeared and went to strike at his neck. As soon as he stepped to the side to avoid the blade, she vanished to her other dagger and slashed the back of his leg. He groaned in pain and quickly turned around to get her back in his sights.

"Fine," he said coldly before he thrust his claymore into the ground. He cracked his neck and put up his metal fists. Vera smiled and spun her daggers around her fingers.

Alice charged through the cloud of smoke her explosion had created with her pointed sword aimed at Barrik's neck. As he stepped to the side to evade the danger, Vincent moved to take a downward slice at her arms. In the blink of an eye, she spun to the side, dodging his attack, and forced her blade down into Vincent's foot. He winced and breathed through his teeth as she ripped it back out.

Barrik took the pointed pommel of his axe and thrust it at Alice's midsection. She jumped high, planted a hand on the grip of his axe, and split her legs to kick them both in the face before she rolled away to safety. Before they could recover, she threw another needle right in front of them. Barrik quickly put up a shield to block the explosion, but was unable to prepare for the attack that followed. Alice appeared at his side with a few swift jabs of her sword into his shoulder. He dropped low with a sweep of his leg she did not see coming. Her feet were taken right out from under her, and just as she hit the ground, Barrik forced his foot into her stomach as hard as he could. He could hear the air leave her lungs as she rolled several feet away from them.

By the time she hopped back to her feet, Vincent was already on top of her with a barrage of slashes. Her movements were sluggish from Barrik's attack. There was no way she could avoid Vincent's blades for long. He missed and missed over and over again, or so she thought. She quickly realized his goal was never to strike her; it was to move her. She found herself in between Vincent's fury and Barrik's rage. Distracted by the monstrous axe that lusted for her demise, she fell victim to a swift slice from Vincent's saber across her arm. A deep wound now leaked blood that trickled down to her fingertips. In a desperate act to turn the tides of battle in her favor, she quickly threw a needle that pierced Vincent's leg.

Frantic to not be blown to pieces, Vincent dropped a saber to pull the needle out of his leg. He could feel it heat up in his hand. He quickly tossed it. "Look out!" he shouted.

Barrik protected himself with one of his shields. Alice dove out of harm's way. Vincent, however, had no chance to escape the blast. All he could do was throw up his arms in front of his face. The force of the explosion sent him crashing through the stalls of a nearby stable. Barrik took a step in Vincent's direction, but was immediately cut off by Alice. He gripped his axe firmly and narrowed his eyes at her as she started to circle him.

Toran and Rinna crouched beside Alexandra and helped her back to her feet.

"Did you guys do what I asked?" she asked quietly, clutching her head.

Toran nodded quickly. "That big guy definitely has a Favor. It has to be either speed or strength-related. Otherwise, there's no way he could move that fast with all that heavy equipment. Even Vera's struggling to keep up with him."

"And what about the girl?"

Rinna shook her head. "I'm sorry, but I don't know. She has to have some kind of Favor, but I can't quite figure out how she's causing those things to explode. Other than that, she seems normal. Well trained and slippery, but normal."

"That's not exactly ideal." Alexandra thought for a brief moment before she continued. "Okay. Toran, do you think you can get through his armor with your Favor?"

"You mean double strike? Yeah, I think so."

"You don't need to name it. Just do it."

He gave her a nod of silent confirmation.

"Rinna, you help the boys. We don't know her Favor, but she doesn't know yours either. Keep yourself hidden until you see a point where you can get the drop on her. Got it?"

"Got it!" Like a mirage in the distance, her visibility quickly faded away until they could no longer see her.

"Okay, Toran, wait for my signal, and then give him your worst."

"Okay!"

With their plan of attack complete, Alexandra rushed back into the battle.

Vera and Qrux stood toe to toe, but neither party could land a meaningful attack on the other. Everywhere Vera's daggers made contact was far too thick for them to do anything other than make a scratch in his armor, while Qrux found her far too challenging to hit, and just when he thought he had her, she would vanish and reappear behind him or to his side. They were locked in a stalemate until, all of a sudden, Alexandra launched from behind Qrux and wrapped her arms around his neck. He reached up to pull her off, but she held on tightly. Vera quickly dashed in and jammed one of her daggers into an exposed part of his midsection, twisted it, and ripped it out with a spray of blood. He groaned in pain and dropped to one knee.

"Now, Toran!" Alexandra shouted.

Toran charged in at the wounded man with a war cry, the tip of his sword aimed at his chest. He thrust it forward into his target, and just as it made its mark, as if he had performed the action a second time without anyone seeing it, the blade struck again, sinking deeper into Qrux's armor.

While their plan was a success, their victory was short-lived—far too short. Toran looked at his sword in Qrux's chest, mortified. He had successfully pierced his armor, but barely. Only the very tip of Toran's blade dripped with blood, little more than a pinprick.

Qrux reached behind himself with both hands and latched onto Alexandra just below her shoulders. In one quick motion, he pulled her over his head and slammed her down onto Toran. Vera charged in, only to be abruptly halted by a metal gauntlet to the face that threw her to the side in a daze.

Qrux, now back on his feet, delivered a powerful kick to Alexandra's face, forcing her into an abrupt darkness. From the ground, Toran stabbed his sword into the wound in Qrux's midsection. He growled, swatted away the sword, and returned a punch to Toran's face. A great mist of blood splattered onto the ground. Toran's world spun as he lay stunned by the hit. Qrux placed his foot on Toran's knee and began to apply pressure. Toran's body filled with panic and pain the harder he pushed.

Qrux leaned in close with his foot firmly planted on Toran's knee. The small eye slit in his helmet was only inches from Toran's face. "I do not *need* to collect all of you," Qrux said menacingly. "And you, most of all, I find to be the most useless." He slammed his foot down and twisted. There was a loud crunch of bone and then... agony.

Alice threw a needle into the ground in front of Vincent and Barrik's charging steps and flipped backward away from the white blast of danger. Before the smoke cleared, the two boys were already closing in on her from both sides. As Barrik readied a mighty swing of his axe, Vincent went to thrust one of his sabers through her chest. Both attacks missed. Alice dove out of the way and out of their reach, but failed to realize she had leaped into more danger. As soon as she went to take another step, both Vincent and Barrik watched as a shining metal gleam suddenly appeared with a swipe down Alice's back. They could see Rinna standing behind Alice as she fell to the ground with a cry of pain, and before she could move again, Rinna bashed her in the head with the butt of her staff. Now Alice lay on the ground, silent and still.

"Hey, thanks," Vincent said, catching his breath.

Before Rinna had a chance to respond, desperate screams of agony from down the road tore through their ears. They turned around and raced down the village street.

Qrux lifted his claymore out of the ground and turned back to Toran, who was writhing with pain. "Allow me to put an end to your suffering," he said as he raised his weapon.

Vera struggled to get back on her feet. Blood now ran down her chin from a split in her lower lip. Her head was pounding, ears ringing, heart racing. Still, she had to do something. She sloppily threw one of her daggers, but by the time it left her hand, it was too late. Qrux's massive sword fell through the air with horrific speed until it found its mark. Toran's screams vanished into an abrupt silence.

Vera shouted in a fit of rage as she appeared in front of Qrux with a fury of attacks. He backpedaled, dodging every one of her advances until he took a giant leap away to create distance. As soon as he saw her throw her dagger, he cut upward through the air. Vera allowed her reckless state to dull her senses and fell for the bait. The moment she appeared in front of him, the end of his sword sliced her open from her lower cheek to her forehead, just above her left eye. Qrux then delivered a kick to her stomach that launched her down the road. Covered in dust and dirt, with blood covering half of her face, she lay utterly still.

Just as Qrux went to take a step in Vera's direction, he heard someone's rapid approach, but he never had the time to evade. From a full sprint, Barrik lowered his shoulder and ripped Qrux from his feet, carrying him through the stone wall of a village home. Stones came crashing down all around them. Barrik ripped off Qrux's helmet and let loose with feral fists of fury into his disfigured face, painting the debris of stone and wooden floorboards with bright red blood.

Vincent ran over to Vera and placed his fingers on the side of her neck. Relief quickly washed over him. She was severely wounded and unconscious, but she was alive. He ripped a piece of cloth from his tunic and wrapped it around her head, covering her left eye.

Rinna knelt beside Toran, but did not find the same relief as Vincent. Toran's chest and back were soaked in crimson. Qrux's sword had pierced straight through his heart. With a quivering lip and tears on her cheek, Rinna cradled his head in her hand and gently closed his light blue eyes for the last time.

"Alex, wake up!" Vincent nudged her urgently. "We need you!"

Alexandra slowly lifted her heavy lids as Vincent helped her to sit upright. Her face was covered in blood that still spilled out of her broken nose. Vincent handed her another piece of cloth that she pressed to her face while she looked at the scene around her—Toran's head in Rinna's lap, and Vera's motionless body not too far away. She panicked and tried to run towards Vera, but was quickly restrained in Vincent's arms.

"Hey, hey, hey, she's okay... ish. She'll live," he said plainly.

"What about Toran?" Alexandra asked frantically.

One look into Rinna's eyes was the only answer she needed. Her heart sank, her eyes filling with tears. "Why? What do they want with us?"

"Hey!" Vincent demanded her attention. "We can ask our questions later, but right now, we need you."

He was right. Now was not the time for mourning. She had to focus. She clenched her jaw and closed her eyes tightly to gather herself. When she opened them again, she looked around once more. "Where's Barrik?"

As soon as the words left her mouth, Barrik came flying through the house's front wall of stone and crashed into the cedar entry gate. The fence collapsed beneath him into splinters and broken boards.

Qrux emerged from the hole he had used Barrik to create with his claymore in his hand. The others rushed to his aid. Barrik rolled to the side to avoid Qrux's downward swing and snatched up one of the thick cedar planks. He planted his feet and twisted his hips forward to bash Qrux in the head. Such force was behind Barrik's hit that the board exploded into wooden bits on impact and knocked Qrux to the side in a daze. Barrik dropped to one knee and spat out a mouthful of blood and saliva.

Vincent came to a halt at his side. "You all right, big guy?"

He grunted weakly in response.

"Barrik, catch your breath," Alexandra said as she stepped forward with a tearful fury in her eyes. "His armor is still too strong to cut through; even Barrik's axe will struggle to make anything more than a dent, but Toran managed to weaken the center of his breastplate. He's also injured in his right hip, so he's going to favor his left side."

"I have a feeling this would cut through him without any issue." Vincent gestured down to the sword on his hip.

Alexandra was quick to deny the thought. "No. We don't know anything about that thing. And she told you not to use it for any other purpose."

"Vince," Rinna started slowly as she climbed to her feet, "what about that thing you did in the cave? His armor holds up against our weapons, but maybe it won't do so well against a blade of energy like that."

"If I can even do it again, I don't know, maybe. I guess there's only one way to find out, but I'm going to need some time to try and find that feeling again."

"I think we can handle that," Alexandra said confidently. "Right, Rinna?"

"Absolutely."

Qrux, still slightly disoriented from Barrik's cedar plank, stumbled to his left just a little too late. Alexandra's sword slid across his upper cheek, slicing him open all the way back to his ear. He fired back with a punch as fast as lightning, straight into her kidney. She dropped to one knee with a forceful groan.

Rinna hopped over her downed comrade to jam the heel of her boot into Qrux's face, forcing him backward. Following through her attack, she thrust the bladed end of her metal staff forward with quick short motions, like she was backing a lion into its cage. Qrux lost his footing, fell backward onto the ground, and quickly rolled to the side to evade her downward slash. He blasted off a desperate swing of his massive weapon in return that howled through the air, but she had already spun away out of his reach.

Rinna stood several feet away from him, perfectly balanced on one foot with the other resting against the inside of her knee. She held her weapon behind her, tucked under one arm with her other raised close to her chest. Her eyes were narrowed and still slightly puffy. With a stance that could easily flow from offense to defense and an expression of wet anger, she dared him to come closer.

Qrux carelessly charged at her with his sword level with his shoulders as if he planned to joust her. His footsteps were heavy and rang with a metallic thud as they drew closer. She waited patiently, and once he was in range, she twirled her weapon, spun low to the ground, and thrust it above her. Qrux hopped to the side to dodge and tried to counter with a kick. Rinna quickly rolled and swiped up to slice open the back of his exposed leg. He charged her again.

She twirled her staff like a windmill as she backpedaled to keep him at bay until his momentum slowed. Now, as she stepped toward him suddenly, she used her Favor to make her weapon vanish from his sight. A metal clink against his gauntlet assured him that although he could not see it, it was still there. He quickly stepped back to try to gauge the reach of her invisible weapon. The more she attacked, the more he grew accustomed to it.

Qrux blocked one of her slashes and countered with a heavy downward swing. Rinna quickly stepped to the side to avoid the danger and make way for Alexandra. The crevices in her left arm still glowed a vibrant white. She slid on the ground past his claymore, and just as she got beneath him, she forced all her momentum into the ground to launch herself upward with a well-placed uppercut that dented his breastplate even further. She rolled low and away from him to avoid retaliation, stopping at Rinna's side.

"Anytime now, Vince!" Alexandra shouted.

Immediately, she realized she had made a mistake. Qrux whipped around to see Vincent perfectly still with his eyes closed. He had not the slightest clue what they were plotting, but he had no intentions of finding out the hard way. He took off.

"Shit!" Alexandra charged after him.

As soon as she caught up to him, she leaped onto his back, wrapped her hands around his head, and jammed her fingers into his eyes. His voice bellowed throughout the empty village in pain. With his free hand, he angrily reached up to grab her by the neck. The very moment she felt the cold metal against her skin, Alexandra leaned in close and sank her teeth into his neck just below his ear. When he ripped her to the ground, she took a mouthful of him with her.

She slammed into the ground with an unforgiving crash that forced her to cough out all the blood and skin in her mouth. Qrux turned and kicked her in the stomach before inspecting the bloodied area of his neck. Before he was able to kick her a second time, Barrik wrapped his arms around Qrux's waist, lifted him high in the air, and forced him into the earth beneath them. The ground ached from the monstrous impact. Still, Qrux could not be stopped. He quickly threw Barrik off him and continued his charge.

Vincent stood motionless with closed eyes and calm breaths. As he slowly breathed in and out, time seemed to slow to a near halt. One by one, he noticed the ability of his senses increasing. A strong scent of iron drifted its way into his nostrils that he tracked behind him to Vera. He could see her injuries as if he were standing right next to her. The split in her lower lip, the deep cut on her face—the more he focused on them both, the more he began to feel her pain as if it were his own. He gritted his teeth and clenched his jaw tightly to bear it. Images of Qrux's claymore cutting across *his* face flashed across his mind and started to break his focus, until a distant strength began to comfort him.

The feeling draped over him as if he were being tucked into bed with a blanket of warmth and security on a cold winter's night. An image of a revitalizing waterfall gently flowing into a cool spring briefly took hold of his mind. It was a place he had never been, yet he felt as though he knew it so well. He heard no words and could not figure out where the image had come from, but somehow, he knew it carried a message of reassurance.

Qrux may have been in a full sprint, but Vincent felt he had all the time in the world. Each one of the man's heavy footfalls crushed the dirt beneath them with an elongated metallic clang that rang in Vincent's ears. Behind the rushing threat, he could tell Alexandra's concern for him was growing from her accelerated heartbeat. Qrux was almost on top of him.

Alexandra's eyes widened with panic as she screamed, "Vince!"

Her call was drawn out, as if she had said it as slow as she could, but Vincent heard her loud and clear. Every one of his bones and muscles swelled with power that flooded his body with a painful burning sensation. His eyes snapped open. Qrux skidded to a halt at the sight of two bright emerald irises that shone with the intensity of the sun.

Vincent pulled back his sabers and slashed at the air before him with all his strength. The light in his eyes seemed to transfer into a vibrant emerald blade of energy that raced through the air. Vincent dropped to his knees, exhausted, and watched as it drew closer and closer to his target until... he missed.

Qrux quickly rolled out of the way, letting the danger soar behind him. Caught off guard, Alexandra had no time to react. Both of her arms shot up as the energy wave crashed into her. Ripped from her feet, she was thrown backward into Barrik and Rinna, who were following close behind.

Qrux turned his attention back to Vincent and walked over to him slowly. "Well now, that was a fancy trick."

Vincent looked up at him from his downed position with no stamina left to even stand on his feet. Up close now, he could see Qrux's disfigured face in detail. A bald head of torched skin and hideous scars that were most likely infected before they completely healed covered every part of his face. The large bleeding cut Alexandra had gifted him only added to the monstrosity. Two of the scars on Qrux's face, however, stood out to Vincent in particular. Two deep parallel lines cut into the right side of his face from his ear to his cheekbone—the mark of a Rogue.

Vincent knew he had no attack left in him, but as long as he drew breath, he maintained his wit. "You roll over into a campfire or something?" he asked with a weak smile.

Qrux growled and slammed a metal fist into Vincent's face. Vincent fell to the side in a daze. His mind scrambled for a way out, but he barely had the strength to keep his eyes open, let alone return with another attack.

Qrux grabbed him by the throat and hoisted him into the air. Vincent still clung to the saber in his left hand as he dangled helplessly.

"I expected more from the son of Victor Raine," Qrux said disappointedly, looking Vincent up and down. "Just hearing your father's name was enough to strike fear into the hearts of the mightiest of men, but you? You're not even half the man Victor was."

Qrux slammed his head into Vincent, spraying a mist of blood into the air. Pain jolted through him, and his world began to spin, his vision fading in and out underneath his heavy eyelids. Qrux's words struck a chord, bringing the saddest melodies of realization to Vincent's blurring mind. He felt like a failure. How had he ever thought he could live up to the memory of his father?

"Maybe you were put here only to receive the punishment for all of the sins Victor managed to escape from with his early demise," Qrux continued to taunt.

Vincent coughed and wheezed in the large man's clutches. Maybe Qrux was right. There was nothing he could do to help Kai, Vera was severely injured, and Toran would never see another sunrise.

Ever since they left Sylva, Vincent felt he had done nothing to prove himself worthy of being Victor's son. Was all of his mother's training for nothing? He should have known he was incapable of completing the task given to him by Larissa. Why did he ever agree to it? Was it arrogance? Was he just too full of himself? Whatever the reason, none of that mattered now. His fate was in the hands of the disfigured man in front of him.

"*He* is going to be quite disappointed when I deliver you to him," Qrux said. "He was hoping for another warrior of value to add to his cause... but you're only a boy." Qrux slammed his head into Vincent again. "Nothing," he growled, "but a useless..." Another slam. "...worthless..." And again. "...good-for-nothing..." One last brutal impact. "...*boy*!"

Suddenly, a splash of blood from Qrux's chest splattered across Vincent's now swollen face. He looked down to see Alexandra's left arm sticking out of Qrux's breastplate. Deep crimson blood dripped off the tips of her dark and jagged fingers. The creviced veins in her skin looked like streams of bright pearl and emerald. Rather than being injured by Vincent's attack, she absorbed it.

Qrux tightened his grip around Vincent's throat and pulled him closer, still refusing to go down. Vincent let go of the saber in his left hand. Just before it hit the ground, Alexandra caught it in her right, and in one fell motion, ripped her arm from his chest and forced the blade through Qrux's midsection from one hip to the other. Qrux fell to his knees, but still gripped Vincent even more tightly. He pulled him close and looked into his eyes as he whispered, "He... will come for you."

Vincent felt the metal fingers begin to loosen around his neck, and as he peered through the red haze covering his face, he could see tears streaming down Qrux's cheeks. The man desperately hung onto his life as he stared at the bloodied boy in front of him, until a dagger raced through the air with an unrivaled fury and sank into the side of Qrux's head. He dropped to the ground in an instant and finally let go of Vincent's neck. Vera had delivered the killing blow. Barrik and Rinna rushed to her aid.

Covered in a foul mixture of his own blood as well as Qrux's, Vincent hunched over to retch and cough until he regained his breath.

Alexandra knelt beside him and placed her hand on his back. "Are you okay?"

No, he thought to himself. He was far from okay. Every part of his body screamed in pain, while his mind was a whirlwind of thoughts and questions he had no desire or energy left to consider. An overwhelming sensation of failure and worthlessness shrouded every fiber of his being. He was saturated with self-doubt and disappointment. So, no, he was *not* okay, but he gritted his teeth, swallowed the pain, and ignored what he was feeling inside. At least for now.

He turned to her with a string of bloody saliva dangling from his lip. He could see that her nose was black and blue with a deep gash across the bridge and dried blood all over the lower half of her face. He gestured to his mouth with his finger. "You got a little…"

She chuckled and softly began to sob as she gently laid her forehead against his shoulder.

Barrik came rushing over to them with Vera cradled in his arms and laid her down gently on the ground. With both her hands pressed against her left eye, teeth clenched, Vera squirmed in pain.

"We need to get her back to the city, fast," Barrik said.

"Is there anything we can do to ease her pain? Or slow the bleeding?" Rinna asked as she caressed the top of Vera's sunset head.

Alexandra stood up with a quick sniffle and clenched her jaw. She pulled Vera's dagger out of Qrux's head, wiped the blood from it, and tucked it in her belt.

"We can look for herbs on the way," she started, "but we need to move. It's almost daybreak, and we have to make as much progress as possible while it's light. We can't go down that cliff with Vera, so we'll have to take the long way around, and with all of our wounds, it's going to be a miracle if we don't run into any horrors at night."

Vincent was crouched next to Toran's body, holding his hand. "What about him?"

Everyone fell silent. Alexandra walked over and knelt beside him. She placed her palm against Toran's freckled cheek. Her lips started to quiver. She clenched her eyes tightly, slowly removed the cherry red scarf from around his neck, and took a deep breath to gather her strength before answering. "We can bring this back to his mother," she said softly with tears in her eyes. "But we don't have time for anything else."

"So, we just leave him to be a feast for the crows?" Vincent questioned disapprovingly.

Alexandra tensed up, fighting back her tears. She forced herself to look away from Toran's body. "We don't have a choice," she answered.

After a moment of silence for their fallen comrade, Barrik carefully scooped Vera up in his arms. As they all started to leave the village, Vincent suddenly realized they had forgotten about someone. He turned around in a panic and looked down the road. "Guys, where's Alice?"

Rinna went to reach for her weapon, but Alexandra stayed her hand. "If she was going to try anything, she would have already. She'd be a fool to try and ambush us herself. Forget about her for now."

Vincent and Rinna uneasily let go of their weapons and continued on with guards raised.

Once they reached the top of the hill overlooking the village, Vincent felt an intangible pull in his mind. The waterfall that had given him strength earlier flashed into his thoughts again. He looked back over his shoulder, but saw nothing other than an empty village he hoped never to see again. However, the farther and farther they walked away, the tighter a gut-wrenching knot wound itself inside his stomach. Something, or someone, called out to him.

CHAPTER 16

ANG in there, Vera," Rinna said with a gentle touch to Vera's head. "We're almost home."

Vera weakly groaned and mumbled deliriously. She had become unresponsive to any of their remarks shortly after leaving the village as her condition continued to worsen. The tone of her sweat-covered skin appeared white and was cold to the touch. While the bleeding had all but stopped from the deep cut on her face, it continued to swell and ooze a greenish-yellow pus. Meditas was close, but haste was of the essence.

Alexandra emerged from the dark bushes and into a sliver of moonlight. "All right," she whispered, "there doesn't seem to be any more of them. Let's keep going."

As they led the others through the night, Vincent remained by Alexandra's side, their eyes and ears constantly searching the darkness for the next set of fangs to leap out at them. They had already endured several encounters. The scent of Vera's injuries wafted through the air, seemingly finding its way into the nose of every nearby horror. Now, every rustle of leaves or shifting of shadows threatened to unleash another nightmare.

Vincent looked over his shoulder, gazing into the darkness that followed closely behind.

"She's going to be okay," Alexandra reassured him.

While he was concerned for Vera, her health was not what continued to steal his attention. The knot in his stomach wound itself tighter and tighter, and the urge to turn back for some unknown reason bordered on irresistible.

"I know, I just..." He trailed off, unsure of how to describe his feelings.

"I heard the things Qrux was saying to you," Alexandra started, her eyes still scanning for danger. "You know none of it was true, right?"

Vincent could not find a response.

"I mean it, Vince," she continued, "you're not worthless. You mean so much to us all. We need you. *I* need you. Don't let him make you think otherwise."

"That's just it, though. You say you need me; I just can't understand why. I couldn't do anything to help Kai or Toran, and Vera's only getting worse. So, if Qrux was wrong, then I'm having a hard time proving that to myself."

"Without you, we never would have beaten him."

"You stopped him, not me."

"With your help!" she exclaimed. "Vince, if it wasn't for your Favor, I wouldn't have had the strength to attack him like that. You gave me the strength to end the fight. Just like you gave me the strength to lead us forward."

"You were already strong enough to lead us."

"If that's true, you helped me see it, because I trust you. Let me do the same for you; trust me when I say you're worth the stars to us... Even when you're being a thorn in my side," she joked.

Just as Vincent smiled softly, the sun began to peek over the distant horizon.

"Thank the stars," Barrik said. "We should be able to make it back to Meditas before the sun sets again, right?"

"I hope so," Rinna answered, clearly suffering from fatigue. "I think I've seen enough horrors for a while."

"It should only be a few more hours," Alexandra confirmed.

"How is she doing, Bear?" Vincent asked.

"I don't know. She hasn't gotten any worse, at least."

"Just a bit further, V," Vincent said softly, his voice carrying a mix of encouragement and weariness.

As the sun rose above the horizon, bathing the landscape in golden light and easing their fears of lurking horrors, the safety of Meditas felt tantalizingly close. Everyone seemed hopeful—everyone except Vincent. A weight lingered in his chest, pulling his thoughts back to the idea of turning around. The waterfall that had steadied him during the battle with Qrux resurfaced in his mind. It had brought him peace and reassurance in the village, but now it felt different—like a source of unease, or perhaps more accurately, a cry for help. And he was beginning to understand where it was coming from.

Kai slowly opened his eyes to the hall of darkness he was still sitting in. Weak from his battle with the Soul Eater, he grunted in pain as he struggled to his feet. He took one final look at Gala's remains, but instead of seeing the skeletal remnants of a loved one, he vividly imagined all of her features as he remembered them. A head of dark, loose curls fell just below her ears and gently lay right on top of her brow, complemented by the soft waves of chocolate that flowed in her eyes. A round nose slightly too small for her face hovered above lips that always seemed to turn up at the corners with the hint of a smile. Kai picked up the two minor axes in her hands, tucked them into his belt, and took a deep breath before he tore his eyes from her to limp his way out of the cave, weighed down by a heavy heart.

Robust gray clouds drifted across a sky hued by a blend of orchids and violets as Kai exited the depths of the earth. While the air refreshed him with the soothing scent of early autumn, every breath he took was accompanied by a sharp pain in his midsection. His hand held his side as he continued to push through the village. The farther he traveled down the dirt road, he noticed things that were not there before—large holes in the ground, crumbled walls, broken gates and doors. The evidence of a battle quickly became irrefutable, and once he spotted the two bodies that lay in the middle of his path, his heart found another weight it would have to carry. A cold face devoid of all color lay on the ground before him. He knelt on both knees next to Toran's body and hung his head in silence.

As the last bit of evening sun left Kai's face, he rose to his feet and examined the other lifeless body. He grew curious at the large hole in the middle of Qrux's chest, unsure as to what could have caused such a fatal blow. The metal from his breastplate peeled outward as if something had exploded from inside it. Beneath Qrux's chin, Kai noticed a patch of dark skin creeping up his neck, barely peeking out beneath his armor. He was infected with the ash.

An exhale of ailing breath escaped Kai's nose. "I wonder," he said out loud as he looked down on Qrux, "did you underestimate them, or did you allow them to defeat you?"

He crouched down and shook his head as he tried to piece everything together. "What brought you here to this end?"

Kai reached forward and gently closed Qrux's eyes with the palm of his hand. "Find your peace among the stars."

He stood up and drew his katana. "Well… it looks like you'll get to feed after all." There was a moment of hesitation. "Truly, I am sorry for this, old friend." Kai lifted his blade and slammed it down into the center of Qrux's head. The moment the blade tasted flesh, the crimson flame burst into existence across the shining steel. As the fire raged on, Qrux's body slowly started to shrivel up as if all of the fluid were being drained out of him. The longer the flames fed, the more ferociously they burned. Kai turned his head away. He was never willing to witness the process.

As the flames continued to shrink Qrux into an emaciated version of the large man he once was, Kai allowed his thoughts to overtake him. So many questions flew through his mind in such little time. Where were the others? Were they okay? What had Qrux been here to accomplish? And how did he know where to find them? Nothing he could think of made any sense to him. He needed more information. All that mattered to him now was the safety of everyone else.

Suddenly, the fire exploded across the blade in a bright red flash as if Qrux's bones were made of flash powder. When Kai turned around, the flame was relaxed, calmly flowing up and down the blade with a satisfied hum, like a soft purr against the steel.

"Finished?" Kai asked out loud.

The crimson flame purred louder.

"The ribs first, if you would. I should be able to manage with the rest."

Like the gentle flow of a small stream, the flame swam up the blade, through the hilt, and into Kai's hand. After a brief moment, once the flame could no longer be seen, Kai sheathed his weapon and leaned his head back to take a deep, painless breath. The several broken ribs he had had only a moment ago were now completely healed.

Qrux's body was reduced to nothing more than a skeleton with a dehydrated layer of skin tightly stretched across his bones. He no longer resembled a man capable of wielding such a massive weapon and heavy armor.

Kai gathered several planks of wood from the wrecked debris and laid them across the ground lengthwise until he had two beds of pine and cedar—one just big enough for Qrux and the other the size of Toran. He respectfully laid both individuals on their designated pyres and lit a flame beneath them—a flame of natural birth.

As both bodies in front of him started transitioning to ash, Kai offered them a few final words.

"Return to the stars, my brothers of light. Carry with you only love, for nothing else will serve you well. May your journey through the darkness be swift, and may the peace you find be everlasting. Return to the stars, my brothers, and when my time has come to venture on, may we find each other once again."

Kai turned away from the orange flames and began his journey home.

While Kai's more troublesome injuries healed, he still struggled through the forest. Fatigue took a strong hold in every part of his body. Most of the cuts on his legs and torso could not fully clot due to his constant movement, which led to a slow but steady loss of blood. He knew he needed more rest before continuing, so at the sound of flowing water, he veered off his path.

When he emerged from the tree line, he was greeted by bright and tiny stars shimmering on the river's surface beneath the light of the moon. The colorful brilliance of fallen leaves, filled with shades of autumn's rainbow, was dulled by the darkness of night as they drifted peacefully downstream. Tree branches high above gracefully swayed back and forth with every chilling breeze that swam through the air.

He carefully made his way down the embankment, ensuring that his footsteps were soft and well placed, as if he were afraid to disturb the environment. As silently as he could, he used the river's cold yet revitalizing water to wash his wounds. Once he was finished, he propped himself up against the bank with his katana in his lap and let the mellow flow of the river sing him to sleep.

Kai's hand shot up to shield his eyes as the early morning sun blinded him awake. He splashed the river's cold water against his face to wash away the lingering remnants of sleep, and as his eyes fully opened, he caught his reflection. They were marked by an incurable exhaustion, his face full of dark scruff, and a head of wet and messy silver strands that fell wherever they pleased. He took a deep breath and made his way back into the forest.

By the time he neared the old Sanorian watchtower, the sun had already begun to sink past the horizon. The closer he drew to the forest edge, the more he could hear the mumble of distant chatter in the air. He stopped. He knew there was no way he had already caught up to the others at his current pace; this had to be someone else. Rather than press on blindly, he sat on the ground, crossed his legs, and closed his eyes. There he sat, perfectly still in the growing darkness, testing the area with his Favor.

He sensed several unfamiliar energies in and around the watchtower. They were spread out in pairs. Some strolled along the tree line, while others were positioned at the top of the watchtower, facing all directions. *Bandits*, he thought—and armed to the teeth, at that. Arrows, swords, and axes were all ready to attack at a moment's notice, as if a rival tribe threatened them. Kai knew he could slip by undetected with relative ease, but saw a potential opportunity for the information he was so desperate for, and he was not about to waste it. Slowly, he lifted himself back to his feet.

"I hope you're still hungry," he said out loud. With his Favor, he masked his energy and seemingly disappeared into the night.

With his presence concealed and his body low to the ground, he could go unnoticed as long as he remained out of anyone's direct line of sight. He snuck out from the trees and carefully maneuvered around the patrol units, slowly making his way to the watchtower, using their crates and wagons as cover. Kai circled to the tower's backside and started climbing his way up the stone wall. As he came to the top, he could hear the conversation between two bandits. He stopped, clinging to the tiny grip and foothold to listen for anything useful.

"You can't be serious?!" one of the bandits exclaimed in shock.

"Keep your voice down, dammit! Why wouldn't I be serious, Daren? You've seen it all for yourself. I can't take being in Enora any longer, and you can't neither. That place is going to get us killed. Look, with the money from this job, we could disappear. You and me. Doesn't that sound better than livin' in a slum of a city where you have to dodge the shit every five steps?"

Daren hung his head. "I don't know, James. Where would we even go?"

"Who cares? We could go north of the Ankar Mountains and disappear into the wild. With all the money this freak is paying us, we could have a fresh start. And this is the easiest job of them all! We don't even have to capture this one. You heard 'im! 'This one, I want dead. Bring me his head, and all of this will be yours.' Did you see all that gold he had?!"

"Yeah, I saw it, but—"

"But what? Why do you always try and find the negative in things?"

"It's just, if he's offering such a high reward, I doubt it will be that easy, you know?"

"Daren, there's twenty of us. No man, Guardian or not, is going to be able to win that battle. And if he takes out a few of the others in the process, well, then that just means we get a bigger cut."

A thud against the wooden floor startled them both. They quickly turned around to see another one of the bandits lying on the floor. James quickly raised the crossbow in his hands and looked around carefully. He walked over to nudge the other bandit with his foot but received no response.

"Is he...?"

"Yeah," James said, confirming Daren's suspicions. He looked around cautiously. "Ring the bell. He's here."

Daren ran for the bell rope on the other side of the tower, but only made it a few steps before his life was threatened.

"Don't move," Kai said firmly.

"James!"

When James turned around, Daren was being held hostage under Kai's grasp, with his blade hovering only a few inches from his neck.

"Let him go!" James demanded.

"I will. I have no intention of harming anyone else. I only want some information, and I'll be on my way."

James narrowed his eyes to better see Kai under the moon and the flickering flames of the two torches.

"Silver hair, wounded, and a shiny katana." James smiled and raised his crossbow. "You're the one we're looking for."

"Put that thing down before you hurt someone," Kai commanded.

"But that's exactly what I'm trying to do."

"You going to shoot your friend to get to me?"

"That'll be up to you," James said as he aimed.

"I only want some answers. Don't make this difficult."

"I'll give you to three. One...!"

Daren's eyes widened. "James, you can't be serious! You're going to hit me!"

"Two...!"

Kai's eyes narrowed at the man, and it was quickly apparent to him that the countdown was for real.

"Three!" James's crossbow launched a wooden bolt with a jagged steel tip through the air. Kai quickly tossed Daren to the side, letting the bolt sink into his right shoulder. Daren scrambled to ring the alarm bell as Kai dropped to a knee.

"He's up here!" Daren shouted over the screaming bell.

All the bandits in the field outside started to storm the watch-tower. Kai heard the wooden door open with a slam, followed by several pairs of footsteps sprinting up the stairs. James loaded another bolt into his crossbow.

"I asked you not to do this," Kai said to him. "I only wanted information."

"Yeah! Like I would have given it to you anyway."

"You still will. You don't have a choice."

"What are you talking about, crazy man?"

James looked into the eyes of the downed man as he awaited an answer and saw something that would haunt him for the rest of his life. There was a flicker of crimson light in Kai's eyes—and then, as fast as a strike of lightning, his features changed. A ghostly white face with venomous eyes as dark as a bottomless pit and a smiling mouth full of misshapen fangs looked back at James with an unquenchable lust for his flesh. It was only a brief moment, but James was struck with such bone-chilling terror that he accidentally fired his crossbow into the floor and started to unknowingly back away slowly.

"Kill him! Kill him! He's some kind of horror!" James shouted frantically. His voice reached an octave that one would think impossible for a grown man.

Bandits, all wearing mismatched armor from various scores, flooded the top of the steps. One charged at Kai with a downward slash of his rusted longsword. When the silver streak of steel from Kai's katana was visible to their eyes, the bandit's longsword hit the ground along with his severed hands. Kai quickly silenced the man's cries of agony by removing his head with one swift slice of his blade.

Another attacker took a careless slash at Kai's midsection with a dull blade that he parried away easily. In retaliation, Kai ripped out the bolt from his shoulder and forced it through the bandit's skull. An arrow hissed through the air right towards Kai's head. Once it was in his range, he snatched it out of the air and hurled it back at the archer, hitting him in the throat.

With a howling war cry, Daren picked up his halberd and took a mighty swing that was well placed. Kai had no choice but to duck underneath the attack, where he met the metal greaves of another bandit. He stumbled back into the wooden guard rail. He recovered just in time to swat away another incoming blade, but was helpless against the onrushing giant.

At full speed, the massive bandit slammed into Kai, breaking the wooden safety barrier behind him. Both of them raced through the night toward the ground. Kai crashed into a wagon full of sacks and small boxes. There was a puff of dust and the sound of jingling items rolling away into the darkness. When Kai rolled over to face the man who had taken him off the ledge, he realized the man had plummeted to his death. His body lay still, his head splattered against a large rock.

As Kai slowly returned to his feet, arrows flew from above that failed to find their mark. It was too dark for archers to see well, and all the debris acted as momentary cover for him. But he could hear that he was quickly becoming surrounded by the bandits still on ground level. He gritted his teeth angrily. "I don't have time for this."

Kai exploded from the rubble, the crimson flame thrashing against his blade. The bandits froze in shock, which Kai quickly took advantage of. He dashed toward them.

Kai may have been outnumbered, but they were outmatched. His speed was incredible. He moved through the night like a red blur. Archers fired aimlessly whenever they could, failing to hit anything other than the ground or the dead bodies of their fallen comrades. With the advances that did come close to him, Kai slipped, ducked, and sidestepped all of their chaotic swings with ease.

Each one of Kai's movements was swift and true. It was as if he had planned out every footfall months in advance and rehearsed them several times before this night. His body flowed like a gentle river, with his fiery blade acting as nothing more than an extension of himself. Every slice was placed with immaculate precision. Blood, limbs, and wretched shrieks of pain filled the midnight air—music to his ears. He twirled, twisted, spun, and rolled to life-ending pirouettes. It was almost as if they were unwillingly dancing with him, assuming their part as the Follow in a waltz of horror.

The bandits' numbers quickly dwindled, as did their morale. Kai pivoted on one foot and spilled the innards of two bandits with a red mist that sprayed into the air. As he slowly rose to his feet, covered in bandit blood, he eyed three trembling men in front of him, two of whom he was already acquainted with. The fiery blade purred calmly at his side. With a burst of misplaced courage, the only bandit Kai was unfamiliar with charged at him with a spear. The other man's head fell to the ground before James and Daren could perceive what had happened.

Kai slowly walked toward them. As the monster approached, panic raged throughout their bodies.

James shakily fired off a bolt from his crossbow that was nowhere close to hitting Kai. Daren suddenly threw down his halberd and fell to his knees, begging, "Please, just let us go!"

"Coward!" James shouted with fear evident in his voice.

Before James could load another bolt into his crossbow, Kai raised his blade to his throat. James nervously looked over the crimson flame that seemed to be desperately reaching for his neck, and when his eyes made their way to Kai's face, he shut them quickly, afraid of what he might see. Stricken with fear, he dropped the crossbow and joined Daren on the ground to beg for his life with a loud iteration of Daren's previous request. "Please, just let us go!"

"I offered you that choice, and you declined," Kai said coldly, not lowering his blade.

Daren remained silent, too afraid to speak.

"But maybe this time, if you cooperate, I'll let one of you live."

Their eyes shimmered with a crumb of hope.

"First, I want to know if anyone else passed through here. Five people, precisely. Younger than myself, and likely wounded. Anything come to mind?"

James shook his head quickly. "No, no, they never came. We were told about them, but they never showed up. I swear!"

Kai thought to himself for a quick moment before he concluded they had to have gone around the tower instead.

"All right, next question: who hired you?"

"We don't know his name," Daren said softly. "He comes and goes like the wind. Tells us where and when to be and who to look for."

"He's hired you before, then?"

"A few times."

"To kidnap people?"

"Always. Well, except for you. You were the first one he told us to kill, and now I think I know why."

Kai lowered his blade slowly. "You've taken other Guardians."

James and Daren could not figure out if they should respond. They stayed silent.

"Where do you take them?" Kai asked.

"Enora. That is, if he doesn't find us and take them himself first," Daren answered.

"Enora," Kai sneered. "That lawless gutter of a city?"

James chuckled. "Hey, believe me, we don't like it either, but it pays."

"What does he want with us?"

"We don't know," Daren said.

Kai raised his blade again.

"Seriously! We don't know," he repeated in a panic.

Confident that there was no deceit in the bandit's eyes, Kai lowered his weapon.

Daren let out an exhale of relief. "I will say this, though. Some-times, we'll see some of the ones we captured fighting in the games, but they never last that long. And when we do see them, they look much different."

"Different how?"

"Something happens to them—something that takes all the light from their eyes. By the time they make it to the coliseum, it looks like they're already dead."

Kai sheathed his katana and slowly turned away from them both, lost in his mind, trying to piece together his thoughts.

James looked at Daren and gestured toward his halberd with his eyes. Daren nodded.

James cleared his throat. "I don't know what makes you so special, but that guy is just as scary. Every time he speaks to us, I feel a chill run down my spine... Not that you'll ever find out!"

Daren lunged forward with his halberd, sinking it into Kai's lower back. Kai's arms fell to his sides.

James hopped to his feet, ecstatic. "HA! We're about to be so rich, Daren, I told you!"

Kai shook his head, disappointed. Before Daren could remove the weapon from his target, the dark red flames that were once thrashing on Kai's katana suddenly raced from Kai's wound up the shaft of the halberd to quickly catch Daren on fire. He dropped his weapon and kicked his feet, screaming on the ground as he rolled around, desperately trying to put out the flames. But no matter what he tried, they never waned. James rushed to his side.

"Help him! Help him! What are you doing?!"

Kai started to walk away towards the cliff, blood steadily flowing out of his back. "Thanks for the information."

The flames suddenly vanished from Daren's body, but his lifeless eyes told James all he needed to know. Kneeling amidst fallen comrades, James stared at his only friend as grief hollowed him out. He may have survived, but now he was alive and alone with nothing left but a bleak, empty future. Anger ignited in James's chest as he turned toward Kai, now a silhouette fading into a distant nightmare. The reward money was all that remained. Gritting his teeth, James rose to his feet and charged after him. Kai had to die.

Kai approached the edge of the cliff and looked around for the path down when he heard the rapid approach of footsteps behind him. Quickly, he turned around with a slice of his blade. All he managed to cut was air. James dove straight at him from a low angle, tackling him off the cliff. Together, they sank into the depths of darkness below.

CHAPTER 17

INALLY," Barrik said as they breached the edge of Thern-ruff Woods to see the towering tree of Meditas right before their eyes. "We made it."

"Let's hurry and get her to Master Darion," Rinna urged.

While everyone else hurried out of the forest toward the city, Vincent remained still, his eyes fixated on the sinking sun. They had made it back to the city. Vera would receive the care she needed, and the others would be safe, but there was still someone else who needed their help.

"Vince, what are you doing? Let's go," Alexandra called to him.

"I'm going back for him," Vincent stated, his firm resolve clear in his eyes.

"For who?" Alexandra asked, confused.

"Kai."

Alexandra stepped closer. "Vince, we don't even know where he is, or even if he's…"

"He is. I know it. I can't explain why, other than I can *feel* it. Just as I'm as sure you're standing right in front of me, I know he needs help. We made it back to the city, but once we walk inside, we won't be able to leave again without the king's permission, and I can't risk that. I may not be as strong as my father, Qrux made that painfully clear, but if I don't try, I won't be able to live with myself."

Alexandra looked deep into his eyes and knew there was nothing she could say or do to change his mind.

"I'll be all right. Trust me," Vincent added reassuringly.

"I know you will be." Alexandra turned back over her shoulder. "Barrik, Rinna, get Vera to Master Darion's."

"What? Where are you going?" Barrik questioned.

"We're going back for Kai," she answered.

"For *Kai*? What are you talking about?!"

"Vera doesn't have time for questions. Just get her there. Vince and I won't be far behind you. Show him the way, Rinna."

"You got it!"

"You're coming with me?" Vincent asked.

"Well, I can't trust you to find your way there and back on your own," she teased. "Besides, you're right. They're safe now. If Kai is out there and needs our help, then we'll bring him back. Together."

Vincent smiled gratefully and nodded his head. "Then lead the way."

A young boy with shoulder-length hair, dark as night, sat on the cold, damp cave floor with tears streaming down his face. Beaten and bruised in the middle of a frightening place he was told never to enter.

"A beast sleeps deep inside, and we dare not wake it," the villagers would say. But this was where he was told to hide. When he could no

longer hear the distant voices outside, he would make his escape. As the adrenaline in his muscles and bones began to fade, grief quickly overtook him.

The final faces of his parents, full of fear and desperation, would forever be ingrained in his mind. They had sacrificed themselves to allow him to escape, but what was he to do now? He had nowhere to go, had nobody else to run to. He was entirely on his own. The hole that now took the place of his heart pulled so hard that he felt it might swallow him, and he wanted it to—*needed* it to. The pain was unbearable. Yet it never ceased.

With clenched fists and gritted teeth, he desperately tried to subdue the insurmountable pain in his chest, but found no success. Anger took a firm hold of his bones and gripped him by the soul. Nothing would please him more than to bring an end to the one responsible for this pain—that gray-eyed man. While the boy's rage continued to consume him, suddenly, all of the hairs on his body shot up in an instant.

He only *thought* he was alone.

"I can smell the lust for blood on you, child," a woman's soft voice trickled throughout the cave.

The boy jumped to his feet, startled. He looked around frantically. "Wh—Who's there?!" he shouted.

A whisper caressed his ear. "Let me heal you."

The boy whipped around, but saw nothing besides the ambient moonlight creeping in from the distant cave entrance. He was sure of what he heard and that it was not just his imagination playing tricks on him. Something was in the cave with him. He could *feel* the lingering presence—a presence that sent a chill straight down his spine. His bones froze with terror, his breaths rapid. His feet stuck to the ground as sweat poured down his face.

"I can give you power." Her voice seemed to come from everywhere.

The boy tried not to let himself succumb to fear. He squeezed his eyes tightly and counted to three in his head. As soon as he hit his mark, he took off toward the entrance, running as fast as he could. With the outside's safety within reach, he heard her voice again.

"Power to avenge those whom you've lost. You needn't hide any longer."

His steps slowed and came to a halt. He stopped himself just before the cave's exit. His heart still pounded, and his body was wracked with fear, but there was something in her voice, something in her words that suggested he could lend her his trust. His curiosity blossomed enough courage for him to turn around. Still, he saw only darkness.

"What kind of power?" the boy asked hesitantly with a sniffle.

In the endless distance, near the back of the cave, a bright crimson flame burst into existence.

Kai's eyes shot wide open to see a dark night sky sparkling with stars above. He turned his head to see James's body grotesquely contorted and still. He groaned in pain as he tried to sit up. His side was bleeding. His left leg was surely broken. A large gash across his right shoulder covered his arm in blood, and every one of his breaths produced an excruciatingly sharp pain in his side. His newly healed ribs were broken once again.

From the ground, he looked up to the top of the cliff. Several broken tree branches indicated the path they had taken from the top. With the quick loss of blood amongst his other injuries, no stamina to move himself, and the location of his katana unknown, he was stuck.

The effect of his injuries had begun to overtake him. The world above began to blur and spin as his eyes grew heavy. He dared not close them, but the battle with fatigue was his strongest yet. His throat felt scorched as he coughed up a mouthful of blood. He rested his head against the cliff as he slowly began accepting his fate. Time passed as he waited to die.

Night turned to day. The warmth of the sun, while it felt nice against his face as he faded in and out of consciousness, did awful things to the smell of James's rotting corpse.

The next time he opened his eyes, it was dark again. There was a rustle in the brush nearby. Kai's head swayed back and forth as he tried to get a look at what moved closer to him. He smiled at the blurred sight of a familiar face—one he had not seen in ten years.

"Victor…" Kai said weakly. "My time for the stars, then…"

"Stars? No, you're not dead yet, old man," a familiar voice said.

"Although he doesn't look far off," someone else added.

Despite his best efforts, Kai could no longer keep his eyes open.

"Hey! Kai! Stay with us, come on, now!" Alexandra knelt over him and looked at his injuries.

"Vince, he's in rough shape. See if you can—"

"Sword…" Kai barely spoke above a whisper.

"Save your breath, Kai, you're gonna be fine."

"Sword… will… help," Kai gasped, each of his words taking a full breath.

"Your sword?" Alexandra looked around, but saw no sign of it. "Vince!"

"On it!" He scrambled around, searching the nearby area for Kai's katana.

Only a few moments passed until a loud, monstrous howl boomed in the air from somewhere nearby. Alexandra quickly stood up, drew her sword, and scanned the area, but it was too dark to see anything.

"Vince!" she shouted, not removing her eyes from the void between the trees.

Vincent suddenly emerged from the darkness with Kai's katana in his hand. "Was that a wretch?"

"I really hope not."

Vincent handed the katana to Alexandra.

"Kai, what do you want us to do with this?"

Another howl that sounded much closer than the last forced Vincent to draw his sabers with a twirl and focus on the tree line, ready for anything to leap out at them.

Kai slowly opened his right hand. Confused, Alexandra placed the hilt of his weapon in his palm. As soon as she let go, he mustered the remainder of his strength to thrust the sword into the chest of the bandit next to him.

"I think he was already dead," Vincent said with a wince.

At the taste of blood, the crimson flame immediately burst across the blade. Startled and slightly afraid, Alexandra fell backward. The flame fed on James's body, pulling his skin tighter and tighter across his bones. Vincent and Alexandra watched in horror as the bandit shriveled up, his body transforming with each passing second. Now, with his skin taut and drained, he barely resembled a human at all. The sight sent a disturbed shiver throughout Vincent's body.

When there was nothing left beneath the tight wrapping of flesh other than bone, the fire slowed to a pulse and quickly entered Kai's body through his hand. After a quick moment, their nearly dead mentor struggled up to his feet. They stared at him, jaws agape, frozen with shock and awe. Vincent fumbled around to find words. "What in the—"

"Not here," Kai said quickly. He sheathed his weapon and extended a hand to Alexandra. She was reluctant to take it.

"Come on. We need to move from here before company arrives."

Kai limped into the trees. Vincent and Alexandra exchanged glances to confirm that they had seen the same thing before they followed behind him.

The three of them traveled silently on guard through the forest for only a short distance. Once they felt safe from harm, they stopped to rest for the night.

Vincent and Alexandra put together a small fire as Kai tended to the wounds he had not yet remedied. The gash on his right shoulder continued to bleed. He held his burning blade to it until the fire had painlessly sealed him up once again. When he sheathed his weapon, he looked up to see Vincent and Alexandra averting their eyes. The lambent orange light from the flickering fire illuminated the dried blood and dark bruises on their faces—but it was the weight in their expressions that caught his attention.

Not only were they broken, they were haunted.

Kai's gaze lingered on Vincent's tightened jaw and the way his hands fidgeted with the hilt of the three-gemmed sword. He appeared like someone else entirely. He was fighting doubts, struggling to reconcile something inside himself. Alexandra's avoidant eyes and slumped shoulders told their own story, one of guilt or uncertainty she had not yet voiced.

"You guys look like you've been through hell," Kai finally said, breaking the silence. "What happened?"

Vincent and Alexandra exchanged a reluctant glance before they took turns recounting the events after their party was separated, sure to give him every detail they could remember. When they were finished, a silence fell over them all. Alexandra's watery eyes returned to the ground while Vincent resumed fidgeting with the sword on his hip.

"Are you still letting Qrux's words torment you now, Vince?" Kai asked gently.

Vincent scoffed. Qrux's words were practically the only thing in his mind.

"Vince," Kai continued softly, "you escorted your comrades to safety and helped take down a man of incredible strength, and if it weren't for your decision to turn back for me, I'd be dead right now. I had no strength left to keep my eyes open, let alone move. Qrux's words couldn't be further from the truth. You're shaping up to be just like your father."

Vincent shook his head in disbelief. "It's hard to feel that way when I'm constantly reminded that I'm nowhere close to as strong as he was."

"Victor didn't gain his strength overnight. It took time, practice—and a lot of sacrifice. This was only your first mission as a Guardian. You'll get there."

Vincent plucked a blade of grass and twirled it between his fingers. "I hope so," he muttered before letting it fall with a sigh.

Kai tilted his head. "What is it?"

Vincent hesitated. "…Are you sure my father was a good person?"

The question caught Kai off guard. "Why would you ask something like that?"

"Qrux said his name struck fear into people, and Alice was yelling that he tortured her and that she wanted to make me pay for it. But I don't know how that would be possible, seeing how young she was. I just…" He paused and exhaled a deep sigh before continuing. "I just wanted to be like him, but I don't know how I'm supposed to do that when I barely remember him. All I have to go on are stories from other people and the things Mom used to tell us." His expression tightened with emotional turmoil. "I just wanted to make them proud, but now…" His watery eyes fell to the ground. "I just feel…lost."

"Vince," Kai started delicately, "do you remember what I said to you outside the king's hall when you first arrived in Meditas?"

Vincent shook his head. "I don't know. You said a lot of things."

"I told you then, as I'm telling you now, the only thing that matters to your parents is how you see them—not anyone else. Do you believe your father was a bad man?"

"No. Of course not."

"Do you think Fira would have remained by Victor's side if he were evil at heart?"

"No."

"Your father was human, Vince. As are you. He made mistakes. As will you. No matter what path we choose in life, we will always be met with difficult choices and no clear answer. And when we're faced with these tough decisions, someone will always feel slighted, no matter what choice you make. A hero to some will always be a villain to others."

"Ghost said something similar to me before." Vincent remembered.

"Although he means well, Ghost tends to be perilously direct with his choice of words. He may be a bit bold and coarse, but in the end, he does what he believes to be right. That's all any of us can do. We use the information and experience we have to do what we feel is best."

"But what if I choose wrong?"

"You might. And if you do, then you'll be faced with two options. You either let your mistake eat you up inside until it wears you down to nothing, or you make it a lesson on how to do better in the future. Own it and watch how you grow, or run from it and see just how hard it is to live."

Kai fell silent for a moment as his gaze lingered on Vincent. He felt a sense of familiarity in the storm behind Vincent's eyes. He knew it well. It was a storm born from carrying too much weight.

"Vince, people are always going to compare you to your father, whether you want them to or not," Kai said quietly. "You look like him, you carry his name, and even though you don't remember much about him, he lives on within you."

Vincent smiled softly, warmed by Kai's words.

"But, Vince," Kai continued, "you're not him."

Vincent's smile quickly faded. He felt as though Kai had built him up just to tear him back down. He was crushed.

"It's not a bad thing," Kai was quick to add, noticing the shift in Vincent's expression. "Fira taught you everything she could—not so you could be as strong as her or Victor, but so you could be stronger. It's noble that you want to be like your father, but instead of walking in his shadow, run ahead and stand beside him in your own light."

"I don't think I know what that means," Vincent responded, his voice heavy with uncertainty.

Kai smiled faintly and sat back against the tree. "In time, you will. Just keep your head up."

His eyes drifted to Alexandra as he addressed them both. "You've dealt with quite a lot these past few days, but don't allow the words of your foes to create doubt in yourselves or the ones you love. Most people would not have walked away from what you have. I'm proud of you all."

Kai's words hung in the air, heavy with sincerity. Alexandra looked up, disbelief etched into her face. "Proud?" she asked, her

voice quivering. "How can you be proud of us when, when Toran..."
She turned away with clenched eyes, biting her lip.

Kai's gaze softened as a flicker of pain crossed his face. He waited, giving her the space to speak, but when she failed to continue, he
spoke gently. "Alex... Hey, look at me." His voice was tender and full
of empathy.

Grudgingly, she lifted her eyes.

Kai looked at her delicately, slowly absorbing the pain and
disappointment she felt. His head moved back and forth almost
imperceptibly. "You can't blame yourself."

Her lips started to tremble uncontrollably.

"It's not your fault," he reassured her.

The light from the fire glistened in her wet eyes as she looked
up into the night sky beyond the trees. She took a deep breath to
loosen the tightness in her chest. "Your last words to me were..." She
swallowed the lump in her throat. "...'Get them home safely,' and we
didn't even make it out of the village before I let Toran..." Her voice
faltered, unable to finish the thought.

Vincent placed a consoling hand on her shoulder. Kai remained silent.

A small hysterical laugh escaped her. "Vera's all cut up and in
terrible condition, I don't know how Vince is still standing, I have
no idea why they even attacked us, and I still don't understand what
happened with the village. And on top of it all, we couldn't even give
Toran a proper burial."

Kai waited a moment before he responded, "Don't burden yourself with this weight. Hey, look at me. I'm serious. You performed
your responsibility, as did Toran. So, I'm proud of him as well. Part
of being a leader is understanding that you *will* lose people. That
much is out of your control. Even when you do everything right
and do everything in your power to save everyone you can, there
will still be loss. Don't allow a crime you didn't commit to hold your
mind hostage. But if you must accept some fault, then understand,
self-forgiveness is only a sin if you treat it like one."

Alexandra continued to hold his gaze.

"And know that I sent Toran to the stars, may he find his peace. It may not be the funeral procession he deserves, but it's the best we can give him."

She nodded and wiped the tears from her cheeks.

Vincent suddenly remembered something he had forgotten to mention during the recount of their battle. "Kai?"

"Yeah?"

"There was one other thing Qrux said to me just before he died: He said, 'He will come for you.'"

Vincent could see Kai grow uneasy. "Does that mean anything to you?"

"All I know is that someone in Enora is collecting people of interest, and the son of Victor Raine would surely make it on that list. That's why those bandits in Thernruff Woods wanted to capture you the night before you arrived in Meditas."

"They were looking for someone else too," Alexandra recalled. "Someone with a blindfold and a... fiery sword." Her eyes widened as she realized. "They were looking for you, weren't they?"

"Yes," he answered.

"They called you something else that night, though. Something like Uda... Uder—"

"Udurim," Kai finished for her. "It's an old Sanorian word that means something akin to 'nightmare.'"

"Qrux called you that too," she remembered. "Is that your Guardian name?"

Kai nodded.

"Seems kind of dark, don't you think?"

"I do. But I wasn't the one who picked it. It was given to me on the battlefield many years ago, and unfortunately, it stuck."

"Okay..." Vincent began to wonder. "I understand why they would go after you, seeing as people all across Sanora seem to know who you are, but why me?"

"Because despite the doubts you're experiencing, someone suspects you to be of great capability, and likely wants you *with* them rather than standing against them."

"With them for what?"

"Ever since your father and those who followed him fought King Netir and his army ten years ago, Dahnkar has been in shambles. If the Abnor fountain's power was truly stolen, it would still take time to rebuild and try again."

"Try again? But wasn't King Netir killed in the war?"

"He was. However, after your conversation with Larissa, the strange kidnappings of Rogues and Guardians, and now what happened with Qrux and Alice, I'm beginning to believe Netir was only a pawn. Or maybe someone is picking up where he left off."

"You're saying someone else is building an army to steal another fountain's power?"

"There's no way to be sure, but it's starting to appear that way. Only this time, they're trying to remove key players on the board before they make their move."

Vincent sat silently for a moment as he tried to piece everything together, until he started thinking aloud, "So, that's why they want you to join them too, then?"

Kai shook his head. "I think it's more likely that whoever this person is would prefer me eliminated entirely. Qrux and Alice only attacked you after I was gone, and the fact that they knew about the Soul Eater leads me to believe that it was a trap meant specifically for me."

Vincent furrowed his brow. "The Soul Eater... I still don't understand. What exactly is it?"

"Soul Eaters are ancient, foul creatures created by Sanorians. Their presence alone is enough to warp the energy of the surrounding environment, causing all kinds of mutations. Animals, weather patterns, and anyone else who spends prolonged time in the vicinity are all affected."

"Like those bear horrors and that poor old woman?" Vincent asked.

"Exactly. They were likely normal bears or wolves until its energy changed them, and she was just a normal villager."

"Why would the Sanorians create something like that?"

"They were supposed to be weapons to help them against humanity's assault, but turned out to be an enemy to them as well. Just like all the other horrors of our world, they don't care where they get their meals from; they just hunger."

"What happens to them?" Alexandra asked softly. "The souls, I mean."

"The souls they consume aren't necessarily destroyed. They're just tethered here to the Soul Eater as a sort of power source," Kai answered.

"Do they ever find their peace in the stars?" she wondered with heavy concern.

"Unfortunately, no. Not unless the Soul Eater is killed."

"That's why you stayed," Alexandra said, realizing. "To make sure Gala and the others could find their peace."

Kai nodded, confirming her assumption. "I wouldn't be able to live with myself if I knew they could never truly rest."

"Qrux and Alice seemed to be aware of that fact," Vincent pointed out. "Is that why you think it was a trap?"

"Yes. Not only did they know about the Soul Eater, but they knew I would stay behind to fight it. And from what you tell me, they also knew that you, the son of Victor Raine, were among the group as well."

"How could they possibly have known all of that, though?" Alexandra questioned.

Vincent remembered the two parallel lines scarred upon Qrux's disfigured face. "Well, Qrux was a Rogue, wasn't he?"

"He was," Kai answered. "While their information on my character likely stems from Qrux's days as a Guardian, that doesn't explain how they knew the rest."

Alexandra looked at Kai curiously. "You knew him, then?"

"In a distant time, we fought alongside each other. He was a good man."

Alexandra was taken aback. "A good man?" she repeated angrily. "He killed Toran! He tried to abduct us, butchered Vera, and set a trap to kill you too! After all of that, how can you sit there and say he was a good man when he was clearly evil?"

Kai allowed silence to fill the air before he replied to her concerns. "Simply because someone stands against you does not inherently make them evil. If you start to assume your reason for fighting is above someone else's, you may find yourself with the mind of a tyrant. Sometimes, people find themselves in a desperate situation with a lack of options. You don't know what decisions you would make if you were faced with the same conflicts. One impossible choice is all it can take to lock someone in a cell of darkness. It is our task as Guardians to be their light and help them out of that darkness if we can, but never condemn them to it."

"So, what are you saying? We should have tried to befriend him? That we should have reasoned with him while his sword was in Toran's chest?"

"No. You did what you had to. All I'm saying is, keep in mind that your enemies are also people. They have values, beliefs, loved ones, something that drives them to make the choices they do. Unlike the horrors that lurk in the shadows of the moonlight who kill for hunger, they're complex." Kai groaned in pain as he repositioned himself against the tree. "Fight for your friends and your beliefs to your last breath, but don't assume that because you fight for your own cause, you are more noble than those who would oppose you. Because if another war truly is on the horizon, you'll come to find there's plenty of evil within the good, and a surprising amount of good within the evil."

There was silence. A long silence. Vincent's eyes drifted to the three-stoned sword as his thoughts spiraled. The mention of war made him uneasy—uneasy because he knew it to be true, and after their battle with Qrux, he felt hopelessly underprepared. He had been powerless to do anything for Toran, and Vera's condition was now out of his control. He felt useless and weak—something he never wanted to feel again.

Vincent looked up at Kai, his eyes filled with a burning resolve to overcome his helplessness. "I don't want anyone else to get hurt," he finally said, breaking the silence. "If war is coming, can you make us ready for it?"

Kai glanced at Alexandra and noticed the same fiery determination in her eyes. "You're never truly ready for war, but I'll do my best. First, though, we need to get back to Meditas and recover. In the meantime, however, I have a question of my own for you, Vincent, if I may?"

"Ask away."

"How exactly did you know I was in need of help?"

Vincent scratched the back of his head, unsure of how to answer. "Well, I felt something… Something familiar that was like a tug or a pull, almost like it was asking for help. I don't know how to explain it, but in my mind, I saw this waterfall splashing into a peaceful spring, and every time I felt it, somehow I knew it was you."

"Do you feel it now?"

Vincent's eyes looked around as he searched for the feeling. "No."

"Close your eyes and focus."

Vincent did as he was told. Kai closed his eyes along with him.

Vincent shook his head. "Still noth… Wait, yes! There it is again! Only it's much stronger. I can feel the warmth of the sunlight… Wait, now it's gone again."

"You're sensing my energy just like in the training yard—only this time, it's much stronger, so you're feeling my emotions as well. Which is how you knew I was in need of help, and also why it gave you strength when you were losing focus. You were picking up on my distress as well as my strength, and from quite a distance at that. Rather impressive."

Vincent slightly wriggled with pride from the compliment. "Why only yours, though? It's not like I sensed anyone else's, and they were much closer."

"Because of how my Favor works," Kai answered with a groan.

"I thought you masked energy. Wouldn't that make it harder to sense?"

"I never said that's *all* I can do. Yes, I can mask energy, but I can also propel it outward to get a read on everything around me. In some ways, it helps me see even better than my normal vision."

"So, you're like a bat?"

"If that's how you want to see it, then sure. To put it simply, when you sense my energy as I use it in that way, it's like I have my door open, and you're looking into my home. For other people, though, their doors are locked, and if you want to see inside, you'll have to conjure a key. Does that make sense?"

Vincent stared at him blankly. "I guess."

Kai chuckled painfully. "We'll work on it. In time, the more you work on your Favors, the more they will grow and develop new capabilities along with you, just like any other skill."

"So, then, that flame on your sword and whatever you did to that bandit—is that also part of your Favor?"

Kai stared plainly into the small fire. "That is something else entirely."

"What *did* you do to him?"

Kai stayed silent, but Vincent and Alexandra's curiosity refused to move on.

"I drained his energy and used it to heal myself... partially."

"How?" Alexandra asked.

Kai grunted as he adjusted his position against the tree. "When I was still a child, there was a cave just outside my village, said to harbor one of the first horrors—a beast of the night that fed off the blood of warriors or anyone unlucky enough to come across her."

"Her?" Vincent suddenly grew excited. "Are you talking about the Red Mother?"

"Red Mother? Why does that sound familiar?" Alexandra pondered.

"Because she's in one of the stories Mom used to read to us all the time. One of me and Vera's favorites."

"Yeah, but that's just a story, Vince."

"Actually..." Kai interjected.

"She's real?" Alexandra looked shocked.

"While the story is an embellishment, as they all tend to be, I assure you she is very real."

Vincent leaned forward suddenly. "Wait... You didn't kill her, did you?" he asked, clearly concerned.

"No, I didn't kill her."

Vincent leaned back up against the tree, relieved.

"I do, however, have her sword and control over her energy and abilities. An overall spike in strength and agility, as well as the power you witnessed, to drain anything with blood to heal myself and replace my own energy."

"Well, that's useful," Vincent said plainly.

"Useful, yes, but an excruciatingly painful way to take someone's life, and an even more disrespectful way of treating the dead. It's not a power I like to use." Kai said disapprovingly.

"Why use it, then?" Alexandra asked.

Without an answer, he peered into the fire, silently watching the faces of all his unfortunate victims flash through the dancing flames.

"We should get some sleep," he finally said, dodging her question. Kai laid his head back against the tree and shut his eyes. Vincent and Alexandra looked at each other and decided to question him no further.

"I'll take the first watch," Vincent whispered to Alexandra.

"Are you sure?"

"Yeah. I'm sure."

"Fine by me," Alexandra said, shrugging. "I'm exhausted." She lay on the ground to toss and turn until she made herself as comfortable as the forest floor would allow.

As the others drifted asleep, Vincent tried to focus on the sounds of the wind in the trees to drown out the growing noise in his mind. It had been several days since they had truly slept, and the more he thought about it, the more he started to prefer the screaming thoughts of self-doubt to what awaited him once he closed his eyes again. He knew the dreams of the Sanorian sword would be there, ready to greet him. He looked down at it, belted to his hip. It was darker than the night's shadows that surrounded him, save for the trim of Sanorian silver. The colorless star stones seemed to pull him in as his eyes wandered over them, each one a beacon of the dreams he dreaded. He was sure he would see their ethereal shine again. See the one who wielded each color. Feel the pain they gave him—such visceral agony.

The vivid memories of each dream lingered, weighing down his battered body even further.

Like Alexandra, he was exhausted. He ached all over—not just from endless traveling, but also from their battles and the wounds they left behind. Weariness had seeped into his bones, heavy and unshakeable. Yet despite his physical need to rest, he avoided shutting his eyes for as long as possible—for as long as his body would let him. As long as his eyes were open, he was unable to dream; he was safe.

But Alexandra eventually relieved him, and his body betrayed him far too soon.

The night's darkness had just begun to fade away when Kai opened his eyes. While the sun was not yet visible, it cast a subtle light that snuck its way through the forest. As the sleep drifted away from him and his senses returned, he could hear Alexandra singing softly.

> *"They smile brightly and bow their heads,*
> *But are they foe, or are they friends?*
> *In this cage where I stand alone,*
> *I'll never know if it's truly home.*
> *I'd rather live wild and free,*
> *Among the birds and the raging sea.*
> *So, should I stay or should I leave,*
> *To become the me I want to be?"*

Her words floated away into the trees where the morning birds began a song of their own.

"Not bad," Kai said.

Alexandra whipped around, startled, and smiled gently. "Thanks, but I don't think I'll be performing anytime soon."

"Why not? It's much better than anything that crazy seaman is wailing in his bar."

"Mancho sings?"

"If you dare to call it that."

She laughed softly.

"Which one was that again?" Kai asked.

"The Tragedy of Lady Altaraya, the young princess everyone is envious of, who struggles to find her place in the world. Nobody quite understands her, and they treat her like a leper because she fantasizes about living outside the kingdom. Eventually, she flees to live on her own, but on the first night she leaves the kingdom, she falls victim to a pack of weren. The outside world was not quite how she pictured it to be."

"I guess it would be hard not to feel a little of that right now."

A short huff of air left Alexandra's nose in evident agreement. She looked at Vincent, still sound asleep, as she fiddled with the Sanorian silver ring on her finger, losing herself in thought.

"You know, we never questioned it," she said, starting to openly speak her thoughts. "Vince was always talking about becoming a Guardian just like his dad, and from the moment our mom told us he didn't have a choice, regardless of what he wanted, me, Barrik, and Vera all knew we'd be here right beside him. It's just…"

"Not quite what you pictured it to be?"

She looked up at him. "I don't really know what I expected. Living the adventure feels much different than reading it."

There was a moment of silence until Alexandra grew a soft smile of remembrance and continued, "She used to read to us every night right after dinner when we were younger. Vince and Vera would marvel over the crazy horrors and weapons the stories spoke about, and Barrik would usually fall right to sleep. His snores almost became part of every book." She chuckled. "But I always loved the songs. Each one became a break for the characters, where all their problems faded away, and nothing other than the lyrics and notes of the melody mattered to them. Almost like they took place somewhere beyond the rest of the story."

She looked down at her left arm, tracing the dark crevices with her eyes. "I know they're just words on a page, but Mom has a way of bringing them to life." She closed her eyes and started to sway back and forth gently, still smiling. "Her voice was soft and subtly powerful for the sad songs, hearty and strong when there was a ballad about a battle, and lively and full of excitement for the ones purely for everyone's entertainment. Once you heard her sing it, that was it. That's how you read those words every time from then on."

Kai sat quietly and continued to listen. Alexandra watched as little smoke trails from the fire's embers swam up above to join the clouds.

"It's funny... Everyone looks at her as nothing more than the fearless leader of Sylva. A strong, intimidating warrior who could win any battle or take on any horror. The village bows to her and speaks to her as if she's royalty, but to us, she's just Mom."

"I think she is more than okay with being 'just Mom.'"

"I know. I just wish everyone could see her the way we do, because she's so much more than a Rogue or a Guardian or Sylva's chief."

"The majority of people will only ever see the mask you wear when you walk among them. Only a few will look beyond and come to know your soul. Those are the ones you'd be wise to keep by your side—the ones who keep you whole."

Alexandra softly shook her head back and forth. "Kai, destroyer of bandits, slayer of Soul Eaters, and master of poems," she teased.

The corners of his lips turned up ever so slightly. "No master here. Just a reader."

"I noticed that."

He shrugged slightly. "Hard for a busy mind to wander."

She watched as he leaned forward with a groan and clutched his side. His silver hair, still wet with sweat and covered in dirt, but without his cloth to hold it all back, gave more shape to his rugged face, full of cuts and dried blood. He was filthy. His breathing not only sounded painful, but looked it too.

"You're not going to die on me, right, old man?"

He chuckled painfully. "I've been in much worse shape than this."

"Okay, good. I was a little worried you might kick off in your sleep."

"If only I could be so lucky." Kai weakly brought himself to his feet, declining Alexandra's offer to help. He looked down the trail, slowly becoming brighter and brighter with the rising sun, when Vincent suddenly jolted awake. His face glistened with sweat, his breaths full of panic. He looked around, momentarily frightened, until he realized he had woken up... finally.

"Are you okay?" Alexandra asked, concerned.

Vincent caught his breath before he answered. "Yeah, just a bad dream." His eyes fell to the Sanorian sword at his hip. He reached up to the center of his chest, where the same blade had been forced through him in his sleep only moments ago. It was just a dream, yet he still felt the dark metal sliding through him. Like a distant memory carved into his body, the painful sensation remained as vivid as the texture of a tree's bark beneath his fingertips, or the slick finish of a polished tabletop.

"That dream have anything to do with that sword of yours?" Kai questioned, demonstrating his perceptiveness.

Vincent hesitated a moment, slowly lowering his hand. "It was one of the same ones as before."

"*One* of them?" Kai asked, surprised.

"One for each of the star stones in this thing," Vincent said, gesturing to the sword. "Except the stones are glowing in the dreams." His hand reached up to his chest again. "And everything feels so real."

"Just more and more questions," Kai said, looking at Vincent's sword curiously. "Come on," he urged with a groan. "We won't be able to find the answer to any of them sitting around out here."

Vincent watched as Kai slowly started down the trail at his injured pace. "You're not going to die on us on the way back, are you?"

Alexandra laughed.

Kai hung his head.

Vincent looked on, confused. "What did I say?"

Alexandra shook her head, ignoring his question. "Let's go."

Before he took a step to follow behind them, Vincent's eyes returned to the dark hilt of the sword that now haunted his every dream.

The three of them pushed through the forest, but since their pace was slowed due to Kai's injuries, their journey back to Meditas took longer than expected. Once they emerged from the tree line of Thernruff Woods, they could see the fountain's tree reaching high above the city toward the stars. As the sun sank into the late evening, they approached the open city gate and began to hear the sound of stressed voices growing louder and louder.

"For the last time, you need permission from King Sentis to leave! Until you have that, we will not let you pass, even if we have to use force. And don't try to bring us another fake scroll!"

"We could have you thrown in the dungeon just for that, you know!" someone else shouted.

"They should be back by now! You can't expect me to sit here and do nothing."

That loud, angry voice sounded familiar.

Alexandra looked at Vincent suspiciously. "I think that's—"

"Put him down!" a guard shouted.

Vincent and Alexandra rushed ahead of Kai and around the corner of the gate to see Barrik holding a guard high in the air by his shoulders. Several others had him surrounded with spears pointed and swords drawn.

Alexandra leaned up against the stone wall with a smile. "You can put him down, Bear."

Barrik looked up and instantly let go. The guard crashed to the ground with a metallic rumble of his armor. He started to run toward them, but before he could take a step, a guard jabbed his spear at him to keep him back. Barrik snatched the weapon from his hands, growled in his face, and snapped it in half over his knee, sending splinters of wood into the air. The guards all backed off and let him through.

As the beast thundered toward her, Alexandra threw up her hands to halt him. "Hang on a second, Bear... Barrik!"

She failed. Barrik scooped her up and squeezed her tightly.

"Okay, okay, put me down," she managed to squeak out.

Vincent laughed, but only for a moment. With his other hand, Barrik yanked him in close. Vincent thrashed his arms against Barrik's chest and back in an attempt to escape, but quickly fell limp, accepting his fate.

Finally, Barrik let go. "What took you guys so long?! I was about to come look for you."

Alexandra looked past him at the group of rattled guards. "I see that."

"Did you guys find Kai? Is he okay?"

Just then, Kai limped his way around the corner of the gate, holding his side.

"Kai!" Barrik exclaimed.

"He's in bad shape," Vincent said with a straight face. "He needs you to carry him to Master Darion."

"Okay," Barrik said as he jogged over to Kai. As he drew closer, Kai looked into Barrik's eyes and let his hand fall to his katana. "Don't touch me."

Vincent and Alexandra started to laugh hysterically. One of the guards ran up to Kai and stood straight with a salute.

"Sir! In the event of your return, we were ordered to send you to King Sentis immediately!"

Kai rolled his eyes as he exhaled his pain and frustration. "Of course you were."

"Barrik, how's Vera doing?" Alexandra asked.

His face quickly fell. "She..." He trailed off.

Concern grew in Alexandra's voice. "She what?"

He hesitated for a moment before answering. "She might have lost the vision in her left eye."

"What?!" Vincent was outraged. "How bad of a healer is this Master Darion?"

"Well, he said if we would have gotten here sooner, it would have been an easy fix, but since so much time had passed, not only did it get infected, but there might be permanent damage. They don't know for sure. All we can do is let her rest. He said he would like to keep her there for a few weeks."

"Weeks?!" Alexandra shouted.

"So, we just have to sit around and do nothing until then?" Vincent asked, frustrated.

The discomfort of helplessness washed over the three of them.

"Right now, we all need to rest," Kai said. "That is the best course of action for everyone. I think the events we experienced are part of a much larger picture we don't yet see. Something on the horizon awaits us, and we'd best be ready when it arrives. So, rest up. We have work to do."

After Kai gave his ominous command, he slowly started walking toward the king's throne room. Every step seemed more painful than the last.

"He's in really bad shape," Barrik whispered, eyeing Kai up and down as he walked by them.

"I'm fine."

"He won't let us help him," Alexandra whispered back.

"Are you sure you don't want Barrik to carry you?" Vincent called after him, trying to lighten the mood.

Kai's only response was to move his hand to the hilt of his weapon.

CHAPTER 18

EEKS had passed since the return of their mission, and with each setting sun, the air grew colder. The fountain's tree stood tall above the city and was the only one that had not forsaken its leaves. Each ray of sunshine offered little more than the illusion of heat. Now, to stay warm, everyone huddled around fires, dressed in thick wool cloaks, or filled their stomachs with ale and wine. People hurried from one location to the next in fear of being frozen solid. Only when they stopped to eye various trinkets and wonders in the market did they allow themselves to linger.

Within the Guardians' barracks, all had been quiet save for the crackling fire in the main room. The cold days had dragged on for everyone as they restlessly recovered until finally, the day had come when they felt they had regained all of their strength.

Three loud booms echoed throughout the empty hall as Alexandra pounded on Barrik and Vincent's bedroom door.

"Come on! Wake up, already!" she shouted.

There was no immediate response. She pulled back her fist, ready to pound on the door again. Just before her hand met the wood, it angrily swung open. Vincent glared at her through narrowed eyes, deprived of sleep. His hair was messy, and his face was full of contempt.

"Why?" he asked her plainly with a shrug of his shoulders.

"You know why," she said with her hands on her hips.

"Can't we just meet you guys at the Broom?"

"No. We all told Vera we'd be there! Don't be such a baby, and hurry up! Rinna's already waiting for us outside."

"Fine," he said with a yawn, rubbing his eyes. "We'll be down in a minute."

Barrik's loud snoring blasted out from behind him. Vincent turned around to see that he was out cold.

"Maybe two," he corrected.

Alexandra raised her eyebrows. "Good luck."

Vincent sneered at her before he slammed the door in her face.

"So rude," she muttered to herself.

It was much more than a few minutes before the boys made their way down the stairs. Alexandra launched to her feet from the sofa. "Finally!"

Vincent waved her off. Snugly tucked into his Sylvan cloak as if it were a blanket, he was reluctantly ready for the icy air. Barrik, however, wore nothing more than trousers and a tunic with the sleeves ripped off just below the shoulders.

Alexandra quickly threw on her cloak as well and hurried to the door. "Okay, let's go!" Her voice was full of excitement and impatience.

They emerged from the barracks to see Rinna standing in the center of the road, wearing a dark tunic with sleeves that draped off her raised wrists down to her calves. A light green godet skirt belted around her waist fell like waves down to the top of her brown leather boots. Her head was tilted back, and her arms were out in front of her. Soft flurries were falling from the overcast morning sky onto her open palms and outstretched tongue.

"There you are, sleepyheads!" she said, full of cheer.

Barrik grunted.

"How are you so cheery this early?" Vincent asked with a yawn.

"It's the first time I've seen snow since I left Nalitay! Each snowflake is like a teeny bit of home," she said with her fingers pinched close together.

Less than impressed by the frigid temperature, Vincent watched his breath as he exhaled. "I don't see what's to love."

Alexandra started to walk down the pathway. "Don't mind him, Rin. He's being a grouch this morning."

"Still having those dreams?" Rinna asked.

"Every night," Vincent answered plainly.

"Is Kai anywhere closer to learning anything about that sword?"

Vincent shook his head. "Not that I know of. He spoke to the Lorekeeper on the other side of the city, and even he found no record of the sword, the people from my dreams, or the Sanorian runes we gave him. All he said was that they looked like names, but nothing he was able to read."

"Well, don't worry too much. I'm sure we'll figure it out soon!" she said reassuringly.

Vincent was less than convinced. "Yeah. I hope you're right."

Rinna turned to Barrik as they were walking. "And what about you? Are you also sleepy?"

"I'm hungry," he replied. He sounded as if he were pouting.

Alexandra turned to start walking backward. "I thought you were supposed to have stocked up for winter?"

Barrik entertained no response.

"Ya know, if you'd let a little sunlight in your room, it would be much easier to wake up in the morning," Rinna advised.

Vincent chuckled. "You're lucky he's awake at all. The rest of his kind are all hibernating."

Unamused, Barrik grunted.

As they continued through the city, the flurries grew in size, but not in speed. The snowflakes gracefully floated to the ground, each one with its own sense of time. Different parts of the city became more and more hidden as they piled on top of one another. The vines that sprawled out across the path and up the walls would soon become pesky obstacles concealed beneath the white powder for people to stumble over. In the market, the snow added an extra chore to the shopkeepers' day—the constant need to sweep away the deceptively heavy gathering of white flakes.

Vincent rubbed his hands together and blew his warm breath on them. He looked at Barrik and Rinna, who both seemed unfazed by the temperature.

"I will never understand how you two don't get cold."

With all the walking, Barrik seemed to have awakened a little. "I like it. It makes Mancho's soup taste even better."

Rinna laughed. "Nalitay is much chillier than this, so this is nothing for me."

Vincent held his hands out in front of his face to check that they were still there. "How did you survive?"

"You get used to it," she said with a smile.

A bit beyond the market, down a street here, an alley there, and around a corner, finally, the healer's ward came into view—a dome of mossy stones slowly being buried by fluffy pearls of snow. Its perimeter was an ethereal garden full of flowers, herbs, and smaller trees, all used for their healing properties. A gated fence of iron, overgrown with vines and bushes, circled the garden until it eventually came to two open doors of gray metal bars that indicated the entrance.

"Rinna!" a healer's apprentice shouted as they passed beneath the archway. The young girl came running over to them. She had two braids in her brown hair that fell to the shoulders of her white robe.

Rinna bent over and placed her hands on her knees with a smile. "Lexa, sweetie! What are you doing out here?"

"Mr. Dary asked us to pick the herbs that haven't gone all wilty yet. Lookie, I made one just like yours!" The girl lifted one of her braids to draw their attention to a ribbon made from stems of small flowers tied in a bow at the tip. Her voice was elated and full of cheer.

Every word raced from her mind to her mouth as if she couldn't say them fast enough. She looked up at Rinna with a full smile, revealing the dimples in her full cheeks.

"Wow! So pretty!" Rinna exclaimed.

"Oh, oh, I have something for Bearie too! Wait here, okay?"

She took off back to a basket on the ground several paces away and pulled something out of it.

Alexandra leaned over to Vincent. "Did she just call him…?"

"Oh, yeah," he said with a grin.

She trotted back and stopped right in front of Barrik with a big smile, keeping her gift hidden behind her back. "You have to close your eyes," she said as she swayed back and forth.

"Uhh, okay." Barrik played along and closed his eyes, getting a teasing taste of sleep until she gave him permission to open them again.

"Okay!"

When he opened his eyes, she held a gleaming blue flower with four surprisingly healthy crescent-shaped petals. The smile on her face was wide enough to reveal a missing tooth in the back of her mouth.

"Oh, that's pretty," he said as he leaned over and gracefully took it from her with the tips of his fingers. He brought it to his nose and took a deep breath.

"Mr. Dary says it's called a moonshade. Do you like it?"

"Yes, I love it. Thank you."

"Yay!" Lexa did a little dance before she ran off back to her basket with a wave.

When Barrik turned back to the others, they were all staring at him with a smirk across their faces.

"Looks like Bearie has an admirer," Alexandra teased.

"That is too cute!" Rinna agreed.

"Stop it. It was very sweet."

Vincent chuckled from the back as they headed toward the dome's entrance. "Berry."

Inside, they were greeted by the distant sound of coughing and moaning from ailing patients somewhere on one of the floors above. The room they stood in was filled with stone tables covered in glass jars that contained various herbs and strange liquids of all colors. The refreshing scent of vanilla and mint wafted through the air from a simmering cauldron beneath the fireplace. To their right, a set of stairs hugged the wall that led to the upper levels. As soon as they started their way up, there was an aggressive slam from above.

"Preposterous!" someone shouted.

"HA! You never stood a chance against me, peasant!"

As they breached the top of the stairwell, they could see Vera and an older man in a silver robe with a well-groomed beard of grays and blacks. They were sitting in the prismatic light that flooded through a colorful stained-glass window, with a game board in front of them.

"How could I cling to a hope of victory with your travesty of regulations? On several occasions, you altered the game's parameters to your own advantage," the man grumbled.

"Sounds like someone is a sore loser," Vera instigated.

"I am more than willing to acknowledge an honorable defeat, but this is hardly close to that."

Vera stood up and placed her hands on her hips with a victorious smile. "So, you admit I won!"

"On the contrary. You cheated, and therefore, by default, I should be named the victor."

Vera crossed her arms smugly. "I don't think you understood the rules."

"An impossible challenge when they're in a perpetual state of change."

Alexandra stepped forward, laughing to herself. "Don't take it personally, Master Darion. Vera most likely didn't know the rules either."

"Well, it's about time!" Vera said as she turned to them with feigned frustration. A thick black cloth covered her left eye and wrapped around her head beneath all the golden strawberry curls in her hair. A deep wound that had already begun to scar ran from her forehead and hooked down to the outside of her left cheekbone.

"The boys didn't feel like waking up," Alexandra said, quick to shift the blame.

"Still don't," Vincent said plainly.

"Still having *scary* dreams?" Vera asked with a sneer as she threw on her cloak.

"Every night."

"Poor baby."

Vincent shrugged. "Meh, I wake up and can still see out of both my eyes, so it's okay."

A hush fell over the room. With jaws agape, Barrik, Alexandra, and Rinna all stared at him in shock. Vera narrowed her eye and quickly launched a game piece at him. He threw his hands up to block the projectile, but found himself defenseless against Barrik's palm as it cracked the back of his head.

"Ow!" Vincent shouted as he started to rub his well-deserved injury.

"That's what you get! Thanks, Bear," Vera said with a smile. She leaned in as she noticed the bright blue flower now resting behind Barrik's ear. "Say, that's cute; where'd you get that?"

"Lexa gave it to him," Alexandra said with a playful smile.

"She calls him Bearie," Rinna quickly added.

Vincent chuckled as he continued to rub his head. "Berry."

"Awww, Bearie? That's adorable!"

Master Darion stepped forward. "Lexa has taken a liking to many of the flowers that grow just beyond our doorstep, but the moonshade is by far her favorite. I would accept such a gift with the greatest of honors."

Barrik's posture straightened with pride as he fiddled with the flower proudly.

"Now, Miss Vera," Darion started, "despite the events of our game, in which you most certainly cheated—"

"Won," Vera quickly corrected.

"Would you care for me to dull the pain once more before you leave? The blend of herbs I have prepared for you will help, but with a significantly inferior effect."

"Yes, please." She stood still, arms at her side, as he lifted the cloth covering her eye and placed his left hand over it. As he began to weave a sign with his other hand, she closed her other eye. A moment later, a gentle green glow was emitted from beneath his palm. Vera started to giggle.

"You are the only patient who finds this amusing," he said with his eyes closed.

"I can't help it, it tickles!"

"Hush."

Vera tightened her lips to conceal her laughter the best she could. After several moments, the green glow faded away, and Master Darion removed his hand.

"There, how does it feel now?"

Vera reached up and poked the surrounding area of her injured eye. "Nope, doesn't hurt at all."

"Wonderful. Now—"

Suddenly, another healer dressed in cream-colored robes with frayed chocolate tassels tied around their waist came storming up the stairs. "Master Darion, sir... two more with the ash just came in, and we don't have anywhere to put them!"

Darion sighed. "Have Felix and Jesse fix them a temporary spot in the flower hall. I'll be along shortly."

"Yes, sir!" The healer bowed and disappeared to the lower level.

Darion shook his head disappointedly with his eyes on the floor.

"Have you found anything to treat it yet?" Rinna asked softly.

"Unfortunately not. We've exhausted all known remedies, but nothing shows any promise. With our more serious cases, we've turned to experimental tactics—with their consent, of course—but those are more or less mere attempts at something rather than nothing at all. But never mind all that, come with me so I can send you on your way."

He led them all down the stairs and across the room to a small table full of glass jars varying in size. The jars clinked against one another as he fumbled around with them, lifting up a few he chose to inspect until he finally found the one he was looking for.

"Ah!" He turned around with a smaller jar of blue-and-white powder. "Ingest no more than a small pinch of this whenever the pain becomes too much to bear."

"What is it?" she asked as she reached for the jar.

His hand quickly recoiled before she could take it. "A powdered mixture of *streya dormianis*, the very moonshade behind dear Barrik's ear, and snow lavender. So, do not mix it with any of that foul poison from that wicked sailor. I do not know what sort of terrible reactions you would have, but I do assure you it would be better not to find out."

He slowly handed Vera the jar. Alexandra stepped forward and inspected the powder alongside her. "So, when will her vision return?"

Master Darion shook another bottle and peered into it with narrowed eyes. "Impossible to know," he said as he set the jar down and returned his attention to them. "Unfortunately, the possibility that it may never return must be accepted."

Everyone fell silent, thinking about what that meant for Vera's future.

"However, time can produce the greatest of miracles. A flower wilted by winter's chill will blossom again with spring's warm rain. And where there is loss, there is always something to be found. That is, if you are willing to…" He turned to Vera with a wink. "…leave an eye open."

She smiled as he continued, "So, fear not, and let time be the healer from this point forward, for it cures ailments even I cannot. For now, enjoy winter's beauty and the company of your comrades."

Vera bowed her head with spirits restored. "We will. Thank you for everything."

"Yes, thank you so much, Master Darion!" Rinna exclaimed. "If you ever need help with anything, let us know right away!"

"You are most welcome. One day I may just accept your offer. Now, go on, leave me to wallow in my defeat." He smiled and ushered them out the door with a wave as they walked down the path.

In the distance, between the falling white flakes, Lexa clapped and jumped up and down when she saw the flower behind Barrik's ear. She wildly waved goodbye to them as they passed beneath the iron archway.

"Freedom!" Vera shouted. She quickly scooped up a handful of snow and blasted Vincent in the face with it.

The others burst into laughter while he failed to fight the urge to smile. Everyone saw his lips begin to curl upward, but just to be sure it did not go unnoticed, Vera called attention to it.

"Ah-ha!"

Rinna nudged him with her elbow. "There he is."

"Shut up," he said with a reluctant grin as he wiped the snow from his face.

"Can we go get some food now?" Barrik asked with desperation in his voice.

"Aww, is the big guy hungwy?" Alexandra teased, poking him in the belly.

He gently swatted away her hands. "Stop it."

"Does Bearie need some soup?"

He sighed. "That's not going away anytime soon, is it?"

Vincent laughed. "Not a chance."

Vera stood next to Barrik with her hand resting high on his shoulder. "I'm with ya, Bearie; I need an ale."

Amazed, Rinna looked at her to see if she was serious. "Uh, Vera, honey, it's not even midday."

"Hey, *you* try being locked up in there for weeks, only being fed herbs and potions. Bleh!" She pretended to vomit.

"Uh, at least you weren't tossed in a dungeon," Vincent interjected.

"You were asleep the whole time, so it doesn't count," Vera said.

"Didn't feel like it."

"Guys…" Barrik was ready to beg.

"Yes, yes, we're going. We just have to make one stop on the way," Alexandra said as she held something out in her hands for everyone to see. Neatly folded in her palms, quickly accumulating white fluffs of snow, was Toran's cherry-red scarf.

The five of them walked down a curved entryway of cobblestone to a small home crafted from long oaken boards. On the porch underneath the snow-covered overhang, swaying gently on a wooden rocking chair, was a woman approaching her later years, warmed by the comforts of a wool robe and a hefty wolf pelt. Smoke rolled out from a white stone chimney directly above her as she made loops and knots with a ball of yellow yarn and two long needles of nickel. As they approached the porch steps, she flashed a welcoming smile that accentuated the crow's feet at the corners of her eyes. "Hello there. May I help you?" she asked in a sweet and tender voice.

Alexandra moved closer, stopping just shy of the first step. "Hi, um, we're sorry to bother you, but would you happen to be Toran's mother?"

The two needles in her hands stopped clicking as she laid them still in her lap. "It's no bother at all, dearie. I am indeed. Were you friends of his?"

"We were, yes. We came by because we wanted to return something of his to you," Alexandra said, starting her way up the steps to the woman. She held out Toran's scarf, its worn fabric resting in her palms, a silent echo of the friend they had lost.

The woman's eyes glossed over as she gently reached for the scarf. "Oh… my boy." Toran's mother let her tearful gaze linger on the scarf in her hands for a moment before she rose from her creaking chair with a sniffle to embrace Alexandra. Although it was slightly awkward, Alexandra gladly returned the gesture as the scents of chamomile and sage pleasantly filled her nose.

"Would you all like to join me inside for some tea?"

None of them had any intention of denying her invitation, but even if they had, the heartwarming look in her eyes would have made it impossible.

"We would love to," Alexandra said with a soft smile.

She hurried over to the door and held it open for them all. "Please, please come in. Have a seat and make yourselves at home. My name is Tila. It's a pleasure to meet you all."

Everyone shook her hand and introduced themselves as they stepped inside and found themselves a seat in the sitting room. Around a circular mahogany table were two large rocking chairs identical to the one on the porch, and a long sofa with olive-colored cushions. In every window, and practically anywhere else there was space, there was either a potted plant sitting on the ledge or a baby bulb growing out of a glass jar filled with water.

"I'm afraid I don't have much to offer you other than the tea, if that's all right," Tila said as she closed the door behind them all.

"The tea is more than plenty, Miss Tila, thank you," Vincent said.

"You're very welcome, dearie. I'll throw the kettle on."

The warmth from the fire crackling in a pit lined with red stone gave them all a comforting sense of home. Although this was their first time here, the cozy atmosphere and familiar scents made it feel as if it were a place they had known their whole lives. The tea, herbaceous and subtly sweet, added to the ambiance with its revitalizing freshness, enhancing their sense of relaxation and belonging.

"This is delicious, Miss Tila. What kind of tea is this?" Vera asked.

"Please, dearies, just Tila. Or if you'd like, you can call me Tilly." She leaned in with a warm smile. "It's a tea I make myself with some of my own herbs you see around you." Her smile widened, and she lowered her voice conspiratorially. "I keep the recipe a secret, so that way, if anyone wants more, then they have to come and visit." As she straightened up, her expression softened. "Thank you for doing so, by the way. You've gifted me with a gracious amount of joy."

The porcelain cup clinked against the small saucer on the table as Alexandra set down her tea. "You don't have to thank us. We're just sorry we didn't come sooner. We wanted to wait until Vera was released from Master Darion's care, so we could all be here."

"The fact that you came at all tells me that each and every one of you has such a sweet heart." Her teary eyes wandered around to each of them. "It makes me so happy to know my Toran was surrounded by such wonderful souls. Even that silver-haired gentle fellow took the time to make sure my boy was lifted to the stars. So, again, thank you."

Two younger boys, both with messy red hair, suddenly crashed through the front door, letting in a flurry of white flakes and a gust of icy air. The first boy sprinted into the kitchen with wet footsteps and ducked behind a chair. The second boy launched a snowball that hit the chair and splattered apart. The flakes of snow on the floor quickly melted into tiny puddles.

"Ha ha, you missed me!"

"You cheater! The stars are gonna curse you now!"

"Boys!" Tila shouted as she rose from her chair. Her voice was stern, but retained its delicate inflection.

Both of them quickly turned to her with fear of inevitable punishment in their eyes.

"How many times have I told you not to bring the snow in the house? And to keep that door closed? We don't have the wood to heat the entire city, do we?"

The boys shook their heads with their eyes locked on the floor.

"Well, then?"

The boy who had fired the snowball hurried over to close the door. "But Momma, we said you can't run inside, and Tinny broke the rules!"

"Trever, you teller!" Tinny shouted in a high-pitched voice.

Tila turned to him. "Is that true?"

"Well, yeah, but—"

"No, there'll be no excuses," Tila said, cutting him off. "Your word is your word. How can you expect to be respected or trusted if nobody can ever believe anything you say?"

"See? I told you!" Trever instigated.

Tila now turned to him. "And you!"

His eyes widened with shock.

"Since when is it okay to point the finger of blame at your friends, let alone your own brother?"

"But we agreed!"

"Yes, and we also agreed there would be no snow in the house—so both of you broke the rules and your word. Now, what do we do when we've done wrong?"

The boys turned to each other, and both apologized before they turned to Tila and apologized to her as well.

"Good. Now find something to clean up all this water, then go wash up before your father gets home."

Tila turned back to the group. "Sorry for all that."

Alexandra laughed. "It's quite all right. I think it's about time we got going anyway."

Tila quickly noticed that Vincent had fallen asleep with his face pressed against his fist. "I'm amazed the boy slept through all the commotion," she said with a soft laugh.

"Barrik, wake him up, would you?" Alexandra requested.

Barrik reached over to give Vincent a light nudge. "Hey, Vince. Wake—"

Vincent suddenly jolted awake, panicked and unaware of his surroundings. He accidentally knocked over one of the teacups as he fell to the floor, hyperventilating.

Barrik quickly knelt beside him consolingly. "Hey, hey, it's okay. Vince, you're okay."

Vincent looked back at Barrik, barely recognizing him in his rattled state.

"We're here, Vince," Rinna said gently as she placed her hand on his shoulder. "You're safe."

Vincent looked around the room at everyone's concerned faces. Realizing he had fallen asleep and there was no longer anything to fear, he relaxed. Barrik assisted him to his feet once his breathing returned to normal.

"You okay?" Barrik asked.

"Yeah, I'm fine. Thank you." Vincent instantly felt a rush of guilt at the sight of the spilled tea all over the floor. He leaned down as his cheeks flushed with embarrassment. "I'm so sorry," he murmured, picking up the porcelain teacup. "Do you have a rag or something I could clean this up with?"

Tila's eyes had widened at Vincent's sudden outburst, but she quickly softened. "Oh, don't worry about it, dearie. I'll get it," she responded, waving away his apology. "That must have been some dream you were having."

Vincent's eyes lingered on the scattered tea leaves in his cup. Their patterns reminded him of the mutilated bodies littered across the battlefield in his dream. "Yeah," he replied, "some dream."

Alexandra and Barrik shared a look of concern before moving to the door.

Everyone hugged Tila as they walked out the door to the snowy porch. There she stood with the door slightly cracked behind her.

Vincent uncomfortably rubbed the back of his head as he looked at Tila with eyes full of remorse. "Again, I'm really sorry about the mess."

Tila's warm smile never waned. "Oh, dearie, you've nothing to apologize for. You be safe now, all right?"

Vincent nodded. The feeling that he owed her something more gnawed at him as he reluctantly stepped off the porch.

"Thanks again, Tilly!" Vera exclaimed as she walked outside.

"Oh, you're very welcome, dearie. Thank you all so very much. I can't tell you how warm you've made my heart. And please, come by whenever you'd like. I'll happily make you some of my secret tea." She winked.

"We'll definitely be back to visit!" Rinna said cheerfully.

From inside, they could hear Trever's voice. "Momma! We don't have the wood to heat the whole city, 'member?"

Tila hung her head with a gentle smile. "Oh, my, these boys… Thanks again, dearies, and please be safe in your travels."

"We will," Alexandra said.

Tila turned around and closed the door, but from outside, they could still hear the muffled sound of her voice: "Let me see your hands. They had better be clean!"

CHAPTER 19

As everyone made their way toward the market, the snow continued to fall, turning the ground beneath them into a mixture of fluffy powder and sloppy footprints. The city seemed brighter and brighter as the sun climbed and reflected off the snow, wherever the clouds allowed it to peek through. More and more people began hurrying from errand to errand as morning transitioned to noon, desperate to remain as warm as possible. With their desire for speed also came the inevitable slip and fall, wetting their clothes and chilling their bones.

With The Wicked Broom in sight, Barrik's stomach began to rumble louder than the great booms of thunder. His pace quickened as the desire for food became almost unbearable.

Just outside the entrance stood a man clad in a midnight-black robe with golden tassels, shouting the same words over and over again. "The ash is only the beginning! Let them save us, our saviors, our beloved gods! Give them your love! Give them your energy, your unwavering fidelity! They will guide us to paradise! May they rise again!"

As they drew closer, Vincent noticed a weathered blue book underneath the man's arm. Nobody seemed to be paying him any attention; they continued hurrying through the market, and some people even bumped into him as they passed, yet he continued his rant. His commitment to his preaching, despite the lack of listeners, sparked Vincent's curiosity. While everyone walked inside, he took a short detour. He slid behind someone trying to haggle down the price of a wicker basket filled with multicolored linens. Slowly, he approached the robed man, finding it increasingly difficult to tear his eyes from the blue book in the man's hands.

"… fidelity! They will guide us to—"

"Who's 'they'?" Vincent asked, interrupting the man.

The man looked at him with horror in his eyes. "You do not know?!"

"Uh, no, sorry. That's why I asked."

"Stay your apologies, child. For it is not your fault, nor be it too late! There is still time for your acceptance!"

"Acceptance of what?"

"The Sanorians, of course!" the man exclaimed, leaning in uncomfortably close. He had a shiny head topped with a small patch of white fuzz, and eyes that were sunken and sleepless. He looked at Vincent intently. His breath reeked with a foul scent Vincent failed to place. He turned up his nose and took a step back.

"Uh…"

"Vince!" Rinna called from the doorway. "You coming?"

"Yeah, I'm coming," he called over his shoulder, unsure if he should take his eyes off of the robed man. The moment he went to turn away, he realized his assumption was correct. The man snatched Vincent by the shoulders and held him in place. The blue book fell to the snowy ground.

"You must accept them! You must! The time is near where it will be too late! They are our saviors! Our creators! Our gods! May they rise again!"

Vincent gently removed the man's hands from his shoulders, ready for any other sudden movements, and backed away cautiously. "Uh, yes, I accept. Thank you for showing me," he said uncomfortably.

"You are welcome! Hurry and tell all those you may! We all may yet be saved!"

Vincent turned around to steal one last look at the man before he stepped inside. The man picked up and dusted off the weathered blue book and returned to his obnoxious preaching. "…only the beginning!"

His words quickly faded with the closing of the door.

Vincent walked across the nearly empty bar to sit down across from Rinna at their usual table in the corner of the room. Bright white light flooded over their table from the window next to them.

"Friend of yours?" Vera asked jokingly.

Vincent shook his head in disbelief. "That strange man has been eating the wrong berries."

Rinna chuckled. "First time seeing one of them?"

"A strange man?"

"No, silly, a devoted."

Everyone looked at her, confused. She felt attacked by their stares. "Okay, I'll take that as a yes."

"What's a devoted?" Vera asked.

"I came across a few of them in some of the towns I stopped in on my way to Meditas, but they were in Nalitay all the time. They're a group of people who are under the impression that the Sanorians are going to come back, and when they do, those who are faithful to them will be saved—cured of all disease and protected from all evil."

"How do they expect an extinct species to come back?" Vincent asked.

Rinna shrugged. "I'm not sure. But they're really not supportive of Guardians either; before or after the war, it makes no difference. They think the fountains' power is evil, and even the killing of horrors is wrong, because all life, no matter how frightening, should be preserved."

Alexandra laughed. "Yeah, that's a nice idea. I wonder how fast they'd change their mind at the sight of a thirsty ghoul."

Vera narrowed her eye and spoke plainly. "They chew on people like sticky sweets."

"They're a bit loony," Rinna said. "Whatever is in that book of theirs seems to turn their heads into mashed potatoes."

Vera softly nudged Barrik in the side with her elbow. "Just like ol' Bearie here."

He gave no acknowledgement. His eyes were fixed on the kitchen door.

Alexandra snapped her fingers in front of him. "Hey, big guy. You in there?"

"Hmm? Yeah, I ordered mashed potatoes. Why?"

Everyone burst into laughter.

"See? I told you," Vera said.

"Huh?" Barrik's eyes darted around the table, full of confusion.

A moment later, a large tray of food hit the table. Everyone was gratefully blasted by steams of heat coming from hot soup, warm bread, mutton, mashed potatoes, and Mancho's famous roast chicken. Barrik's eyes lit up like fireworks.

"'Ere ye go, everyone!" Mancho said with a wide smile.

Vera leaned in across the table. "Can we have some ale too, Manch?"

"Well, o' course ye can! Wouldn't be much of a celebration o' yer health without some ale, now, would it?"

"My thoughts exactly," Vera agreed, sitting back and crossing her arms proudly.

Before he could return, a familiar voice appeared out of nowhere. "Room for one more?"

Alexandra almost choked on a piece of bread. "Kai?!"

Vera smiled. "Wow, old man. Never thought we'd see the day where you'd actually join us."

As Kai pulled up a chair to the end of their table, he noticed Vincent sitting silently and fidgeting with his food. While everyone else still bore slight bruises or cuts from their mission, Kai's face was the only one that had completely healed.

"What? I can't enjoy a mediocre meal and some of Mancho's infamous ale?" he asked defensively.

"…Me…iocre?" Barrik questioned with a mouthful of food.

"Now, would ye believe it?" Mancho sounded surprised as he set down two pitchers of ale and a handful of mugs. Vera's remaining eye practically launched from her skull with excitement. "It be good ta see ya when there be no business talk fer once." Mancho rested his hand on Kai's shoulder.

"Actually, I do have some things I'd like to talk to you about."

"Aye, I know. Just wanted ta hear ye say it. I'll go grab ye a mug."

He was gone and back again in a flash, practically shoving the mug in Kai's face. As Kai started to pour some ale into his mug, another empty one appeared right next to his. Kai followed the thick arm attached to it until he met Mancho's massive grin. He shook his head and filled his up as well. As soon as he set down the pitcher, Mancho slapped him on the shoulder, splashing some of Kai's ale onto his lap.

"Before we get ta the business, it be a proper time fer a toast, doncha think?"

"Yeah, you're probably right, Mancho." Kai rose to his feet as Vera quickly reached out to refill her already empty mug. "First things first: it's great to have you back, Vera."

"Aye!" Mancho initiated a group sip before Kai continued.

"Since we're all finally together again, I would like to commend you all on the completion of your first mission as Guardians. You've all grown exponentially since your arrival here, and I couldn't be more proud."

"Aye!" Another sip.

"A comrade was lost." A melancholic silence quickly fell over the table. "There is nothing any of us can do to change that. We'll train to continue our growth, to save as many as we can, but until the day comes when we can save everyone, the way to remember those we've lost is not through avoidance of their memory, but by continuing to cherish the ones we had. In that way, they'll never be forgotten." He took a deep breath and raised his mug. "To Toran."

Alexandra stood up after they sipped. Kai's eyes were dry, but the sadness in them was visible behind a thin layer of armor. Alexandra raised her mug with tears in the wells of her eyes, but a look of strength and confidence. "To Gala and her team."

Kai gave her a grateful nod.

"Fer those who drink no more," Mancho said as he dumped a splash of his ale out onto the floor. Everyone followed the gesture.

"And to those who still can." He held his mug out in the center of the table.

They all clashed their mugs together and took a large gulp before Kai and Alexandra sat back down. Mancho sipped from his mug again and disappeared quickly to tend to something in the kitchen.

Only a few moments passed before Kai noticed that Vincent's mind still seemed to be elsewhere. "You all right, Vince?" he asked, concerned.

Vincent looked up from his untouched food. "Yeah, I'm all right."

Alexandra recognized the guilt in his voice. "Vince, that wasn't your fault. You know that, right?"

"I know," Vincent answered plainly.

"What happened?" Kai asked inquisitively.

Vincent hesitated, not wanting to answer, as if speaking about the event at Tila's house would force him to relive it.

"He fell asleep at Tila's," Alexandra answered for him. "Barrik startled him awake, and he spilled some tea. It wasn't a big deal."

"Did you have another dream?" Kai wondered.

Vincent nodded slowly, still playing with his food.

"Which one was it this time?"

"The one where I get tortured over and over again."

Kai remembered Vincent telling him the star stones were different colors in each of his dreams. "What color is the star stone in that one?"

"Red."

Kai's silence stretched out as he searched for an answer to Vincent's problems. Rinna, watching him, broke the tension.

"Would there be any herbal remedies to stop him from dreaming?" she asked.

"Oh, yeah!" Vera exclaimed. "I'm sure Master Darion could whip you up something, Vincey."

"That actually isn't a bad idea," Kai agreed. "Maybe if we stop the dreams from happening until we can figure out why you keep having them, you could get some decent rest."

"I'm willing to try anything at this point, so if you think it will help..." Vincent shrugged his shoulders. "I'm in."

"Good," Kai said with a nod. "In the meantime, try to keep your head up. I'm certain Toran's mother holds no negative feelings toward you and wouldn't want you to ruminate over something so trivial."

"She did reassure you it was no problem," Barrik reminded him.

"Right," Alexandra seconded. "So, eat. We can't have you sleepy *and* hungry. You're already grouchy enough," she teased.

Vincent chuckled, beginning to feel a little better. "All right, all right." His eyes wandered around to everyone looking back at him with warm expressions. "Thank you," he said to them all.

Mancho suddenly reappeared next to the table and noticed that the food had barely been touched. "Oy, what's this? Ye all too good fer me cookin', eh?"

Vincent smiled softly. "No, no. Nothing's wrong with your food, Manch."

"Well then, dig in before it gets cold!"

They spent the rest of their day drinking and eating around the table. More and more people wandered in, until eventually, the bar was full of loud voices and hot dishes. Even the local bard sporting a bright blue feathered cap and striped tunic to match found his way in to strum away on the strings of his lute. It felt like half the city was inside The Wicked Broom, hiding from the cold. For a moment, the liveliness seemed to chase away the growing chill in Vincent's mind.

As the day passed, the conversation somehow turned into everyone interrogating Rinna about Nalitay, forcing her to share more and more details about her home city. She spoke of a large statue in the village square, mountainous terrain that was perilous to travel through without a guide, snow that rarely faded from the trees, lakes that were frozen almost year-round, and the energy waves Vera was obsessed with that could be seen in the sky nearly every night.

"Do you know if Salivan is still around?" Kai asked.

"Who?" Rinna questioned.

"Salivan Moorsaan. He was the barkeep for the Crow's Beak." Kai's words were beginning to sound slightly elevated.

"Oh, I'm not sure. That's the pub my father always goes to, but I never ventured in long enough to remember anyone's name. I'm sorry."

Kai waved away her apology. "Ah, no worries."

"You've been to Nal...itay?" Vera asked with a hiccup as she leaned in to refill her mug again.

"Is that your fifth?" Barrik asked.

"Sixth," she said proudly.

"Maybe you should..." He slowly reached for the pitcher. She quickly guarded her precious ale and hissed at him.

Kai leaned back in his chair. "I've been all over. Dhankar, Enora, Limfas, Abnor, Nalitay, Sylva... I've even gone beyond the Ankar Mountains."

"Aye, that be where ye slayed yer first Soul Eater, ain't it?"

Thoughts of Kai's first Soul Eater encounter—and the pain that came with it—briefly resurfaced. He hesitated before answering. "Indeed."

"How *do* you kill them?" Vincent asked.

"It's more like unmaking them," Kai said. "The Sanorians created them using a blood seal and a single soul. To unmake one, you need to undo that seal."

"Oh, so it's like a craftsman's seal?" Barrik assumed.

"Yes, but a little more complicated. You have to get close enough to place a seal of your own on it, and then activate it with fire."

Vincent chuckled. "I guess it's a bad day for the Soul Eater when you show up."

"What do you mean?"

"You can fight blindfolded and carry a fiery blade. You're kind of their worst enemy."

"While that's true, it doesn't make it easy. Each one I've fought has left me on the edge of the stars."

Alexandra started to wonder. "Wait... how many of those things have you killed?"

Everyone watched and eagerly waited for Kai to finish drinking from his mug.

"That makes four," he finally said.

"Four?!" everyone echoed.

"Aye, most people don't even live ta run away, let alone killin' 'em," Mancho said as he proudly rested his hand on Kai's shoulder, although he did not seem particularly receptive.

"All by yourself too!" Rinna exclaimed.

"Mmm, not quite," Kai said.

Everyone looked confused.

"Actually, that last one was the first I've killed by myself."

"You mean there are others who can fight them?" Vincent asked, surprised.

"I've heard rumors of others with the ability to do so, but I only *know* of one."

Mancho snarled. "Aye, that sly fox be the worst."

Vincent raised an eyebrow. "You mean the one in the dungeon? What's his Favor?"

Kai stared blankly into his half-empty mug. "I could never figure it out. He never told me—or anyone else that I'm aware of, for that matter—but he doesn't even need to close his eyes. He can stare right at those things, perfectly still, and smile. If I'm completely honest, in a way, he frightens me more than they do."

Mancho snarled again, "He don' even have a soul ta steal, that be why." Disgust remained clear all over his face, until it was redirected to the shouting of other patrons demanding his services from across the bar. "Aye, ye drunken fools..." His mumbling faded into the noise of the crowd as he walked away.

"Anyway," Kai said, "I should be going. It's a little late for me."

"Uh..." Barrik pointed to another round of food being delivered to the table by a younger man with dark hair and a sloppy white apron.

Kai was baffled. "When did you even order this?"

"Now you *have* to stay and help us," Alexandra said with a devious smile.

Kai looked at Barrik, who was already digging in. "I doubt you're going to need it. I'm fairly certain he could finish this all himself."

Barrik chuckled with a mouthful of food. "Pr...uh...ly."

Kai shook his head and filled another mug. "I'll stay until this mug is empty."

As evening turned to night, everyone continued to enjoy the feast. Vincent and Rinna, sitting on either side of Kai, would distract him and swap out his mug for one of their fuller ones every time his ran low. It only took a few times before he no longer remembered his original intent to leave and began filling it up himself. While all the hot food and warm bodies kept everyone heated, once the sun sank beyond the horizon, the only source of light came from lanterns suspended on the walls and support pillars around the bar.

Mancho eventually came back around and slammed two more pitchers of ale down on the table. Vera, with red cheeks and a large smile, immediately snatched one to sloppily refill her mug, splashing ale everywhere. Vincent and Barrik fought over the last piece of roast chicken while Kai and Rinna were deep in conversation. Alexandra leaned across the table before Mancho walked away again.

"Say, Manch," she said with a curious and hopeful look in her eyes.

"What can I do fer ya, me girl?"

"Kai tells me you're quite the singer."

Kai broke off mid-sentence to snap his attention to her. All of his senses seemed to return in an instant. "Please don't do this to me," he begged.

Too late. Mancho had already turned to him with a smirk. "Oh, did ye, now?"

Alexandra gestured to herself with her left arm, uncovered by her rolled-up sleeves. "Songs happen to be my favorite part of stories."

Mancho's smirk quickly grew to a wide and friendly smile, showing a few golden teeth. "Well, then, me girl, ye've come to the right place."

"Oh, no…" Kai groaned as he leaned his head in one of his hands.

Mancho cleared his throat and pounded his meaty fist against the wall twice. All the noise in the bar came to an abrupt halt. Everyone at the table and at the bar were all focused on Mancho. He gave a look to the bard, who twisted the tuning knob of his lute and nodded soon after. With the strum of the bard's lute, Mancho started to speak with a rhythmic flow to his words.

"All the bucks…"

"Yo!" all the men shouted. The strum of the bard's lute followed immediately after.

"Raise yer cups."

All their mugs shot high in the air. Another strum of the bard's lute.

"It be time ta drink the night away."

"Yo!" They all took a large gulp and slammed them down at the same time.

"Now the ladies…"

"Yo!" Alexandra, Vera, and Rinna all eagerly participated with wide smiles.

"Fer whom I be crazy,
Drink 'til ye've nothing left ta say."

Most of the women sipped and slammed their mugs down; only a small group of women in the back protested his lyrics. He simply waved off their frustrations and continued after the sound of the lute.

"Ye have no fear
When ye come in here,
So, let me hear ye's shout and cheer."

Those who were familiar with the song slammed their mugs down twice before the chorus. Most of the bar roared and swayed to the words while the lute picked up into a cheerful tempo.

> *"Ye come into The Wicked Broom*
> *Ta wash away yer doom an' gloom.*
> *An ale or wine,*
> *They're both divine,*
> *So, don't be shy,*
> *Tilt 'em back and have yerself a time."*

The lute slowed down.

> *"Now, ye might be thinkin',*
> *A bowl o' soup,*
> *Or a nice roast chicken,*
> *Or maybe ta fill yer belly full o' beer.*
> *So, undo a button,*
> *And have some mutton,*
> *While ye lend ol' Mancho yer ear."*

Slam! Slam! The lute picked up again.

> *"Ye come into The Wicked Broom*
> *Ta wash away yer doom an' gloom.*
> *An ale or wine,*
> *They're both divine,*
> *So, don't be shy,*
> *Tilt 'em back and have yerself a time."*

Slam! Slam!

Mancho wrapped his arm around Kai and forced him to join in for the chorus. Kai glared at Alexandra, who was consumed by her smile. By now, the entire bar was singing loud enough for the whole city to hear.

"Ye come into The Wicked Broom
Ta wash away yer doom an' gloom.
An ale or wine,
They're both divine.
So, don't be shy,
Tilt 'em back and have a time,
Until the night need say goodbye."

Mancho finished with a bow and a gracious smile to Alexandra as the bar applauded and cheered.

"That was fantastic, Mancho!" she exclaimed as she rose from her seat, clapping.

"Thank ye, me girl. Used to sing all the time back when yer pop was around, Vince, me boy. Ahh, good times they were, eh?" He gave Kai a little shake.

"Embarrassingly enough, yes, we did," Kai said, placing his fingers on his temples.

"Ahhh, ye be too rigid ta this day."

Alexandra looked at Mancho suspiciously. "What other songs do you know?"

He grew a mischievous smile.

As the night fizzled on, the bar slowly emptied. People scurried home as fast as they could without slipping on the icy terrain. Barrik was slurping hot stew with his eyes half closed, and Vera passed out on his shoulder. Alexandra and Mancho were slurring songs from old stories with arms wrapped around each other, while Kai was sprawled out over the back of his chair. A night at The Wicked Broom was ending as it was known to, and as much as the day had been a distraction to the growing worries in Vincent's mind, he found it was only temporary.

As he stared into the frothy ripples of golden ale in his mug, Vincent's thoughts screamed louder, demanding his attention. He still wondered what Alice had meant when she accused his father of torturing her. How could it even be possible? He wondered about

Qrux's final words—*"He will come for you"*—and who he was referring to. Would this person really seek him out just because of who his father was? And if Kai was right and someone was collecting people for another war, how were they supposed to prepare for it? And if he were to stand in his own light like Kai had said, how was he supposed to do that? He had so many questions, and with his inability to sleep at night, he barely had the energy to think about them.

It had been several weeks since his encounter with Larissa, but he was certain that if there was a way he could speak with her again, she would at least be able to tell him about the dreams that continued to haunt him every night. And while she might have been able to provide insight into his condition, there was someone else he longed to speak to much more—someone who would be able to give him direction no matter what obstacle he faced: his mother. He felt he needed her guidance now more than ever. There was no way of telling what she would say, but he knew her words would have a special effect on his troubled mind. Even though her advice was blunt and maybe even a little harsh at times, he missed it dearly.

Vincent suddenly felt a hand gently touch his shoulder, jolting him out of his mind. He looked up, startled.

"You okay?" Rinna asked with a softness in her eyes.

Vincent briefly shook away his dissociation before answering. "Um, yeah. Yeah, I'm fine, I was just admiring the color of Mancho's ale."

Rinna raised her eyebrow at him suspiciously. "What a strange way of saying you don't want to tell me what's on your mind."

"It's not that—"

Rinna started laughing before he could finish his thought. "I'm only teasing. I know there's a lot on your mind. Mine too," she said, her expression softening in a way that suggested he was not alone. "But it's late, and I'm getting sleepy, so I think I'm going to head back."

Vincent tried his best not to sound disappointed. "What? Had enough of Alex and Mancho butchering songs?"

She laughed again. "Be nice! They sound great."

He threw his hands up as if to defend himself. "Whatever you say. Have a good night, Rinna," he said warmly.

"You too," she responded softly. Her eyes darted from him to the floor and back to him as she flashed him a quick smile before heading out the door. When the door closed, Kai sluggishly brought himself to a semi-upright position, almost falling onto the table.

"Hey, you... C'mere," he said with a half-hearted wave.

Vincent looked around, confused. "Me?"

"Obvee-usly."

"Uhh, okay?" Vincent scooted in closer.

"Ya shouldn't... never let... let the lady walk home alone," he struggled to say.

"I'm sure Rinna can handle getting back home by herself."

Kai's head swayed in a small circle as he tried to look at Vincent. "Doesn't mean... she wants to."

Vincent thought about his words for a moment. He turned to his left to see Barrik dozing off with his spoon in his hand, with Vera still passed out on his shoulder, drooling. Alexandra and Mancho were still swaying back and forth, singing together.

After taking a quick sip from his mug, Vincent left the bar and followed after Rinna. Kai let his head fall onto his crossed arms, and as he heard the door close once more, a soft smile grew across his face.

Snow crunched beneath every step as Vincent ran through the cold night, doing his best not to slip on the icy ground. As he approached the market, he could see that Rinna had already made it to the far side.

"Hey, wait up!" he shouted.

He continued to run, but once he reached the other side of the market, she was gone. He spun around in a circle as he searched for her, but he saw nothing other than falling snow and empty roads.

"I was wondering when you'd catch up," Rinna said as she suddenly appeared from the veil of her Favor, leaning against the wall beside him.

"Well, I figured if you were going to freeze to death out here, you wouldn't want to do it alone."

"Wow, how valiant of you," she replied, playfully rolling her eyes.

He bowed. "Thanks, I thought so too."

She shook her head as they started to walk together. While the lanterns that hung on the stone walls lit their path, they were hardly a considerable source of heat. Snow continued to fall, and this late in the night, most of the city had been covered. An icy blanket had tucked in people's homes until the sun would rise to melt it all away. Cushions of white powder had accumulated on the rocking chairs, which would make for a wet and chilly seat.

Rinna took notice of Vincent marveling at his surroundings. "Don't get this much snow in Sylva?"

"It snows, but no, not this much." Vincent breathed into the palms of his hands and rubbed them together.

"If you think this is a lot, wait until you see Nalitay. One day, I'll show you. That is if you can stand the cold long enough without turning into an icicle."

"My fingers and toes already are, so we might as well complete my transformation."

She laughed. "You're such a baby."

"Hey, it looks nice. It just doesn't feel nice."

She leaned closer to him. "Baby."

He chuckled. "Whatever."

"You know, I've been meaning to tell you—I think I'm starting to get the hang of the fire sign you showed me."

"Oh, yeah?" Vincent raised an eyebrow. "Been practicing, have you?"

"Yup! Tell me if you think this is fast enough." She focused for a moment, her hands moving with almost flawless execution as she performed the sign. Vincent watched intently, genuinely impressed by how smooth and quick her movements had become.

"Well, what do you think?" she asked proudly.

"Yeah, I'd say that's pretty good. Have you tried it on your blade yet?"

"I did, but I'm only getting sparks."

"You really have to clear your mind."

"I guess that's the easy part for you, then," she teased.

"Wow, okay. You know, I think you're spending a little too much time with Vera and Alex. Looks like their sassy remarks are wearing off on you."

"You're pretty sassy yourself, you know?" she shrugged. "Besides, I kinda like it."

Vincent felt a euphoric warmth bubbling inside his chest. "Yeah, me too."

As soon as they returned to the barracks, Vincent hurried to the fire to get as close as possible without burning himself. Other than the pops and snaps from the fire, the place was dead silent.

"Thank the stars this fire is always burning."

Rinna laughed at his desperation. "Well, I'm off to bed," she said, stepping closer. Leaning in, she pressed her ice-cold lips against his cheek. "Thanks for freezing with me." Her cheeks turned pink as a soft smile lingered on her face.

Vincent quickly swallowed the lump in his throat. "So, you admit it was cold?"

She shook her head, still smiling. "Goodnight, Vince."

His heart pleasantly attacked the inside of his chest as he watched her walk up the stairs. The purple ribbon in her hair was slightly covered by a few fluffy white flakes that had yet to melt. When she was finally out of sight, he did his best to try to find where she had placed his breath.

Chapter 20

VERYONE stood in the snowy training yard, basking in the golden rays of the midday sun. With his hands clasped behind his back, Kai barked his instructions at his subordinates.

"All right…" Kai's voice was stern and serious. "Now that you're all rested and back to your usual strength—"

"Minus an eye," Vera quickly interjected, fiddling with the patch covering the wounded side of her face.

"Your new usual, then," Kai corrected himself before continuing. "Since you're all officially Guardians, I'm going to treat you as such. Right now, we know someone in Enora is collecting Rogues and Guardians and killing those they cannot, but we don't know why. However, I think it's best if we prepare for the worst."

"You really think another war is coming?" Rinna asked, concerned.

"Hopefully not, but moving forward with the possibility at the front of our minds will only benefit us. One of my old mentors used to say, 'If you don't want to get wet, don't wait until it rains to seek shelter. Even if you never see another battle, your strength will only ever serve you well.'"

"All right, then, Kai," Alexandra started, "what do you want us to do?"

Kai began pacing back and forth as he spoke. "While you're all gifted in weapons combat and against a normal soldier, I like your odds. But against a Rogue who is skilled with their Favor, I'm not as confident."

"Ouch," Vera said.

"I meant no offense," Kai reassured her. "Don't get me wrong, Qrux was a formidable opponent, and you all fought well. However, it took all of you to defeat him. I need you each to be able to fight one or two Rogues with the same capability as Qrux, by yourself."

"Is that even possible?" Vincent muttered.

Kai quickly shot Vincent a glance. "Your father could do it. And I'm certain Fira could do it even now, after all these years."

Vincent straightened up, feeling slightly guilty for his remark. "Teach us."

"First, I need you to let go of that self-doubt. You've barely scratched the surface of your capabilities." Kai's gaze shifted, lingering on each of them in turn. "And that goes for all of you. Your Favors will grow with you, but only if *you* grow. They won't evolve on their own. Don't allow the darkness in your mind to become a cage for your potential. Understood?"

Everyone nodded their heads to confirm that they had absorbed his words.

"Good," Kai said, clapping his hands together. "Now, Vince, I want you to sit there and focus on my energy, as well as that of whoever is challenging me. Differentiate between the two until you can visualize them in your mind. Everyone's energy will appear different, whether that be a color or an image in your mind, like the waterfall you've already become familiar with. The more you attune yourself to sensing energy, the more it will become second nature to you. This is *your* Favor, nobody else's. If you hone it, you can use it to forge your own path. Got it?"

"Got it!" Vincent eagerly kicked away the snow on the ground to make a semi-dry spot to sit. He crossed his legs and waited for further instructions.

Kai turned to the other four. "As for you all, I'll need a sparring partner."

Alexandra eagerly stepped forward, moving her arm in small circles. "I'll take you on, old man."

"All right, then," Kai scoffed and softly smiled. "You ready, Vince?"

"Ready!"

"Alex?" Kai asked softly. "Are you ready?"

A confident grin swept across her face. "Are you?"

Kai's eyebrows rose at her confidence. He assumed a stance with his arms out in front of him, his left hand forward and his right hand back, with both palms raised toward the sky. "Show me what you got."

Vera, watching from the perimeter of the training yard, hopped up and down, teeming with excitement. "Oh, Bearie, doesn't this just remind you of being back home sparring with Mom?" After a moment passed and still she heard no response, she turned to find Barrik chewing on a half loaf of bread. "Where'd you get that? Gimme some!"

Barrik ripped off a small piece and handed it to her.

Vera inspected the tiny piece of sourdough with a frown. "I'm not a mouse, you know! Just split it with me!"

"No way. I'm starving," Barrik replied, holding the bread tighter.

Vera jumped onto his back, clawing desperately for the bread locked in Barrik's hands. Rinna did her best to pull Vera down, but ultimately decided to back away without getting injured.

"Just give me a bigger piece, you ogre!" Vera exclaimed, still flailing on his back.

"Fine!" Barrik had given up. He ripped the loaf in half and handed it to her over his shoulder. "Here."

Vera snatched it from him and hopped down, grinning triumphantly. "Aww, yiss!"

Barrik watched as she took an aggressive bite out of her half. "You're an animal, you know that?"

Vera stuck her tongue out at him before taking another bite and returning her attention to the fight.

Alexandra put up her fists with her right hand forward and her left hand back. She lifted her heels from the ground and launched forward off her back foot, throwing a right jab at Kai's head. He barely moved—a gentle, quick tap to her attack, just enough to knock it off course. Quickly, she fired back with a left hook. He promptly stepped back and chopped down on her arm.

She jumped back and eyed him, analyzing her instructor. From the times they had sparred before, she knew he was strong and quick, but not quite as fast as Fira. She was never able to land a hit on Fira when they sparred, but she began to wonder just how close Kai was to her skill. The ultimate goal was to learn more about her Favor, but now she had another.

Kai braced himself as he was charged with a salvo of jabs—highs, lows, middle, all just as fast as the last. He was nimble on his feet, dodging left and right, only knocking her attacks to the side when he needed to. His aim was her left arm and nothing else, but she left him no room to strike. At first, Kai thought she was overexerting herself, but he was quick to remember just who had trained her. She could keep this up much longer. Every one of her jabs was well placed and lightning fast. Her arms were like loaded cannons, rapidly firing her fists that flew through the air. If he was even the slightest bit careless or made any sort of misstep, she might...

Crack! A straight right landed directly in his stomach. As he hunched over with a loud groan, another hook came directly at him. He dropped back, placed his hands in the snow, and swept at her legs with a kick. She hopped away. Kai brought himself to his feet and squinted at her arm. He only managed to hit it a few times, but now, it was clear that the crevice-like veins had a subtle white glow. He could stop, but now he had a score to settle. He lifted his hands, but left them open, heels raised, eyes narrowed. Locked in.

"Getting serious finally?" Alexandra asked with a confident smile.

"Experimental," he corrected with a smirk.

"Pfft."

To her surprise, he charged.

While Kai and Alexandra were exchanging blows, Vincent tried to focus on their energies. Kai's was easy to recognize, since he was already familiar with it. When he locked onto it, images of the warm spring and flowing waterfall took over his mind. The sound of water trickling into the small pool soothed him, while the light from the sun in his mind warmed him, despite his legs being wet and cold. The more he latched onto that feeling, the more he felt as though he were somewhere else. More and more, he reached out, but found no sign of Alexandra's energy.

Jabs, hooks, elbows, knees, even his head—Kai made his entire body a weapon. Alexandra hopped, dodged, ducked, and rolled out of the way when she could, but found herself forced to block more than she would like. He was quick, leaving her no opportunity to return fire. He was not about to let her land a hit like that again. His fighting style was much different than Fira's, but his attacks were still tactfully placed, just the same. She had to find an opening to turn the tide before…

Crash! A kick landed right in her gut, knocking her feet out from under her. Kai stepped away immediately after.

"All right, that's enough."

Down on one knee, Alexandra took a second to regain her breath fully. "You hit way harder than Mom does," she said with a cough.

Kai chuckled. "No, I don't," he said firmly.

"Why'd you stop?"

"Look at your arm."

She looked down to see all of the deep veins across the dark and scaly skin glowing a solid white.

"How does it feel?"

She opened and closed her hand a few times while rotating her whole arm. "Maybe a little warm?"

"Did you notice anything during our fight?"

She shook her head. "Nothing."

"Hmm…" Kai thought to himself for a quiet moment until Alexandra's curiosity could wait no longer.

"What is it?"

"You're struggling to grasp the feeling of energy absorption. Right now, you only take in what is forced onto you, but I'm wondering, if you were exposed to a prolonged source of energy, would you find a way to take it for yourself?"

"Okay, but how would we do that, exactly?"

Kai placed his hand on his katana.

Alexandra quickly understood what he intended to do. "You want me to play with fire?"

"It will likely be excruciating. But in my experience, extreme measures produce the fastest results. We don't have to do it, obviously; I'll leave it up to you."

She paused for a moment—not to debate whether or not she wanted to, but to work up the courage to do so.

"If you think it's worth a try, then I'll do it."

He nodded, drew his weapon, slashed open his palm, and smeared the blood across the blade. As soon as it ignited, Barrik, Vera, and Rinna stood frozen—witnessing the crimson flame for the first time.

Kai held the burning blade straight out in front of him. Alexandra walked up next to it.

"Kai, what are you doing?!" Barrik shouted from the side. They ignored him.

"When you're ready, grab on for as long as you can handle. Don't overdo it."

As the fire thrashed across the blade in a volatile dance, Alexandra's heart began to speed up. She looked to Kai, then back to the fire, and took a deep breath. She opened and closed her hands and shrugged away her hesitation. With her left hand, she reached out and wrapped it around the blade. She instantly dropped to one knee, not from the pain, but from the power. Her jaw clenched, her hand tightening around the blade. She gritted her teeth. Her breaths turned short and quick. She did whatever she could to deal with the pain.

With no luck in locating Alexandra's energy, Vincent remained focused on the cool, balmy spring of Kai's energy. Finally, he began to feel something else. In the center of the water, a doorway seemed to manifest out of thin air—old stone, dark and damaged from decades of weather and time. It was connected to nothing, just a door that grew in size, as if he were walking closer to it the more he focused on it.

While the fire was hot, it did not hurt in the way Alexandra expected. Rather than burn the surface of her arm, it felt as though something were clawing from the inside, desperately trying to rip its way out. Kai studied her arm as she endured the agony. The veins in her arm were steadily glowing brighter and brighter, whirling streams of white and red.

"Focus, Alex! Don't let it force its way in, *pull* it in!"

She shouted, desperate not to let go before she figured something out.

"Control your breaths. Look beyond the pain. What else do you feel?"

She breathed in and out through her teeth, trying to rid herself of the uncomfortable sensation with every exhale. Sweat ran down her face. Her arm was screaming, her heart slamming against her chest. Her head felt like it was going to explode. She argued with her entire body and mind, which demanded release. She refused to listen.

I can do this, she told herself. *Look past the pain. Pain. Past it. Focus... Focus... Focus...* She continued to push her body to its limit.

The stone door in Vincent's mind was all he could focus on now. While he still felt Kai's energy, there was no sign of the tranquil spring he had seen in his head a moment ago. He felt as though he were standing right in front of the door, so what was left but to peek inside? As soon as he desired to know where the door led, it burst open, pulling him in.

All traces of Kai's energy vanished. A new energy replaced it—a beautiful darkness that gifted him with an unfamiliar craving. He scanned the area in his head, but saw nothing. He tried to open his eyes, but it was as if he were in a dream where his screams had no voice. He could no longer control his body in the training yard.

"Cute, young, and powerful. How familiar," a woman's soft voice called to him.

He whipped around several times. Still, only darkness.

"How did you stumble in here, human?"

What is going on? he thought. *I was just in the training yard; I couldn't have fallen asleep. Where am I? Who is talking to me? "Human"...?*

"So many questions, so fast. Hush your mind." The same voice came, like a mother's gentle whisper as she put her children to sleep with a bedtime story.

She can hear me?

"Yes, I can hear your thoughts. Clear as the morning sun. Now, tell me, how did you make it in here?" Her voice echoed throughout his mind.

"I don't even know where here is," he spoke out loud, or at least he thought he was.

The veil of darkness lifted to reveal a river, flowing gently downstream to somewhere unknown. Rocks and pebbles glistened just under the shallow water's surface beneath him. Fluffy green grass on the embankments to either side of him led up into dense woods of tall, strong trees full of bright leaves.

"You've found yourself in my boy's soul."

Vincent turned around to see a tall woman with long black hair curling past her exceptionally pale face to her waist. A crimson dress rested on her shoulders, exposing her neck and collarbone. It draped past her hips to layers of flowing ruffles that eventually graced the river's surface where she stood.

"Your boy's... soul?" Vincent shook his head, confused. "You mean Kai?"

"Yes."

"I'm in his soul?"

"Well, not physically, of course," she said with a warm smile.

Vincent looked around the area, taking it all in before he looked back at her. "You called him 'your boy'... Who are you?"

"My name is Lady Machaya."

Vincent's eyes widened. *"You're* the Red Mother?"

Her smile vanished. The world around him flashed to an image he could not retain any details of, other than a feeling of loss.

"Don't call me that!" Her voice became rough and firm, threatening.

"I'm sorry," he was quick to say. "I meant no offense; I'm extremely honored to meet you." He meant it.

Her smile slowly returned. "So, can you please tell me how you got here?"

"I, uh... I'm not entirely sure, to be honest. I was focusing on Kai's energy, and then a doorway appeared. Now, here I am."

"Accidentally, then?"

"Yeah."

"Power you don't yet have full grasp of."

"Uh, yeah, I guess so."

She started to step closer to him through the water. He grew uneasy, but not afraid.

"So, if this is Kai's soul, what are you doing here?"

She stopped.

"If I may ask," he added quickly.

She continued walking again, only answering his question once she stood shoulder to shoulder with him. "We share his body."

"I'm sorry, you what?"

"Our souls both exist inside of him."

Just as Alexandra was reaching her limit, she caught a glimpse of a sensation buried far beneath the fiery claws of pain in her arm. She likened the feeling to a gust of wind against her palm, or rather, *into*

it. Her grip tightened around the blade as she tried to focus, but the feeling started to drift away. She started to loosen her hand instead, slowly lifting her fingers from the blade until only her palm lay against it. Now, with her hand relaxed, it felt as if an air current were flowing directly into her arm. While the pain still lingered, it became a fraction of what it was a moment ago. Slowly, she rose to her feet.

"You mean Kai has two souls?" Vincent asked.

Machaya said nothing. She placed her hand on Vincent's chest—a hand of soft skin, cared for like one of royalty, with neatly trimmed nails that carried a glossy sheen to them. Trapped inside his own mind, he still felt her palm as if he stood right in front of her. She leaned in close to his ears.

"Did you seriously believe you could come here and take *my* power?"

Nothing made any sense to him anymore. "What? What power? I'm not here for anything like that. I don't even know how I got here, or where here is."

The environment around him switched in an instant. The trees went up in flames, burnt to a crisp, until they were dead white. The sky turned orange and filled with smoke. The ground became ash. The river ran dark red.

"LIAR!" Her now rough and raspy voice rumbled through his mind like an earthquake. Her hand shot up to his throat. The claws that were now at the ends of her fingers dug into his neck with enough force to crush a boulder. She held him at arm's length. Her face was now pale enough for him to see the black veins beneath the skin. Her venomous eyes turned dark and hungry. Every tooth in her mouth became fangs, sharp as daggers. The red dress burst into crimson flames with the same shape across her body. Her dark hair flowed behind her head as if it were underwater.

"No, no, no, I... I swear! I didn't even know you were alive until a moment ago."

"I've drained the life from mightier men than you in seconds, and you would be no different. However, for your transgression, I am going to savor you." Every S left her lips like the hiss of a snake. Her jaw unhinged as she opened it wide to clamp down on Vincent's neck. She gnawed on him like a dog's favorite bone. He felt—every—single—fang.

Kai watched, full of amazement, as the flame before them began to engulf Alexandra's arm. It seemed to be almost leaving his blade, like she was *stealing* the fire.

"Astonishing," he said under his breath.

"KAI!" Barrik shouted.

"She's fine. She's getting the hang of it." He was too focused to turn away.

"It's Vince!"

He snapped his attention away. Vincent was laid over on the ground. His whole body thrashed uncontrollably.

"Alex, let go!" Kai ordered in a hurry.

Both of them sprinted over to the other three, who were huddled around Vincent, unsure of what to do.

"Move, let me see him," Kai commanded in a rush. He knelt down and inspected him.

"What happened?" Alexandra asked in a panic.

"I... I don't know. One minute, he was fine, and then..." Vera trailed off, shaking her head.

Vincent's eyes shot wide open. They were bloodshot, the emerald green of his irises rapidly being consumed by a bright crimson. Kai immediately understood what had happened. He leaned in close to Vincent's ear and gently laid his hands on his shoulders.

"Vince, listen to me. She can't harm you if you don't let her." His voice was calm and soft, despite everyone's panicked state.

"She?" Rinna echoed.

"Kai, what are you—"

"Hush!" he snapped at Vera before she could finish.

"Grab onto my voice, Vince. You're with us in the training yard. You're safe. Come back to us."

Kai's words seemed to come from everywhere in the smoky sky. There was no following them. He was unable to move or do anything at all but stand still in the bloody river, the main course of this woman's feast. Even his cries of agony held no sound. Once again, he was trapped in a nightmare.

Kai tried over and over, but there was no change in Vincent's reactions—at least, not for the better. Blood began to spill out of his nose and leak from his eyes. A soft grumble in the sky above drew his attention. Dark gray clouds were forming in the clear sky directly above them. He looked back down at Vincent.

"Alex, come here."

She quickly knelt next to him.

"Place your left hand on his chest."

She did as he instructed. The veins in her arm were gleaming crimson and white with a subtle flow to them. "Okay, now what?"

"You're going to have to gently release the energy from your arm into him."

"What? How? I've only done it when hitting people! How am I supposed to—"

"Relax, Alex. Take a breath. Close your eyes and picture something flowing. Like pouring ale from a pitcher into a mug, your hand being the pitcher. If you actually push into him too, it might help you get a feel for it."

"Okay." She closed her eyes and did as he said. She could feel Vincent's body thrashing beneath her. Her focus was unsteady. Frustrated, she shook her head. "It's not working! We gotta do something else."

"Alex, you have to relax. You can do this. Vincent's mind has traveled too far. He needs something to pull him back."

Barrik rested his hand on her shoulder. "You can do it."

Alexandra took a breath and tried to relax a little. After a moment, the rivers of white and crimson in her veins began to slowly fade to a lambent white-and-red light that emerged from beneath her palm.

Vincent could feel his body growing weaker. His legs no longer possessed the ability to stand on their own. Machaya held him upright as she continued to feed on him. His arms went numb. The surface of his skin felt ice cold. His blood overflowed and spilled out of her mouth, seeped between her fangs, and trickled down his neck all the way to his fingertips. A steady drip of blood splashed into the river. He began to think this was his end, until something warm washed over him.

The feeling not only heated his skin, but brought a familiar warmth to his heart, as if he were being softly covered with a blanket of nostalgia. The sound of a crackling fire blocked out the squelching beneath his chin. The more he gave the snaps and pops of the embers his attention, the louder they grew, until for a split second, he caught a glimpse of their source.

Where was that? I have to go back, he thought.

"You're not going anywhere," Machaya snapped, just as she drilled her claws into the sides of his head.

He ignored her words as best he could and returned his focus to the fire. Every pop and crack came with a flash of the noises from his home in Sylva. The familiar sensation grew until Machaya and his surroundings were all quickly yanked away from him. In a brief instant, he found himself somewhere else once again. On a sofa, he sat in front of the nostalgic flames as they performed their dance of comfort and safety. Alexandra's energy wrapped him in a cloak of tranquility, until finally, he shut his eyes.

Vincent shoved everyone aside as he launched from his back. Hunched over in the snow, he vomited up a mouthful of blood and gasped for air. The others backed away and gave him his space. Once his breathing slowed back to a normal pace, Alexandra knelt in front of him.

"Are you okay?"

"Yeah... I think so."

Barrik plopped down next to him. "Gave us quite the scare, bud."

"No kidding," he replied, wiping his mouth with the back of his hand. "Do you remember when you and I mixed up which mushrooms Mom told us were edible?"

"I try not to."

"Well, this was way worse than that."

"What exactly happened?"

Vincent shook his head, unsure. "I think I just met the Red Mother."

Vera's face quickly lit up with excitement. "Wait—you mean like from the stories?" She never gave Vincent a chance to answer before rattling off more questions. "Did she have a mouthful of bloody fangs? Eyes blacker than night? How long were her claws?" She suddenly gasped dramatically. "Did she try to eat you?!"

"Yes, she did," Vincent answered gravely.

Vera's hands launched up to briefly cover her mouth, agape with shock. "I'm so jealous!"

"Who is the Red Mother?" Rinna asked.

Vera slowly turned to her, mortified by her question. "You don't know?!"

"No, sorry, I'm not familiar with that story."

"The Red Mother was one—"

"Wait, wait, wait!" Vera quickly cut Vincent off before he could begin. "Let me tell it!"

Vincent rolled his eyes. "Fine, go ahead."

Vera leaned in close to everyone as if she were about to haunt them with a ghost story. She cleared her throat and tried to make her voice sound eerie and ominous. "The Red Mother was one of the first humans to drink from the fountains created by the four fallen stars. Twisted and mutated in a horrible way by the amount she consumed, no longer did she hunger for steak and taters. Water would boil in her mouth, leaving her with an unquenchable thirst, until she eventually realized that only the hearts and blood of men would satisfy her gluttonous needs. At first, she stuck to battlefields, too afraid and too good-natured to take the lives of the living; she scavenged through remnants of dead bodies to feed herself. However, due to the many years of cannibalism—or the mutation of the fountain's water, nobody knows for sure—her outer appearance began to reflect the horror inside. Her eyes became endless pits of dark terror. Her skin turned paler than the dwellers in the mountains. Each tooth was a fang sharp enough to pierce armor crafted by the finest Sanorian blacksmiths. Rumors of this new horror spread across the land until, eventually, they hunted her. After years—"

"Are you going to tell us the whole story?" Alexandra interrupted.

"Rinny doesn't know it! Shut up and let me finish," Vera said, clearing her throat again. She continued, "After years of fleeing from isolation to isolation, she grew angry with the world. Finally, after being cornered and left with no other options, she took her first life, and with it, she discovered the taste of fresh blood—a rich and sweet delicacy she would crave until the end of her days. Every time she was challenged from then on, it would end with her covered head to toe in their blood, thus granting her the name the Red Mother."

Vera leaned back and smiled proudly.

"She sounds horrific," Rinna finally said after a moment of silence.

"Was she just like the stories, Vincey?" Vera asked.

"She was," he answered. "But she does not like being called the Red Mother one bit."

"She prefers Lady Machaya," Kai said plainly.

"Uh, yeah, I found that out the hard way."

"Why?" Barrik asked. "What happened when you called her the Red Mother?"

"She tore into my neck like a rabid dog."

"Just like the stories," Vera whispered to herself.

Alexandra shook her head, unable to make sense of the situation. "I don't understand how you met her, though. You never left the training yard."

"I don't know either, but when I was trying to sense your energies, I found a doorway and kind of walked through it. I found her on the other side, where she told me I must have stumbled in accidentally with a power I don't yet understand, and that she and Kai..." He briefly paused, realizing that what he was about to say felt ridiculous. "...share a body?"

"Share a body?" Alexandra repeated, looking at Kai for clarification.

"Oh, now *that* I have read about somewhere," Rinna started to say softly. "When two energies are compatible, they can combine into one, if both parties are willing. Depending on what region the story is from, though, the idea of it changes a little. Soulmates is the most common—that I've read about, anyway—where a child becomes the soul that was merged together. Although, Kai's situation sounds much different."

Kai shook his head. "Unfortunately, I'm afraid there's no beautiful love story to tell like the tales you're referring to, Rinna. And while they get some of how it works right, most of it is embellished and romanticized."

"So, what did happen?" Rinna asked.

Kai let out a deep breath and joined the rest of them by sitting down on the snowy ground. "She was dying and found me when I was still a boy. I was young and desperate, injured with a vulnerable heart. She took advantage of my lust for revenge and naivety by offering me the power to avenge the people of my village, as well as my family." Kai stared into the white flakes slowly accumulating on the ground, thinking about all of the consequences that came from one decision. "Never once did I question the price I would have to pay."

Alexandra gently leaned into his line of sight. "If it wasn't love, then how did she merge with you?"

"She killed me."

Everyone was bewildered by his answer.

"You look pretty good for a dead guy," Barrik offered.

Kai looked up at him through his eyebrows. "She slashed my throat and waited for the moment the light in my eyes darkened. Everything went black, and once I awoke, her presence has been with me ever since. I don't fully understand how, but that never mattered, because now, she and I are forever together."

"Sooo..." Vera was almost afraid to ask. "Do you also feed on people, like her?" She leaned back with a widened eye, awaiting his answer.

Kai stared at her blankly, stunned briefly by her words. "No, Vera. I don't eat people."

She let out a small breath of relief.

"I do, however, live with her bloodlust in the back of my mind. The longer I go without feeding her through my blade, the worse it gets."

Rinna grew uneasy. "You... *feed* her?"

"I feed her. She grants me her power."

A large smile grew across Vera's face. "Amazing," she whispered.

Vincent still felt puzzled. "Kai, I still don't understand how I saw her in the first place."

"The same way you spoke to Larissa. Your mind is not bound to the same limitations as your physical body. Think of it like straying into a dream, except the reality of it is, you *did* go somewhere else in a sense, just not physically. You went further than I thought you would on your first attempt, and for that, I sincerely apologize for my underestimation of your capabilities."

"Teach me how to never experience that again, and we'll call it even."

Kai chuckled. "Deal." He stood up, made his way to the center of the training yard, and put his katana, which lay on the ground, back in her sheath. In the sky above, the clouds that had formed were dissipating, allowing the sun to peek through once more. It was barely noon.

"Who is guarding the fountain tonight?" Kai asked, not removing his eyes from the sky.

"Me and Rinna," Barrik said.

Kai turned to them mischievously. "Then you're up next."

CHAPTER 21

VER the next several days, Kai helped guide everyone in the growth of their Favors. Alexandra focused on pulling in energy beyond when she was purely taking damage. While following Kai's advice, Vincent was careful not to dive too deep again as he absorbed and sensed the energy around him and everyone else's. Quickly, he was able to implement it while engaged in combat, rather than only while sitting still. Barrik worked to grow the size and number of shields he could produce. While he found it relatively simple to make more than one, three was his current limit, and he could not make them big enough to prove useful. Rinna fought to extend the duration of her invisibility, as well as to conceal other people. While there was no indication that she would be able to do so, Kai insisted she continue to try.

Everyone slowly made improvements to their abilities—everyone except Vera. She grew frustrated with her lack of progress, until Kai finally gave her the push she needed. She stood across from him in the center of the training yard as everyone was pelted by morning flurries. Vincent sat in his usual spot with his legs crossed and eyes closed. Snow was quickly piling on top of his head and shoulders.

"All right, Vera." Kai pointed to the side of the training yard. "Throw one of your daggers over there."

In a flash, the dagger flew from her lower back and stuck straight into the fence. She spun the other one around her finger until he gave her the next location.

"Now throw that one…" He turned around, looking for another spot. "…over there." He pointed far behind himself.

She hurled it past him, and he watched as it sank into the bulls-eye of an archery target near the perimeter. He turned back to her to see a wide and confident smile.

"Now what?" she asked.

Kai pulled his headband down over his eyes, sat down, and crossed his legs. "I want you to relocate back and forth between the two until I tell you to stop."

She shrugged. "Okay." She vanished. In the time it took to blink, she reappeared next to the dagger stuck in the fence. She waited a brief moment before relocating to the archery target. She vanished again. From the target to the fence, fence to target, back and forth, she performed her Favor's trick until finally Kai stopped her.

"Okay, that's enough," he called out.

She halted her movements and leaned up against the fence.

"Vince, what did you notice?" Kai shouted over to him.

He took a second to think through the last few moments before he answered. To him, nothing seemed out of the ordinary, but Kai's question made him doubt his own perception. Maybe he had missed something.

He shook his head. "I don't know. I couldn't sense anything unusual. Her energy just switches spots."

"Exactly."

"Uh…" Vincent was lost.

Kai lifted his headband and rose to his feet. He turned to Vera, drew his katana, and stuck it in the ground. "Teleport to me, Vera."

She looked at him, confused. "I can't."

"Try."

Reluctantly, she followed his instructions. She gave her best effort and focused on his weapon, but after several moments without results, she gave up.

"See? I can only do it with my daggers."

"What is different between your daggers and my katana?"

"Mine don't feed a blood-eating horror?" she said with a playful smile.

Kai hung his head. "No, try again."

Silence floated in the air until Rinna chimed in. "Vera, aren't all of your weapons enchanted?"

"Yeah, so?"

Alexandra's eyes lit up. "V, they on—"

"Hush!" Kai cut her off before she could finish. "Let her figure it out on her own. Vera, why can only you four wield one another's weapons?"

"Because… they only respond to our energies."

Kai narrowed his eyes with a grin. "You think it's a coincidence that you can teleport to the very daggers you keep on your back?"

He could see Vera slowly starting to catch on. "So… you're saying I can teleport to them because they respond to my energy?"

"Mm-hmm."

"So, if that's true, then…" She trailed off momentarily as she finished the puzzle in her mind. She closed her eyes, and just like before, she vanished—only this time, she appeared somewhere other than beside either of her daggers.

Kai closed his eyes, relieved. "Finally."

The others started to look for her, until…

"Hiya, Bearie!"

"Woah!" Startled, Barrik whipped around to see Vera standing behind him with a devilish grin.

Alexandra shook her head and smiled with amazement. "So, you can instantly relocate to anything that responds to your energy?"

She vanished.

"Yup!" she said as she appeared right next to her.

"That's awesome!" Vincent said.

Vera appeared right in front of him, flicked him in the forehead, and vanished once more. The others laughed.

"Never mind, I hate it," he pouted, rubbing the minor injury.

Filled with excitement, she continued relocating from person to person over and over again.

"Don't you get tired from that, Vera?" Rinna asked.

"Not really. I feel it a little bit, but I recover pretty quickly."

"And distance doesn't matter either?"

Vera shook her head. "It doesn't seem to. Doesn't matter how far…" Her eye suddenly lit up. Something clicked in her mind. She looked at the ground, closed her eye, and vanished. Everyone looked around to see where she would appear, but after several moments, there was no sign of her. She was gone.

Barrik grew worried. "Where'd she go?"

"Other than all of your weapons, do you know of anything else that responds to her?" Kai asked.

They thought for a moment until Alexandra smiled and shook her head. "I know where she is… Lucky."

Vera's sudden appearance caused a light brown horse to rear right in front of her. She dove out of the way just as it came down. When she rose to her feet, her vision blurred as dizziness overtook her. The air felt slightly warmer against her skin as she began to fall over. Something stopped her gently just short of the snow-dusted ground as someone caught her and cradled her closely.

"You're okay, baby. I got you. You're safe." A woman's hurried voice was the last thing she heard before a curtain of darkness draped over her.

As Vera slowly came to, the scent of horses, oak, and a subtle hint of vanilla made its way to her nose. Along with it came a deep sense of comfort and a rush of nostalgia. It smelled like the peace and innocence of childhood. It smelled like home.

She lay on her back in a bed with a familiar warmth. She sat up and looked around the room. A few feet away, on the other side of the room, another bed was neatly made with a quilt and a feather pillow resting at the foot. A candle burned beneath the soft white light of the moon that snuck in through the only window. The sound of clinking dishes and footsteps came in through the cracked-open bedroom door from somewhere down the hall.

She swung her legs to the edge of the bed and stood up momentarily before stumbling back down. Her legs were far too weak to hold her up without assistance. Her entire body was exhausted. It felt as though she had not slept for a whole moon cycle. Even after the long hunting trips where Fira had kept them up for days, she had not experienced such fatigue.

In order to maneuver herself around, she leaned against the wall as she made her way out of her room and down the hall. The moment she turned the corner into the kitchen from the sitting room, she was ambushed.

"You're awake! Here, let me help you." Fira rushed over to help her to the table.

As soon as Fira was within reach, Vera used what little strength she had to throw her arms around her mother. She exhaled a long, deep breath of comfort. Fira was taken aback for a brief second, only momentarily caught off guard, before she wrapped one arm around Vera and gently ran her fingers through her hair. A moment of blissful silence filled the room.

"I missed you," Vera finally said with her face buried in Fira's embrace. Her hair fell down just by Vera's nose. With every inhale, she smelled the sun, still lingering on every golden strand.

"I missed you too," Fira replied delicately. "Are you okay?"

Vera nodded with a smile and an eye welling with tears of joy. "Yeah, I'm okay. Everyone's okay."

"Your grandfather only stepped out for a moment. Why don't I put on some tea, and you can tell us everything, if you're up for it?"

"Yeah, that sounds good."

Fira helped Vera to the table before she turned to throw on the kettle. It was only a short time before the scent of lavender and honey wafted throughout the room—Vera's favorite. The steam from her cup curled up, warming her face and filling her nose with a soothing aroma.

Just then, the front door creaked open, letting in a gust of winter's chill. Charlie entered, brushing away the flurries resting on the top of his midnight head, making new additions to his few strands of silver. His face lit up at the sight of Vera hovering over her tea.

"Oh, pumpkin, you're awake!" He quickly slipped off his snow-covered boots and rushed over to plant a kiss on the top of her head. She smiled. He gave her a gentle squeeze and patted her on the shoulder twice before he sat down across from her.

"Just in time," Fira said as she started to pour out the hot tea.

"Oh, thank you, my dear." Charlie let the hot steam wash away the icy chill on his face.

Huddled around their teas, the three of them shared a moment of silence. There were so many questions on everyone's mind that they were unsure where to begin, until Vera softly took the lead.

"How long was I out?"

"Almost two full days," Fira answered.

Vera whistled with amazement.

"Scared me and Nexella half to death, you suddenly appearing like that. She almost stomped you out."

"She scared me, trying to crush me like that!"

"As happy as we are to see you, how *did* you get here?"

Vera pointed to the necklace hanging around Fira's neck. The four-star stones were still shining with their designated glow: green for Vincent, blue for Alexandra, red for Vera, and yellow for Barrik.

"I teleported to the star stone."

"Uhhh, okay, you lost me," Charlie said.

Vera explained how her Favor worked, as well as everyone else's. She told them about the training they had been doing with Kai and how she had just figured out a new part of hers.

Charlie exhaled after a warm sip of his tea and looked at Fira. "How fitting of a Favor for Barrik, wouldn't you say?"

She smiled. "Almost too perfect."

"A gentle giant, as they say. I'm glad to hear all my grandchildren are okay. When you showed up out of the blue like that, we thought something was wrong."

Vera shook her head. "No, there's nothing to worry about. We're all okay. Well, mostly." She gestured to her left eye.

"May I?" Charlie asked.

Vera okayed him to inspect it further. He stood up and made his way around the table. With gentle fingers, he lifted the small patch of leather. She squinted.

"Does it hurt?" he asked.

"No, not anymore. Everything is just extremely bright. Like I have that side of my face pressed up against a star."

Her eye had lost all of its color. The ring of soft cocoa that was once there was entirely faded beneath a cloud of gray. Light from the lanterns hanging around the kitchen reflected off of it, giving it a glisten similar to the sheen of a pearl.

"But you can't see anything at all?" he asked as he gently laid the patch back over her eye.

Vera shook her head. "Master Darion said it's possible my vision may never return to normal."

Charlie sat back down and sipped his tea, slowly sifting through his thoughts.

"How did it happen?" Fira asked.

Vera took a deep breath and started from the beginning. She told them all about their mission, from Vincent's sword, to the imps, the two mystery attackers, and Toran. She went on and on, careful not to spare any details of their adventures since they had embarked on their journey.

"Wow," Fira said, shocked. "That's a lot for only a couple of months."

"Yeah," Vera said as she stared into her tea.

"Well, it's late, and I'm afraid you're going to need all the rest you can get, because after breakfast tomorrow, you have to return."

"Already?" Charlie asked, disappointed.

"She can't stay here, Dad, you know this. If I had to guess, Tahara already knows she's gone. If she stays much longer, she's likely to be labeled a Rogue."

Vera set down her tea. "How would she know I'm gone?"

"The lady has a Favor of her own. She calls it her connection to the fountain, but it allows her to detect your energy within a certain radius, which is essentially the city limits."

"They failed to mention that part in the ceremony."

"It isn't exactly something she advertises. Otherwise, people might actively search for ways around it."

"How do you know about it then?"

Fira smiled. "Her true loyalty belongs to the fountain. However, since the king protects it, and therefore her, she reports directly to him. Many years ago, before the war, Sentis would spill all kinds of secrets to Victor, which Victor then told me."

"That Victor could charm just about anyone. He did overturn your heart as well, if I recall correctly," Charlie said in remembrance.

Fira laughed softly. "That's true. He wasn't afraid to take advantage of that ability either."

"No, he was not."

"All right," Fira said as she stood up and pushed in her chair, "it's time you get your sleep."

Vera went to stand up, but her fatigue quickly brought her back down in her seat. Charlie and Fira both helped guide her into bed.

"Goodnight, pumpkin," he said with a kiss on her head.

Fira gave her a smile just before she shut the bedroom door behind her. The soft moonlight that leaked in through the window and the gentle breeze against the glass acted quickly to put her into a deep sleep.

The following day, Vera woke to the sound of bacon being crisped in the kitchen. Waking up back in her bed after her short yet long time away from home felt surreal, as if she had consciously walked through a dream. Not eager to leave, she savored every step on her way to the table. Her bones still felt heavier than usual, and her muscles felt scorched.

When she turned the corner, Charlie launched from his seat to help her sit down.

"You should have called for us! We would have gladly come and helped you."

Vera smiled. "I know, Gramps, but I was okay. Thank you."

"Still, asking for help isn't a bad thing, you know."

"I know," she said, sitting down.

"How do you feel?" Charlie asked from his usual seat at the head of the table.

Vera moved her arm in a circle. "I'm fine. I could probably take down a pack of weren by myself."

Fira set down a plate of eggs, bacon, and crispy golden potatoes in front of her. "I hope that's actually how you feel, because it's only going to get worse before you *truly* feel better."

"Whaddaya mean?" Vera asked with a piece of bacon hanging from her mouth.

"You pushed your body past its limit just to get here, and now you're about to do it again before you fully recover. You're going to need as much strength as you can muster. So, eat up."

Vera started to shovel food into her mouth.

"And you'll probably need something to throw up," Fira added.

Vera gulped. "This doesn't sound fun."

Fira laughed. "Of course not, but what did I always tell you?"

Vera sighed and repeated the words that had been said to her hundreds of times: "You can't go beyond your limits if you're unwilling to see where they begin. Yeah, yeah, I know."

"You don't always have to be so hard on them, you know?" Charlie said.

Fira pointed at Vera with her fork. "You heard what they all went through in just a few months, didn't you?"

"Well, yeah, I was right here."

"Well? They're alive, aren't they?"

He sighed in defeat. He might not have liked Fira's methods, but she was right; all of his grandchildren were alive.

Vera motioned to get another plate of food. Fira quickly shot up and reached for her plate. "I'll get it, hon."

Vera handed it over.

The clink and clang of silver against ceramic bounced through the kitchen as they all enjoyed their meal. When it was finally time for Vera to leave, they all went out back in the yard, where she gave her goodbyes to everyone, including Nexella. Vera patted the long bridge of the horse's chestnut nose. "Goodbye, Nexy. Sorry for scaring you."

An exhale and flap of her lips was Nexella's only response.

"You ready?" Fira asked.

Vera breathed in Nexella before she turned around. "No," she answered with a smile.

Fira smiled at her and pulled her in. "I'm so proud of you."

Vera held her tightly as her eyes welled up. Her bones might ache, her muscles might burn, but no matter what she felt, leaving would remain the hardest part.

"Give everyone a hug for me, okay? Including Vincent—and when he tries to pull away, just hang on tighter," she joked.

Vera chuckled. "I definitely will."

"And hey…" Fira gestured to Vera's wounded eye. "No more overreaching. Know your limits, yeah?"

"I thought I was supposed to find them to exceed them?" Vera said with a smug look.

"Only when it's safe to do so."

Vera hugged her fiercely once more. When she pulled away, she turned and wrapped her arms around Charlie. He let out an elderly groan from the impact. The stubble on his face scratched the side of her cheek.

"Oh, I hate to see you go, little pumpkin."

"I know, Gramps, me too."

She pulled away with a smile and a sniffle. Wiping the tears from her cheek, she looked at them both and stepped back. "Okay, I'll see you soon."

Fira and Charlie both nodded, and a moment later, she was gone.

Kai's katana crashed into Barrik's energy shield and bounced out of his hands.

"Nice one, Bearie!" Alexandra shouted.

Barrik rolled his eyes. "Isn't that getting old, already?"

Alexandra turned to Rinna for her opinion. She shrugged. "I think it's cute!"

Vincent chuckled. "Berry."

"You hush, lover boy!" Barrik fired back, putting a quick end to Vincent's amusement.

Kai paid no mind to their squabbles. "Your shield is much stronger than before, and you seem to be able to conjure it with much less effort."

"Thanks."

"Just keep working on making multiple, and I'm sure you'll see some progress."

Barrik nodded and moved to retrieve Kai's weapon for him.

Sitting in his usual spot in the training yard, Vincent started to sense a familiar energy approaching them from the east. "Guys!" he shouted. "Vera's back!"

Everyone turned and looked around. There was no sign of her.

"Uh, are you sure, Vince?" Barrik said doubtfully.

"I'm positive. She should be right..." Vincent pointed to the gap between Alexandra and Rinna. Just before he could finish his sentence, Vera appeared and immediately dropped to her knees.

"Vera!" Alexandra exclaimed as she moved to embrace her.

"Told you," Vincent muttered with a yawn.

Rinna quickly noticed the paleness in Vera's face. "Are you okay?" she asked.

Vera tried to warn them with a frantic wave before she fell to all fours and let loose the contents of her stomach. Her entire body screamed with every retch. Her throat began to burn worse than her muscles. Once she finally stopped hurling, she fell over in the snow next to a puddle of blood and bacon bits.

"What happened?" Alexandra asked.

Vera's eyes were unbearably heavy. Her bones felt as if they had all been trampled on, while her muscles were simultaneously being torn apart. "I'm... fine," she said weakly—just before slipping unconscious.

Rinna knelt down beside her and placed the back of her hand against her forehead. She felt as hot as the sun.

"Is she going to be okay?"

"She'll be fine," Kai said reassuringly. "She pushed herself far beyond her body's limit. She just needs to rest. Take her back to the barracks. I imagine she'll be out for a few days. We can pick everything back up tomorrow."

Barrik gently scooped her up in his arms and started his way back. Everyone gathered themselves and followed behind Barrik.

"Vince," Kai called after him.

Vincent stopped in his tracks and turned around. "Yeah?"

"How did you know Vera was coming back, let alone exactly where she would appear?"

Vincent scratched his head as he remembered. "Well, at first, I just felt her presence—kind of like she was standing right next to me. Like how I can tell everyone's behind me now. But then that feeling just sort of shifted to one location."

Kai placed his hand on his chin and studied Vincent for a moment.

Vincent looked at Kai curiously. "What is it?" he asked.

Kai shook his head softly. "I was just thinking… if you could somehow find a way to apply that to combat, predicting your opponent's moves before they make them, that is. It would be quite challenging to counter. Even for me."

"So you're saying if I get good at it, I'll be stronger than you?" Vincent joked with a grin.

"Now let's not get ahead of ourselves," Kai responded playfully. "You first have to be able to use it in combat."

"How do I do that?"

"It could just come naturally to you, but you know what's always great for evolving your Favors?"

Vincent rolled his eyes. "Putting me into a stressful situation."

Kai chuckled. "Now you're getting it. Since Vera was the one you were able to sense to that extent, we'll work on it with her once she recovers." Kai urged him onward with a nudge of his head. "Catch up with the others and let me know if her condition worsens at all."

"We will," Vincent answered with a nod.

Just as he started his way back to everyone else, Kai called after him again. "And Vince…"

Vincent turned around. "Yeah?"

"Get some sleep."

Vincent scoffed. "I'll try."

He turned away with a sigh and raced back to the group, the cold snow crunching beneath his every step. He wondered if his lack of sleep was really becoming that apparent to everyone. His dreams continued to haunt him every night, and while Master Darion was working on a blend of herbs to ease his restless nights, Vincent had little faith they would work. The longer the dreams continued, the more he felt like his only answer was to talk to Larissa. Somehow, he had to see her again.

"What did Kai want?" Rinna asked him as he caught up to them.

"Oh, just to marvel over my incredible abilities," Vincent responded sarcastically.

"No wonder it was such a quick conversation then," Alexandra teased.

"Ha ha, very funny."

Rinna snickered.

"How's she doing?" Vincent asked, looking down at Vera, passed out in Barrik's arms.

"I think she's just exhausted," Barrik answered.

Vincent shook his head with jealousy. "Mom probably fed her breakfast too. So unfair."

"You think Mom's breakfast is worth the condition she's in right now?" Alexandra asked.

Barrik and Vincent raised an eyebrow at each other, turned back to her, and spoke in unison. "Absolutely."

Alexandra shook her head with a gentle smile. "Yeah, you're right," she said softly.

CHAPTER 22

FEW days after Vera's return, she finally began to show signs of recovery. She spent most of the day sleeping, but when she did wake, she was pleasantly surprised to find that there was always warm tea by her bedside, thanks to everyone's collective efforts.

While she was unable to partake in training or perform her duties of guarding the fountain, Kai had another mission for her. He brought her stacks of old books and scrolls gifted to him by the Lorekeeper, each pertaining to Sanorian history. Some were purely works of myth and legend, while others contained detailed accounts of battles and the spotlighted warriors who fought in them. While the war records she found rather entertaining, the texts regarding the translation of the Sanorian language to the speech of man bored her half to death, but those were the ones Kai had instructed her to focus on.

She pored over them for hours, desperately trying not to fall asleep. She compared each of the runes to the ones Vincent and Alexandra had replicated from his three-gemmed sword and the ones from the tomb. While she found some similarities, there were no exact matches—nothing to make sense of. The lack of information on the runes, the sword, Larissa, or any of Vincent's dreams left a twisting knot in Kai's stomach that continued growing. Too much was unknown, and Vincent's condition only worsened.

Tired from his late-night watch at the fountain, Barrik sluggishly opened his bedroom door to a sight he was no stranger to. Vincent was thrashing underneath his covers, muttering to himself in his sleep.

Barrik rushed to his side. "Vince, hey, wake up." Bariik leaned over him to gently shake him awake by his shoulders. "Vince."

Vincent launched up from his bed. "Get away from me!" he shouted, throwing Barrik to the ground with one arm. Barrik crashed onto his backside and sat there, stunned.

The horror in Barrik's eyes quickly brought Vincent out of his hypnagogic state. He rushed to help him back up. "I'm so sorry, Bear. Are you okay?" he asked in a hurry.

"Yeah, I'm fine. You just scared me to the stars, that's all." Barrik could see the blatant fatigue all over Vincent's face. "Why don't you sit down?"

He helped Vincent to his bed and sat down beside him. "I take it the herbs Master Darion gave you aren't working?"

Vincent scoffed and leaned over to his nightstand, grabbing something. He handed Barrik an empty glass vial with a few black and brown specks of powder remaining at the bottom.

"You took all of it? I thought he said only to take a pinch or two?"

Vincent shrugged. "That's what I've been taking, but it hasn't worked. When I woke up earlier, I just took the rest of it."

"And it still didn't help…"

Vincent shook his head. "Not even a little," he replied, looking down at his trembling hands. He was drenched in sweat. His body ached from all the involuntary muscle contractions during his nightmares. His heavy eyes wandered to the sword at the end of his bed, lingering over each star stone without its light. It was a relief to see them gray and faded. But what started to concern him was his yearning to hold it. He imagined hearing the *shing* of the dark metal as he released it from its scabbard. His fingertips practically salivated at the thought of wrapping around its grip. His muscles begged to feel its weight, as if they would remember a strength he had long forgotten. The newly visceral desire unnerved him—so much so that it was the only piece of his condition he was afraid to divulge.

Vincent tore his eyes from the sword to see Barrik dozing beside him. He nudged him slightly. "Hey, big guy. Go get some sleep."

Barrik looked around, a tad frazzled, and yawned. "Can I get anything for you?" he asked, rising from Vincent's bed.

"No, I'll be fine. You've done enough already. Thank you, though."

"All right. Good night, bud."

"Good night, Bear."

Vincent sat on the edge of his bed for a while, staring at the floor, dissociating. He was exhausted. He wanted to sleep. He *needed* to sleep. But he was scared. He fought against his sinking eyelids for as long as he could, just like every other night.

When Vincent explained to Kai that the herbs had no effect, even once he took the whole bottle, Kai only grew more uneasy. The herbs had been used in the past to put soldiers who were mentally scarred from battle into the deepest sleep of their lives, and it worked every time. Nothing was making any sense to him, and with every passing day, he only found more questions. Even though he knew Ghost was out gathering information for him, he felt as though he was uselessly waiting around for something to happen. At least if there was a clear conflict, he could act on potential solutions. But for now, he was stuck. Waiting for answers. Waiting for the next move. And he hated it. All he could do was try to keep his mind busy.

Kai sat on the burgundy sofa next to the crackling fire in the barracks, poring over book after book, amassing a significant tower beside him. Alexandra was leaning over the long center table across from him, scribbling on a piece of parchment with a quill and ink.

Barrik and Rinna entered the quarters, bringing a snowy gust of wind that swept through the sitting room. The chilling breeze stirred the air, flipping several pages of Kai's book and prompting Alexandra to press her hand firmly on her letter to keep it in place.

"Welcome back," Alexandra said. "Bear, did you get Vera her soup?"

"Of course," he answered, lifting a wooden bowl with steam rolling out of the tiny gap beneath the lid.

"Find anything, Kai?" Rinna asked as she shut the door behind her.

"Nothing worth mentioning," he replied as he returned to his original page. When he looked over at them, he noted their disregard for the icy temperature. Barrik stood underneath the entryway in a brown doublet with the sleeves cut off, while Rinna wore a flowing gown of olive and amber belted at the waist with no jacket or cloak.

"You two are going to catch a cold if you don't start dressing properly," Kai admonished.

Alexandra laughed. "You tell 'em, Mom!"

Kai shook his head.

Rinna looked around the room. "Where's Vince?"

"He already left for watch," Alexandra answered as she continued writing.

"Ugh, I told him to wait for me."

Alexandra chuckled. "He doesn't listen well. And he probably got lost, so you might want to hurry and catch him."

Rinna rolled her eyes and ran up the steps to switch into her armor and grab her weapon. When she came back down the steps, she raced for the door. "Hey, guys, Vera's tea is getting a little cold. She's still sleeping, but maybe make her some more in a little bit?"

"I can do that," Barrik said.

Alexandra finally dropped her quill. "Okay, finished. Now we just need Vince to write his part. Rin, will you remind Vince not to forget, so we can send this letter out tomorrow?"

"Who is it for?"

"Our mother."

"Sure, I'll remind him, but only if you tell her I said hello."

Alexandra picked up the quill and said out loud as she wrote. "'P.S. Rinna says hello.' Done."

"Great! All right, I'll see you all later."

The door opened again, letting the chill of a cold winter's eve spread throughout the room once again. Barrik plopped down on the sofa and rubbed his stomach proudly. "I swear I'll never tire of Mancho's stew. Tender meat, nice and salty, with potatoes of delicious golden flavor."

Kai peeked at him from behind his book. "I'm curious: how long do you typically go without thinking about food?"

"I'll let you know when I stop."

"*If*," Alexandra corrected.

With a hurried slam, the doors suddenly burst open again with a freezing chill. In the doorway stood a Meditas soldier, frantic and glistening in sweat. "Kai! Thank the stars!"

"What is it, Alvi?" Kai asked as he rose from his seat.

Alvi shut the door, hurried over, and rested his hands on his knees to briefly catch his breath. "I was sent to request your help, sir!"

"What can I help you with?"

"A few missing persons, sir. Last known whereabouts in western Thernruff. A patrol party as well as a scouting party."

"How long have they been gone?"

"The scouting party left just before sundown. The patrol party was supposed to return by supper."

"Hmm…" Kai turned and looked at Alexandra as he wandered through his thoughts.

"What are you thinking?" she asked.

"I'm not sure yet," Kai answered, returning his attention to Alvi. "Do you have any other information for me?"

"We received a report from a panicked merchant earlier today about a pack of ghouls lurking in Thernruff, but—"

"Ghouls don't travel in packs," Kai said, finishing Alvi's sentence.

"Right, sir. But his description matched a ghoul perfectly, if my memory serves me correctly."

Kai thought quietly to himself for a moment. "Okay. Prepare two horses, preferably Alamahn and Mastala. We'll meet you at the western gate."

"Yes, sir!" Alvi gave him a firm salute and ran back out the doors.

"You think a pack of ghouls is actually out there?" Alexandra asked.

"Pack or not, that's irrelevant. A patrol party and a scouting party should still be able to handle a few ghouls with relative ease, if that is the case. And even if they were all amateur swordsmen new to combat, at least one of them would have fled to safety."

"That's true. More bandits, maybe?" Alexandra guessed.

"Perhaps." Kai shook his head with a puzzled look on his face. "I don't know. Something doesn't feel right. I want someone to stay with Vera, so Alex, you're with me. Barrik, just make sure Vera gets her tea."

"You don't want me to come with you?" he asked, surprised.

"Alex and I are more than capable."

Barrik shrugged. "Okay."

Kai turned to Alexandra. "Go get your things and meet me out front."

She nodded and stormed up the stairs.

Kai and Alexandra raced together through the city. Both of them were dressed in their leather armor bearing a symbol of the fountain's tree burned into the breastplate. By the time they reached the western gate, two guards were already waiting for them just in front of the doors of iron bars with reins in their hands. Two horses stood next to them, tall and lean with powerful legs. The one on the left was a white-spotted caramel with a golden mane, while the other was dark enough to be mistaken for the first one's shadow. Both of them were saddled and ready to go.

Before Alexandra tried to mount the horse on the left, she gracefully slid her hand down its nose and patted its cheek. "What's his name?"

"That is Alamahn. He's light on his feet and is no stranger to battle," Kai answered as he climbed into Mastala's saddle.

"Nice to meet you, Alamahn. I'm Alex."

Alamahn nudged her and flapped his lips. She rolled the left sleeve of her gray tunic up above her elbow and hopped into Alamahn's saddle. When she reached for the reins in the guard's hands, he pulled back slightly when he saw her dark and mutated left arm.

"You look like half a ghoul yourself," he said nastily.

Alexandra snatched the reins from him, but gave no further acknowledgment.

Once Kai saw she was up and ready to go, he leaned in close to Mastala's ear and whispered, "To the light beyond the stars, or there and back again to the warmth of home's fire." Mastala flapped her lips and brushed away a bit of snow and dirt beneath her hoof. "We ride!" Kai cried.

With a kick of their heels and a flap of the reins, they were off.

The moon continued to rise above as they rode onward toward the forest. Without a single cloud in the sky, the moon's light washed over the land freely. The speed at which they traveled made the night air feel even colder against their faces. The closer they drew to the edge of Thernruff Woods, the taller the trees seemed to grow, as did the darkness between them.

At the edge of the woods, they slowed to a halt. Kai closed his eyes and sent out his energy in search of anything notable.

Alexandra gave him a moment before she asked, "Anything?"

Kai shook his head. "Definitely no bandits nearby."

"What about anything else?"

"A smaller horror's energy is much more challenging to detect, although seeing as it's an alleged pack, I thought this scenario might yield different results."

"What makes it harder? Because they don't have as much energy?"

"Maybe. Truth is, that is one of the many mysteries of energy I have yet to find an answer to."

"Wow. Just when I was starting to think you knew everything."

"Almost everything," he said with a wink.

"So, now what do we do?"

Kai ran his hand along Mastala's neck and gave her a gentle pat. "We'll hand this part over to them."

They started trotting along the edge of the forest slowly, listening to and feeling Alamahn and Mastala's reactions. At first, they moved along as if they were on nothing more than a routine patrol, until Alexandra felt Alamahn start to tremble.

"Kai," she whispered.

He stopped, hopped down, and walked over to them. He placed the palm of his hand on Alamahn's chest. He could feel his accelerated heartbeat and shaking muscles. The horse snorted.

"Hop down, Alex," he said with an extended hand. "Remarkable, isn't it?"

"What is?"

"Their natural senses far exceed ours, even with all of our abilities." Kai patted Alamahn on the chest and handed his reins to Alexandra. They hitched the horses to two trees along the edge of the forest and unsheathed their weapons slowly, careful to make as little noise as possible. The forest was too dense for the moon to provide enough light. Kai ignited his katana, while Alexandra used the fire sign to turn her sword into a torch.

"Stay close to me," Kai whispered. Shoulder to shoulder, they ventured forth together into the darkness.

Vincent stood next to Tahara, dressed in his leather armor with his two sabers behind his back and the Sanorian sword belted on his hip. They were looking up at the fountain's tree and discussing its ability to retain its leaves when Vincent suddenly stopped and turned around.

"What is it, child?" Tahara asked.

"Well, it's about time you caught up," Vincent said to Rinna. Even though she was entirely concealed, he looked right into her eyes.

She released her Favor, revealing herself. "You're getting pretty good at that. I was trying to spook you."

Vincent shrugged. "Guess you'll have to try a little harder next time."

Rinna placed her hands on her hips. "Speaking of next time, maybe next time I tell you to wait for me, you'll actually listen!"

Vincent scratched the back of his head, guilty. "I was supposed to wait for you?"

Rinna shook her head with a soft smile. "Unbelievable."

"Welcome, Rinna, dear," Tahara said with open hands and a gentle bow. Moonlight shimmered off the speckles of silver in her light green gown. The amber river of hair atop her head flowed gracefully until it disappeared behind her shoulders without a trace. Only the circlet of silver flowers on her head prevented it from falling to her face.

"Thank you, Tahara."

"Now, as I was saying, Vincent," Tahara continued with her wispy voice, "trees rid themselves of their leaves to conserve energy. Since this one has access to an endless supply of it, there is no need. Nor do the leaves falter and change color." She turned with an open palm to the pool of water behind them. "Only if this pool of water were to run dry would we begin to see the leaves fall."

"Like in Abnor?" Vincent asked.

"I would suspect a similar occurrence, correct. However, I have not had the luxury of witnessing any other fountain's beauty, so I speak no more than speculation. What has stripped the life and color from the neighboring lands of Abnor is unknown to me. But fret not, young Raine, the balance will come, and Abnor's grace will be restored. For now, trouble yourself not with needless concerns of such tragic events." She placed a hand on both Vincent and Rinna's shoulders. "It is a beautiful night, so please enjoy it. I'll take my leave."

Vincent and Rinna walked around the outer edge of the fountain's cliff, weaving in and out of the spidery roots that reached out from the tree's base as they talked through the night. The icy winter breeze continued to sweep across them, turning their cheeks red and their lips slightly numb. From this height, all of the lanterns lit around the city resembled tiny orange stars, no bigger than a crumb of bread.

The few people who wandered about appeared small enough to be accidentally stepped on. They could see all the way up to the tall city walls, but beyond the turrets and guard patrols atop the battlement, there was nothing but endless darkness.

"Oh, before I forget," Rinna said suddenly, "I'm supposed to remind you to finish your part of your mother's letter."

"Alex finally finished what she wanted to say? She's been writing that for the last two days."

"Well, she wants to send it out tomorrow, so you have to do it tonight."

Vincent rolled his eyes. "Of course... she does," he said with a yawn.

"Still not sleeping any better?"

"No. I wake up feeling like I was chasing chickens all night."

"Chasing chickens?"

"What? You've never had to catch a chicken before?"

She chuckled. "No, can't say I have."

"Lucky. I'd rather deal with those imps over chickens any day of the week. They're annoying and filthy, but wow are their eggs tasty!"

Rinna roared with laughter. The sound of her elation filled him with such warmth that he found himself smiling uncontrollably.

When she finally simmered down, she wiped her eyes and chuckled once more. "I wonder if the alchemist has a potion that would give me the ability to look inside your mind."

"Oh, you don't want that. I don't think you'd be able to handle my thoughts."

"Why not?"

"Because you don't have any experience with chasing chickens," he joked with an exaggerated and silly grin, which brought a smile to her face.

Even with all the bare trees, the moonlight provided less and less visibility the farther into the forest Kai and Alexandra trekked. They moved in silence, their eyes scanning the darkness carefully. Kai listened for any movement after every few steps. Nothing. They saw nothing, heard nothing. Other than the two of them, there was no sign of life except for the pit growing in their stomachs. They knew something lurked in between the trees. Like eyes lingering on them from a distance, they *felt* a presence.

Kai stopped in his tracks, causing Alexandra to bump into him suddenly. He said nothing. She followed his line of sight to the ground at their feet. A trail of blood, as if someone were dragged by their feet, disappeared behind a fallen tree. They followed it.

Kai hopped over the tree first and maneuvered his blade around like a torch to illuminate the area. As soon as Alexandra made it to the other side, she shot her hand up to cover her nose. She gasped as soon as she saw what was causing the horrid stench. They had found what was left of the scouting party.

Blood was splattered all over the ground and the nearby trees. Weapons and limbs lay scattered throughout the area. To their right, a scout's body had been brutally ripped in half at the waist, her innards leaking out, and a look of terror burned into her face. Alexandra wanted to vomit. Kai knelt next to an arm, still clutching a sword in its hand. It had been cleanly severed from the body, which he found peculiar. Horrors bit, tore, and clawed their victims apart—there was nothing precise about their attacks. Which meant one thing: this wound was caused by a blade.

Alexandra looked around. "Could ghouls really do all of this? Kai, this doesn't—"

A quick rustling of branches silenced her words. Something darted through the shadows. Kai whipped around. Nothing.

Another one, this time with a low grumble. Several silhouettes shifted around them. Alexandra's eyes skipped from tree to tree, searching for which gap the danger would emerge from.

"Alex, place your back to mine," Kai said hurriedly. "We're surrounded."

The two stood together, slowly stepping in a circle with their burning blades ready, painting the area in orange and red light.

Suddenly, a high-pitched shriek screamed through the woods, forcing them both to wince. Several more quickly followed. Multiple horrors started to emerge from the shadows as if it were the signal to attack. Each one towered above them, a mutated and deformed skull with long, emaciated bodies and charcoal skin that flaked like burnt chicken. Their arms dangled down past their knees, with long, jagged fingers curled into thick palms. Ghouls. Kai was right; they were surrounded. Several pairs of fiery yellow eyes stared at them, hungry and ready to strike. Stuck in the center of a circle of ghouls, there was no escape.

They pushed off each other and charged at their enemies. Kai turned his body sideways, letting a slash of claws pass right by him. He quickly brought down his blade, swiftly detaching the long arm. He put an end to the ghoul's loud shriek of pain with a thrust through its heart. Its whole body was engulfed in crimson flames as it fell to the ground.

Alexandra dropped to her knees and slid beneath two pairs of claws slicing for her head. She halted her movement and thrust her sword into her target's chest. The Sanorian rune at the base of her blade shone a light orange and acted as a catalyst to the flame already burning. She ripped out her blade with a twist and stepped to the side as the burning ghoul dropped over like a felled tree.

From behind her in the depths of darkness, a ghoul kicked Alexandra in her side, launching her into the fallen tree. The back of her head slammed against the bark with a crack. She felt something warm run down her back beneath her tunic. While ghouls were slow, their attacks hit with a force nearing the kick of a horse. Their claws were serrated and foul to the touch of human flesh.

Before she could shake off the hit thoroughly, a pair of yellow eyes appeared in front of her. Claws sank into her right shoulder. She cried out in pain.

"Alex!" Kai shouted. Too many ghouls stood between him and her. All he could do was watch.

The ghoul unhinged its jaw to reveal three uneven rows of jagged teeth. As they clamped down, Alexandra shoved her left arm in its mouth. Each tooth latched on, but barely sank in. With the horror clamped down, she forced her sword through its head. It let go and backed off with a wail. She quickly rose to her feet with a slice to its neck. The decapitated body fell to the ground and started to twitch. With her sword flipped upside down, she slammed it into its heart, engulfing it in bright orange flames. The light in the eyes of the head that lay several feet away slowly faded. Steam rolled from the sizzling wound on Alexandra's shoulder as she rolled it around and spat out a mouthful of blood.

An upward slice from Kai's crimson blade split a ghoul into two fiery halves. He twirled his katana and thrust it behind him through the chest of another. Its claws just missed his back as it fell. He turned to see the last ghoul make a fiery fall in front of Alexandra's feet.

"You okay?" he asked.

"Yeah, I'm okay." She reached behind herself to the back of her head and winced. Her fingers were red. "Bastard got me pretty good, though."

Kai looked around. "Well... I guess—"

A thunderous boom in the distant sky in the direction of Meditas drew their attention. They turned. Through the naked trees, high above the city, dark clouds rumbled. The vibration crashed into Kai's chest with an aggressive familiarity, forcing his heart into the depths of his stomach.

"Strange. There wasn't a cloud in sight when we left," Alexandra said.

"Something's wrong. We need to—"

Another high-pitched shriek cut him off. Two more ghouls appeared out of the darkness. Alexandra could see the look on Kai's face—a look she had only seen once before, down in the cave, when he forced them to flee from the Soul Eater. Something she was not privy to filled him with a similar sense of panic.

"You go. I can handle these two," she said as she stepped forward.

"You sure?"

"Yeah, I'll be right behind you."

Kai nodded his head and took off toward the horses. From the moment they had received the report of the missing scouting party, something had scratched at the back of his mind. Something felt... *wrong.* The closer he drew to the forest's edge, the more his stomach turned. Branches and twigs snapped beneath his feet as he ran.

When he emerged from the trees, he saw them. Clouds hovered high above the fountain's tree, cracking with static flashes of lightning. Every growl of thunder brought with it an unwelcome reminder of someone in his past.

Victor. Something *was* wrong. He hopped on Mastala's back and raced toward the city.

The warm tea gave a friendly warmth to Vera's palms. She took in a deep breath of mint and honey.

"Thanks for the soup, Bear. It was really tasty."

"Don't mention it. How are you feeling?"

She slurped from the cup and exhaled a revitalizing warm breath. "Better. But my bones still feel achy, and I think I could sleep for another week."

"That's what you call better?"

"Better than launching up everything in my stomach every hour."

"Gross."

She slurped from the cup and looked out the window. Thunder rumbled in the sky outside.

"A *pack* of ghouls, you said?" Vera asked.

Barrik nodded. "They don't know for sure, but a full scouting party and a patrol party are missing."

"Over a couple of ghouls?"

Barrik shrugged. "Like I said, they don't know for sure."

"Why didn't you go with?"

"Kai told me to stay here and get you your tea. I think he wants you to keep reading."

Vera pouted. "Ugh. These books are so boring! I think the more I read them, the more I start breathing through my mouth."

Barrik held up his hands defensively. "Yeah, I know, but just remember, it's for Vince."

"I know, I know. He could do his own reading too, ya know."

"I don't think he could even read a page without falling asleep."

"Does he even know how to read?" Vera teased with a mischievous smirk.

She looked out the window at the clouds above and took another sip from her tea. Lost in her thoughts for a brief moment, she started to giggle.

"What's so funny?" Barrik asked.

"Can you imagine Vincey's face if he saw an entire pack of ghouls?"

They both started to laugh until a loud boom from outside rattled the window, demanding their attention.

"What was that?" Vera asked, concerned.

Barrik rushed to peer out of the window.

Kai flapped Mastala's reins. Her hooves clopped against the dirt trail with tremendous speed. In the sky, below the gray clouds, something whistled through the air. He was too far away to see the projectile, until all of a sudden, it exploded. Like a firework during a celebration, orange and red sparks burst into the night sky. His eyes widened, his jaw creeping open in shock. It was the warning signal from the fountain. They were under attack.

"No…" he whispered to himself in disbelief.

He kicked into Mastala, begging her to go faster if she could. She had to. He needed to get there. He was almost at the city gates.

High in the distant sky were the dissipating remnants of a reddish-orange explosion.

"I think that's the fountain's signal!" Barrik exclaimed.

"As in…?"

"We're under attack!"

"Who's up there right now?"

"Vince and Rinna!" Barrik said in a hurry. He quickly moved for the door, but stopped and turned back to Vera. "V, please stay here." He begged her with his eyes. She was in no condition to fight. Deep down, he knew what she would likely do regardless of his words, but even if there was a chance of her staying, no matter how small, he had to reach for it.

Nothing else was said between them beyond the silence of a nod. He rushed out of the room.

There was nothing to think about. She set down her cup on the nightstand and threw off the covers. She had been bedridden long enough anyway, she thought. She threw on her gear. There was no reality where she would sit idly by and do nothing. If they fought, they fought together, like always. Her daggers slid into their sheaths on her lower back as she looked out the window. She tilted her head over her shoulder to whisper, as if Barrik were still in the room. "I'm sorry, Bear."

Then she vanished.

CHAPTER 23

INCENT and Rinna stood at the fountain's edge next to one of the flickering torches.

"I don't think I'll ever tire of this view," she said as she gazed out into the city.

Soft lambent light from lanterns and torches all around gave the snow-tipped houses and shops a subtle orange hue. The small specks of various lights made it seem as though some of the stars gracefully fell from above to find a peaceful resting place on the city floor.

She shook her head. "Beautiful."

A small smile crept across Vincent's face as he admired the city's reflection in her eyes. "Yeah, it's…" Vincent trailed off and whipped around.

Rinna looked at him. "What is it?"

"I…" He looked over the area.

She put a hand on his shoulder. "Vince?"

"I don't know, exactly, but I *feel* something. Something…" He quickly drew his sabers. "Something is here."

Rinna looked around for anything out of order, but found nothing noteworthy. "Where?"

"Everywhere. Come on."

"Hey, wait!"

She followed behind him as he ran across the snow-covered grass. Tahara turned around, startled to see Vincent with his weapons drawn.

"Young Raine, may I ask what it is you are doing?"

"My lady, something is here that I believe means to harm either you or the fountain." Vincent turned around and placed his back to Tahara. Rinna pulled her long weapon from her back and stood next to him side by side.

A gentle hand fell onto both of their shoulders. "Children, please. Sheathe your weapons. I assure you, everything is fine. I would sense anything or anyone's presence long before anyone else."

Vincent turned to her. Maybe it was the smile on her face or the confidence in her words, but whatever the culprit was, he doubted himself. Maybe he was paranoid. The troubled sleep had finally caused his senses to dull, and he now imagined things that were not there. He started to relax.

Just as he went to sheathe his sabers, a thud of metal hit the ground nearby.

"What was that?" Rinna asked.

A cry of pain came from a guard on the opposite side. Vincent was right. Everyone drew their weapons and looked around for what was hunting them.

"Stay behind us, my lady," Vincent said.

Another scream from a guard slowly faded away as they fell from the edge to their death.

"Children, you need to fire a warning signal to the rest of the city," Tahara whispered.

A gust of wind suddenly rushed over them all. All of the flames were extinguished in an instant. Darkness befell them until Vincent lit his sabers with the fire sign. Another guard suddenly dropped to the ground. No matter where they looked, they saw no sign of an attacker.

"Okay, Rinna, you stay here and protect Tahara. I'll fire the—"

Before he could finish his words, a gust of wind blew past his face. Behind him, he heard the slice of a dagger. He turned. A deep cut in Tahara's throat let loose a waterfall of dark red that dyed her gown. She choked on blood, air, and final words as she fell to the ground. Vincent lunged to catch her before her impact.

A sword appeared out of thin air, right in front of him, and sliced up the right side of his torso. Another rush of wind followed that knocked him to the side with what felt like a kick. He rolled, stopping just short of the edge. He could see one of his sabers fall far into the darkness below. Quickly, he rose back to his feet and scanned the area. He started to focus. He still sensed the same thing as before. An unknown energy was all around them, like a fog covering every part of the ground they stood on. He was unable to pinpoint a single location, until... He ducked beneath a slice to his neck and dove away from the edge.

"Vince! What is it? Can you see anything?" Rinna shouted.

"No!"

All at once, just briefly before the attack, he felt the fog converge into a single spot—just like when he had sensed Vera. When he rose to his feet, he sensed the fog again. This time, he was ready. Clouds began to form above as Vincent pulled in energy around him. He waited for the next attack. Once again, the fog converged—only this time, it was right in front of Rinna.

"Rinna, move!" Vincent shouted.

She dove to the side just in time. When she rolled to her feet, she looked around.

"Vince, I don't see anything!"

"Then don't let them either!"

Rinna immediately understood what he meant and concealed herself.

"You're able to sense *my* Favor?" A man's voice came from everywhere.

Vincent wandered around in a circle, looking for the assailant.

"*You* must be the son of Raine."

Behind him! Vincent turned with a slash. Nothing.

"With such strength, it's no wonder my Qrux never returned to me." The voice sounded close and far away at the same time.

Vincent barely raised his saber in time. His guard was sloppy; the attacker's blade swiped across his arm, cutting him open.

"Vincent, she said your name was?" The voice echoed.

Vincent felt another attack coming. He parried and followed with a thrust. He was sure it went right where the fog was focused, but his blade found no target. He could sense where the attacks were coming from, but how was he supposed to hit nothing? He stepped slowly in a circle again, unsure of where the next attack was to come from. Behind again! He rolled out of the way and released a blade of green energy from his saber. Another miss.

"Well, now, that shows some promise. Perhaps even the potential to surpass the father. You'll make a fine addition to my collection, Vincent Raine."

Potential to surpass the father? The words rattled through him with a ferocious discord. This person had given him recognition—real recognition—an affirmation of his strengths, but from an unwanted tongue. It felt wrong—tainted even. He shook the thought away. Now was not the time for pride or doubts. Only survival.

"You're not collecting anyone tonight," Vincent fired back.

Another convergence. This time, a man appeared a few feet in front of Vincent. He was hidden beneath a dark, tattered hooded cloak, his face covered by the same white mask Alice had worn. The mystery man walked toward him with no weapon. Vincent released a crescent blade of energy right at him. The man did not even bother to dodge. It looked as though he had just walked right through Vincent's attack.

The man stepped quickly to close the distance between them. Vincent slashed at the oncoming foe. Just before he made contact, a short sword with a white hilt appeared in the man's hand as if it were unveiled by a windy curtain. He blocked the attack with ease and placed himself face to face with Vincent. Moonlight slipped between the two eye slits in his mask, allowing Vincent a quick glimpse of the menacing darkness beneath. A brief look was all he got, but it was enough to chill his bones with fear. The man's eyes were full of bloodlust and murderous intent.

Vincent pushed off of him and hopped back. This time, the cloaked invader remained in his current form. He marched toward him again. Both parties exchanged a series of attacks, neither able to land a hit. The sky above rumbled with thunder and flashed with sparks of lightning.

Still cloaked with her Favor, Rinna picked up a bow and one of the fountain's arrows. For the flash powder inside to explode, she had to light the fuse, and with all the torches extinguished, there was only one way she could do so. She focused herself and quickly weaved a sign with her fingers.

Vincent and the assailant continued to dance around each other until Vincent stood just in front of the fountain's water. Something made him feel drawn toward the mystery attacker. He felt connected. On a level, he did not quite understand, as if his heart or soul were pulled toward the man. Maybe he was someone familiar beneath the mask, or maybe it was something else.

"Ah, so your skill with a blade is up to par," the cloaked invader said.

"Who are you?" Vincent interrogated.

"My identity will not be of aid to you."

A loud whistle screamed out and away from the fountain through the night sky. They both turned to see Rinna standing with a bow in her hand. A loud boom in the distance vibrated throughout the air. The explosion briefly cast them and half the city in a bright red-orange light.

Vincent took advantage of the distraction. He thrust his saber forward, aiming right at the man's torso. Distracted, he never saw it coming. Vincent's blade found its mark, although something was strange; his blade went right through him again. It was in him, yet Vincent never felt any impact. There may as well have been nothing there.

The mystery man hung his head, disappointed. "I really wish you had not done that. For a moment, I was enjoying myself."

In a flash, the mystery man swung a heavy backhand into Vincent's face, knocking him to the side. His other saber fell silently to the snow-covered ground. He picked Vincent up by the neck and tightly squeezed the air from his lungs.

From behind the man, Rinna appeared out of thin air and thrust her blade through him, making a crucial mistake. Her blade went through him entirely, just like Vincent's saber, as if he were never there, and sank into Vincent's stomach. She was stunned, immobilized with horror.

"Now look at what you've done," the man said. He fired back an elbow into Rinna's face, knocking her backward and away from her weapon. He turned around and let Vincent fall to his knees. Next to the fountain's water, he placed both of his hands over his lower abdomen, which was now quickly spilling blood between his fingers.

"That is quite the Favor," the man said, looking down at Rinna. He delivered a powerful kick to her face. Everything blurred as she tried her best to remain conscious. "How about I bring you with me? Hmm?"

"Don't touch her," Vincent said weakly, back on his two feet. Thunder raged in the sky above as he reached for the three-gemmed sword on his hip. Before he was able to draw it, in an instant, the man glided back to him and lifted him by his throat again.

"What do we have here?" the man said as he looked down at the sword on Vincent's hip. Much to Vincent's surprise, he unsheathed it easily for his further inspection. Vincent watched as the runes on the sword lit up just like they had when he first held it in his hands.

"So," the man said as he maneuvered the sword in his hands, "she finally chose someone? Looks like I'm not the only one interested in you." He looked Vincent up and down. "I'd love to carry this blade myself, but…" He leaned close to Vincent's ear. "We mustn't take what isn't ours."

As Rinna succumbed to darkness, she could do nothing but watch through blurred vision as the man thrust the sword through Vincent's chest, piercing his heart.

Vincent's arms fell to his side. He remained suspended in the air by his throat, motionless. The masked man threw Vincent's limp body into the fountain's water and turned back to the unconscious Rinna. He leaned over her. "How much will it take to break you, I wonder?"

As he reached for Rinna's body, something from his side suddenly knocked him several feet away from her. Vera stood over Rinna with tears welling in her fierce gaze.

"And who might you be?" the man asked.

She stood perfectly still with both her daggers drawn, her heart pounding in her chest. She had arrived just in time to see the horrifying moment: the masked man plunging Vincent's sword through his heart. The sight seared into her mind, freezing her in place. Fatigue and a storm of emotions wracked her body, but she could not afford to falter. Every instinct and muscle in her body screamed at her that a head-on fight would not be to her advantage. All she needed to do was protect Rinna. The warning signal had been shot, and help was on the way. Stalling the attacker was her only mission now.

"Not the kindest of introductions, I might say," the man said as he dissipated back into the wind.

Vera looked around in a panic. A kick from seemingly nowhere launched her several feet back. As she climbed back to her feet, the masked man was right before her face. She froze with terror as his cold hand graced her cheek.

"Such a dangerous face," he said softly.

Vera snapped out of her daze and rolled away. He reached for her as she did so, only managing to grab the cloth around her head, uncovering her left eye. When she turned back to him, something was different. The vision in her left eye was not gone; it had changed. Instead of darkness and shadows cast by dim moonlight, she saw everything around her clearly. The moon's light shone much brighter over a world of black and gray. Everything was void of color, except for two silhouettes—a violet one covering Rinna's body, and a white one covering the mystery man, both of which had a steady hum. She watched the white silhouette walk toward Rinna's on the ground.

"Stay where you are, and I'll let you live," the man called to her.

The white silhouette bent over to pick up Rinna. Vera threw both of her daggers on either side of the masked man and vanished. She appeared right next to him and took a swipe at his legs, but just like with Vincent and Rinna's attacks, her blade went right through as if he were an illusion. She disappeared and tried again. Another miss—only this time, she noticed that where her blade struck, a gap suddenly appeared in the white silhouette and then returned right after. She had to try again. She threw her dagger, but when she tried to relocate to it, she failed. Her body gave out. She dropped to her knees and vomited. Her muscles screamed. The man kicked her away from Rinna and stood over her.

"Remember, I offered to spare your life. This is your fault," he said as he seemed to pull a sword out of thin air. To her right eye, the blade seemed just to appear, but to her left, it was like millions of tiny bright stars gathered in his hand to form the weapon.

He raised the sword.

Behind him, Vera saw another silhouette rapidly approaching—a darker one that almost blended in with the shadows. The masked man's blade fell with a metallic clang.

Ghost now stood at her side.

"Back away from them!" someone shouted.

Vera turned quickly to the top of the steps. Kai hurried toward them. Machaya's flame thrashed across the blade at his side.

"Tsk, tsk, tsk. It seems I have lingered too long. I must say, you have become quite a nuisance. I was certain a Soul Eater would take care of you, but no matter. I guess one will have to do."

The man swiped his blade at Ghost, but found nothing but air; however, Ghost was not his target. The man faded into the wind until he appeared over Rinna and huddled over her. A breeze quickly swept through that seemed to take them both with it. Vera watched in horror as Rinna's violet silhouette drifted away with the mystery man, like smoke trails fading into the wind. There was no sign of either of them. They were gone.

Kai sprinted over to Vera's side. "Are you hurt?"

Vera shook her head as she stared at the spot where Rinna had been only a moment ago, but could find no words.

A crowd of guards stormed up the steps; behind them was Barrik. He stopped in his tracks, frozen with shock.

"Kai, sir!" One of the guards stood next to him with a salute.

"Fetch Master Darion, and... clear the dead."

The guards ran down the stairs to do as they were instructed, silently passing Barrik by. Still frozen, he was afraid to move, as if getting any closer would make the scene before his eyes more real. His lips quivered. Tears filled his eyes. He felt a weight in his chest he knew he would never have the strength to wield.

"... Bear."

He turned. Vera was on the ground next to Kai, tears streaming down her face. He rushed over to her side and looked her over. "Are you okay?" He pulled her into his arms before she could answer.

She gently shook her head in his arms. "No." She gripped him tightly as she sobbed.

Barrik looked around the area that was now the remnants of a battlefield. Ghost stood at the water's edge, locked onto Vincent's floating body. Tahara's corpse lay only a few feet away from him. Kai lowered himself to a knee and placed his hand on Barrik's shoulder, but once Barrik realized Kai was there...

"Kai?" Barrik asked softly.

Kai looked at him with watery eyes.

"Where's Alex?"

Alexandra ripped her sword from the final ghoul. Its dark blood splattered across her face as its body ignited in flames. With no other threats in sight, she started to catch her breath. She surveyed the rest of the forest around her. It was silent.

Just as she took a well-earned deep breath of relief, a loud explosion drew her attention. Orange light snuck into the woods between the trees. Her eyes widened. She sheathed her sword and ran.

Her feet slammed into the ground. She pushed as hard as she could. Tree after tree flew past her until she burst out of the woods. The clouds above the fountain were beginning to fade. She hopped on Alahman's back and begged him with the reins to go faster than he ever had before. No amount of speed was enough. The closer she grew to the city, the farther away she felt.

By the time Alexandra reached the western gate, the clouds were gone. She slapped the reins again. Together, she and Alamahn raced through the city, his hooves pounding against the ground.

"Move! Get out of the way!" she yelled at the people standing outside, gazing high in the sky at all the commotion.

At the bottom of the fountain, she hopped off his back before he came to a complete stop. Something caught her eye as her feet hit the ground—something that felt worse than a kick to the stomach. One of Vincent's sabers rested at the bottom of the steps—its star stone dark, void of his green light. Her throat tightened as she feared the worst. She gritted her teeth and rushed up the stairs.

Step after step, the winding staircase went on and on and on. Her heart raced, pounding against her chest. Sweat poured down her face. Finally, the top of the stairs came into view. For a moment, however brief, she hoped they would continue on forever.

At the top of the steps, she slammed into Kai's hands.

"Alex, Alex, listen," he said, trying to find the proper words.

Her hands momentarily rested on his shoulders as she looked past him. In her heart, she already knew. She looked around desperately. Vera had her head buried in Barrik's arms, but once she met her eyes, nothing more needed to be said. She turned back to Kai, her eyes flooded with tears. He was speaking to her, but she heard nothing. The world had lost its sound.

Over his shoulder, she caught a small glimpse of the fountain. When Vincent's body came into her view, her entire world slowed almost to a full stop. Kai held her tightly to keep her in place—or rather, he tried. She shoved him to the side and ran. If it had not been for Ghost, she would have continued on into the water. Just as she reached the edge, he kicked her behind the knee and wrapped his arm tightly around her neck. She squirmed. Threw her head back, scratching and clawing at his arms. She violently thrashed in Ghost's restraint, but no matter what she did, he never let go.

Vincent was right in front of her, the Sanorian sword still buried in his chest, but there was nothing she could do. Her silent screams of agony filled the night. Defeated, she fell limp in Ghost's arms. No longer concerned that she would throw herself in the water after Vincent, he finally let go and backed away. She fell forward to the ground, too weak to hold herself up.

The horrific scene blurred behind all her tears. Her lips quivered. Her breaths were ripped from her chest. Her stomach twisted into knots of pain and grief. Her thoughts tore her apart. She should have been here. She wished she had never come up the steps. Never left Sylva. Never became a Guardian. She wished Fira had never taken them in. She wished for anything that would rid her of this pain. No matter what she wished for, she was left with the truth.

She was helpless.

All she could do was watch as Vincent's blood dyed the fountain's water, shifting from a crystal blue to a deep red. And as the life drained from his body, the star stone in the pommel of his sword began to glow—a bright blue.